ULTIMATE FANTASTIC FOUR

THE FANTASTIC

ULTIMATE FANTASTIC FOUR

THE FANTASTIC

writers
BRIAN MICHAEL BENDIS
& MARK MILLAR

pencils
ADAM KUBERT

inks
DANNY MIKI
AND JOHN DELL

colors
DAVE STEWART

letters
CHRIS ELIOPOULOS

assistant editor
NICK LOWE

editor
RALPH MACCHIO

special thanks to
MACKENZIE CADENHEAD
& C.B. CEBULSKI

collections editor
JEFF YOUNGQUIST

assistant editor
JENNIFER GRÜNWALD

book cover designer
PATRICK McGRATH

book interior designer
MEGHAN KERNS

creative director
TOM MARVELLI

editor in chief
JOE QUESADA

publisher
DAN BUCKLEY

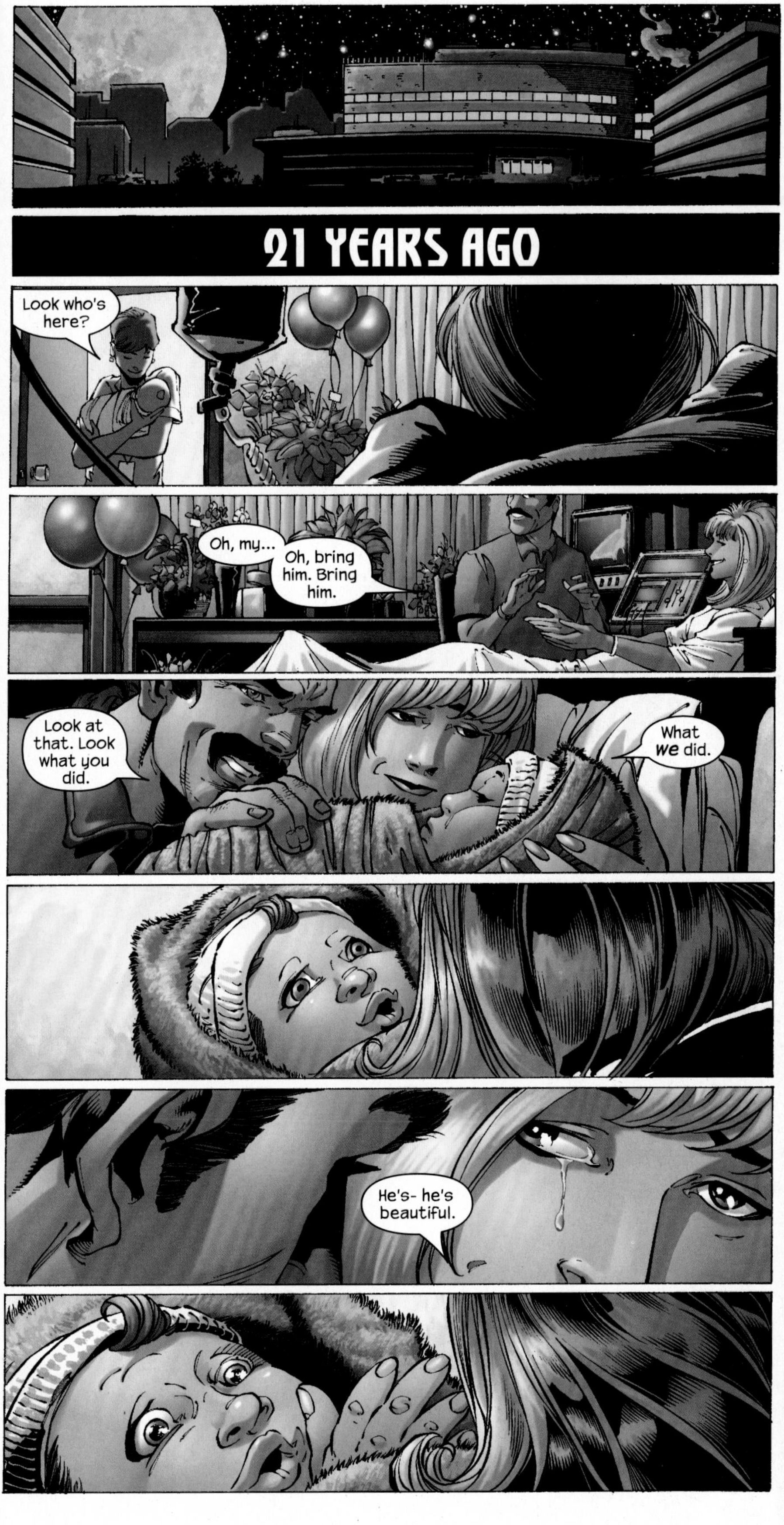

21 YEARS AGO
Look who's here?
Oh, my...
Oh, bring him. Bring him.
Look at that. Look what you did.
What *we* did.
He's- he's beautiful.

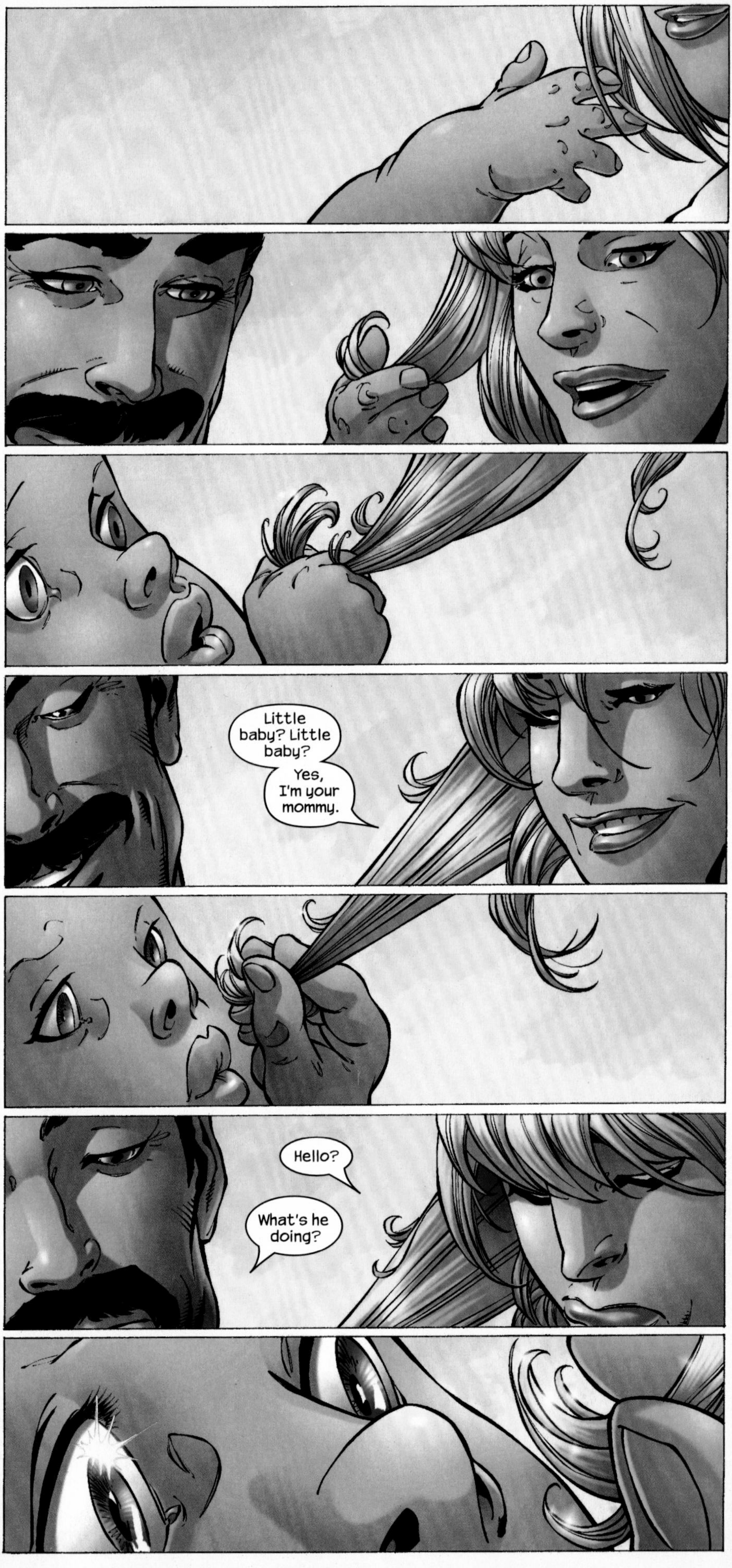
Little baby? Little baby?
Yes, I'm your mommy.
Hello?
What's he doing?

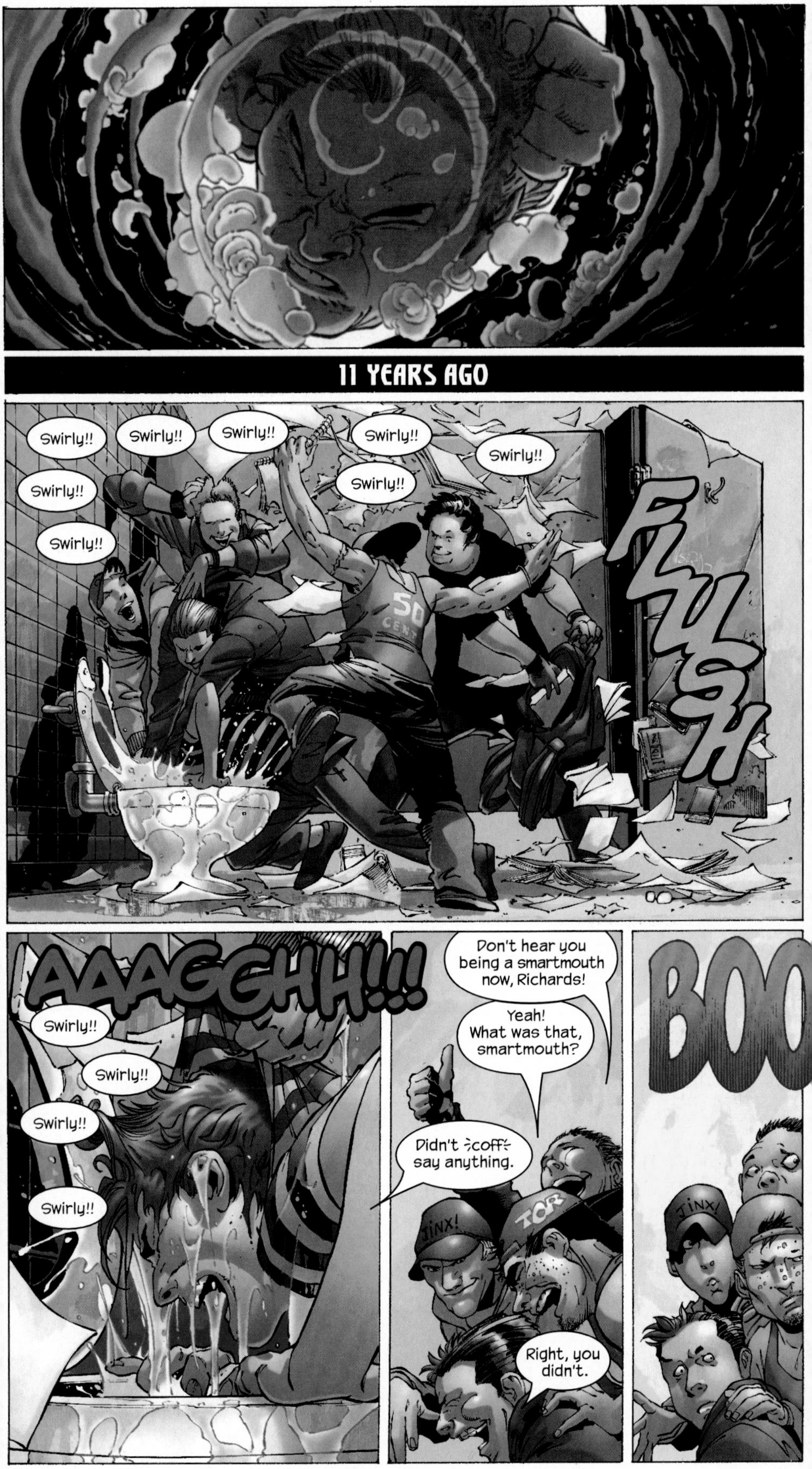
11 YEARS AGO
Swirly!!
Swirly!!
Swirly!!
Swirly!!
Swirly!!
Swirly!!
Swirly!!
FLUSH
AAAGGHH!!!
Swirly!!
Swirly!!
Swirly!!
Swirly!!
Don't hear you being a smartmouth now, Richards!
Yeah! What was that, smartmouth?
Didn't ~coff~ say anything.
Right, you didn't.
BOO

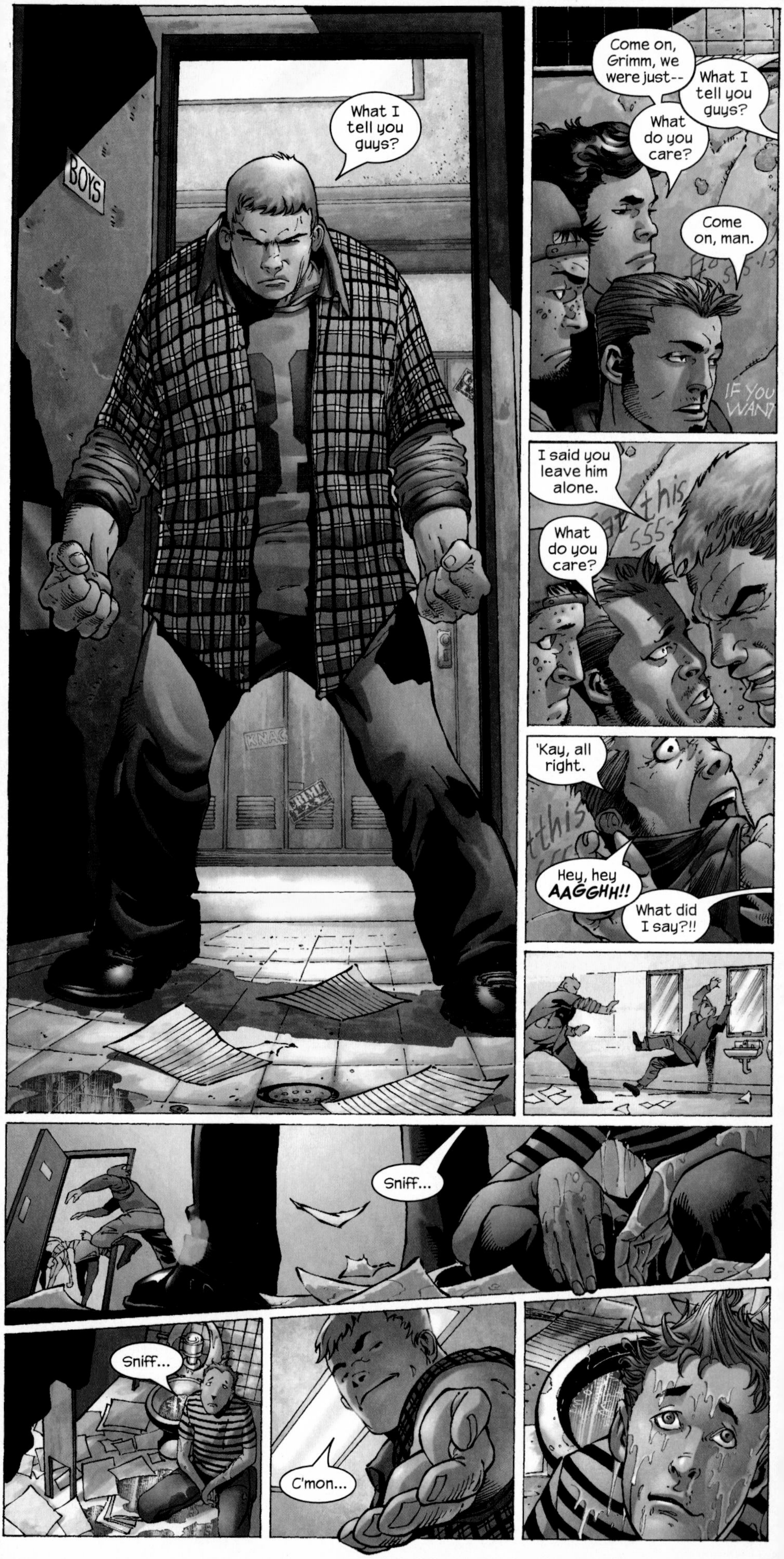
BOYS
What I tell you guys?
Come on, Grimm, we were just--
What I tell you guys?
What do you care?
Come on, man.
IF YOU WANT
I said you leave him alone.
What do you care?
'Kay, all right.
Hey, hey **AAGGHH!!**
What did I say?!!
Sniff...
Sniff...
C'mon...

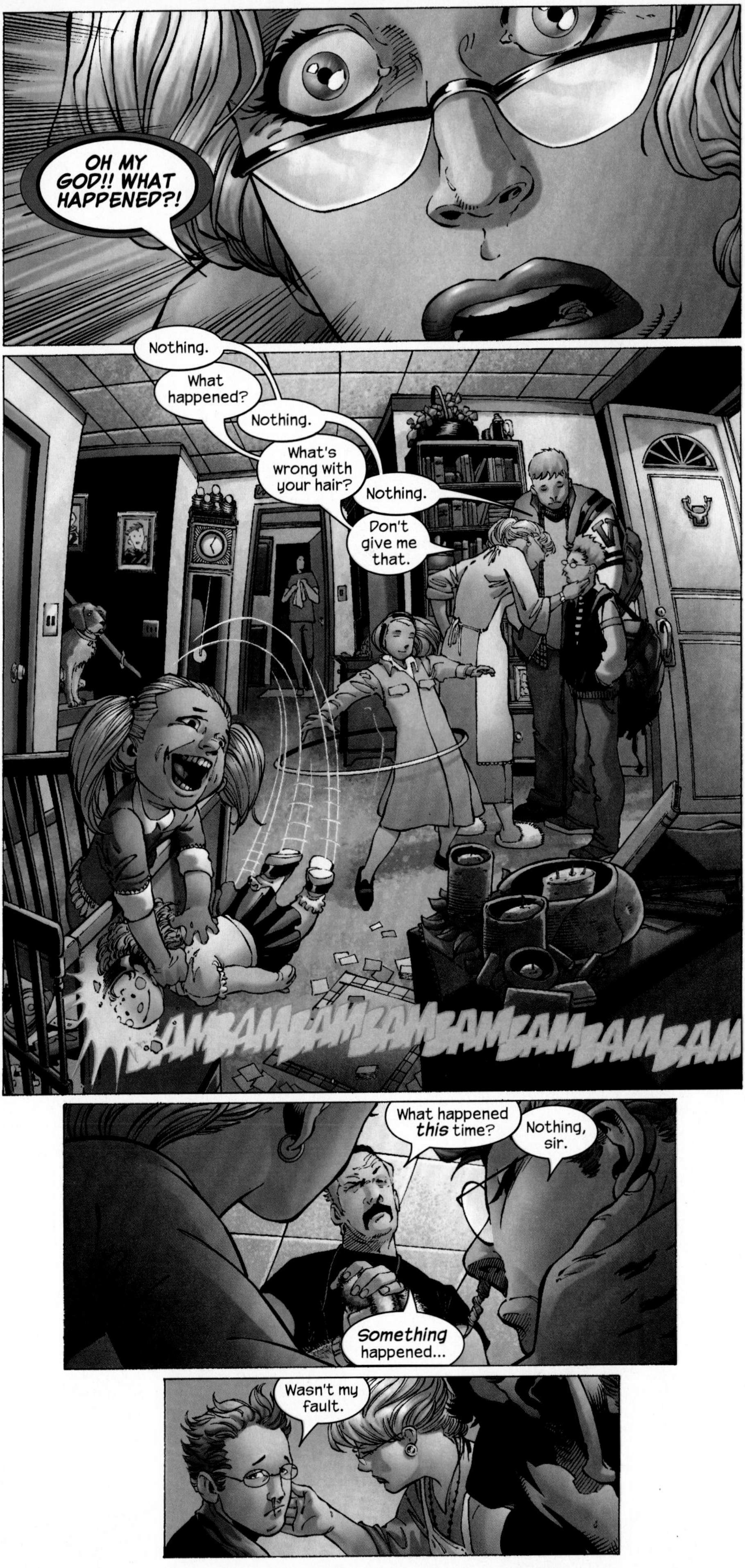
OH MY GOD!! WHAT HAPPENED?!
Nothing.
What happened?
Nothing.
What's wrong with your hair?
Nothing.
Don't give me that.
BAMBAMBAMBAMBAMBAMBAMBAM
What happened this time?
Nothing, sir.
Something happened...
Wasn't my fault.

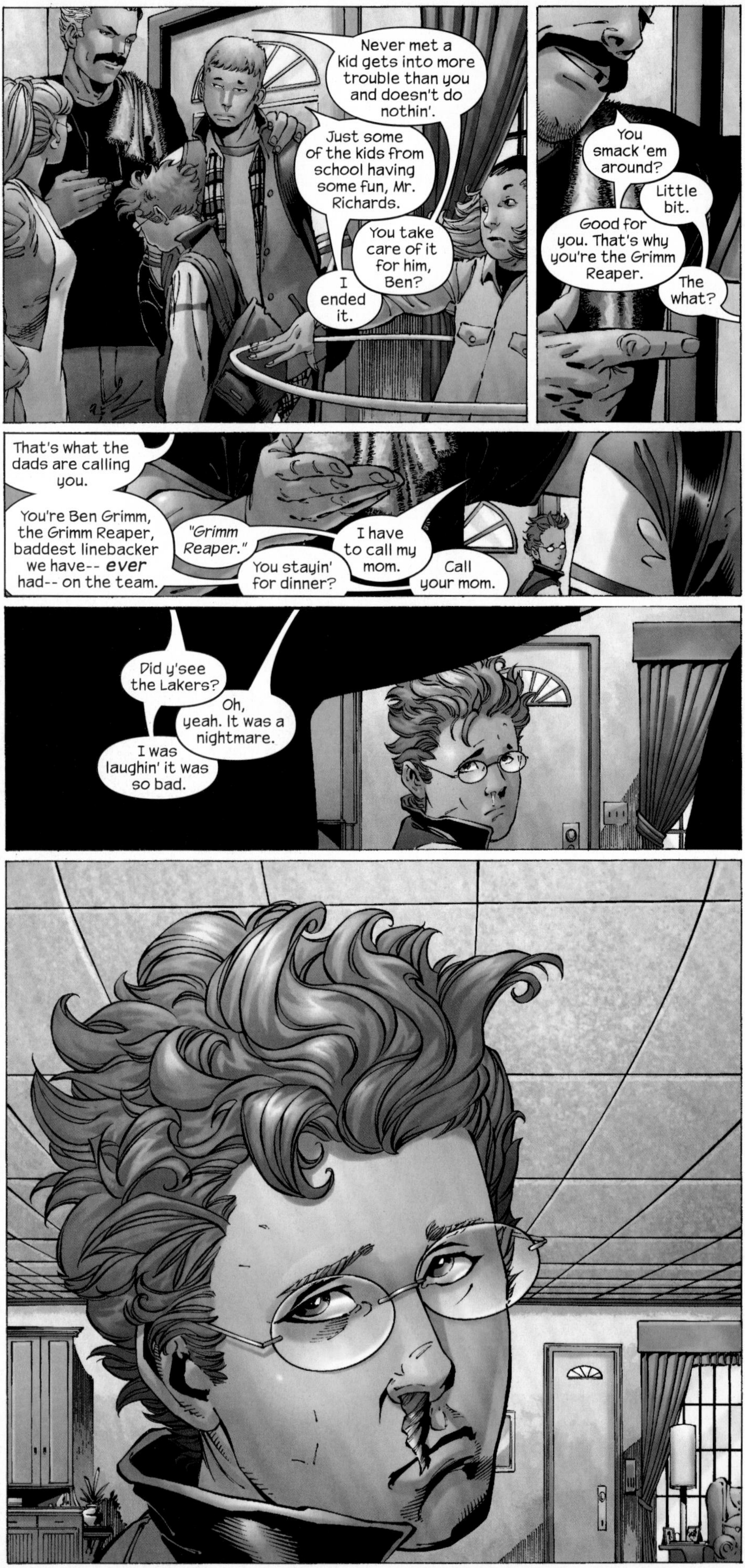

Never met a kid gets into more trouble than you and doesn't do nothin'.
Just some of the kids from school having some fun, Mr. Richards.
You take care of it for him, Ben?
I ended it.
You smack 'em around?
Little bit.
Good for you. That's why you're the Grimm Reaper.
The what?
That's what the dads are calling you.
You're Ben Grimm, the Grimm Reaper, baddest linebacker we have-- **ever** had-- on the team.
"Grimm Reaper."
You stayin' for dinner?
I have to call my mom.
Call your mom.
Did y'see the Lakers?
Oh, yeah. It was a nightmare.
I was laughin' it was so bad.

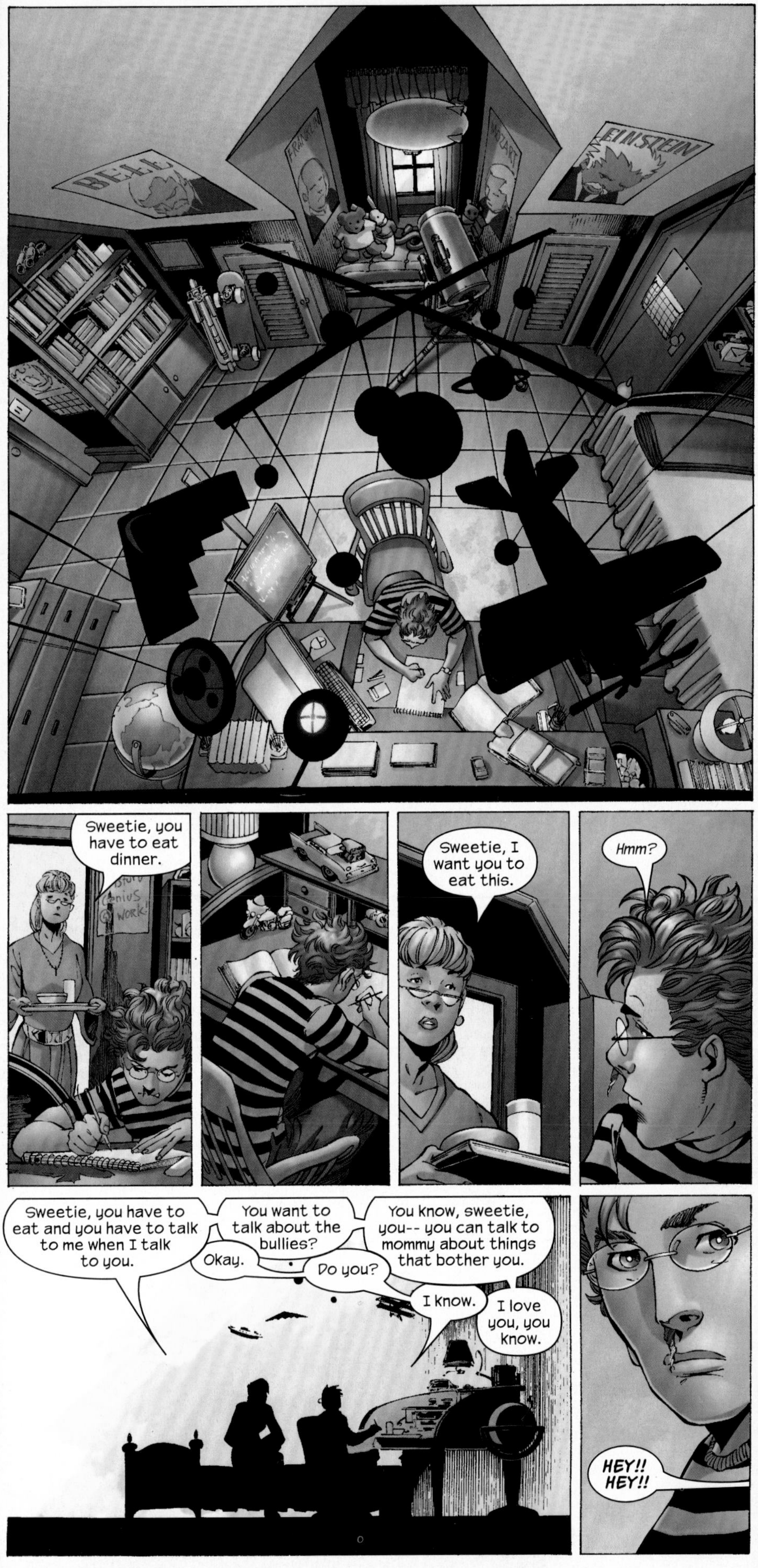
BELL
FRANKLIN
MOZART
EINSTEIN
Sweetie, you have to eat dinner.
Sweetie, I want you to eat this.
Hmm?
Sweetie, you have to eat and you have to talk to me when I talk to you.
Okay.
You want to talk about the bullies?
Do you?
You know, sweetie, you-- you can talk to mommy about things that bother you.
I know.
I love you, you know.
HEY!! HEY!!

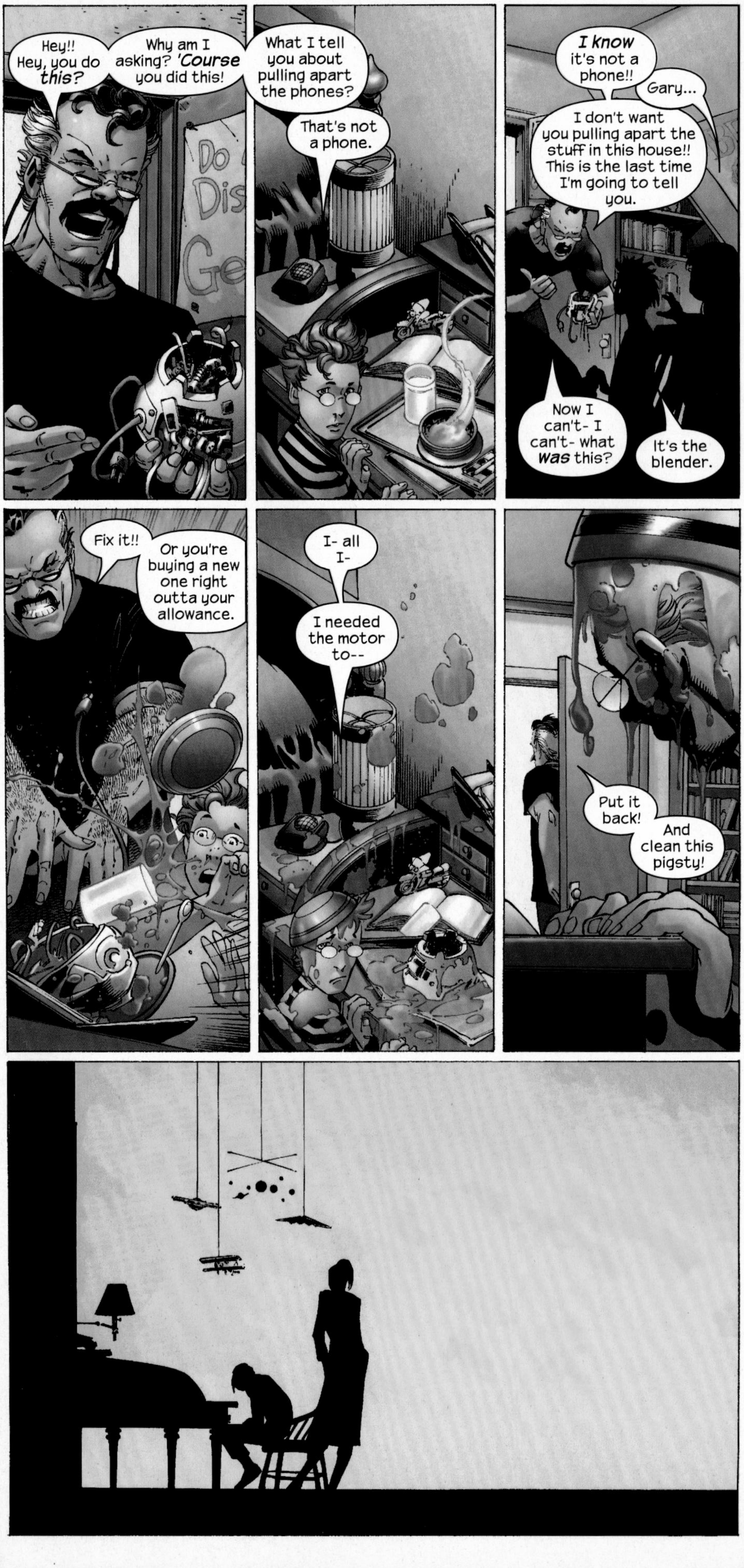
Hey!! Hey, you do this?
Why am I asking? 'Course you did this!
What I tell you about pulling apart the phones?
That's not a phone.
I know it's not a phone!!
Gary...
I don't want you pulling apart the stuff in this house!! This is the last time I'm going to tell you.
Now I can't- I can't- what was this?
It's the blender.
Fix it!!
Or you're buying a new one right outta your allowance.
I- all I-
I needed the motor to--
Put it back!
And clean this pigsty!

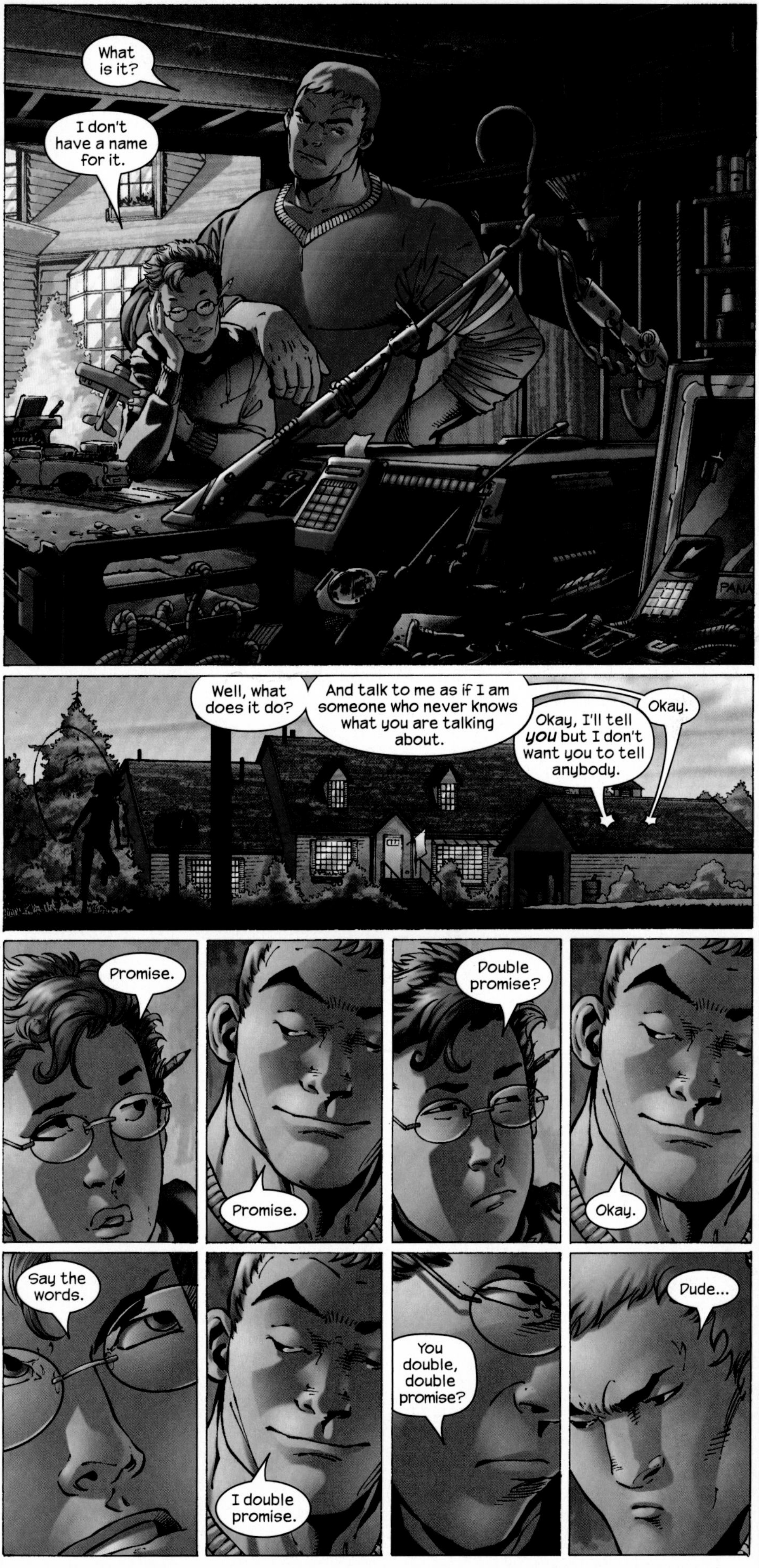
What is it?
I don't have a name for it.
Well, what does it do?
And talk to me as if I am someone who never knows what you are talking about.
Okay.
Okay, I'll tell *you* but I don't want you to tell anybody.
Promise.
Promise.
Double promise?
Okay.
Say the words.
I double promise.
You double, double promise?
Dude...

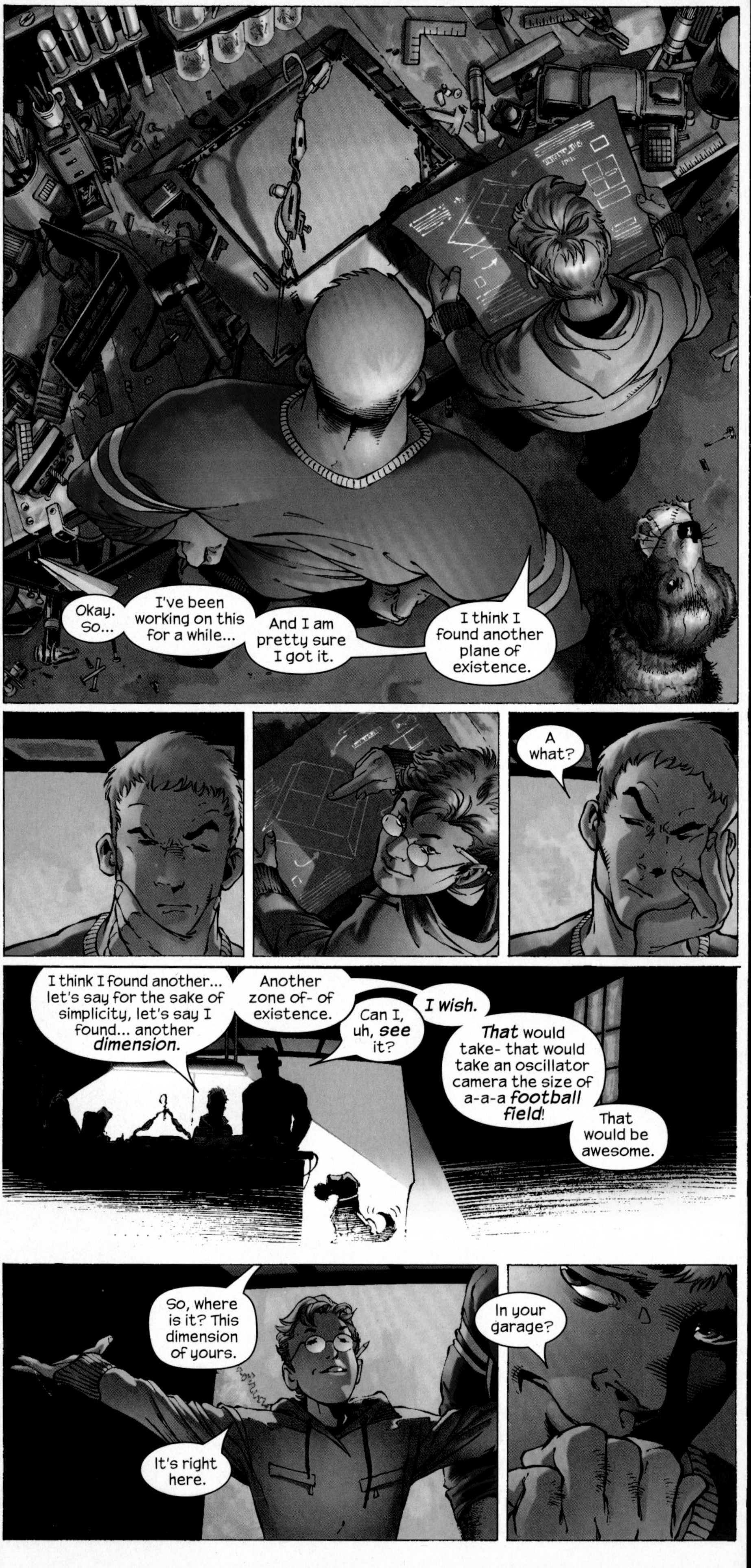
Okay. So...
I've been working on this for a while...
And I am pretty sure I got it.
I think I found another plane of existence.
A what?
I think I found another... let's say for the sake of simplicity, let's say I found... another *dimension.*
Another zone of- of existence.
Can I, uh, *see* it?
I wish.
That would take- that would take an oscillator camera the size of a-a-a *football field*!
That would be awesome.
So, where is it? This dimension of yours.
It's right here.
In your garage?

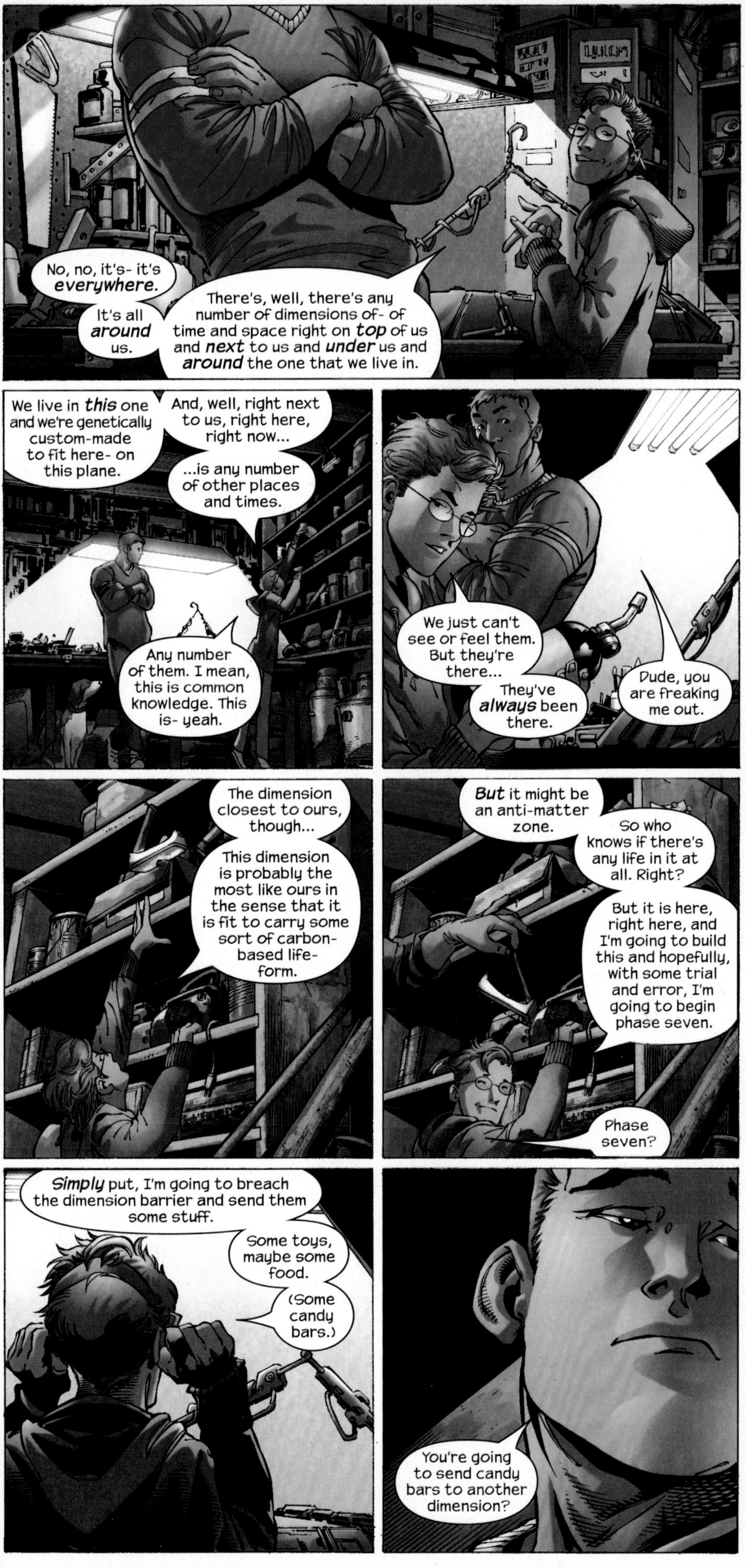

No, no, it's- it's *everywhere.*
It's all *around* us.
There's, well, there's any number of dimensions of- of time and space right on *top* of us and *next* to us and *under* us and *around* the one that we live in.
We live in *this* one and we're genetically custom-made to fit here- on this plane.
And, well, right next to us, right here, right now...
...is any number of other places and times.
Any number of them. I mean, this is common knowledge. This is- yeah.
We just can't see or feel them. But they're there...
They've *always* been there.
Dude, you are freaking me out.
The dimension closest to ours, though...
This dimension is probably the most like ours in the sense that it is fit to carry some sort of carbon-based life-form.
But it might be an anti-matter zone.
So who knows if there's any life in it at all. Right?
But it is here, right here, and I'm going to build this and hopefully, with some trial and error, I'm going to begin phase seven.
Phase seven?
Simply put, I'm going to breach the dimension barrier and send them some stuff.
Some toys, maybe some food.
(Some candy bars.)
You're going to send candy bars to another dimension?

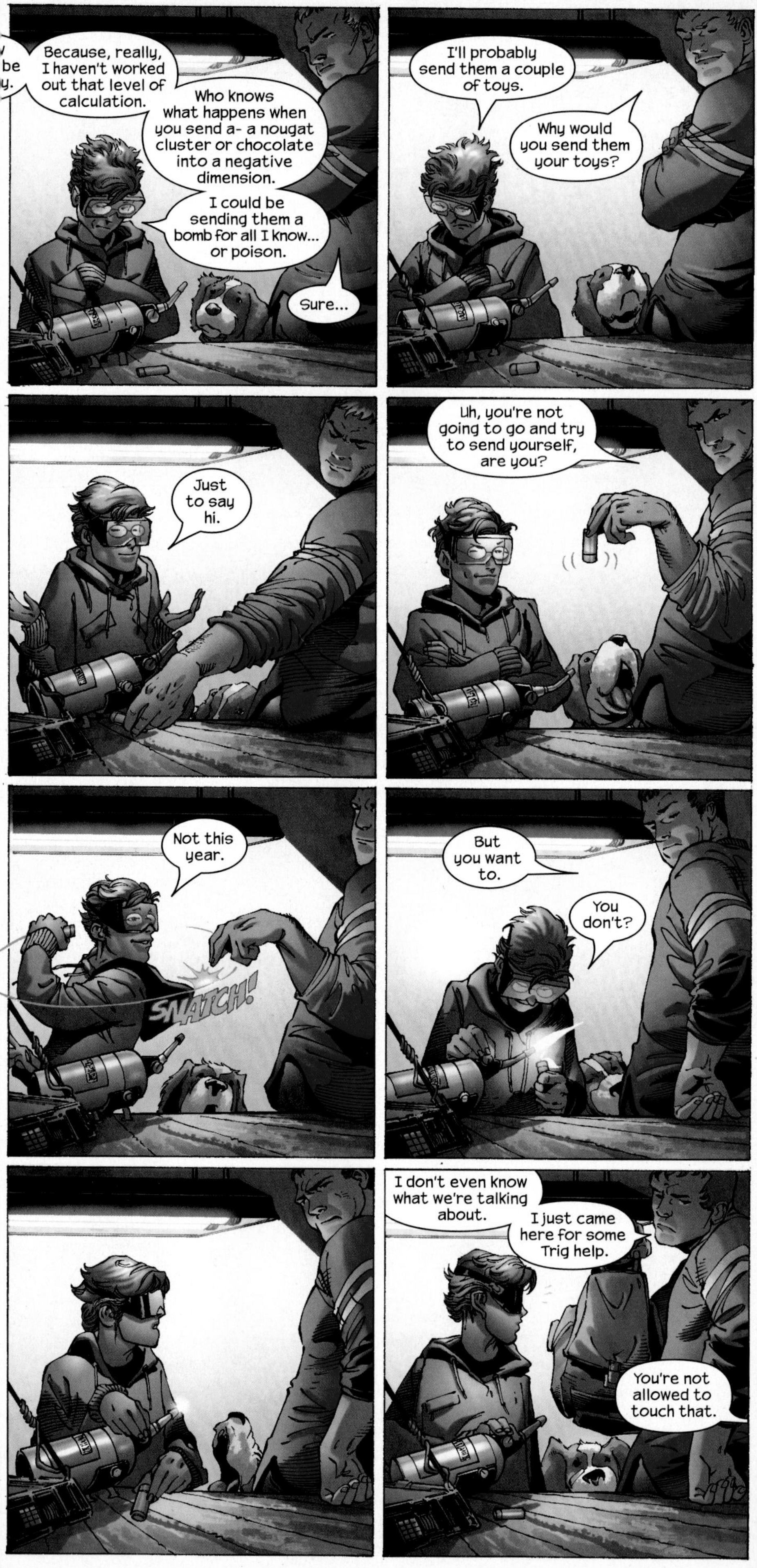
be
y.
Because, really, I haven't worked out that level of calculation.
Who knows what happens when you send a- a nougat cluster or chocolate into a negative dimension.
I could be sending them a bomb for all I know... or poison.
Sure...
I'll probably send them a couple of toys.
Why would you send them your toys?
Just to say hi.
Uh, you're not going to go and try to send yourself, are you?
Not this year.
SNATCH!
But you want to.
You don't?
I don't even know what we're talking about.
I just came here for some Trig help.
You're not allowed to touch that.

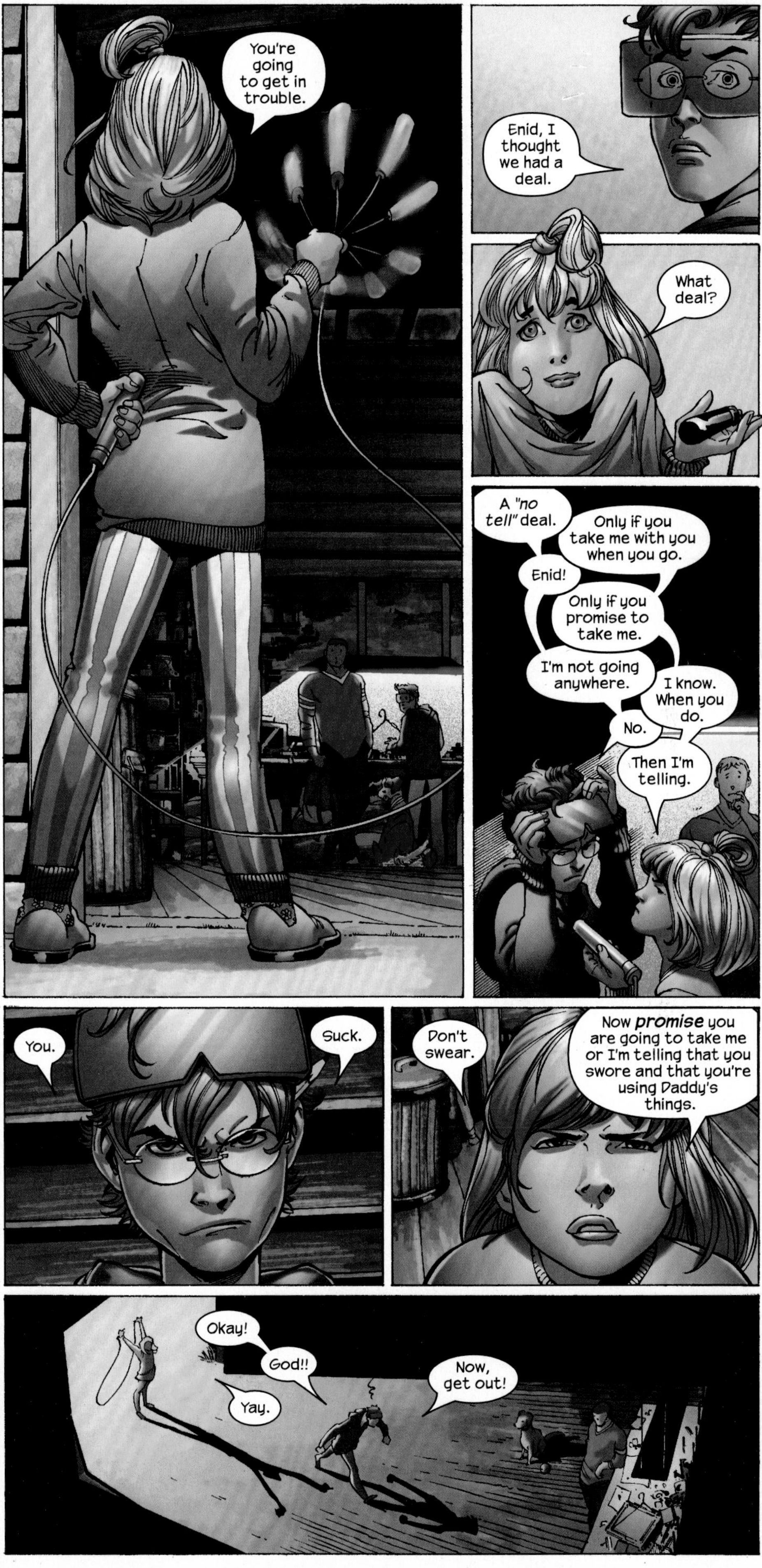
You're going to get in trouble.
Enid, I thought we had a deal.
What deal?
A "no tell" deal.
Only if you take me with you when you go.
Enid!
Only if you promise to take me.
I'm not going anywhere.
I know. When you do.
No.
Then I'm telling.
You.
Suck.
Don't swear.
Now **promise** you are going to take me or I'm telling that you swore and that you're using Daddy's things.
Okay!
God!!
Yay.
Now, get out!

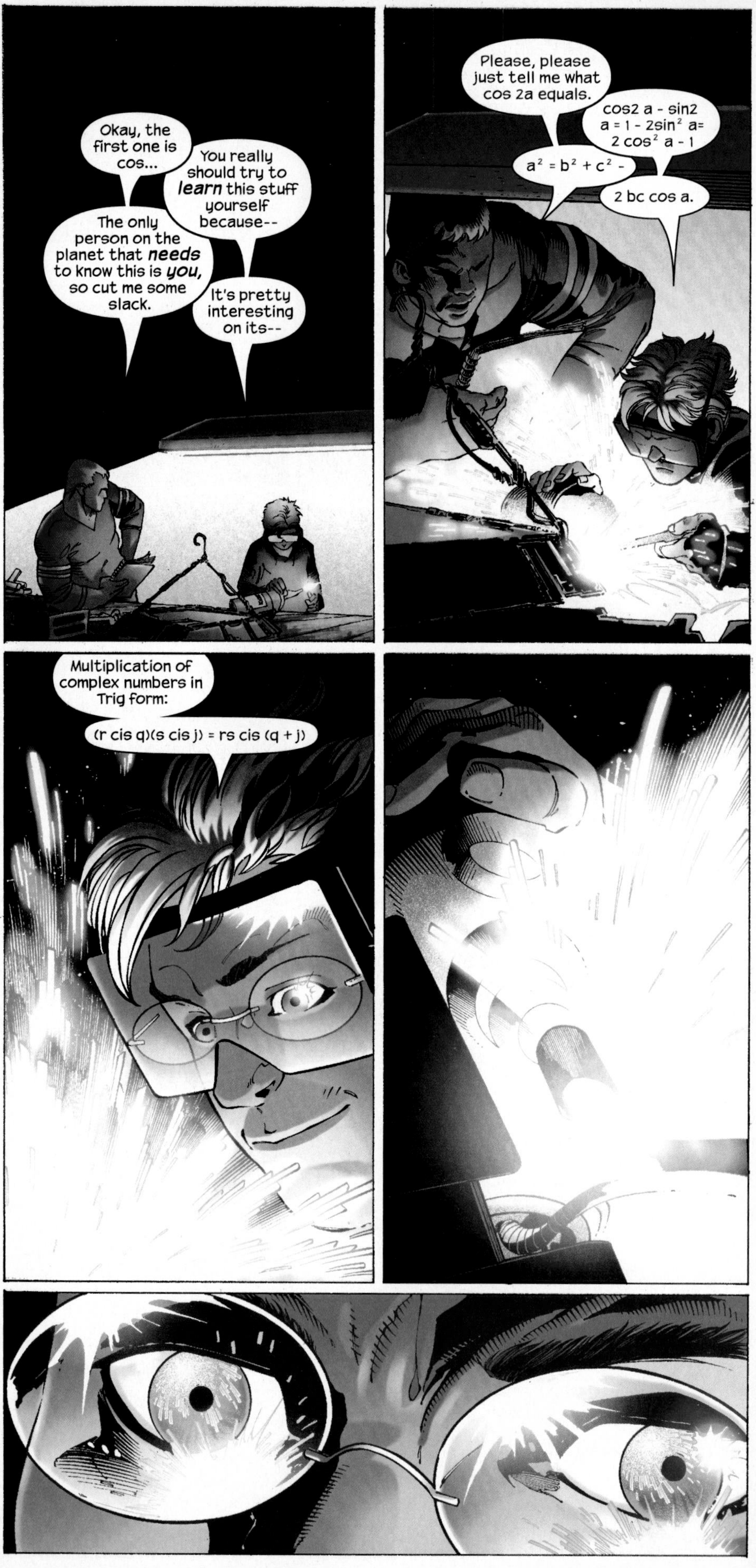
Okay, the first one is cos...
You really should try to *learn* this stuff yourself because--
The only person on the planet that *needs* to know this is *you,* so cut me some slack.
It's pretty interesting on its--
Please, please just tell me what cos 2a equals.
cos2 a - sin2 a = 1 - 2sin² a= 2 cos² a - 1
a² = b² + c² -
2 bc cos a.
Multiplication of complex numbers in Trig form:
(r cis q)(s cis j) = rs cis (q + j)

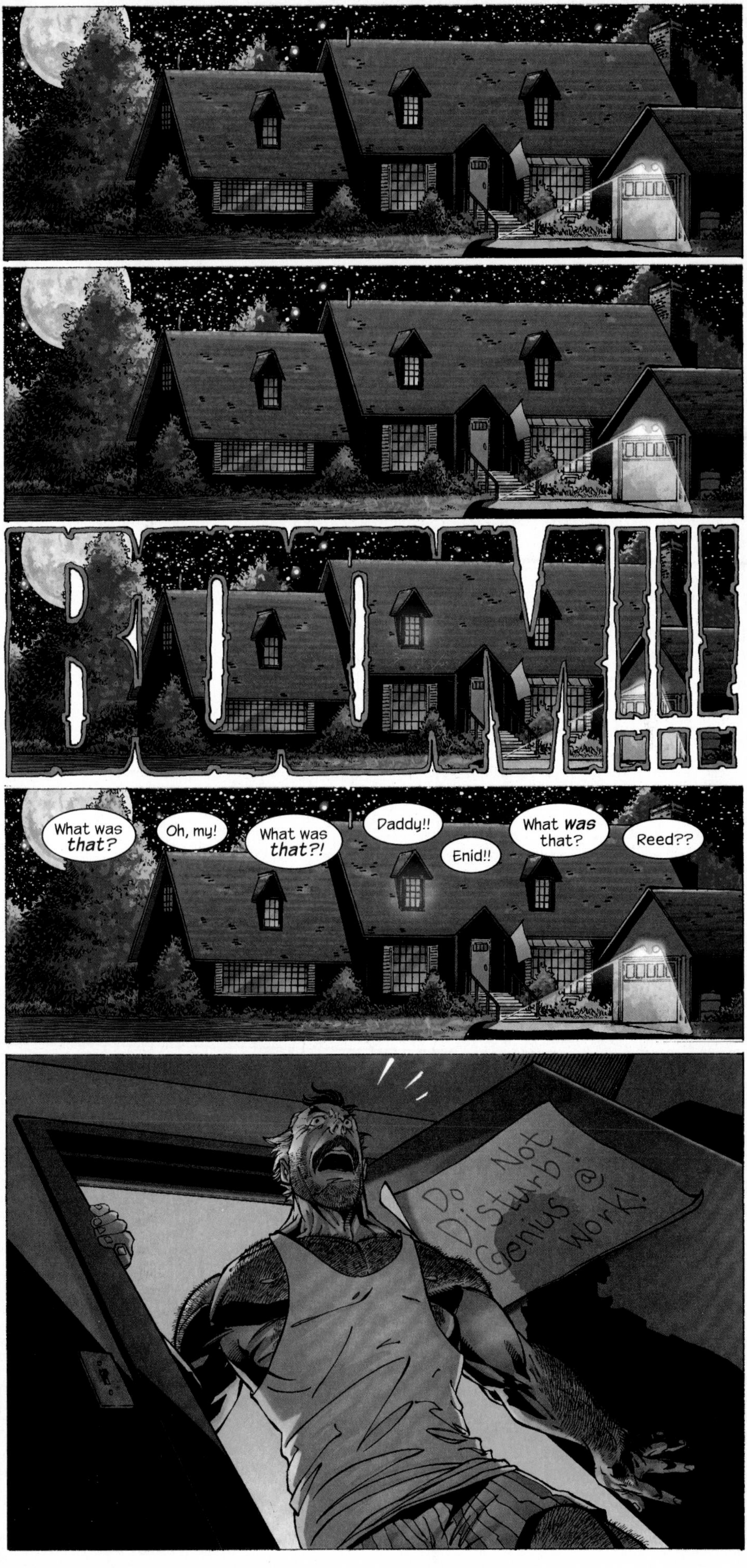
BOOM!!!
What was that?
Oh, my!
What was that?!
Daddy!!
Enid!!
What was that?
Reed??
Do Not Disturb! Genius @ work!

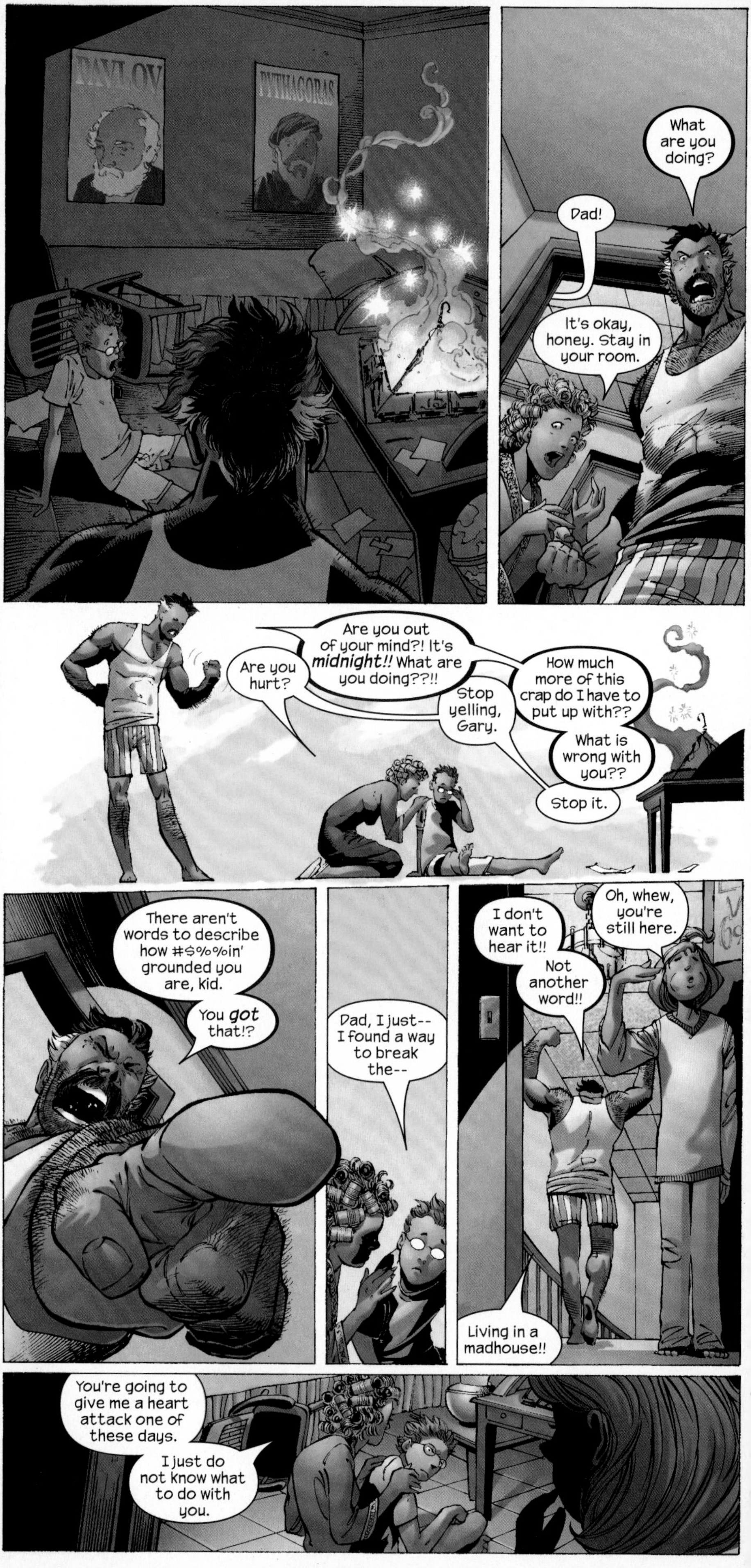
PAVLOV
PYTHAGORAS
Dad!
What are you doing?
It's okay, honey. Stay in your room.
Are you out of your mind?! It's *midnight!!* What are you doing??!!
Are you hurt?
How much more of this crap do I have to put up with??
Stop yelling, Gary.
What is wrong with you??
Stop it.
There aren't words to describe how #$%%in' grounded you are, kid.
You *got* that!?
Dad, I just-- I found a way to break the--
I don't want to hear it!!
Oh, whew, you're still here.
Not another word!!
Living in a madhouse!!
You're going to give me a heart attack one of these days.
I just do not know what to do with you.

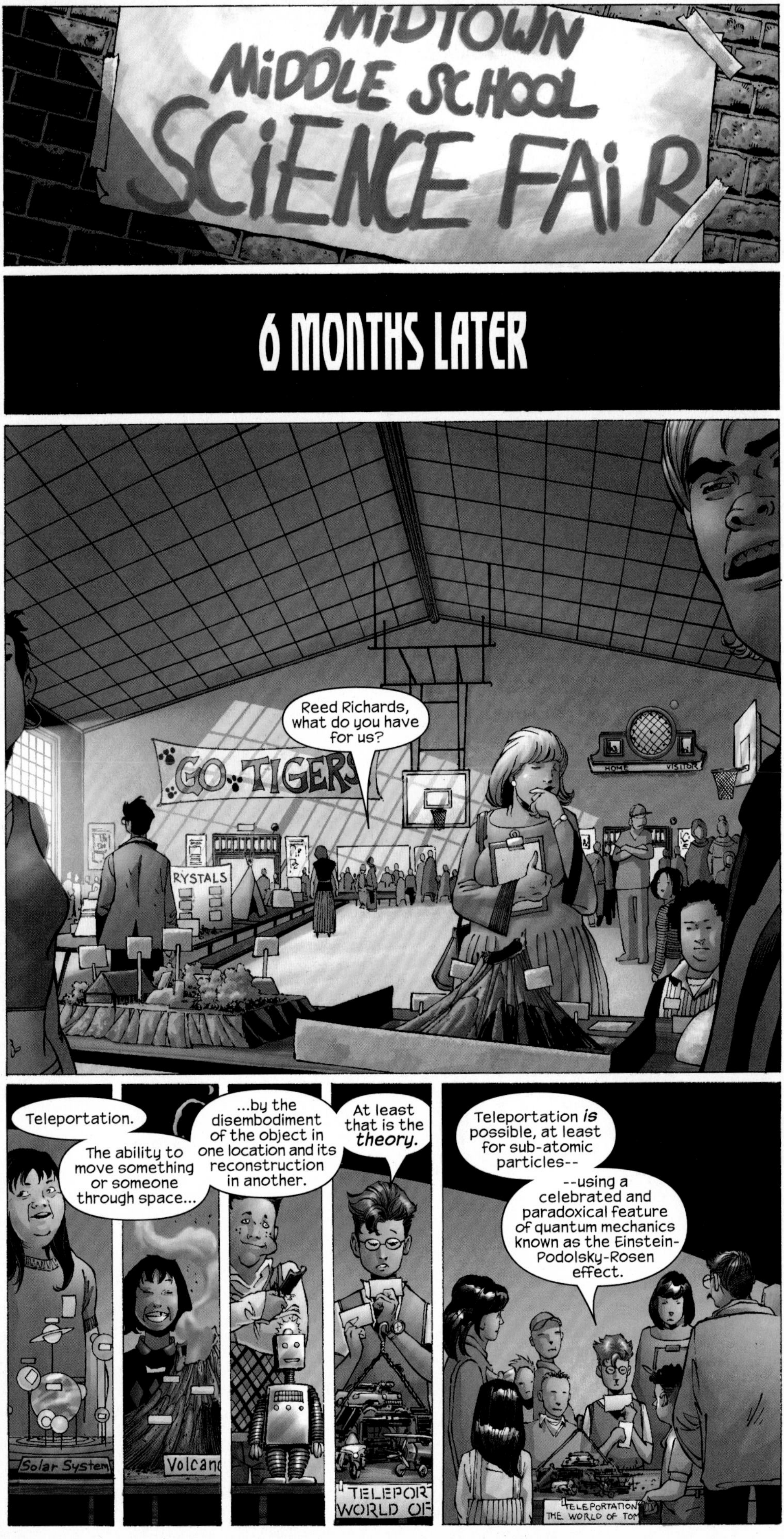
MIDTOWN MIDDLE SCHOOL SCIENCE FAIR
6 MONTHS LATER
Reed Richards, what do you have for us?
GO TIGERS
HOME VISITOR
RYSTALS
Teleportation.
The ability to move something or someone through space...
...by the disembodiment of the object in one location and its reconstruction in another.
At least that is the *theory.*
Solar System
Volcano
TELEPORT WORLD OF
Teleportation *is* possible, at least for sub-atomic particles--
--using a celebrated and paradoxical feature of quantum mechanics known as the Einstein-Podolsky-Rosen effect.
TELEPORTATION THE WORLD OF TOM

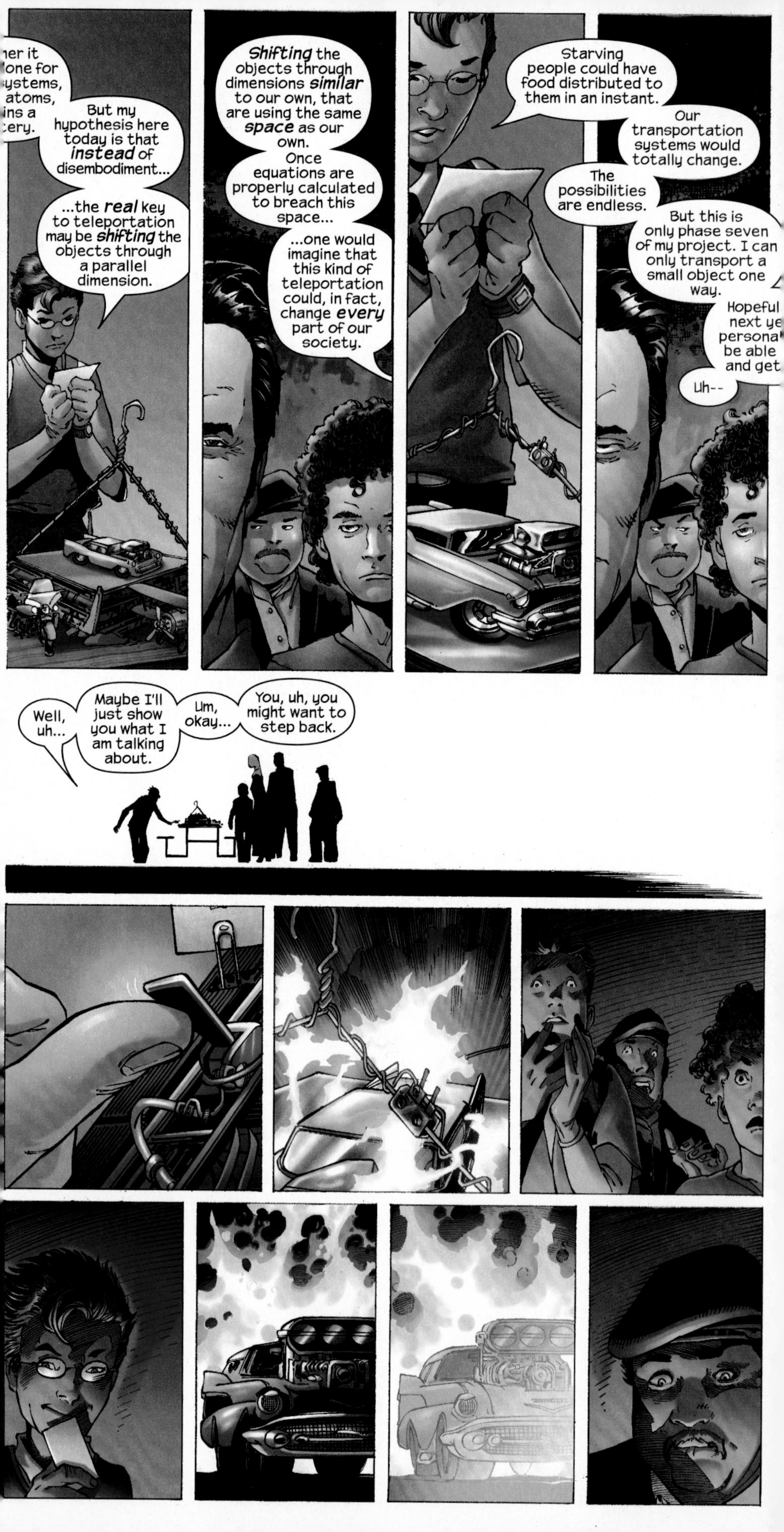
But my hypothesis here today is that instead of disembodiment...
...the real key to teleportation may be shifting the objects through a parallel dimension.
Shifting the objects through dimensions similar to our own, that are using the same space as our own.
Once equations are properly calculated to breach this space...
...one would imagine that this kind of teleportation could, in fact, change every part of our society.
Starving people could have food distributed to them in an instant.
Our transportation systems would totally change.
The possibilities are endless.
But this is only phase seven of my project. I can only transport a small object one way.
Uh--
Well, uh...
Maybe I'll just show you what I am talking about.
Um, okay...
You, uh, you might want to step back.

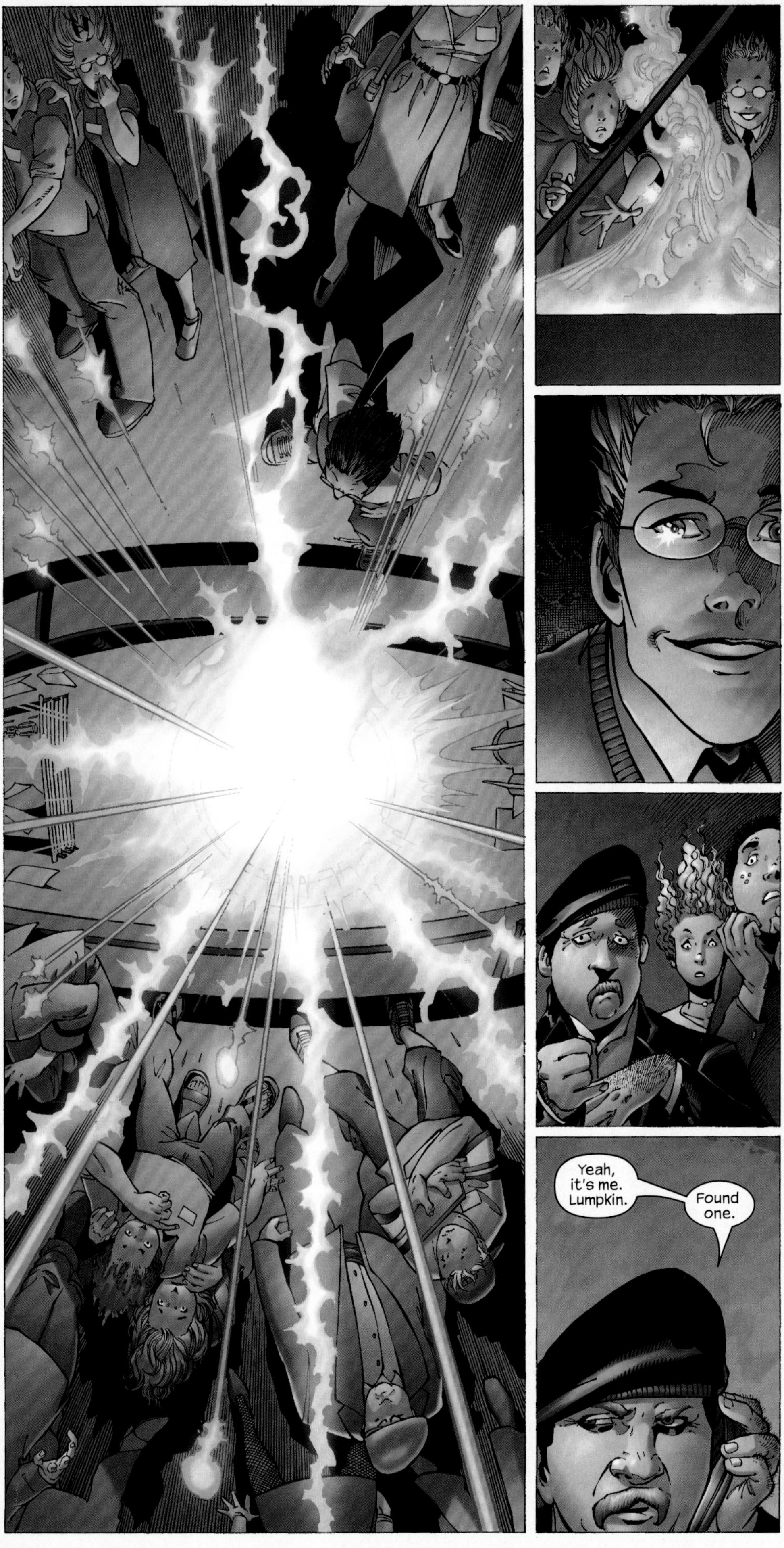
Yeah, it's me. Lumpkin.
Found one.

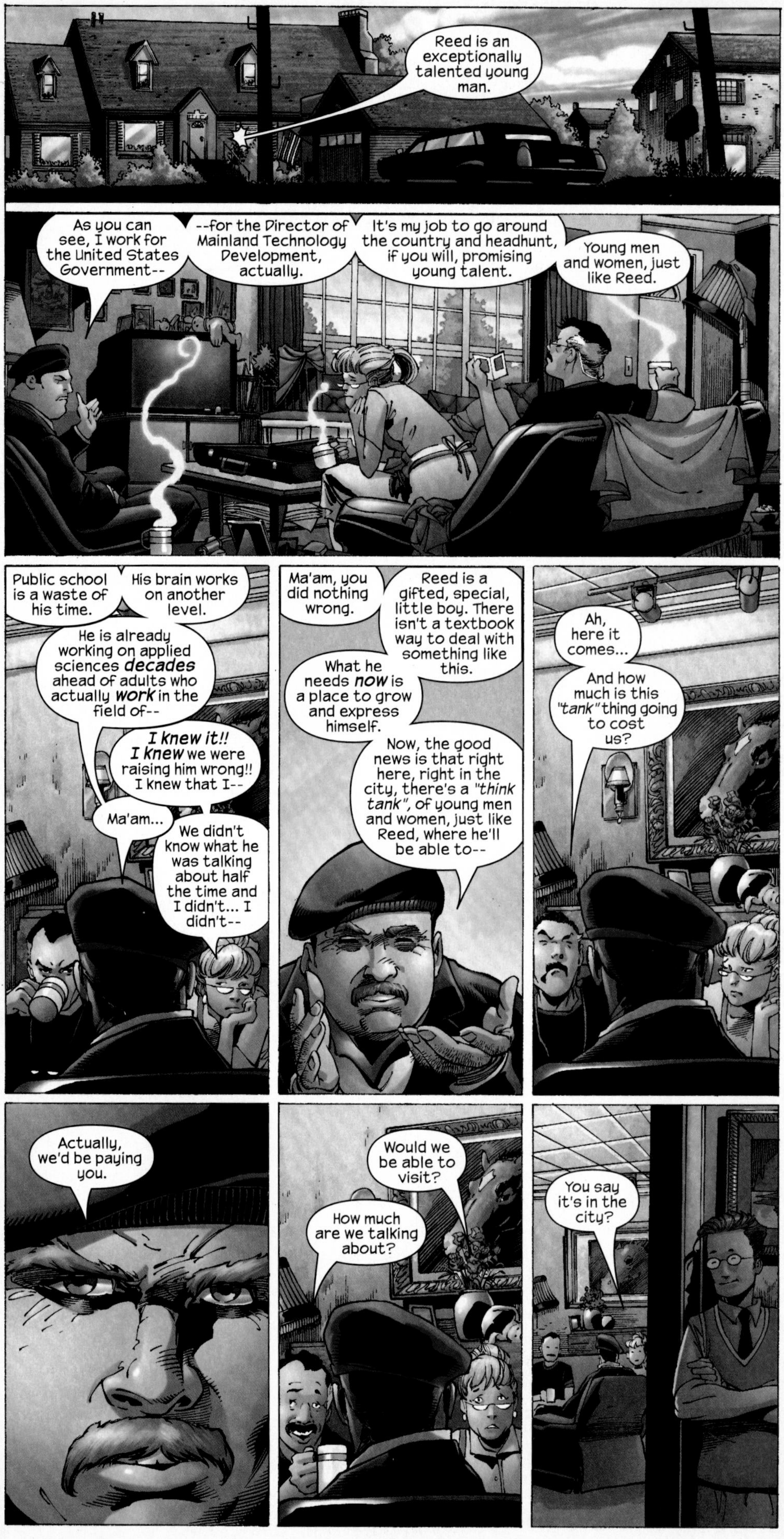

Reed is an exceptionally talented young man.
As you can see, I work for the United States Government--
--for the Director of Mainland Technology Development, actually.
It's my job to go around the country and headhunt, if you will, promising young talent.
Young men and women, just like Reed.
Public school is a waste of his time.
His brain works on another level.
He is already working on applied sciences *decades* ahead of adults who actually *work* in the field of--
I knew it!! I knew we were raising him wrong!! I knew that I--
Ma'am...
We didn't know what he was talking about half the time and I didn't... I didn't--
Ma'am, you did nothing wrong.
Reed is a gifted, special, little boy. There isn't a textbook way to deal with something like this.
What he needs ***now*** is a place to grow and express himself.
Now, the good news is that right here, right in the city, there's a *"think tank"*, of young men and women, just like Reed, where he'll be able to--
Ah, here it comes...
And how much is this *"tank"* thing going to cost us?
Actually, we'd be paying you.
Would we be able to visit?
How much are we talking about?
You say it's in the city?

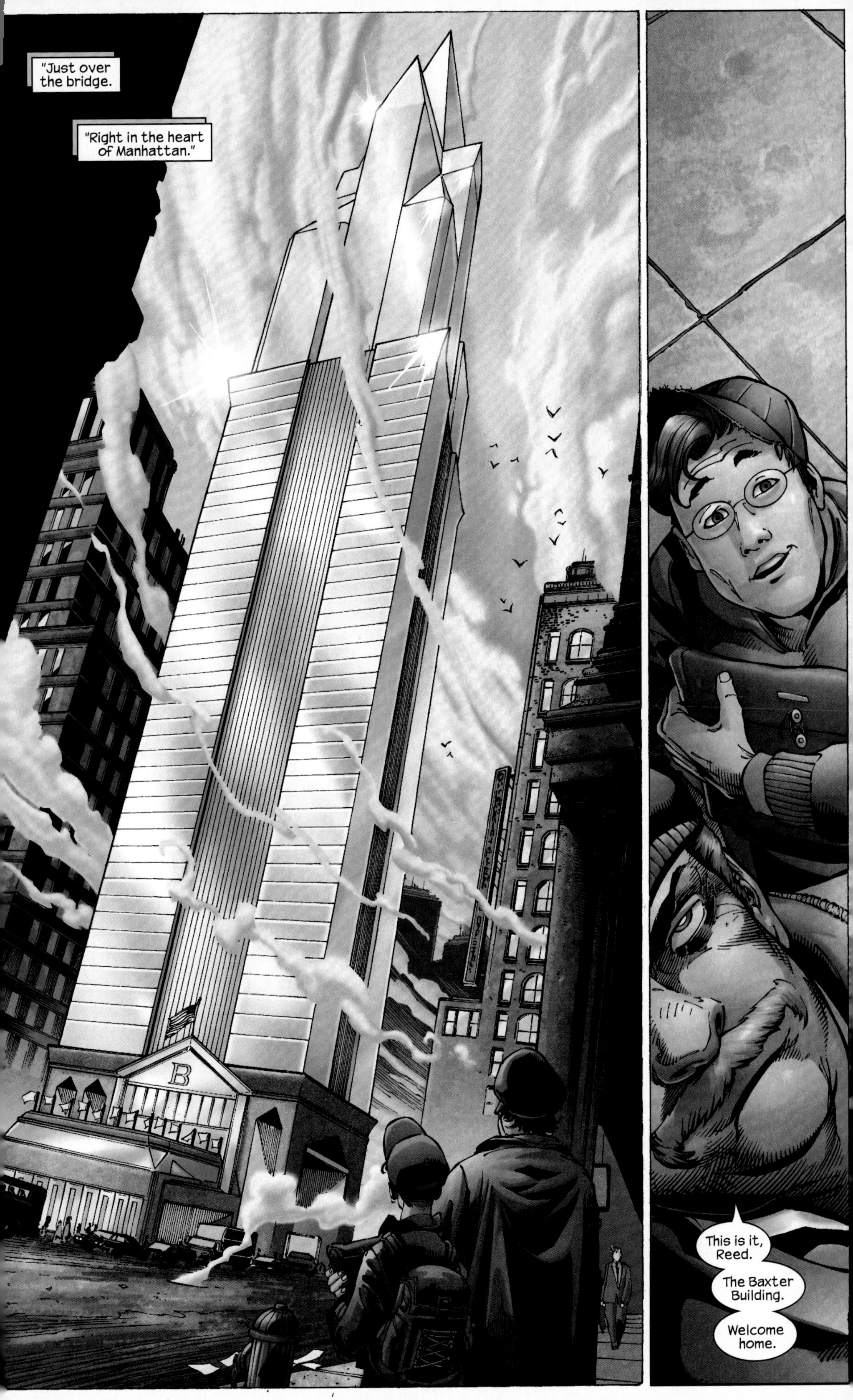
"Just over the bridge.
"Right in the heart of Manhattan."
B
This is it, Reed.
The Baxter Building.
Welcome home.

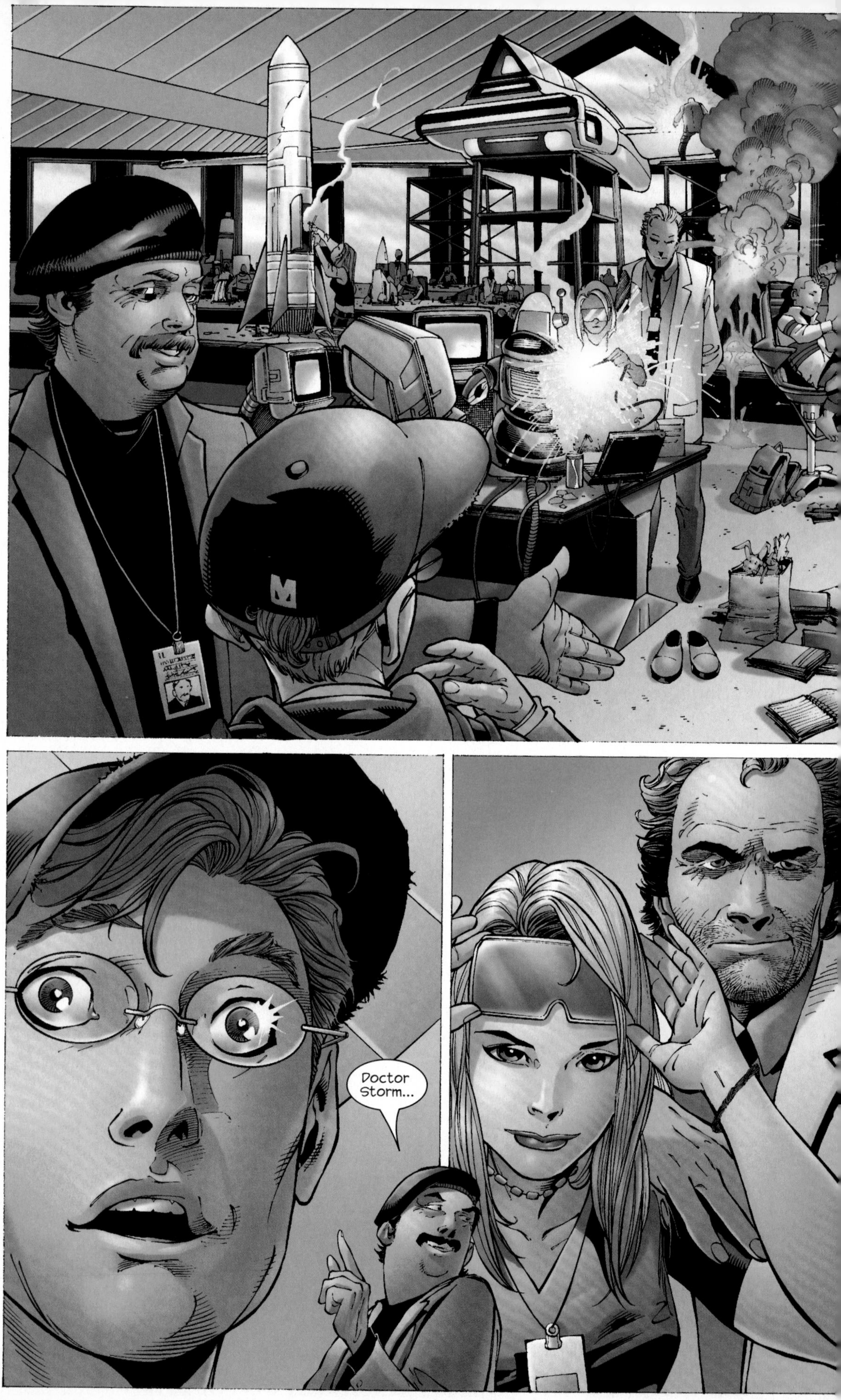
Doctor Storm...

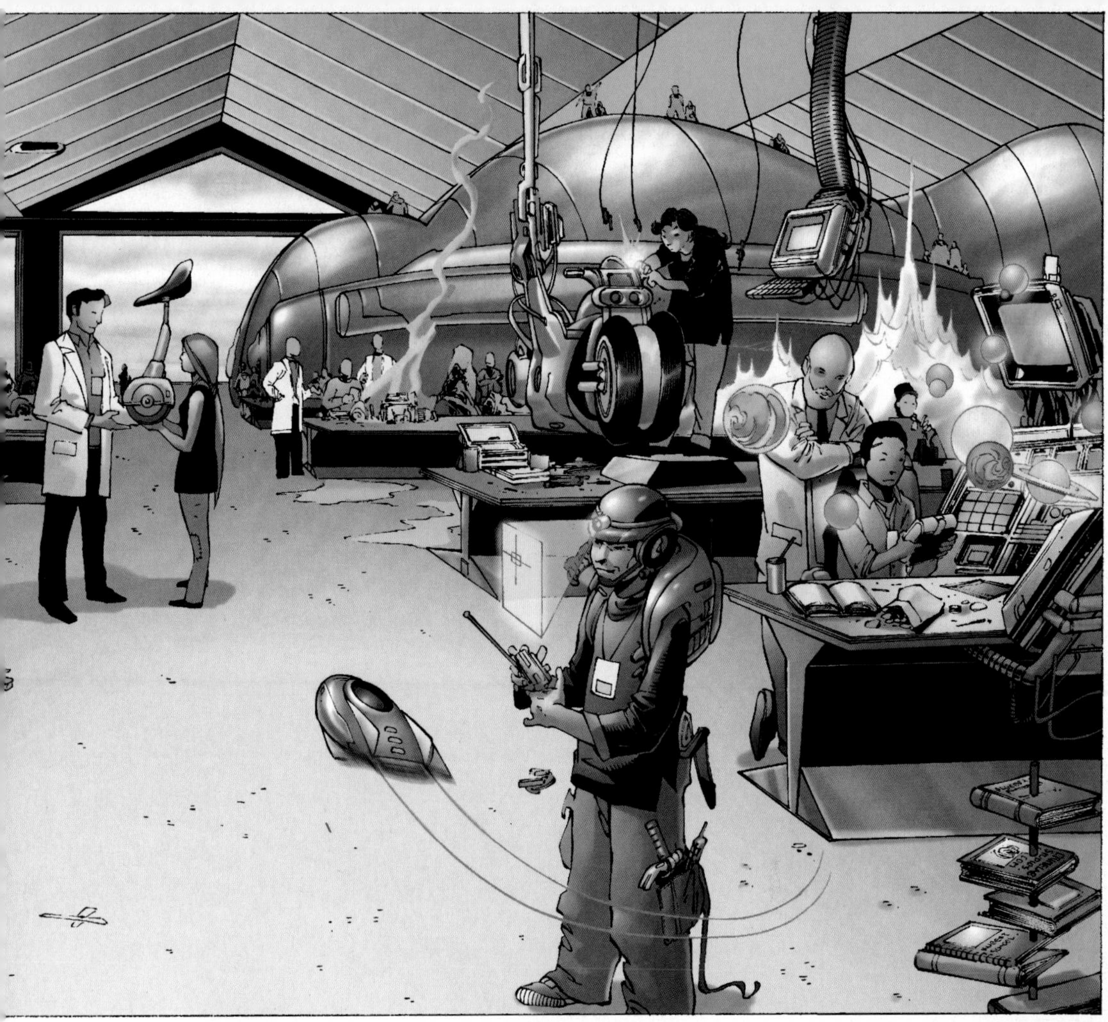

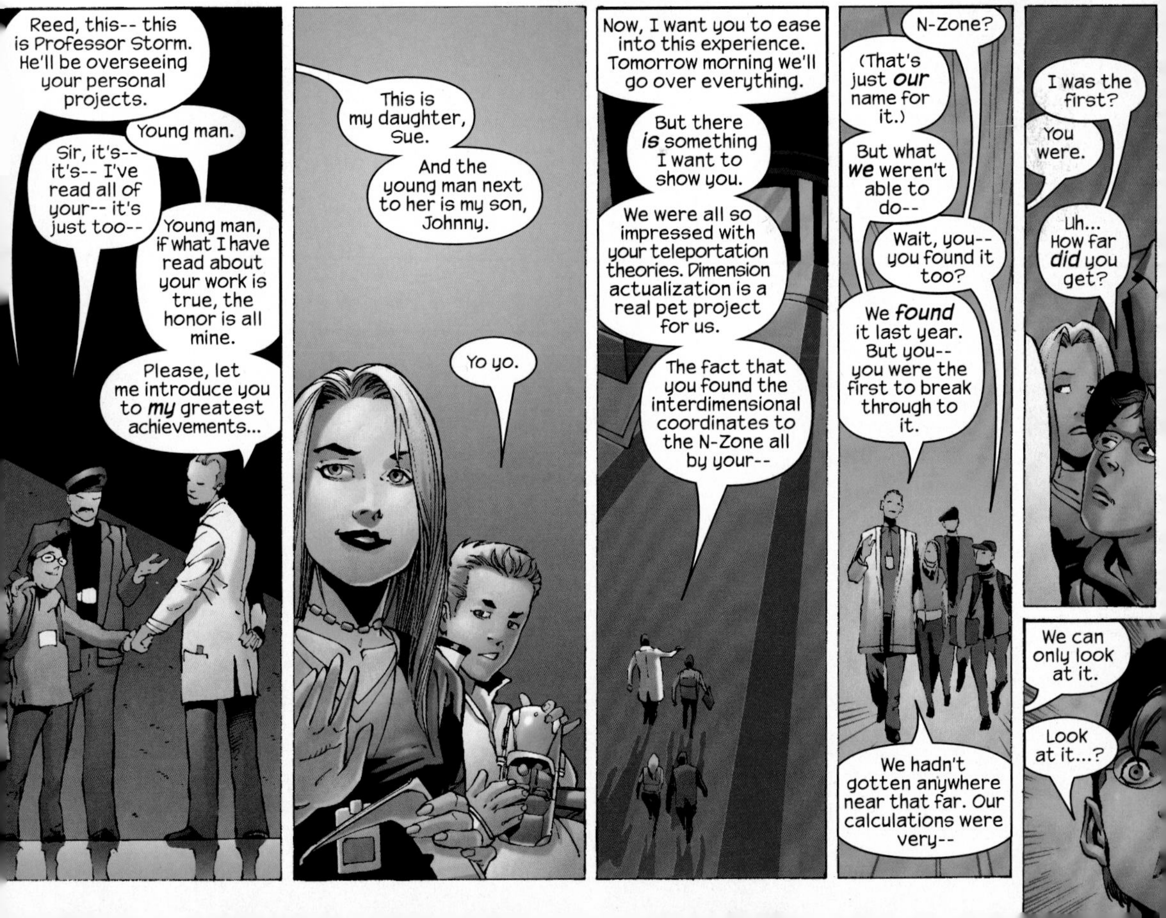

Reed, this-- this is Professor Storm. He'll be overseeing your personal projects.
Young man.
Sir, it's-- it's-- I've read all of your-- it's just too--
Young man, if what I have read about your work is true, the honor is all mine.
Please, let me introduce you to *my* greatest achievements...
This is my daughter, Sue.
And the young man next to her is my son, Johnny.
Yo yo.
Now, I want you to ease into this experience. Tomorrow morning we'll go over everything.
But there *is* something I want to show you.
We were all so impressed with your teleportation theories. Dimension actualization is a real pet project for us.
The fact that you found the interdimensional coordinates to the N-Zone all by your--
N-Zone?
(That's just *our* name for it.)
But what *we* weren't able to do--
Wait, you-- you found it too?
We *found* it last year. But you-- you were the first to break through to it.
We hadn't gotten anywhere near that far. Our calculations were very--
I was the first?
You were.
Uh... How far *did* you get?
We can only look at it.
Look at it...?

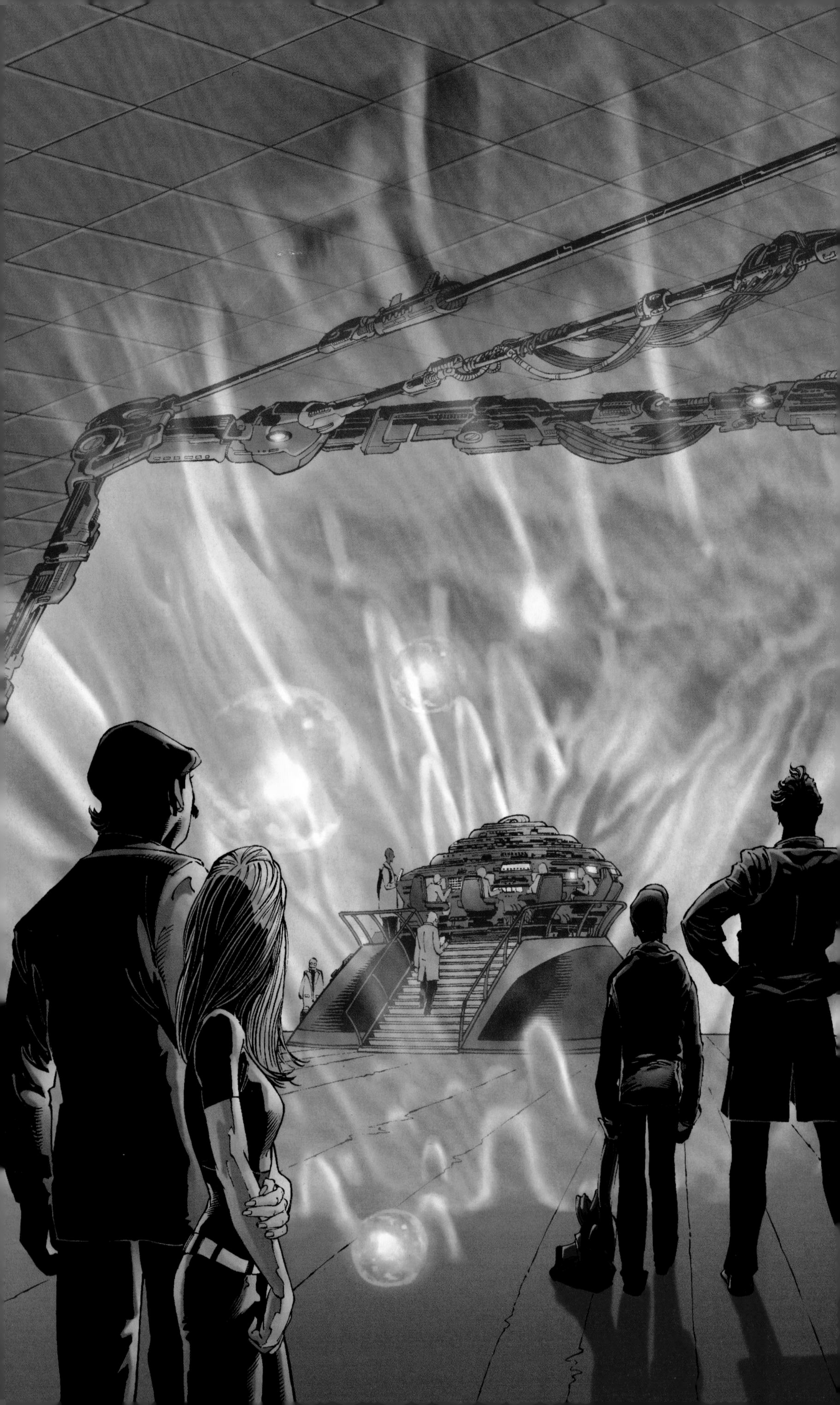

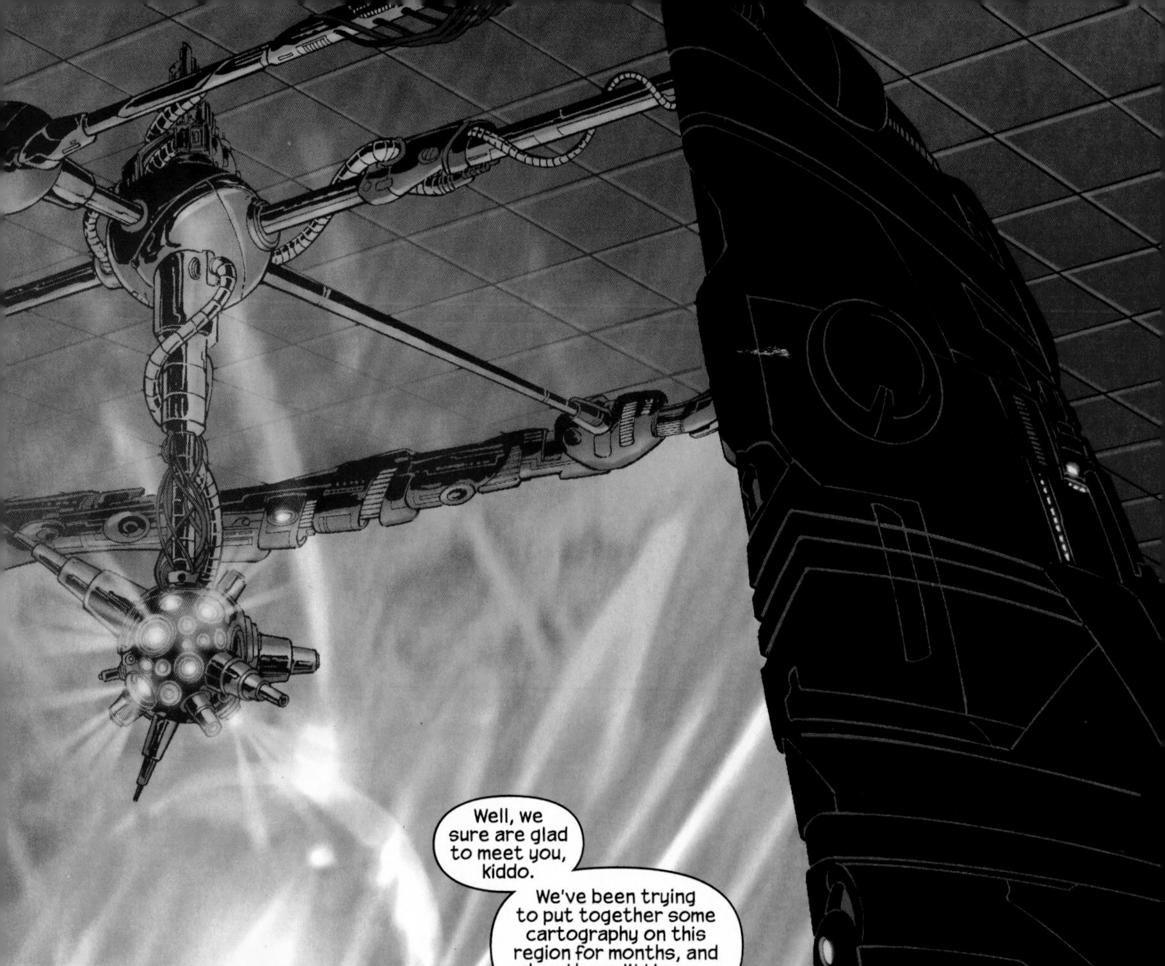
Well, we sure are glad to meet you, kiddo.
We've been trying to put together some cartography on this region for months, and when these little cars started appearing...
...we thought we'd gone *nuts.*

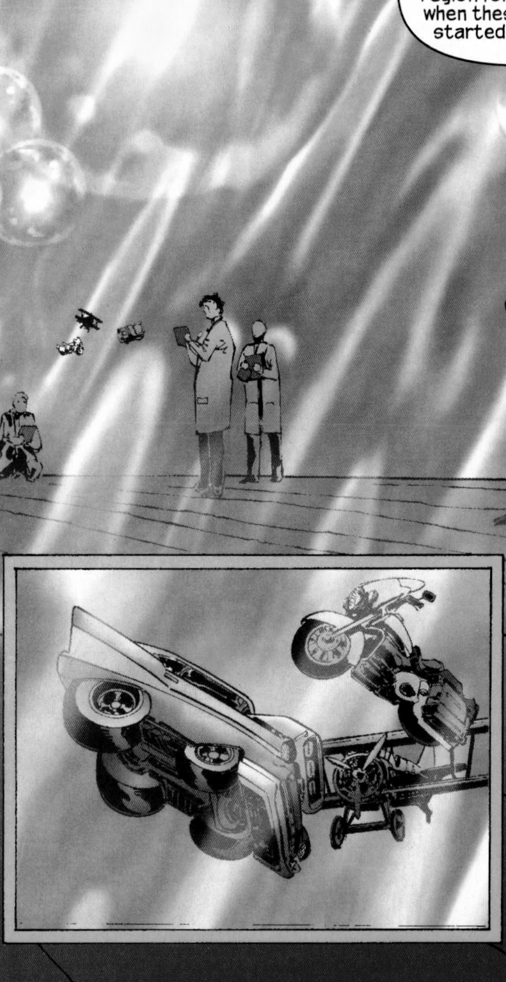

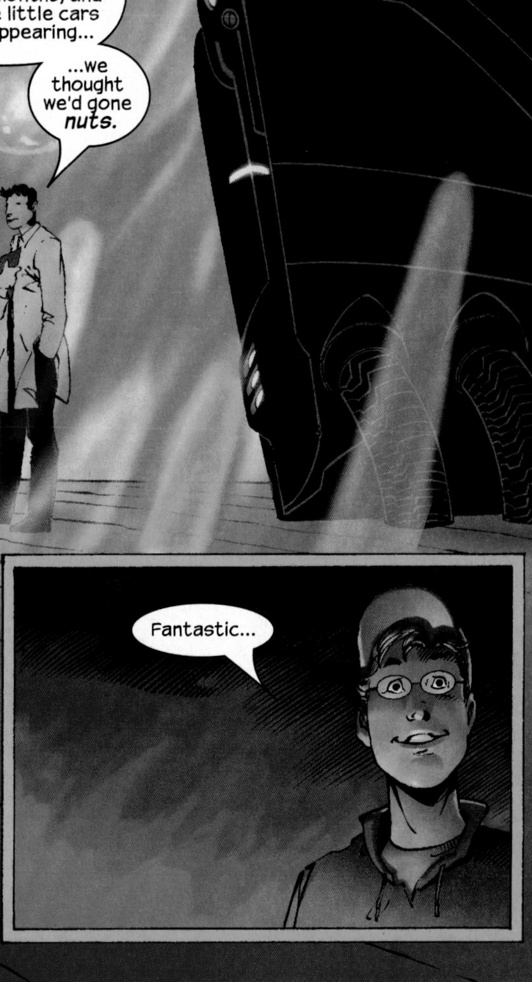
Fantastic...

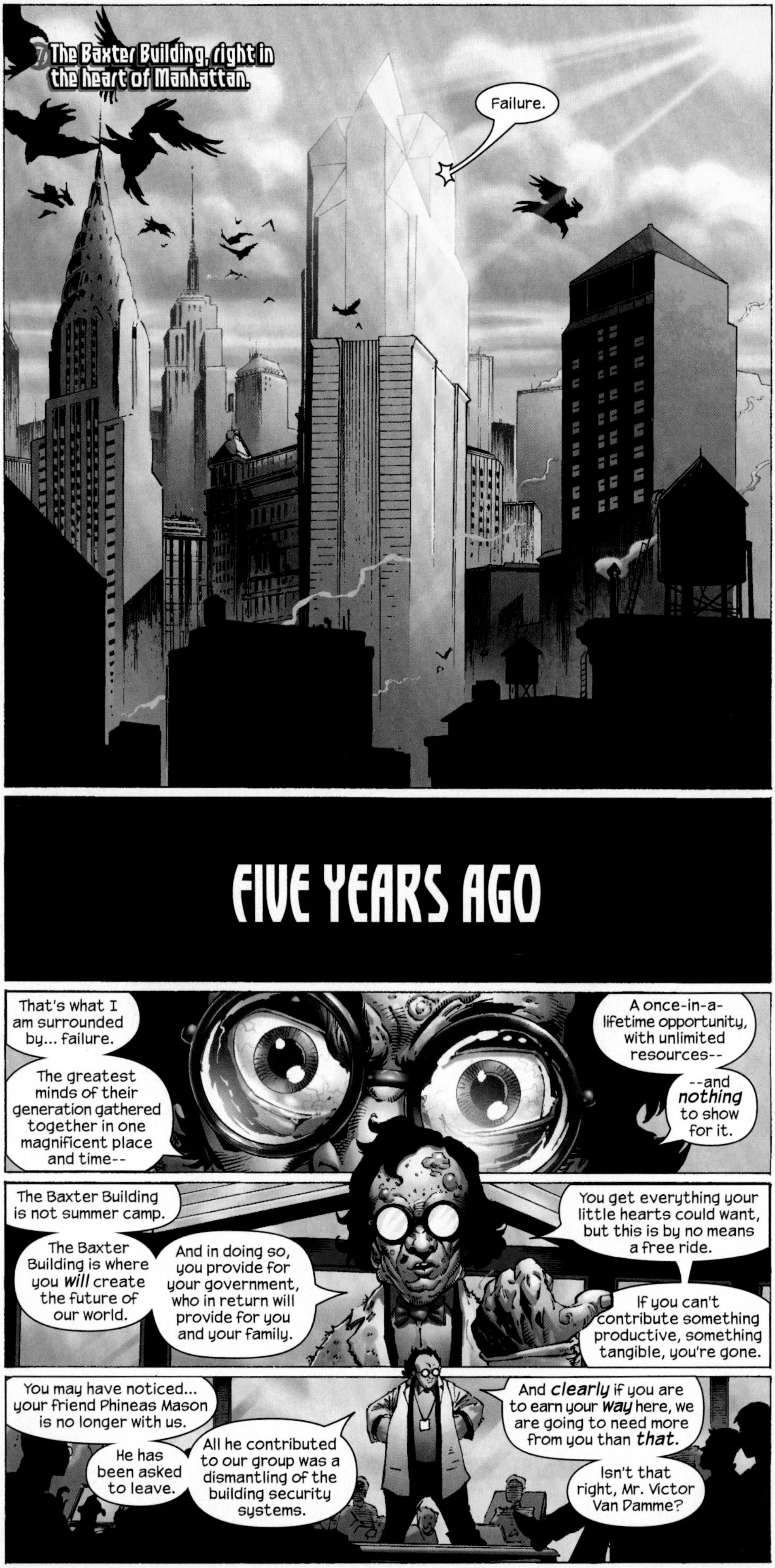
The Baxter Building, right in the heart of Manhattan.
Failure.
FIVE YEARS AGO
That's what I am surrounded by... failure.
The greatest minds of their generation gathered together in one magnificent place and time--
A once-in-a-lifetime opportunity, with unlimited resources--
--and *nothing* to show for it.
The Baxter Building is not summer camp.
The Baxter Building is where you *will* create the future of our world.
And in doing so, you provide for your government, who in return will provide for you and your family.
You get everything your little hearts could want, but this is by no means a free ride.
If you can't contribute something productive, something tangible, you're gone.
You may have noticed... your friend Phineas Mason is no longer with us.
He has been asked to leave.
All he contributed to our group was a dismantling of the building security systems.
And *clearly* if you are to earn your *way* here, we are going to need more from you than *that*.
Isn't that right, Mr. Victor Van Damme?

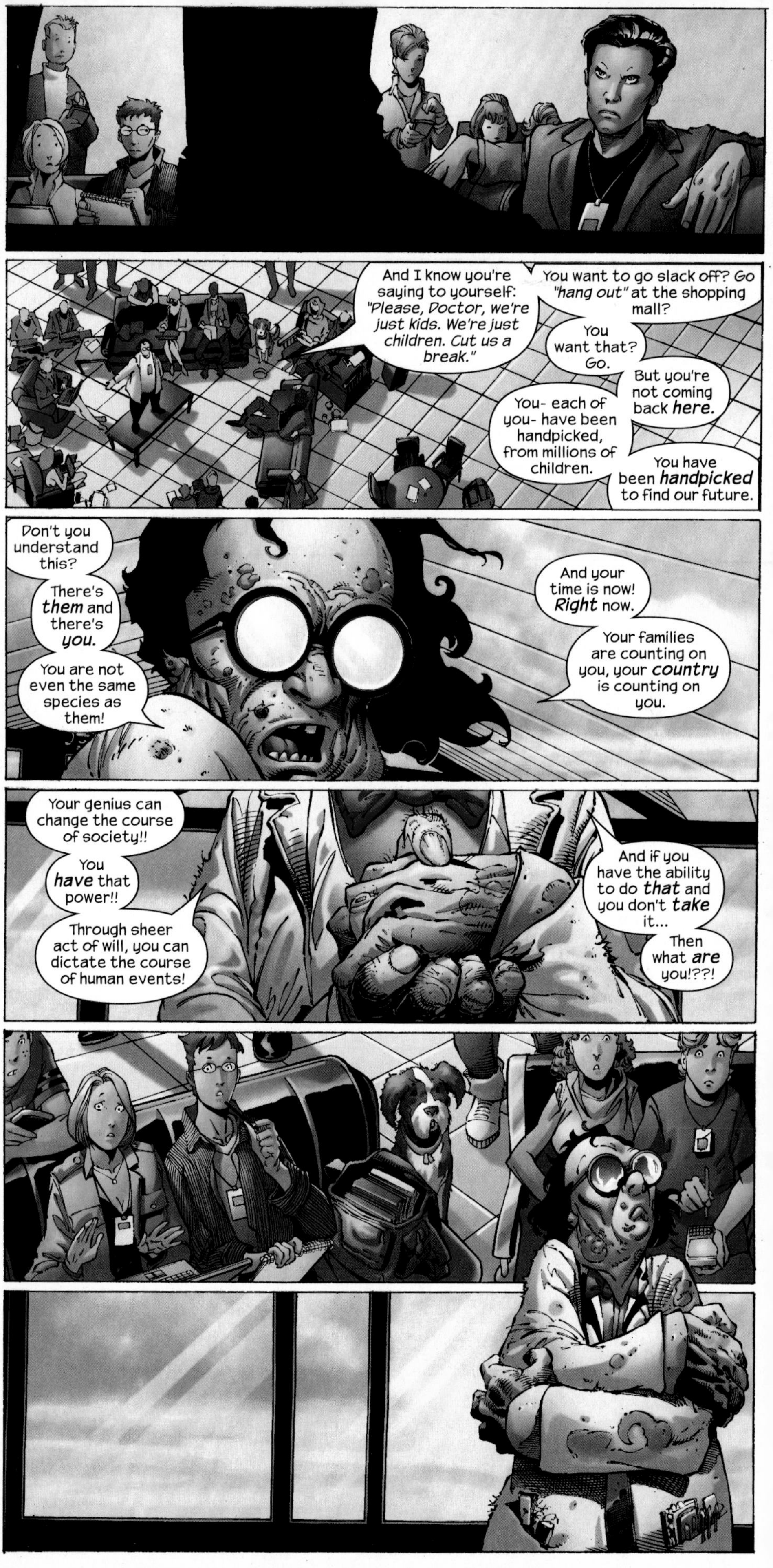

And I know you're saying to yourself: "Please, Doctor, we're just kids. We're just children. Cut us a break."
You want to go slack off? Go "hang out" at the shopping mall?
You want that? Go.
But you're not coming back here.
You- each of you- have been handpicked, from millions of children.
You have been handpicked to find our future.
Don't you understand this?
There's them and there's you.
You are not even the same species as them!
And your time is now! Right now.
Your families are counting on you, your country is counting on you.
Your genius can change the course of society!!
You have that power!!
Through sheer act of will, you can dictate the course of human events!
And if you have the ability to do that and you don't take it...
Then what are you!??!

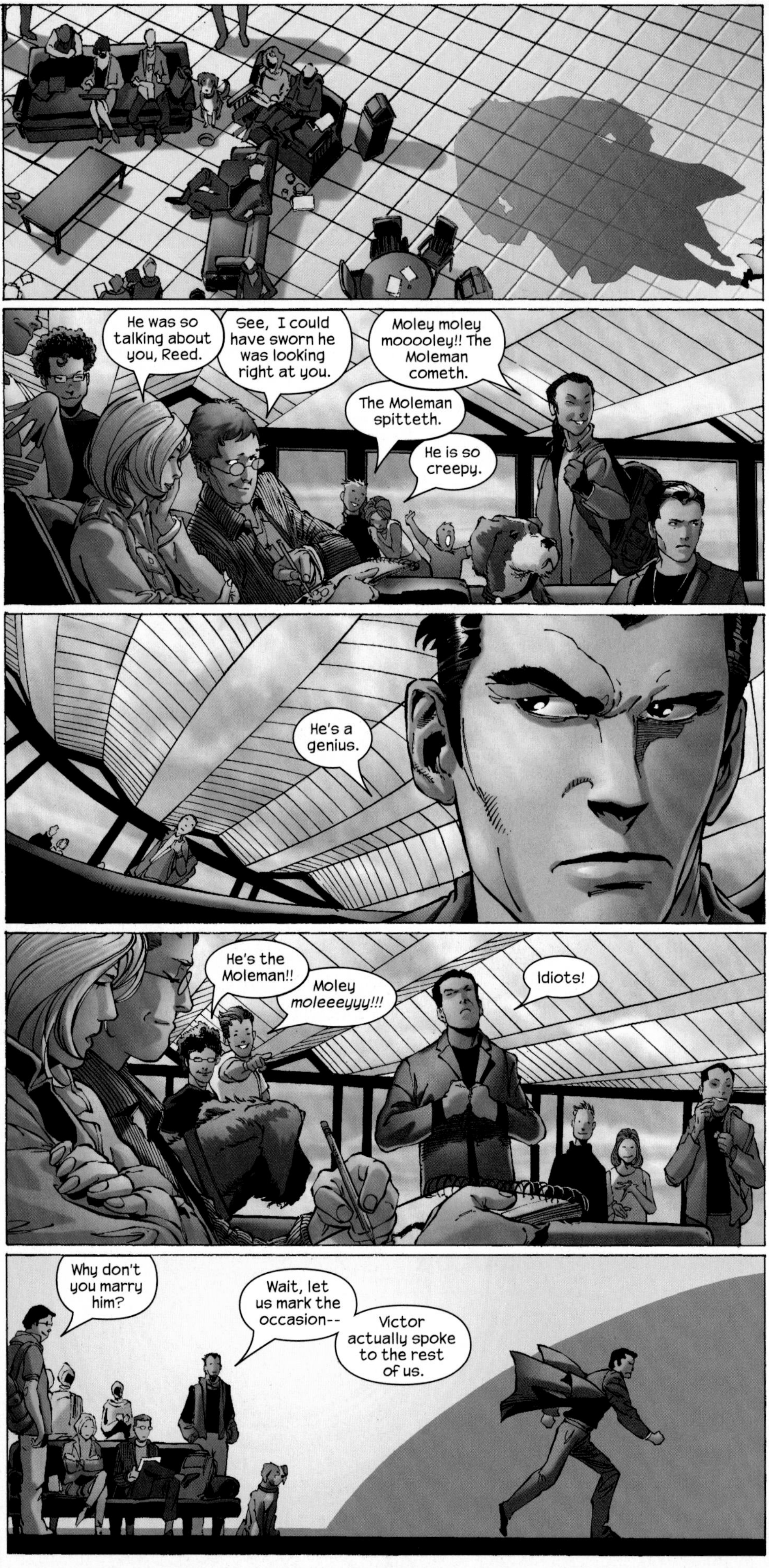

He was so talking about you, Reed.
See, I could have sworn he was looking right at you.
Moley moley moooooley!! The Moleman cometh.
The Moleman spitteth.
He is so creepy.
He's a genius.
He's the Moleman!!
Moley *moleeeyyy!!!*
Idiots!
Why don't you marry him?
Wait, let us mark the occasion--
Victor actually spoke to the rest of us.

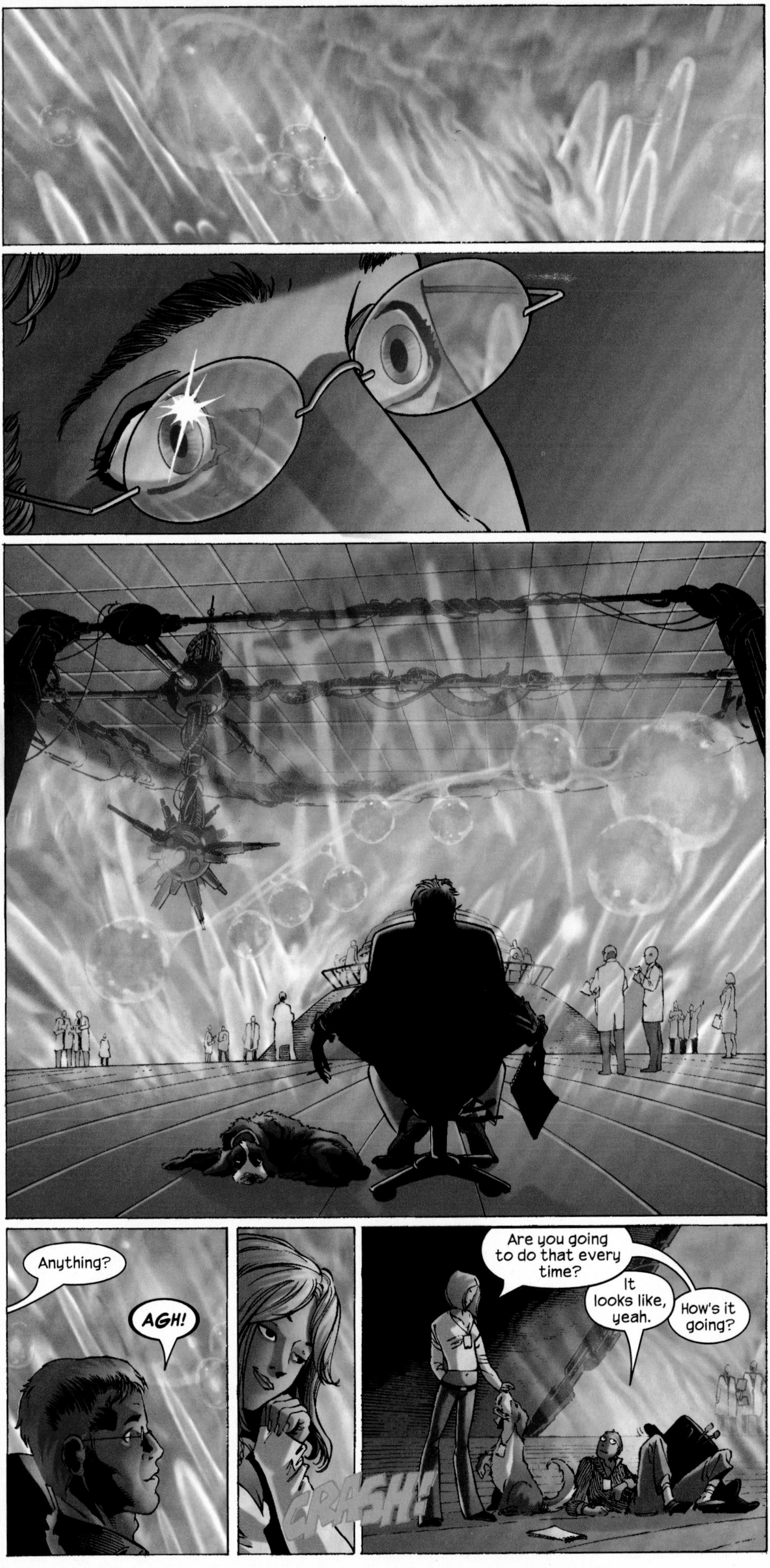

Anything?
AGH!
CRASH!
Are you going to do that every time?
It looks like, yeah.
How's it going?

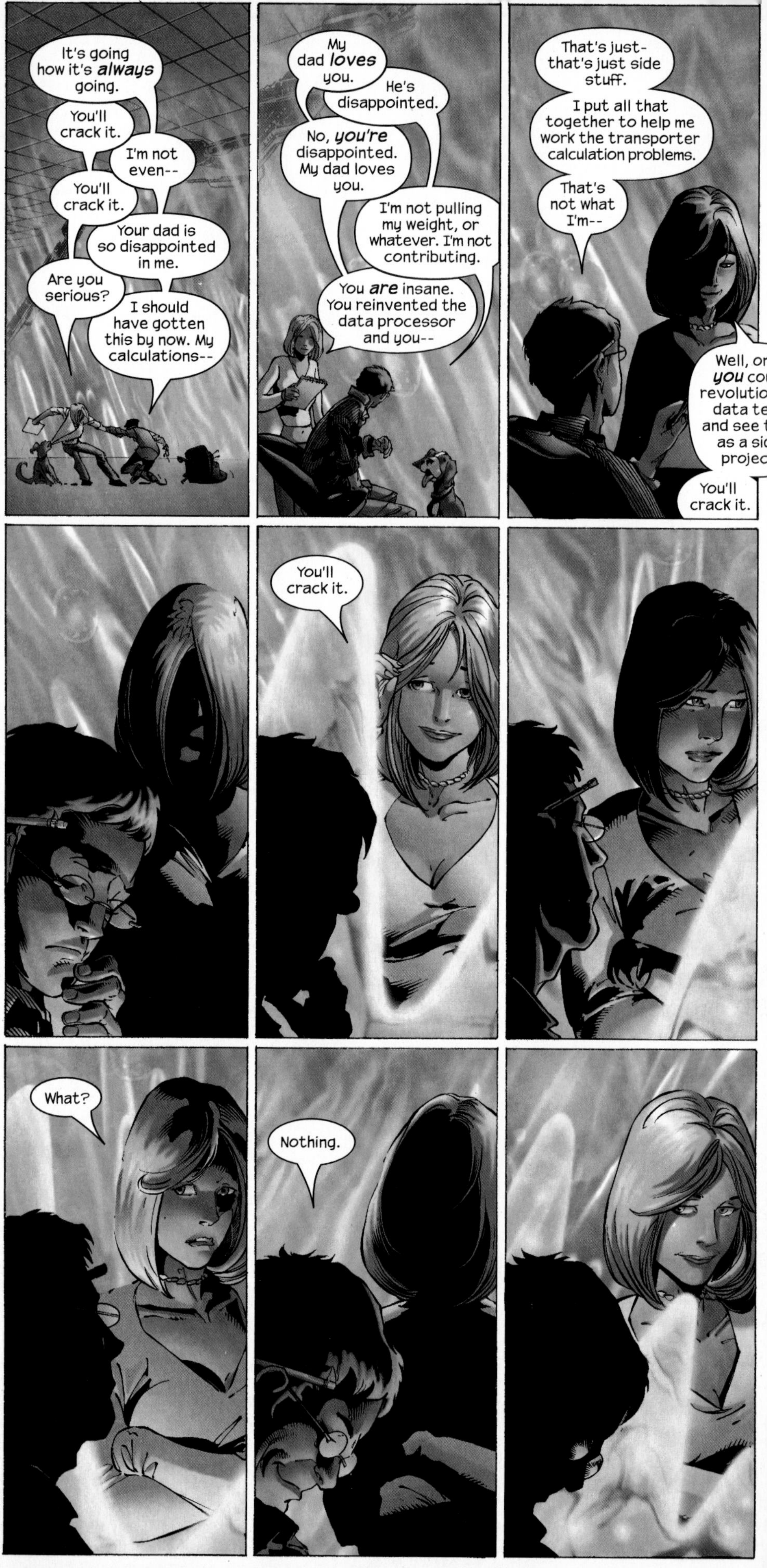
It's going how it's *always* going.
You'll crack it.
I'm not even--
You'll crack it.
Your dad is so disappointed in me.
Are you serious?
I should have gotten this by now. My calculations--
My dad *loves* you.
He's disappointed.
No, *you're* disappointed. My dad loves you.
I'm not pulling my weight, or whatever. I'm not contributing.
You *are* insane. You reinvented the data processor and you--
That's just-that's just side stuff.
I put all that together to help me work the transporter calculation problems.
That's not what I'm--
You'll crack it.
You'll crack it.
What?
Nothing.

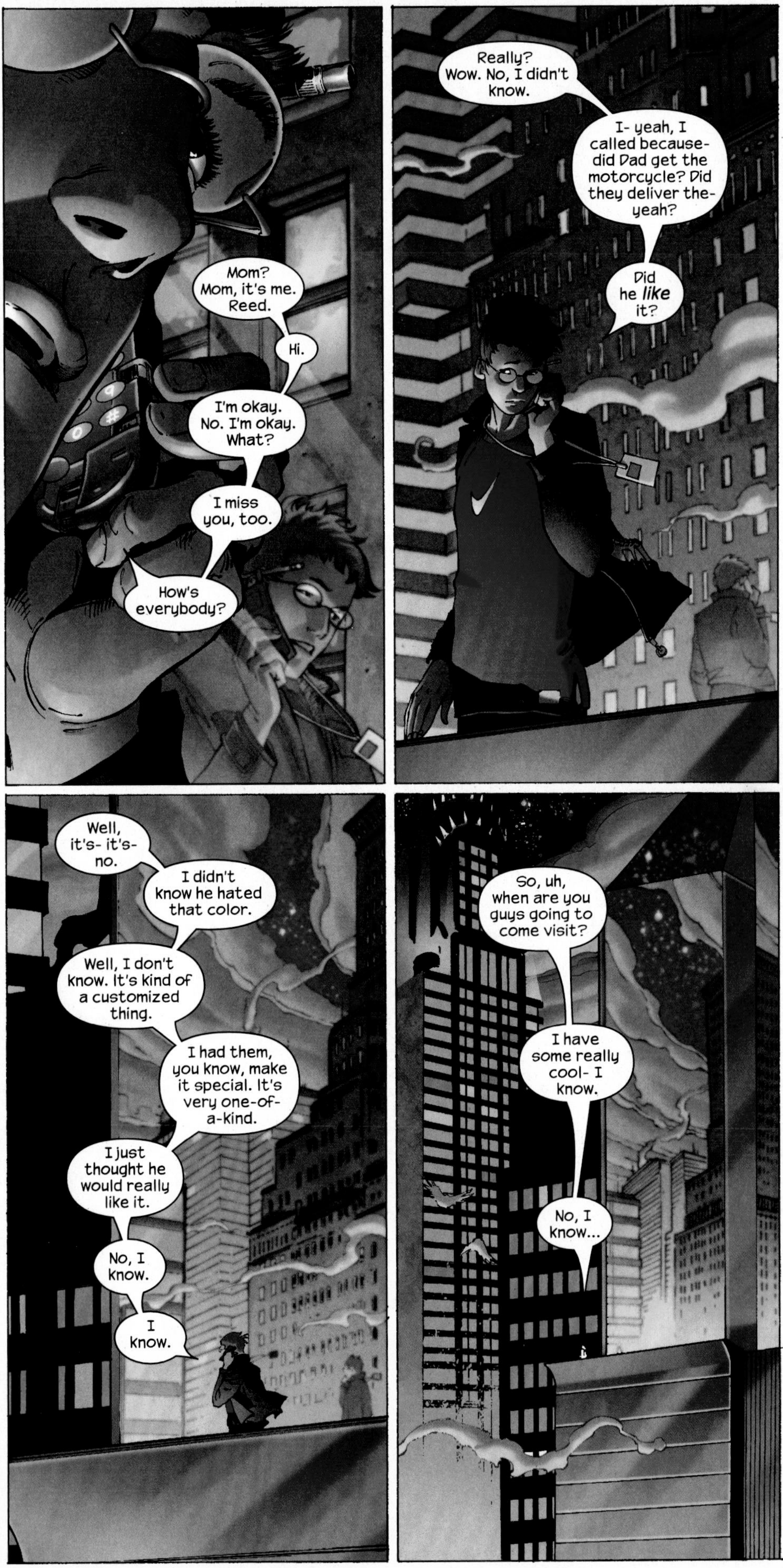
Mom? Mom, it's me. Reed.
Hi.
I'm okay. No. I'm okay. What?
I miss you, too.
How's everybody?
Really? Wow. No, I didn't know.
I- yeah, I called because- did Dad get the motorcycle? Did they deliver the- yeah?
Did he *like* it?
Well, it's- it's- no.
I didn't know he hated that color.
Well, I don't know. It's kind of a customized thing.
I had them, you know, make it special. It's very one-of-a-kind.
I just thought he would really like it.
No, I know.
I know.
So, uh, when are you guys going to come visit?
I have some really cool- I know.
No, I know...

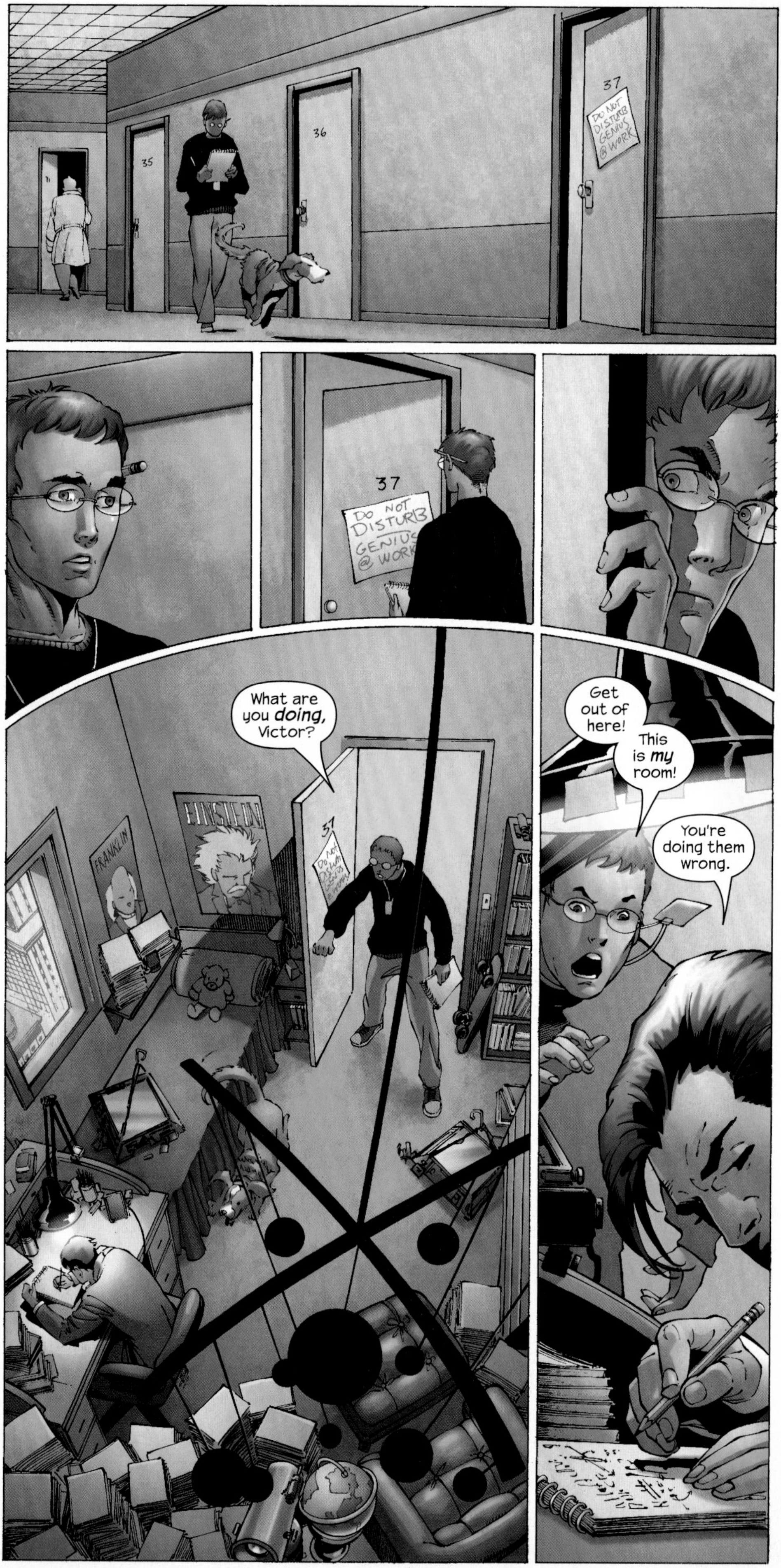
37
DO NOT DISTURB GENIUS @ WORK
36
35
37
DO NOT DISTURB GENIUS @ WORK
FRANKLIN
EINSTEIN
What are you *doing,* Victor?
Get out of here!
This is *my* room!
You're doing them wrong.

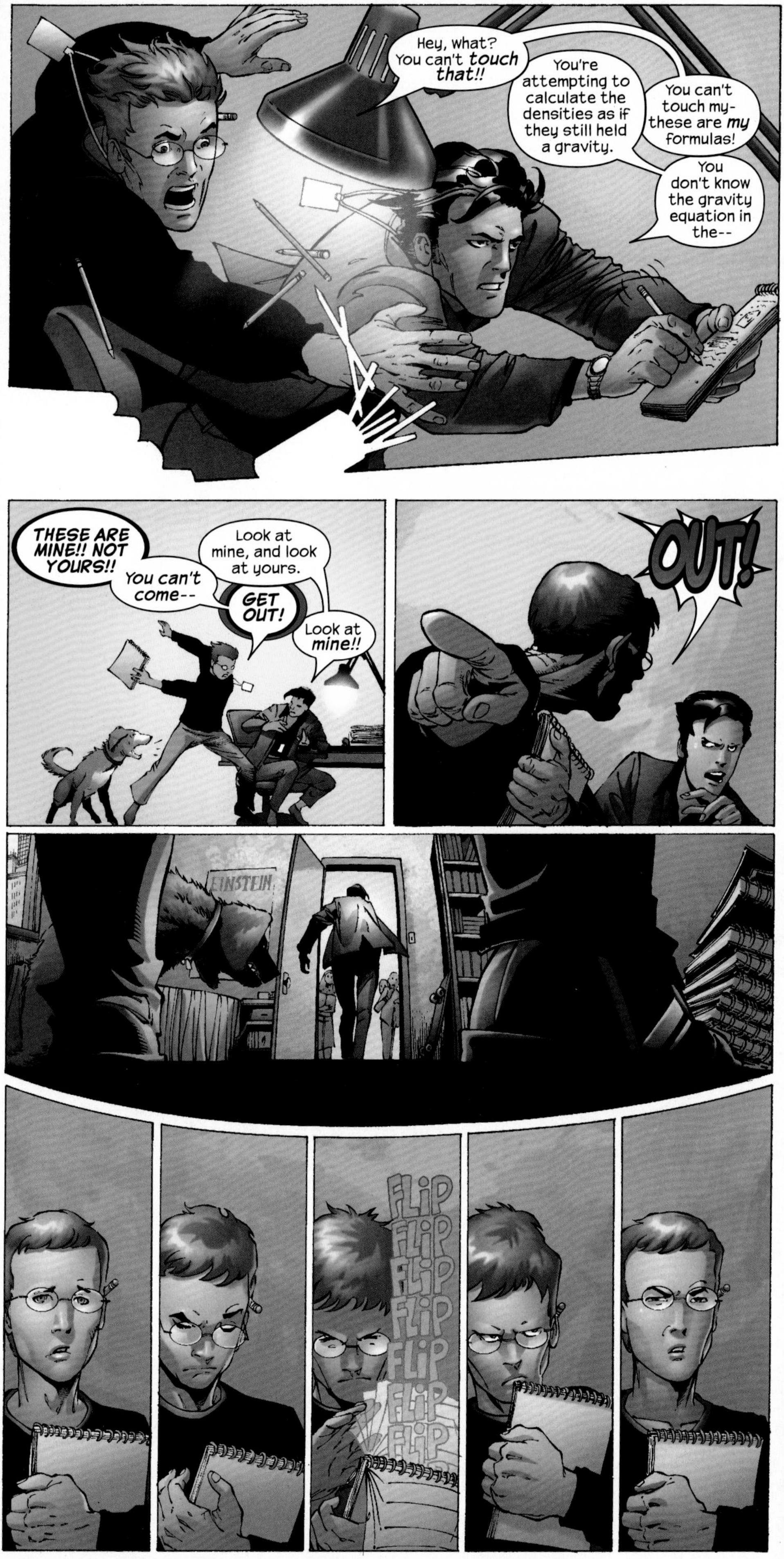

Hey, what? You can't touch that!!
You're attempting to calculate the densities as if they still held a gravity.
You can't touch my-- these are my formulas!
You don't know the gravity equation in the--
THESE ARE MINE!! NOT YOURS!!
You can't come--
Look at mine, and look at yours.
GET OUT!
Look at mine!!
OUT!
EINSTEIN
FLIP
FLIP
FLIP
FLIP
FLIP
FLIP
FLIP

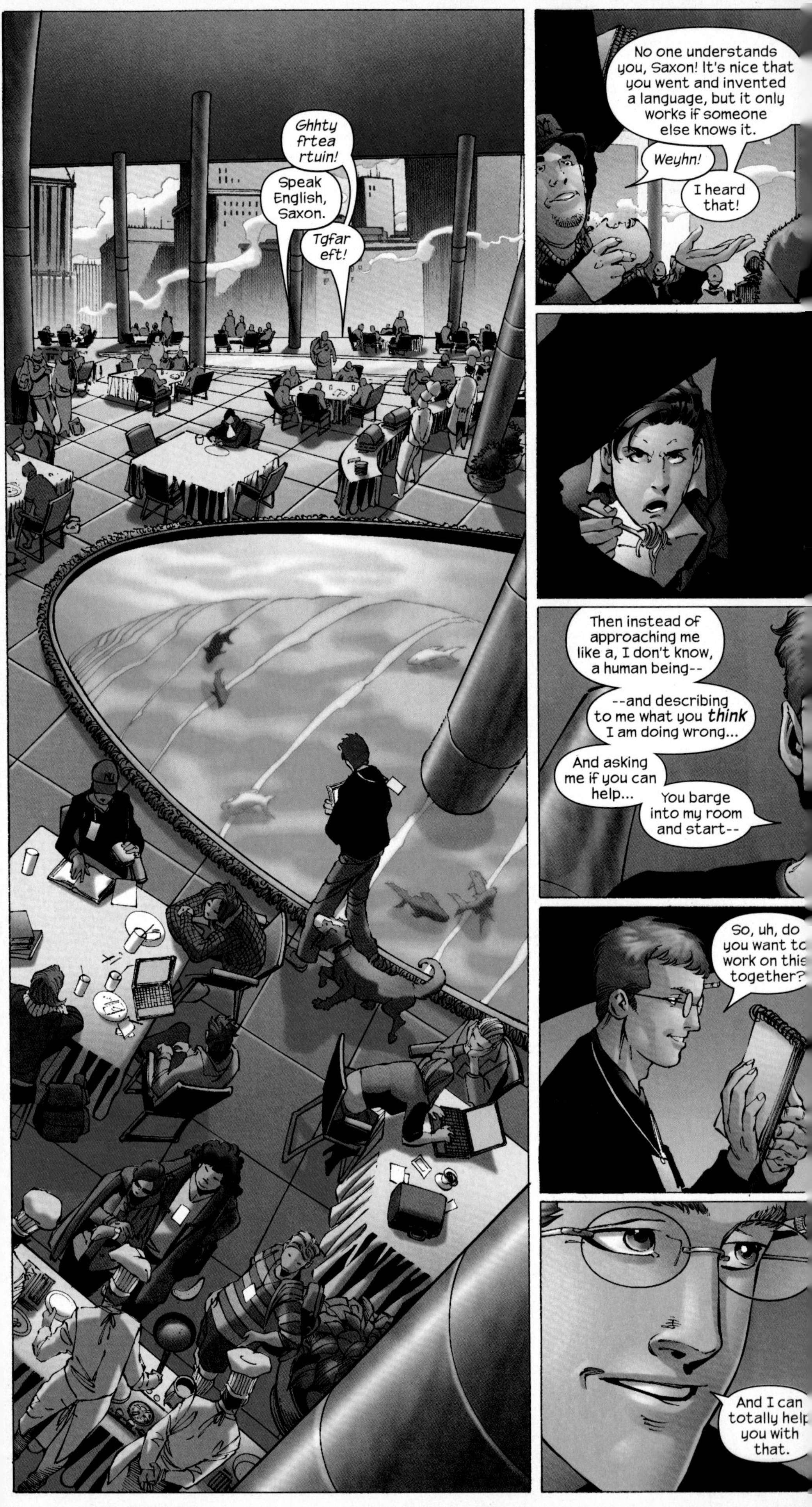

Ghhty frtea rtuin!
Speak English, Saxon.
Tgfar eft!
No one understands you, Saxon! It's nice that you went and invented a language, but it only works if someone else knows it.
Weyhn!
I heard that!
Then instead of approaching me like a, I don't know, a human being--
--and describing to me what you *think* I am doing wrong...
And asking me if you can help...
You barge into my room and start--
So, uh, do you want to work on this together?
And I can totally help you with that.

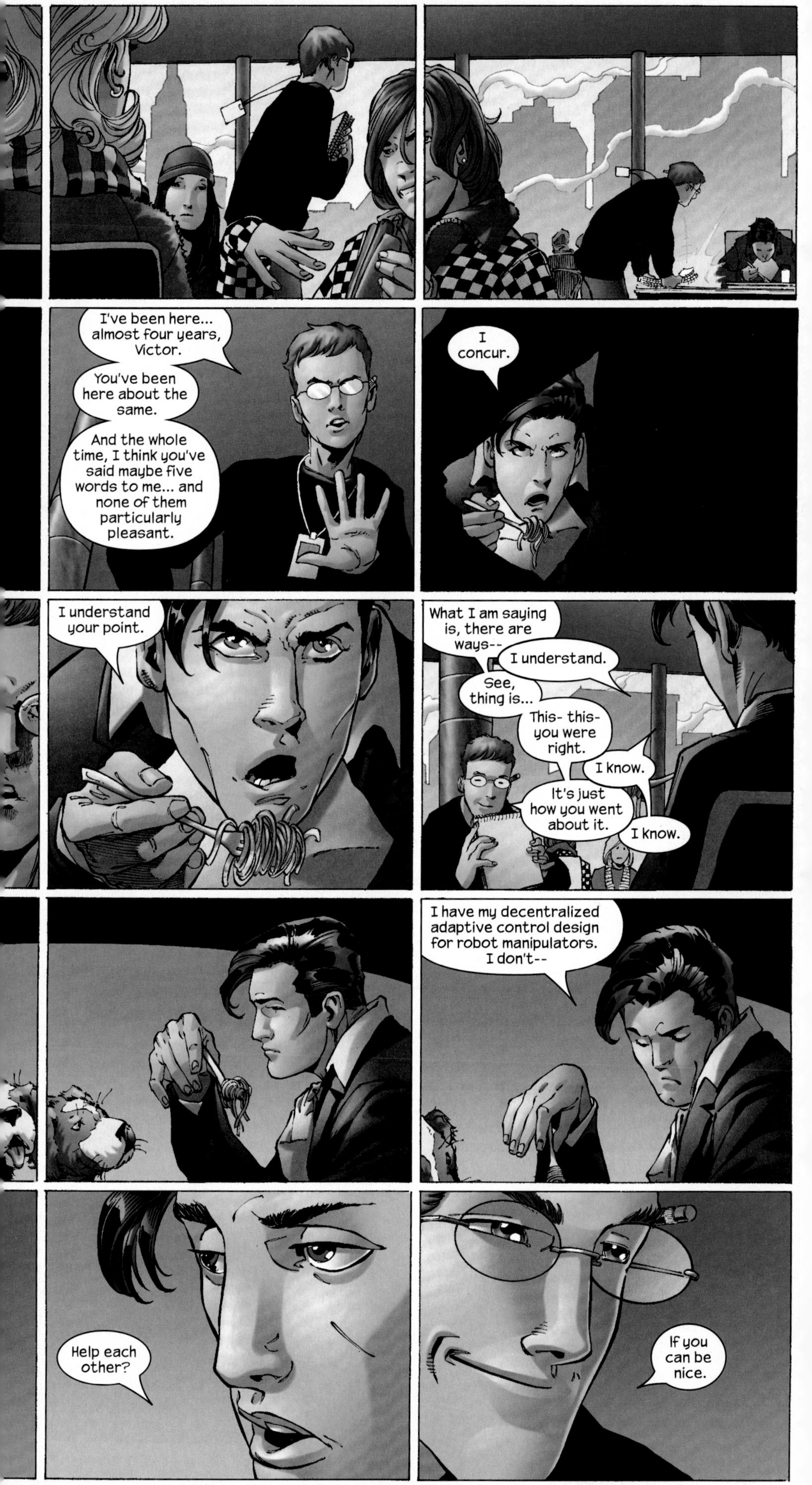

I've been here... almost four years, Victor.
You've been here about the same.
And the whole time, I think you've said maybe five words to me... and none of them particularly pleasant.
I concur.
I understand your point.
What I am saying is, there are ways--
I understand.
See, thing is...
This- this- you were right.
I know.
It's just how you went about it.
I know.
I have my decentralized adaptive control design for robot manipulators. I don't--
Help each other?
If you can be nice.

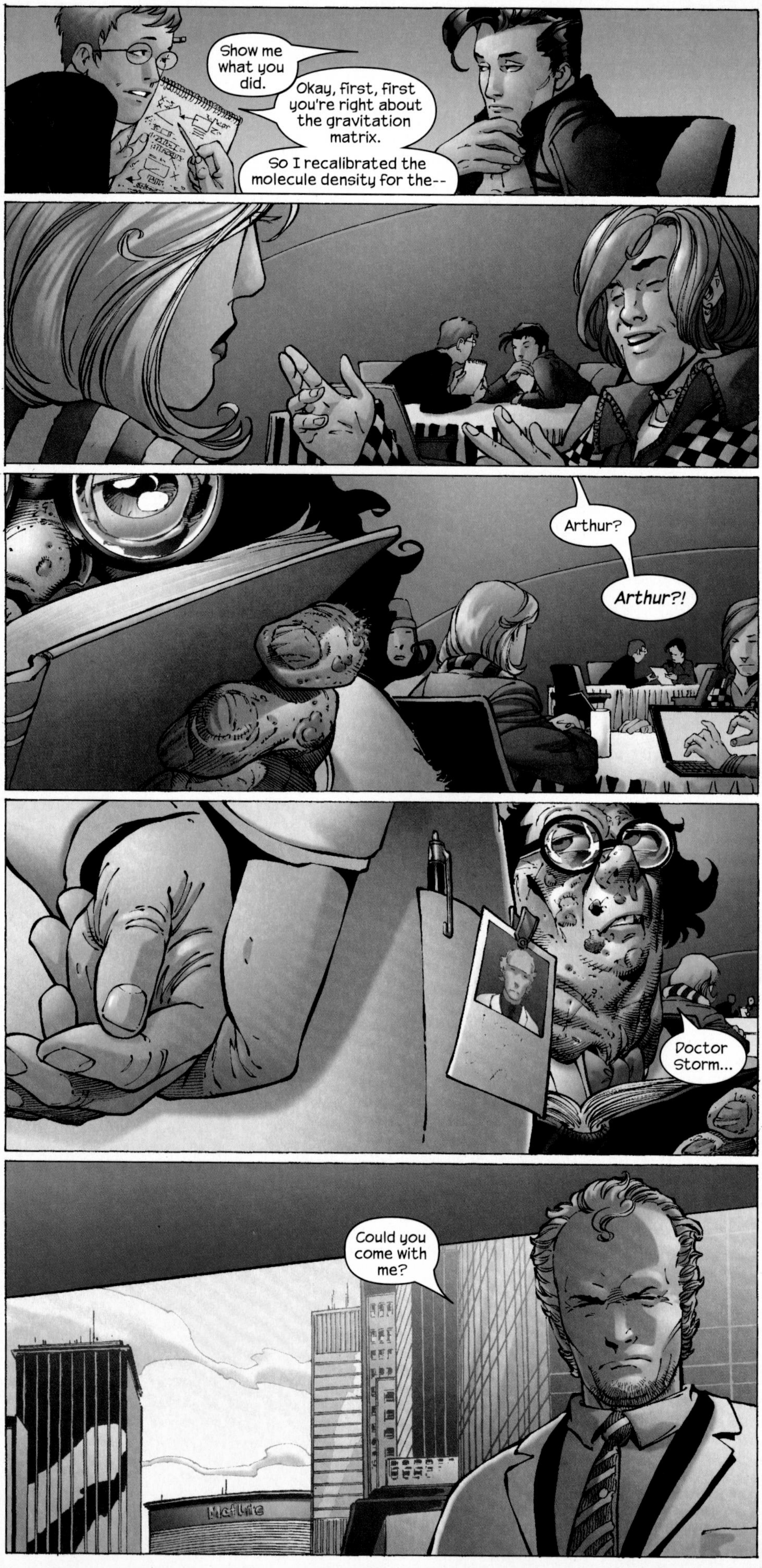
Show me what you did.
Okay, first, first you're right about the gravitation matrix.
So I recalibrated the molecule density for the--
Arthur?
Arthur?!
Doctor Storm...
Could you come with me?

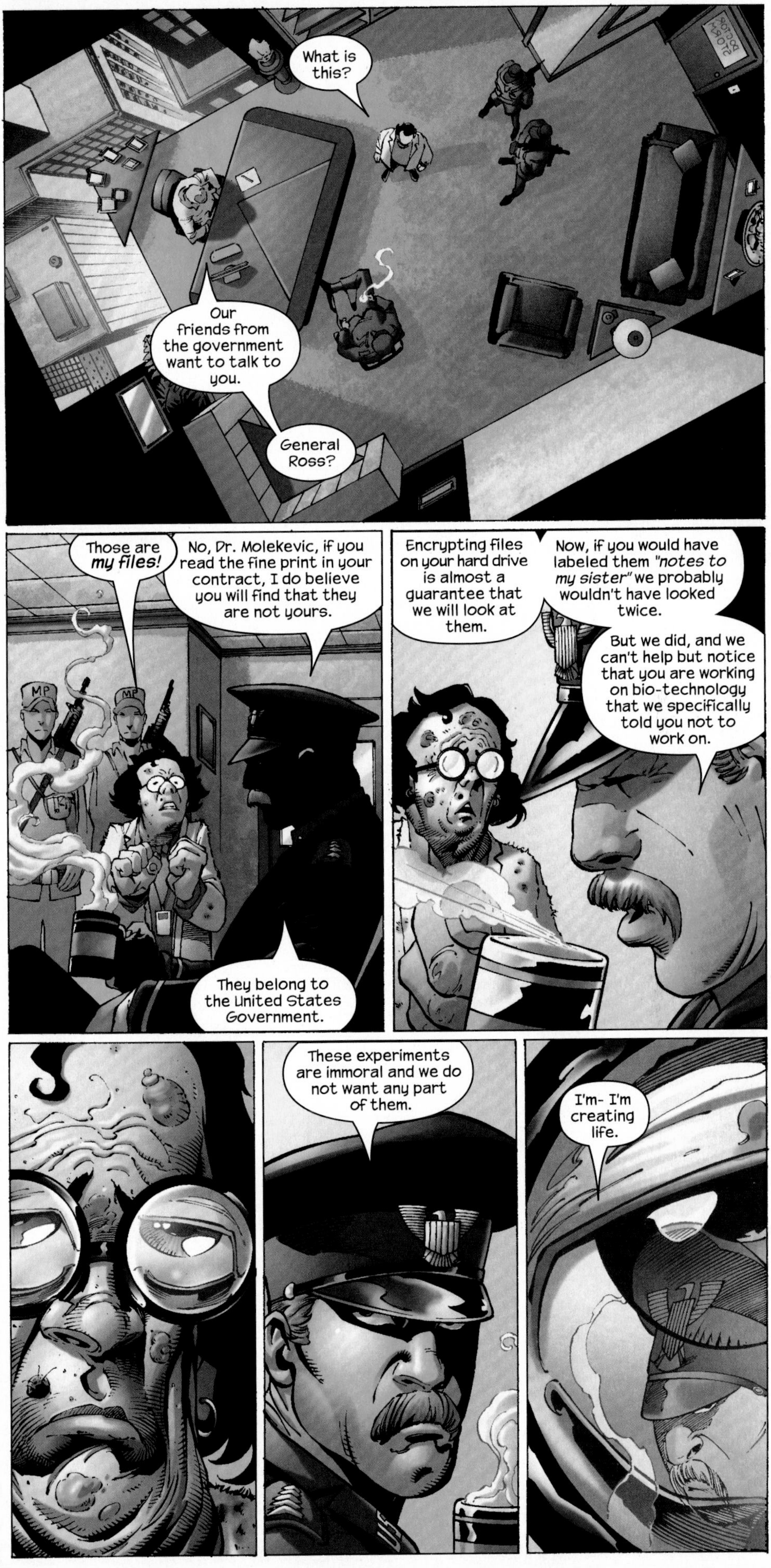

What is this?
Our friends from the government want to talk to you.
General Ross?
Those are *my files!*
No, Dr. Molekevic, if you read the fine print in your contract, I do believe you will find that they are not yours.
They belong to the United States Government.
Encrypting files on your hard drive is almost a guarantee that we will look at them.
Now, if you would have labeled them *"notes to my sister"* we probably wouldn't have looked twice.
But we did, and we can't help but notice that you are working on bio-technology that we specifically told you not to work on.
These experiments are immoral and we do not want any part of them.
I'm- I'm creating life.

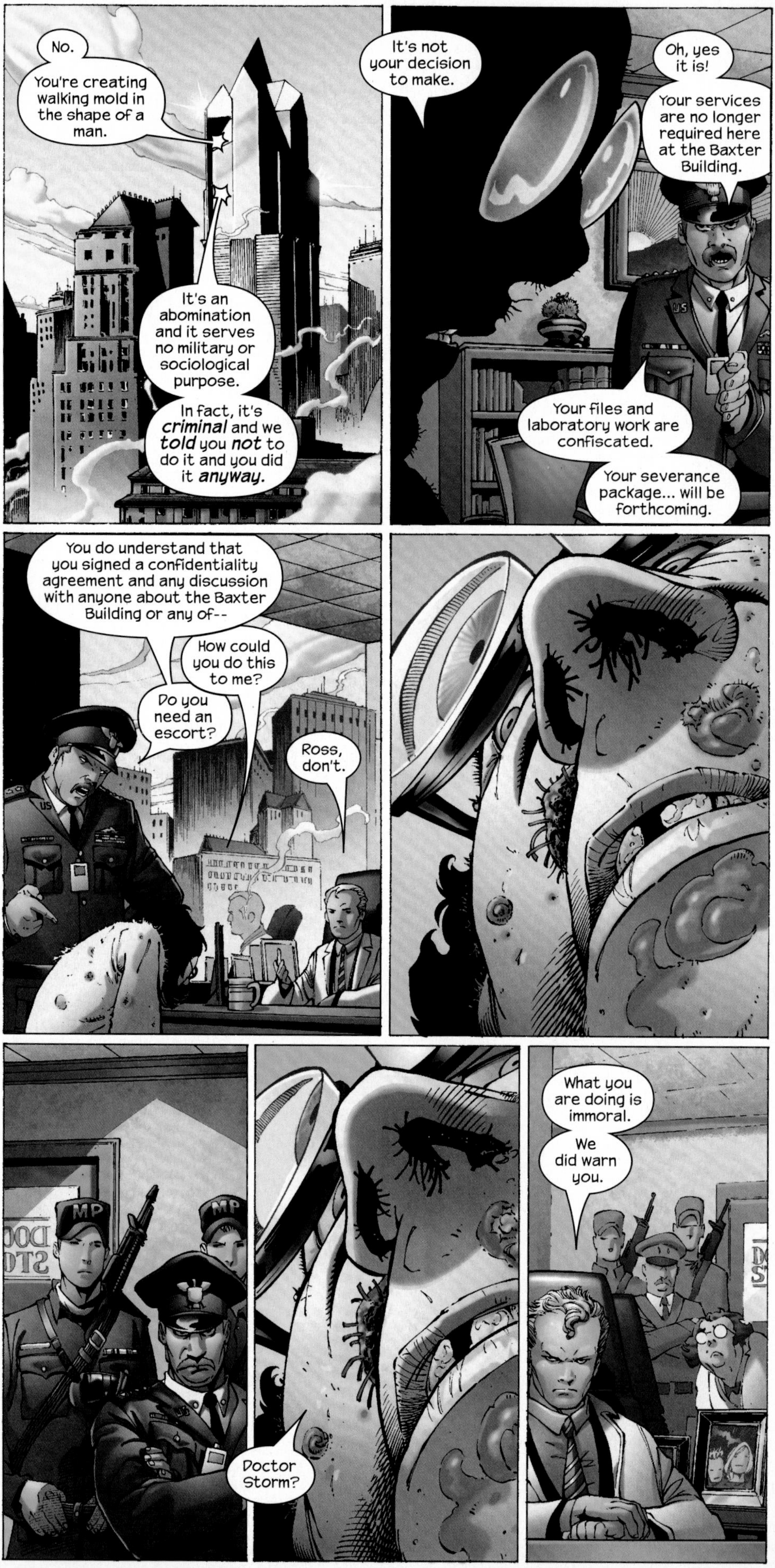

No.
You're creating walking mold in the shape of a man.
It's an abomination and it serves no military or sociological purpose.
In fact, it's *criminal* and we *told* you *not* to do it and you did it *anyway*.
It's not your decision to make.
Oh, yes it is!
Your services are no longer required here at the Baxter Building.
Your files and laboratory work are confiscated.
Your severance package... will be forthcoming.
You do understand that you signed a confidentiality agreement and any discussion with anyone about the Baxter Building or any of--
How could you do this to me?
Do you need an escort?
Ross, don't.
Doctor Storm?
What you are doing is immoral.
We did warn you.

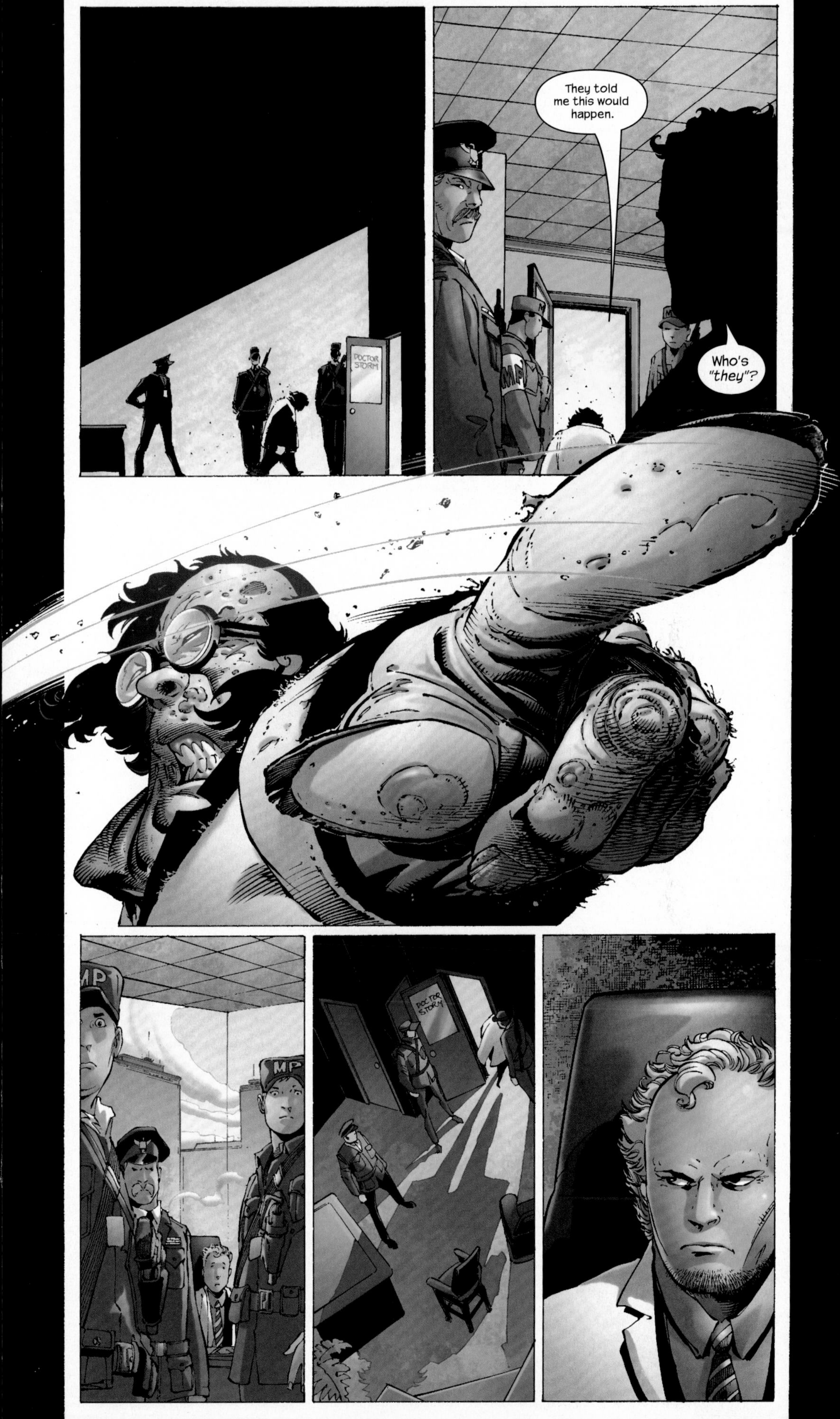
DOCTOR STORM
They told me this would happen.
Who's "they"?
MP
MP
DOCTOR STORM

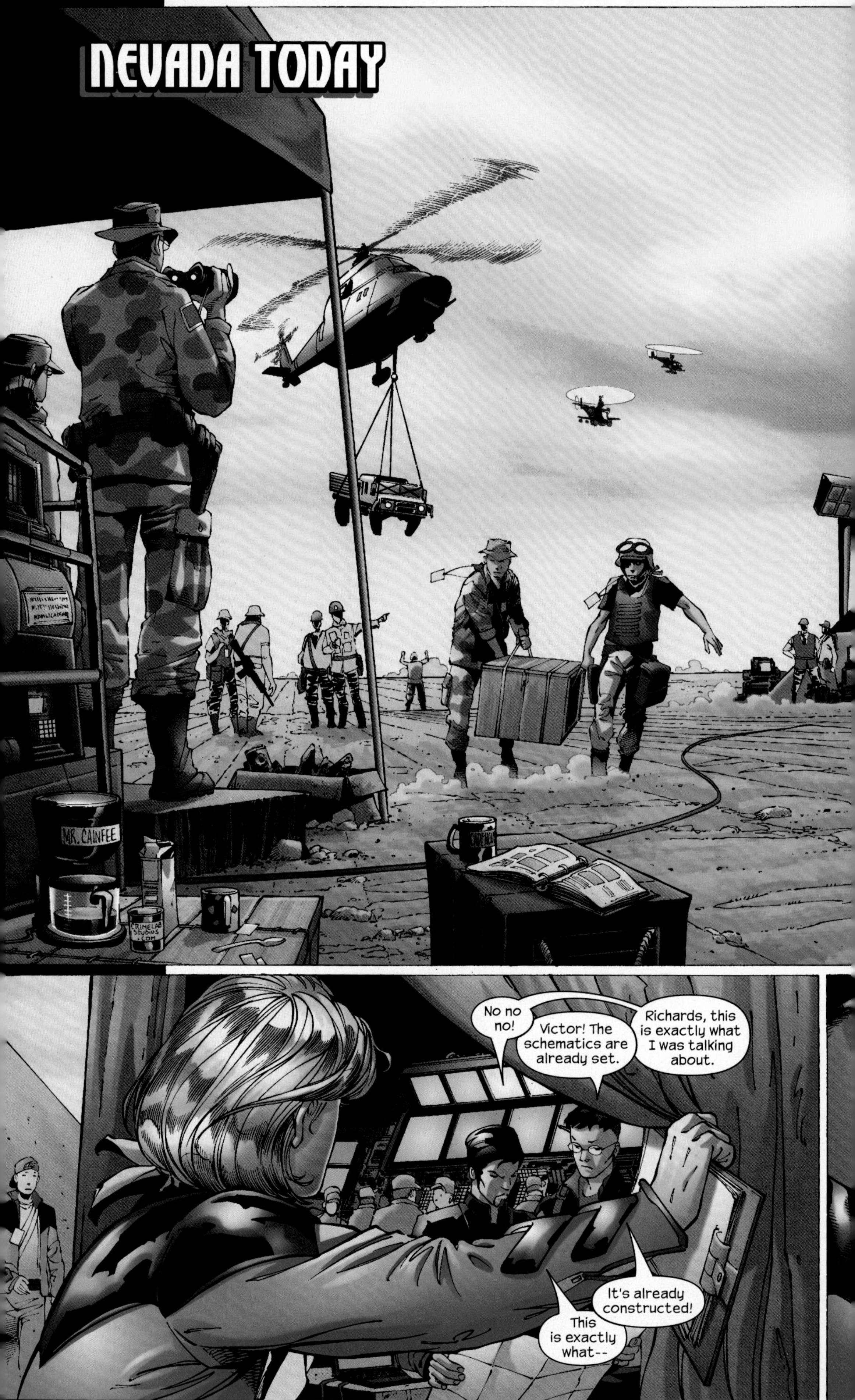
NEVADA TODAY
MR. CAINFEE
CRIMELAB STUDIOS .COM
No no no!
Victor! The schematics are already set.
Richards, this is exactly what I was talking about.
It's already constructed!
This is exactly what--

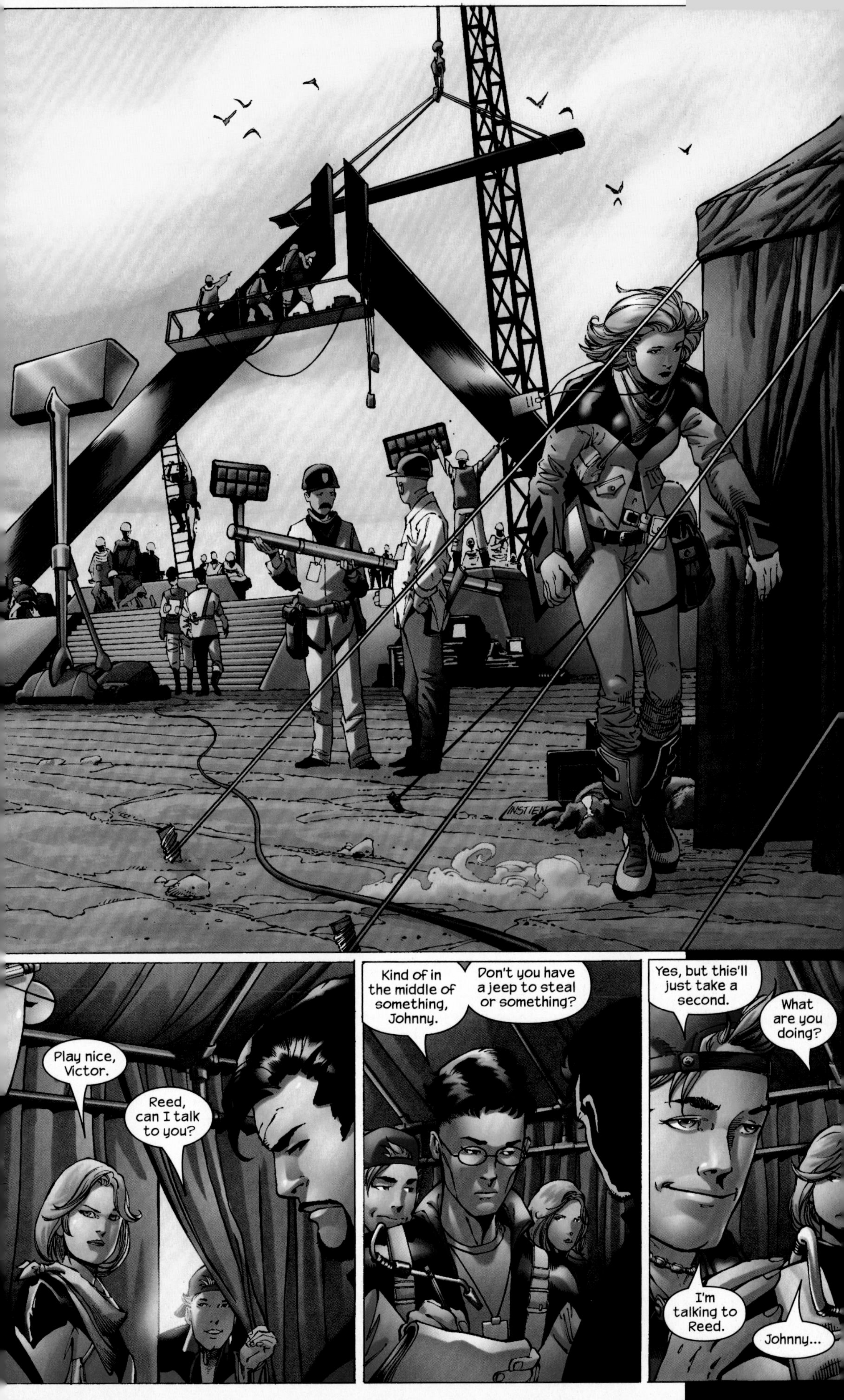
Play nice, Victor.
Reed, can I talk to you?
Kind of in the middle of something, Johnny.
Don't you have a jeep to steal or something?
Yes, but this'll just take a second.
What are you doing?
I'm talking to Reed.
Johnny...

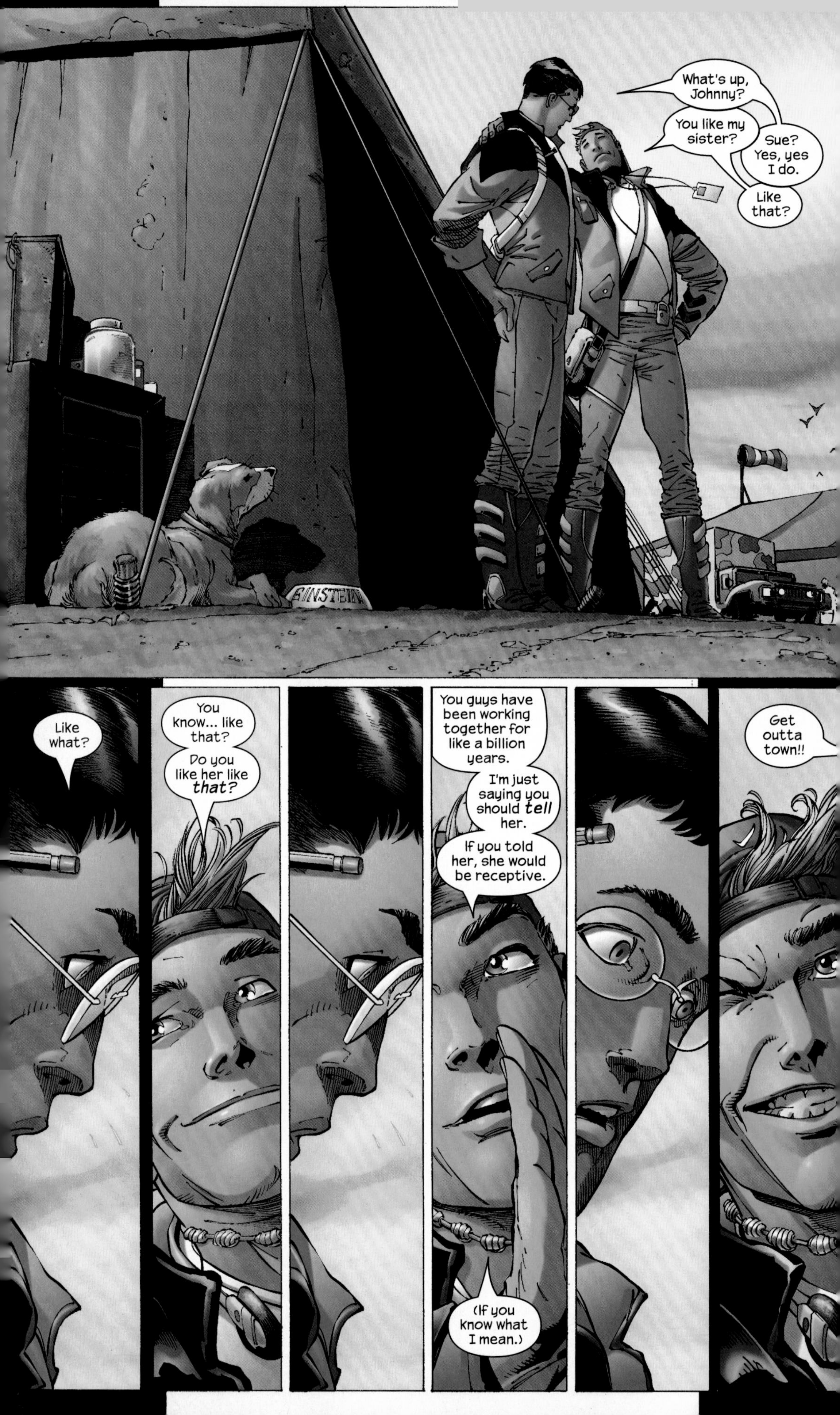

What's up, Johnny?
You like my sister?
Sue? Yes, yes I do.
Like that?
Like what?
You know... like that?
Do you like her like *that*?
You guys have been working together for like a billion years.
I'm just saying you should *tell* her.
If you told her, she would be receptive.
(If you know what I mean.)
Get outta town!!

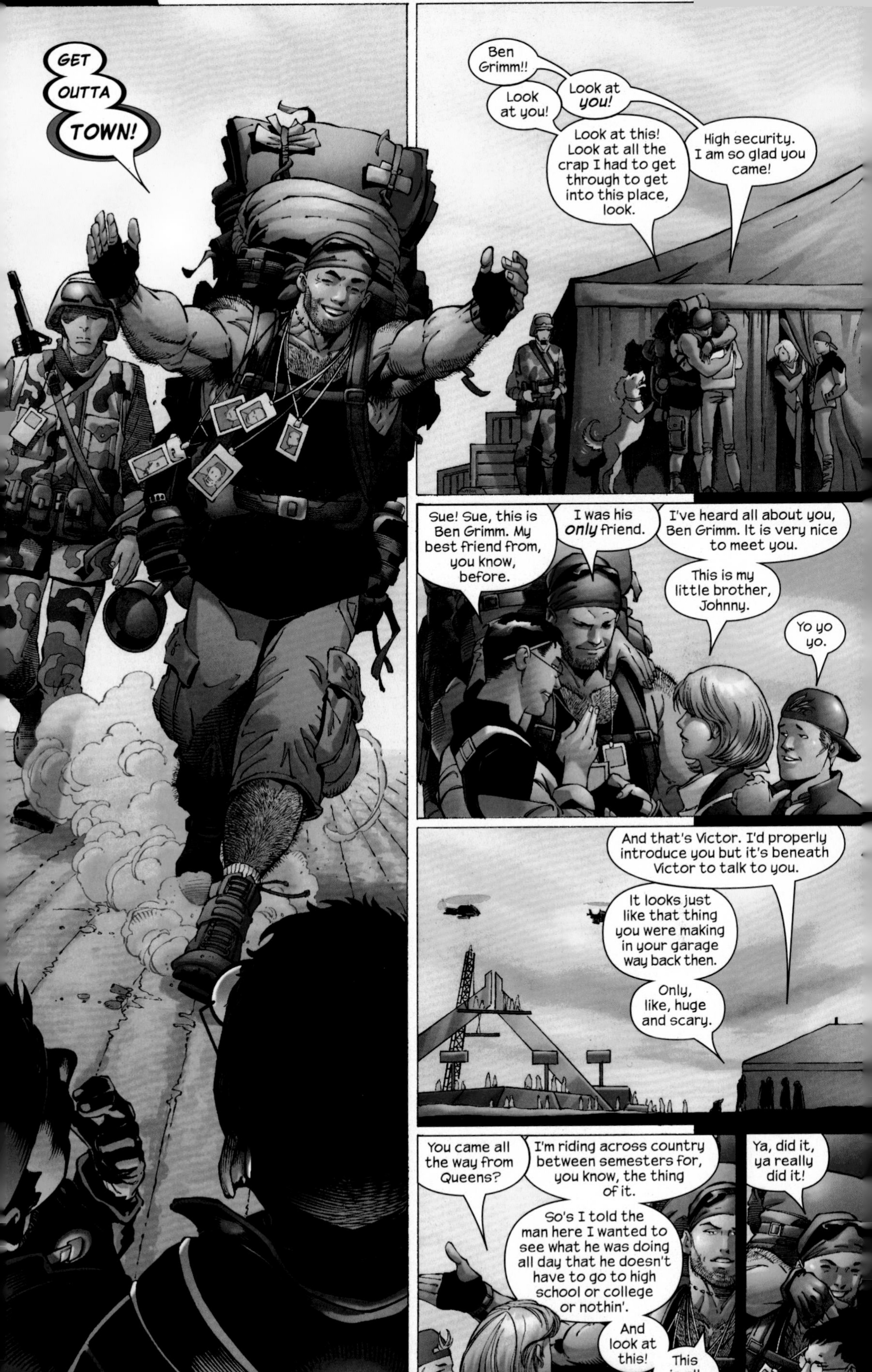

GET OUTTA TOWN!
Ben Grimm!!
Look at you!
Look at *you!*
Look at this! Look at all the crap I had to get through to get into this place, look.
High security. I am so glad you came!
Sue! Sue, this is Ben Grimm. My best friend from, you know, before.
I was his *only* friend.
I've heard all about you, Ben Grimm. It is very nice to meet you.
This is my little brother, Johnny.
Yo yo yo.
And that's Victor. I'd properly introduce you but it's beneath Victor to talk to you.
It looks just like that thing you were making in your garage way back then.
Only, like, huge and scary.
You came all the way from Queens?
I'm riding across country between semesters for, you know, the thing of it.
So's I told the man here I wanted to see what he was doing all day that he doesn't have to go to high school or college or nothin'.
And look at this!
This is all you?
Ya, did it, ya really did it!

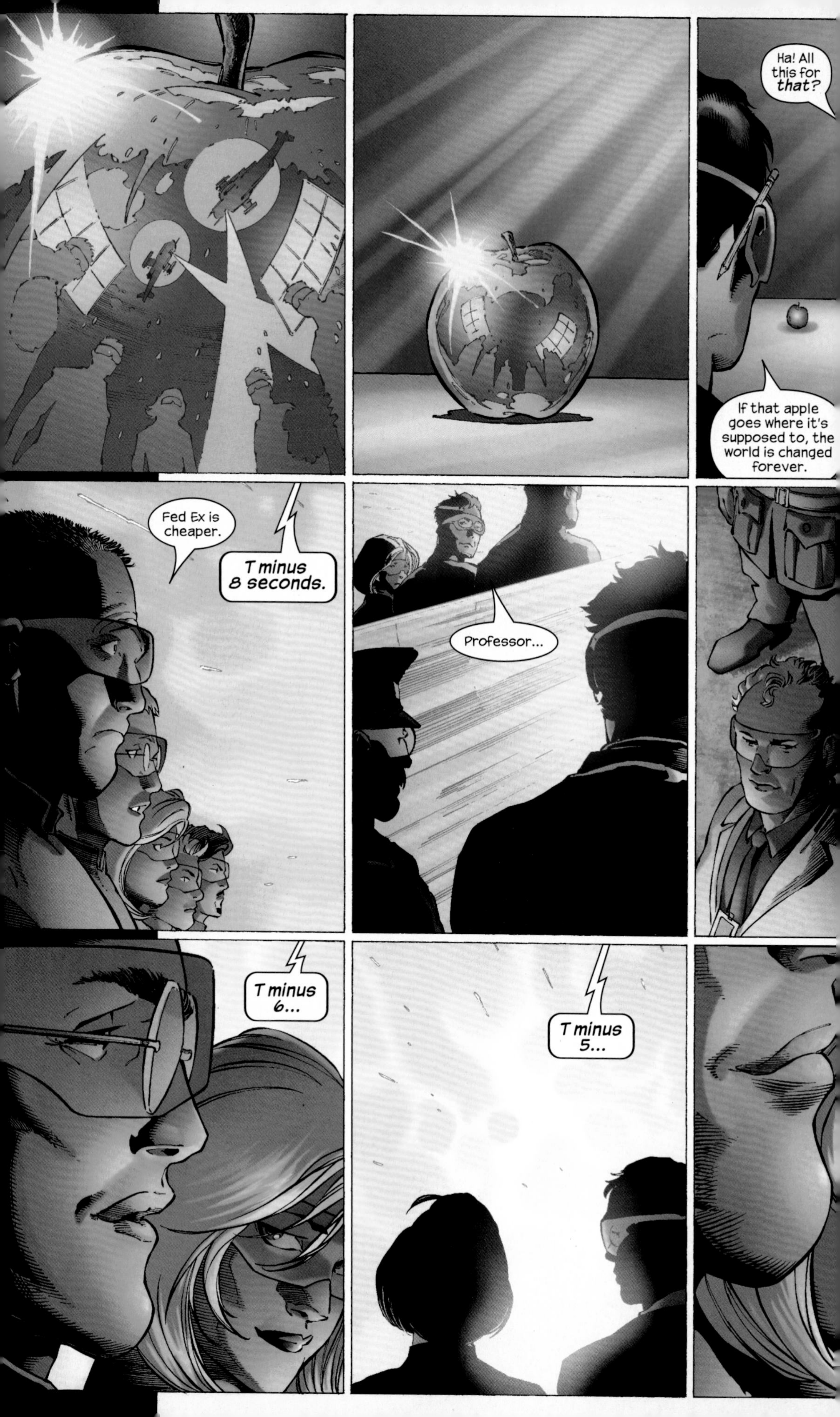
Ha! All this for *that?*
If that apple goes where it's supposed to, the world is changed forever.
Fed Ex is cheaper.
T minus 8 seconds.
Professor...
T minus 6...
T minus 5...

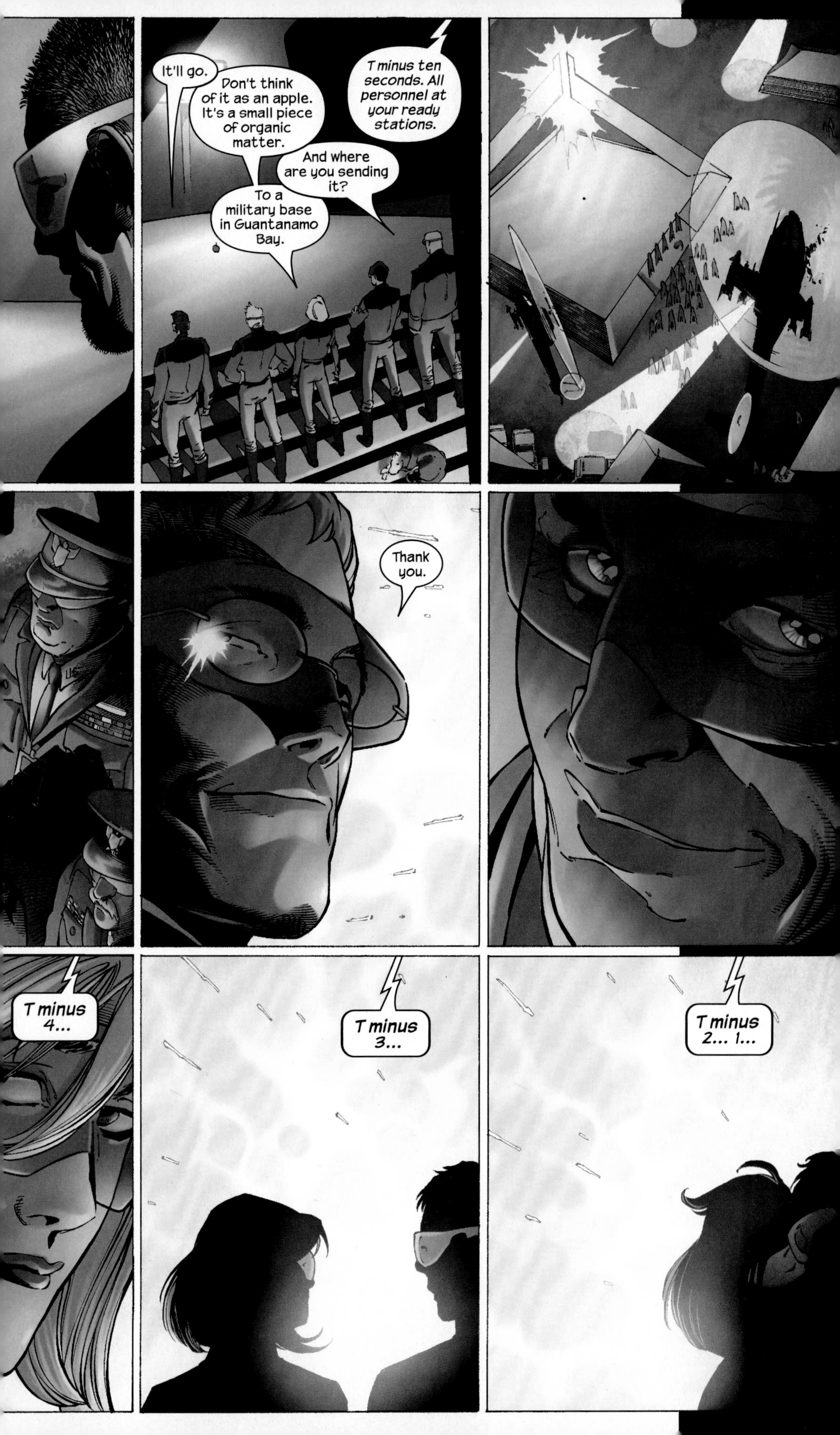
It'll go.
Don't think of it as an apple. It's a small piece of organic matter.
T minus ten seconds. All personnel at your ready stations.
And where are you sending it?
To a military base in Guantanamo Bay.
Thank you.
T minus 4...
T minus 3...
T minus 2... 1...

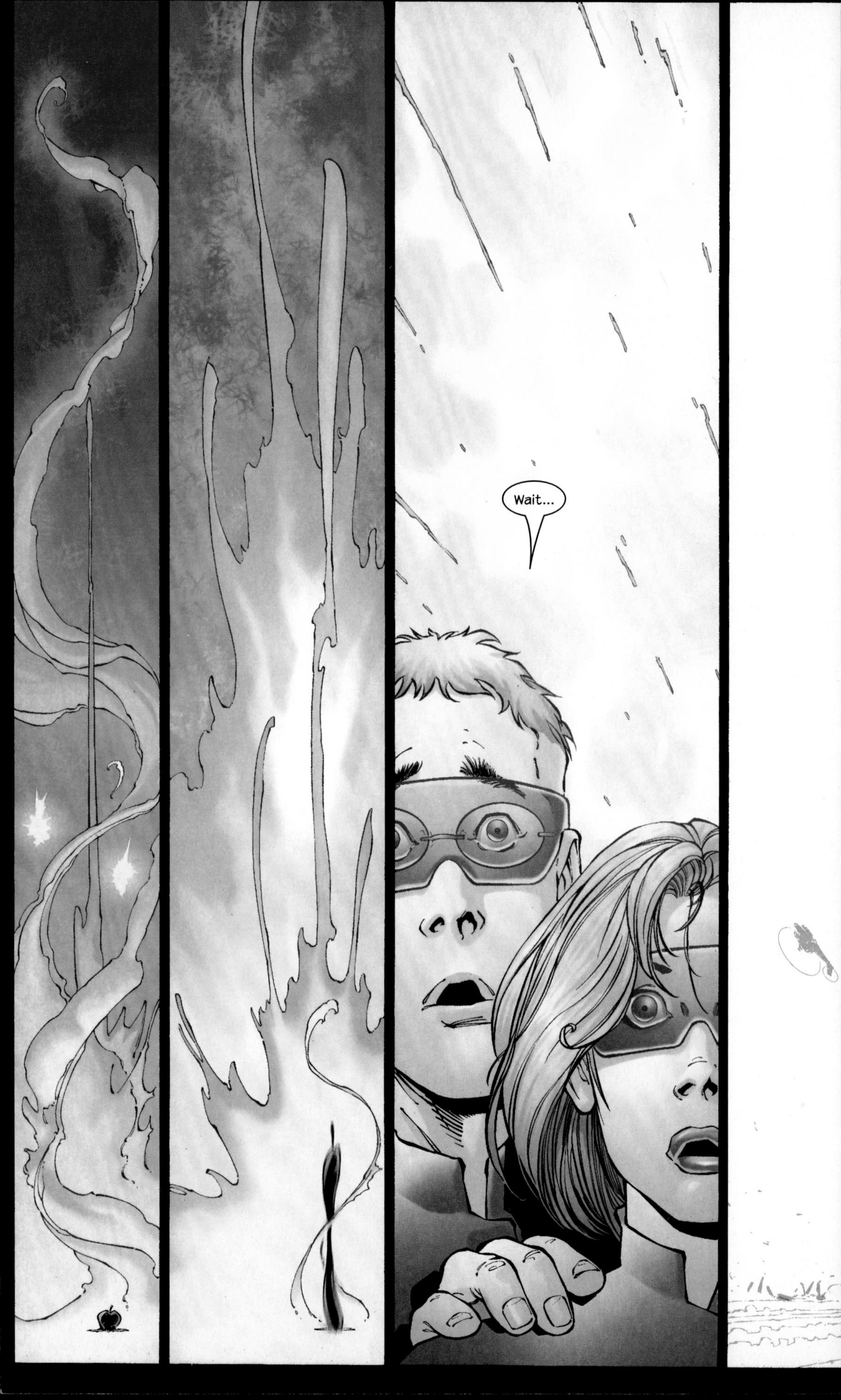
Wait...

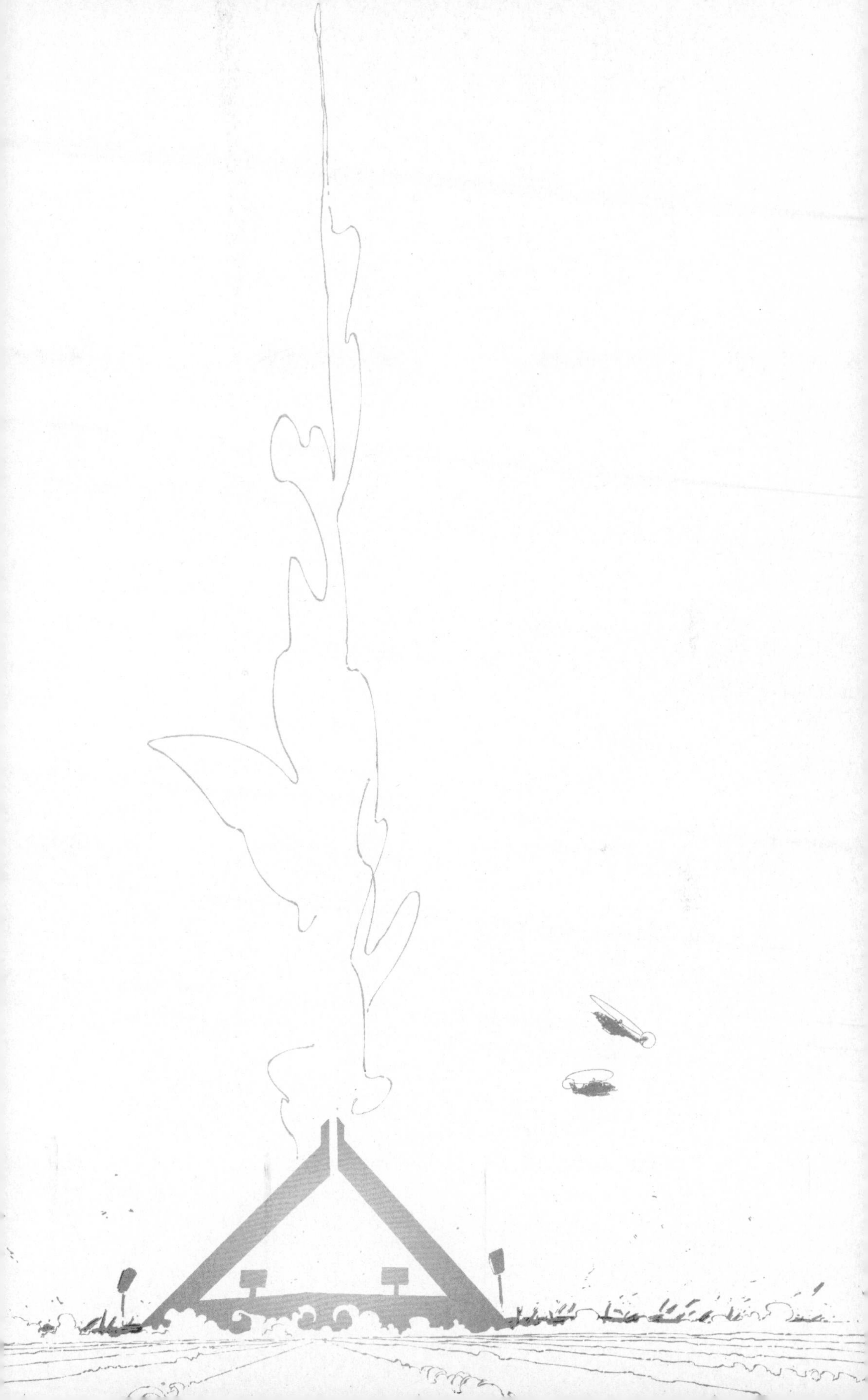

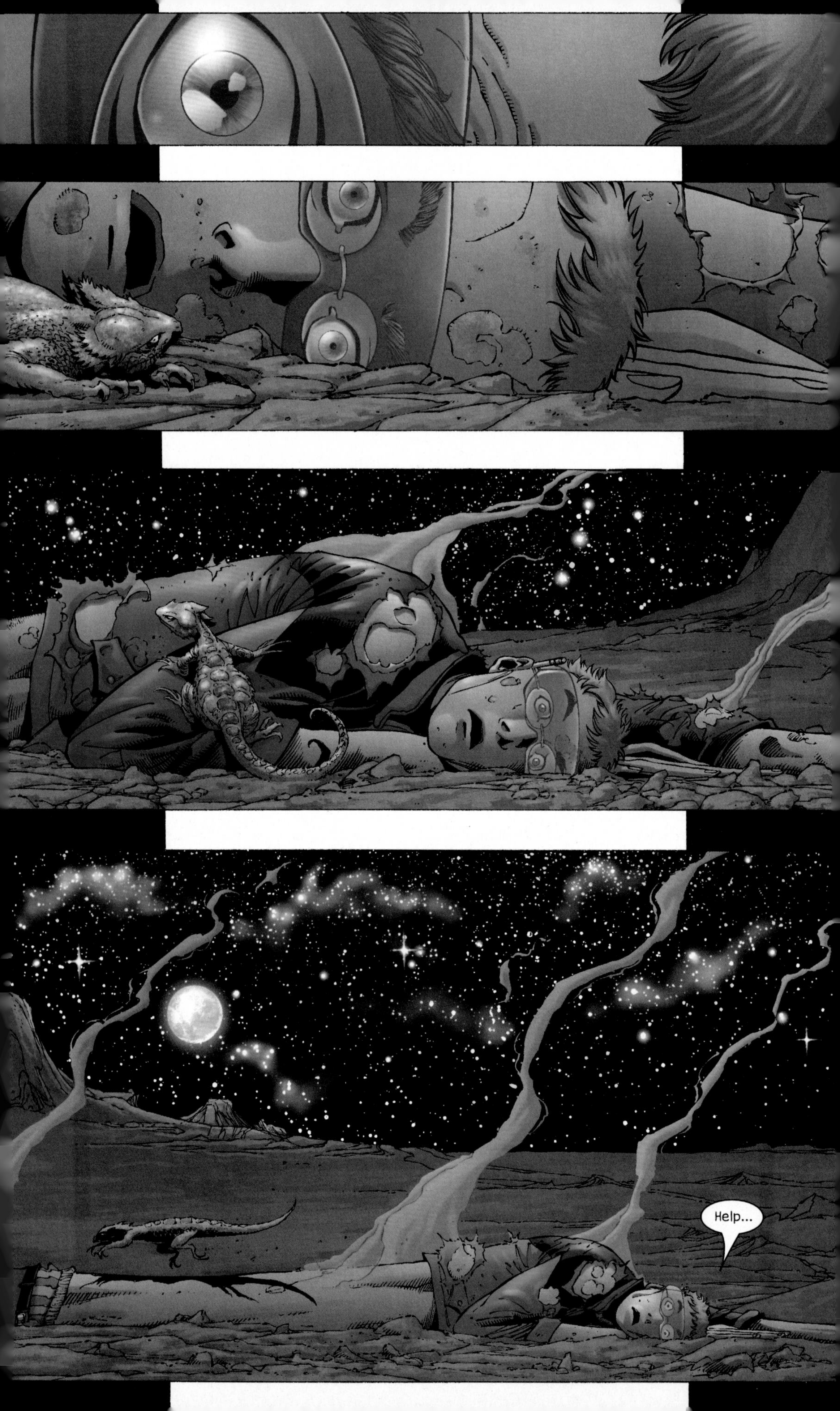
Help...

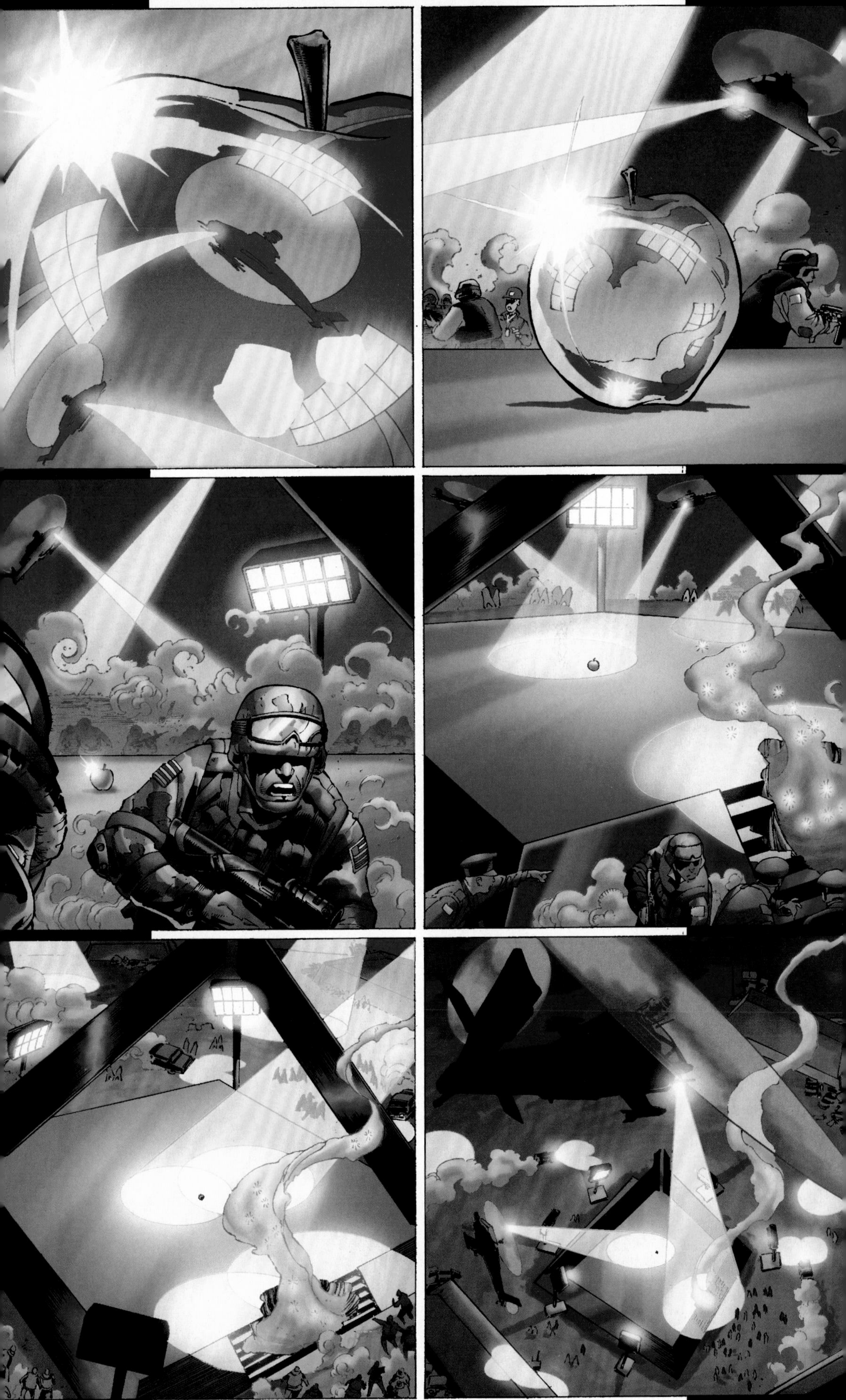

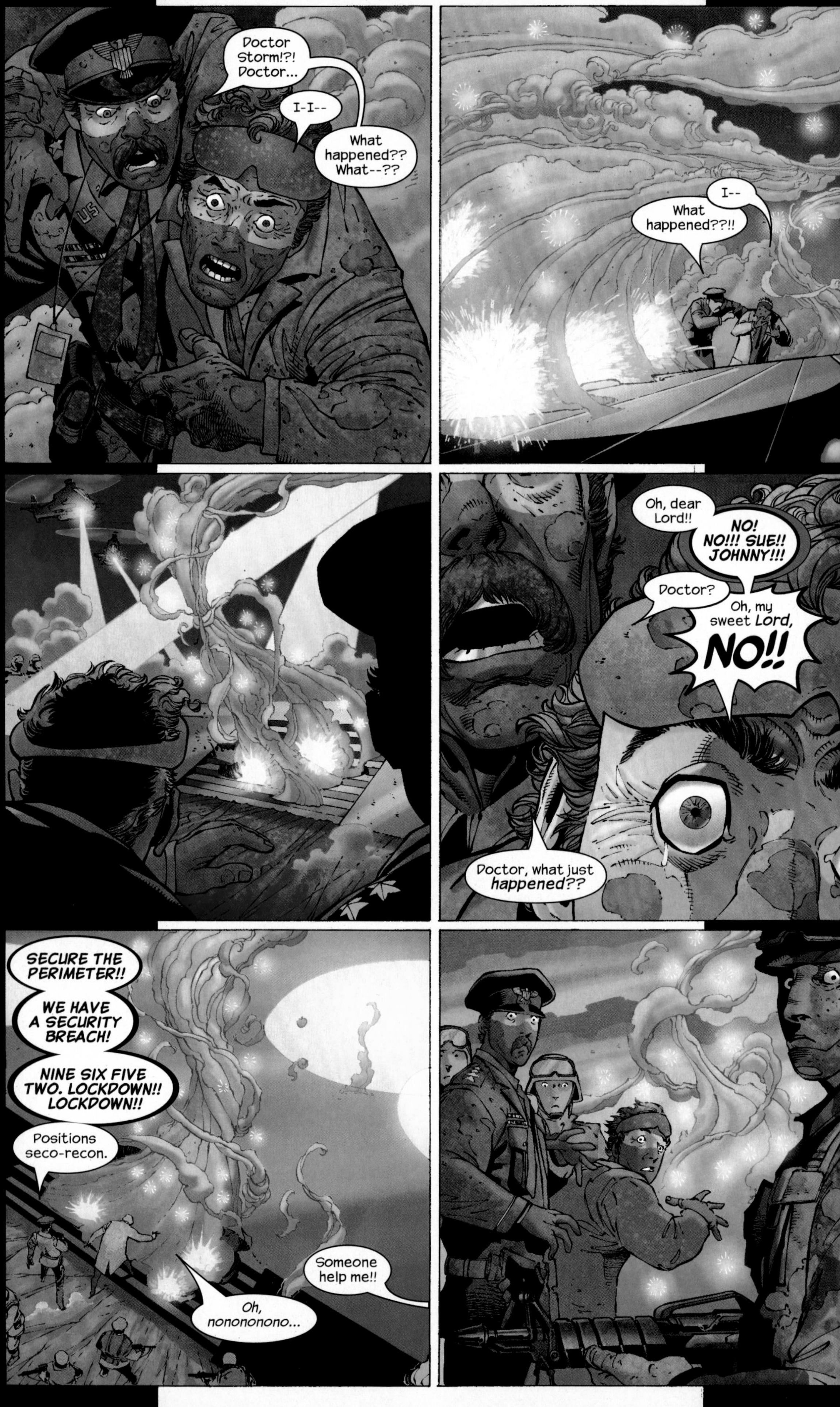
Doctor Storm!?! Doctor...
I-I--
What happened?? What--??
I--
What happened??!!
Oh, dear Lord!!
NO! NO!!! SUE!! JOHNNY!!!
Doctor?
Oh, my sweet Lord, NO!!
Doctor, what just happened??
SECURE THE PERIMETER!!
WE HAVE A SECURITY BREACH!
NINE SIX FIVE TWO. LOCKDOWN!! LOCKDOWN!!
Positions seco-recon.
Someone help me!!
Oh, nonononono...

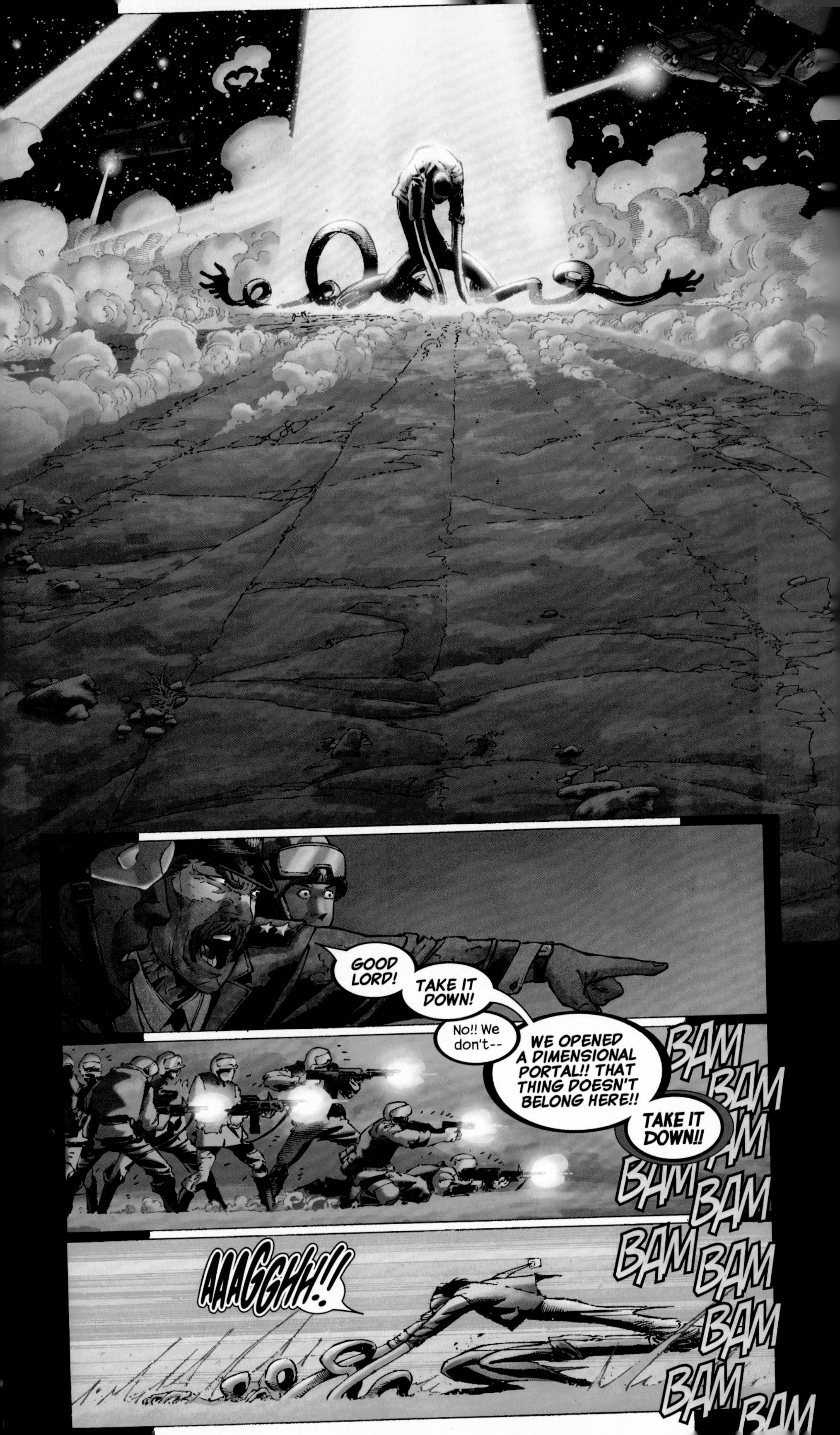
GOOD LORD!
TAKE IT DOWN!
No!! We don't--
WE OPENED A DIMENSIONAL PORTAL!! THAT THING DOESN'T BELONG HERE!!
TAKE IT DOWN!!
BAM BAM BAM BAM BAM BAM BAM BAM BAM BAM BAM
AAAGGHH!!

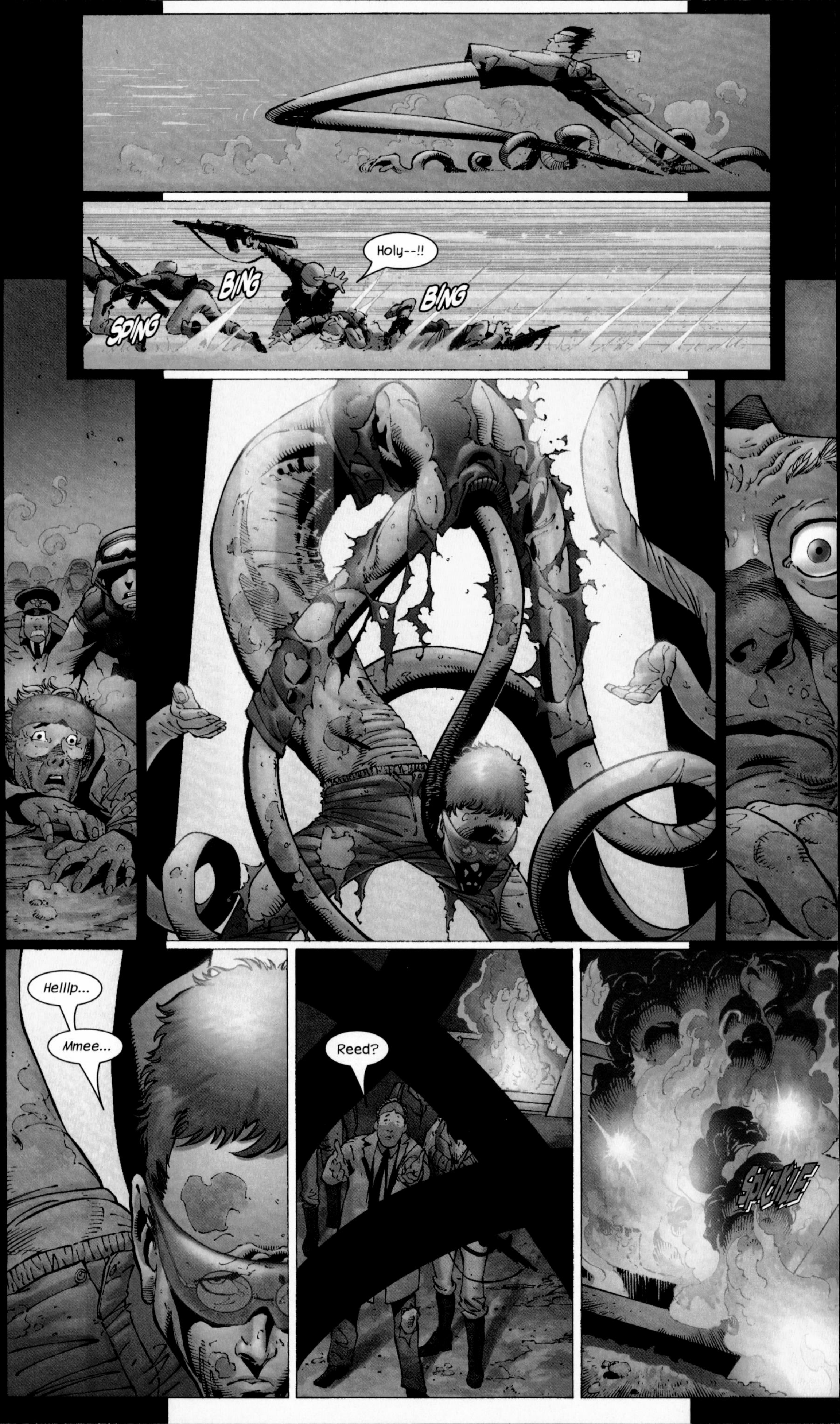
Holy--!!
BING
SPING
BING
Helllp...
Mmee...
Reed?
SPICKLE

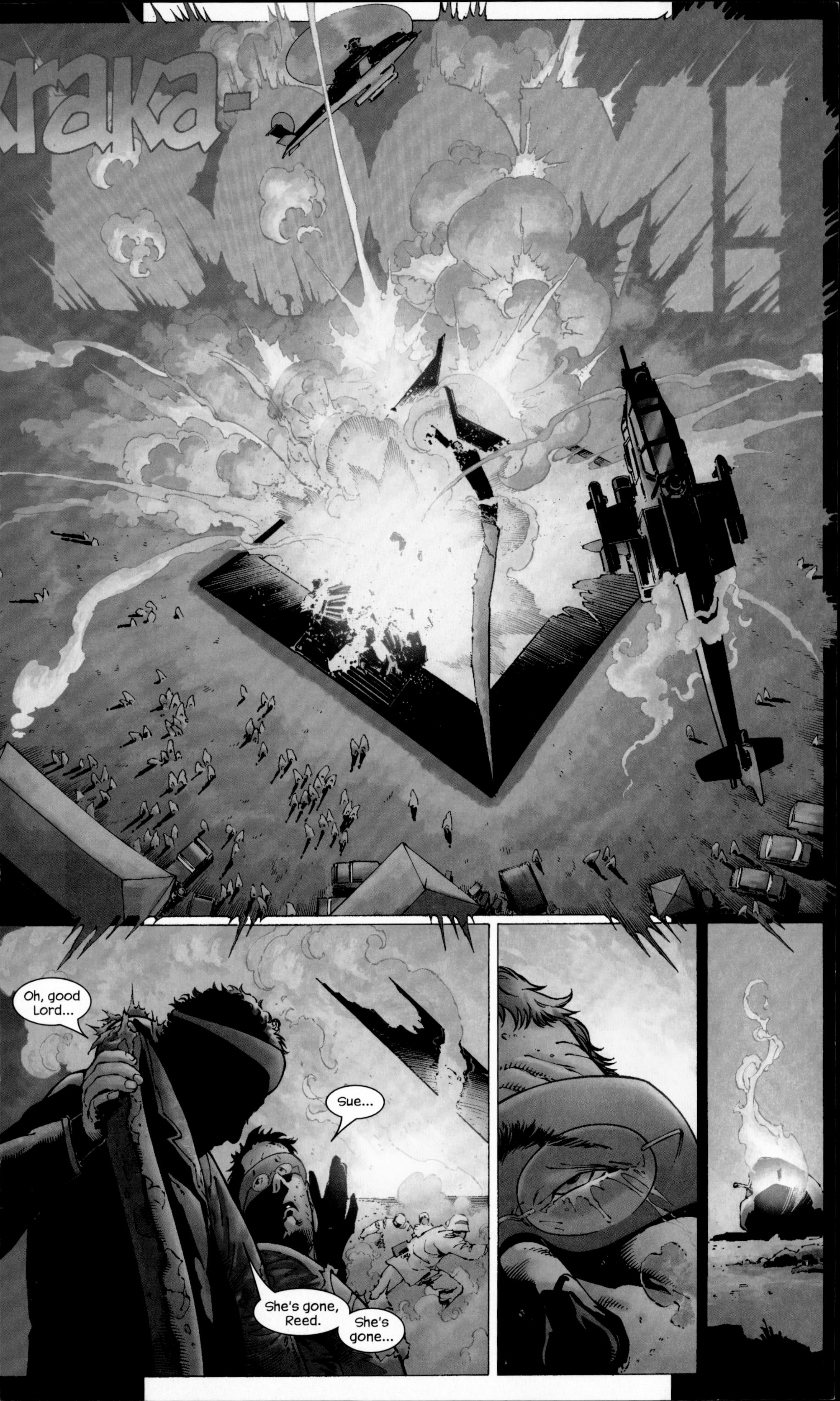
kraka-BOOM!
Oh, good Lord...
Sue...
She's gone, Reed.
She's gone...

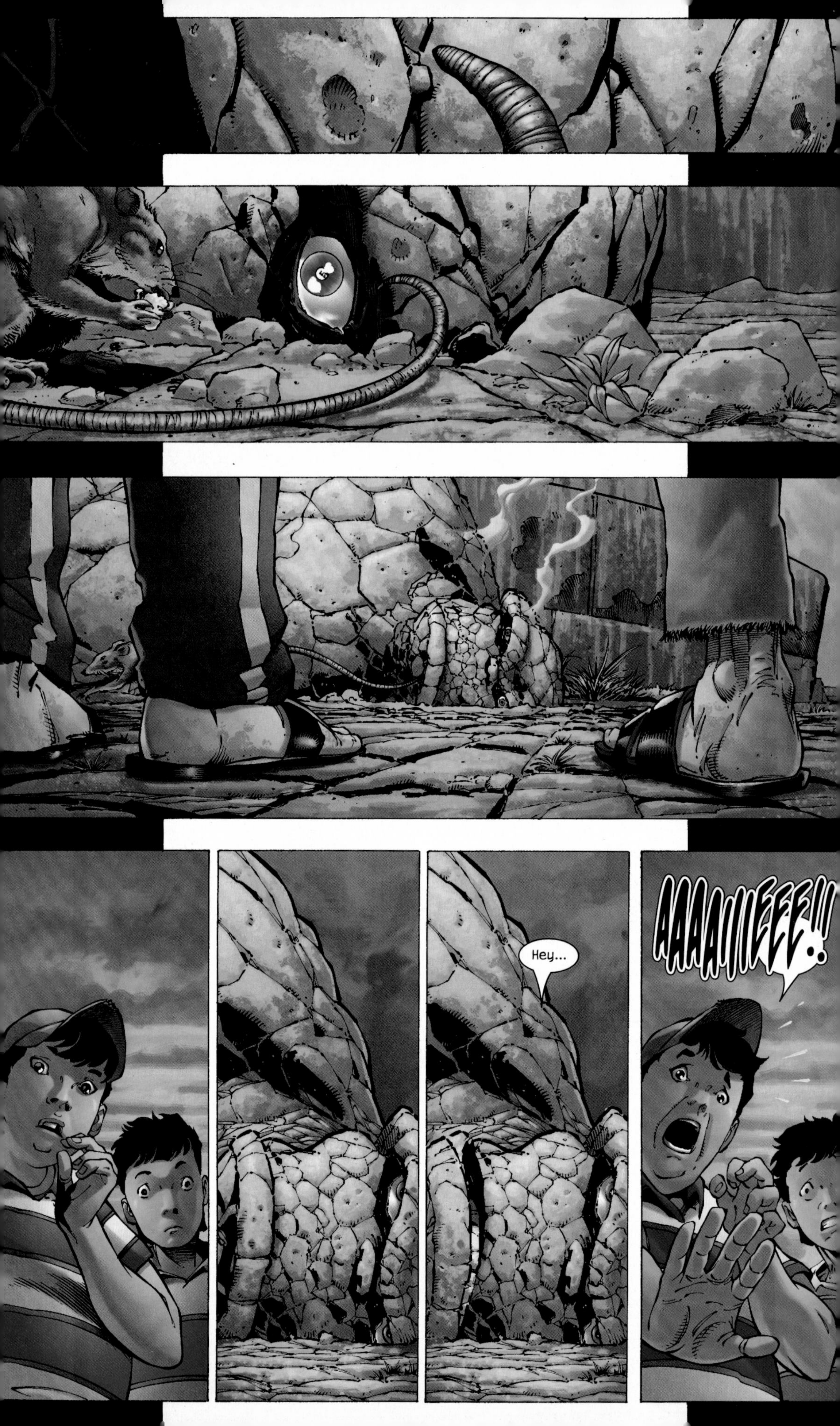
Hey...
AAAAIIIEEE!!

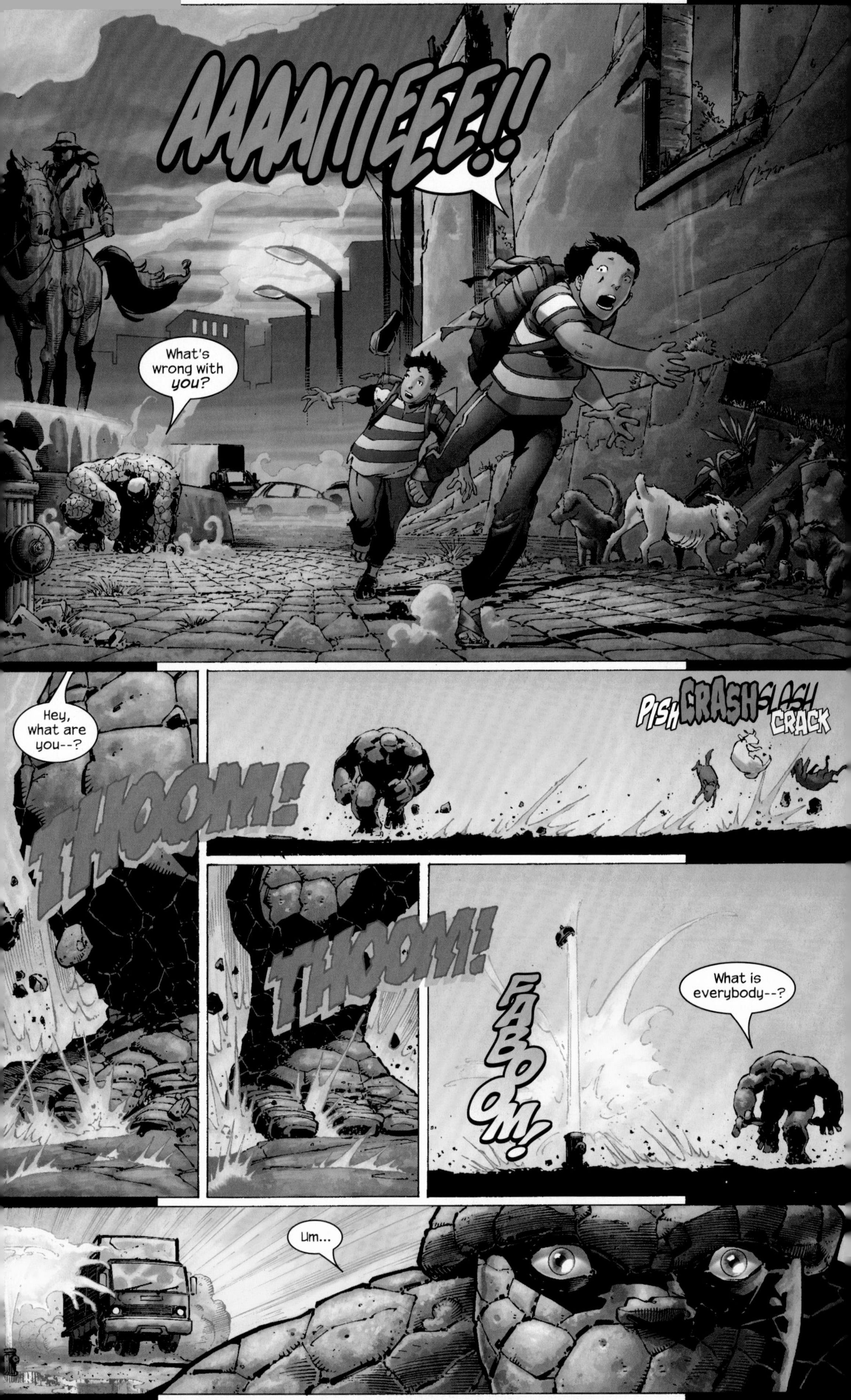
AAAAIIIEEE!!
What's wrong with you?
Hey, what are you--?
THOOM!
PISH CRASH SLASH CRACK
THOOM!
FABOOM!
What is everybody--?
Um...

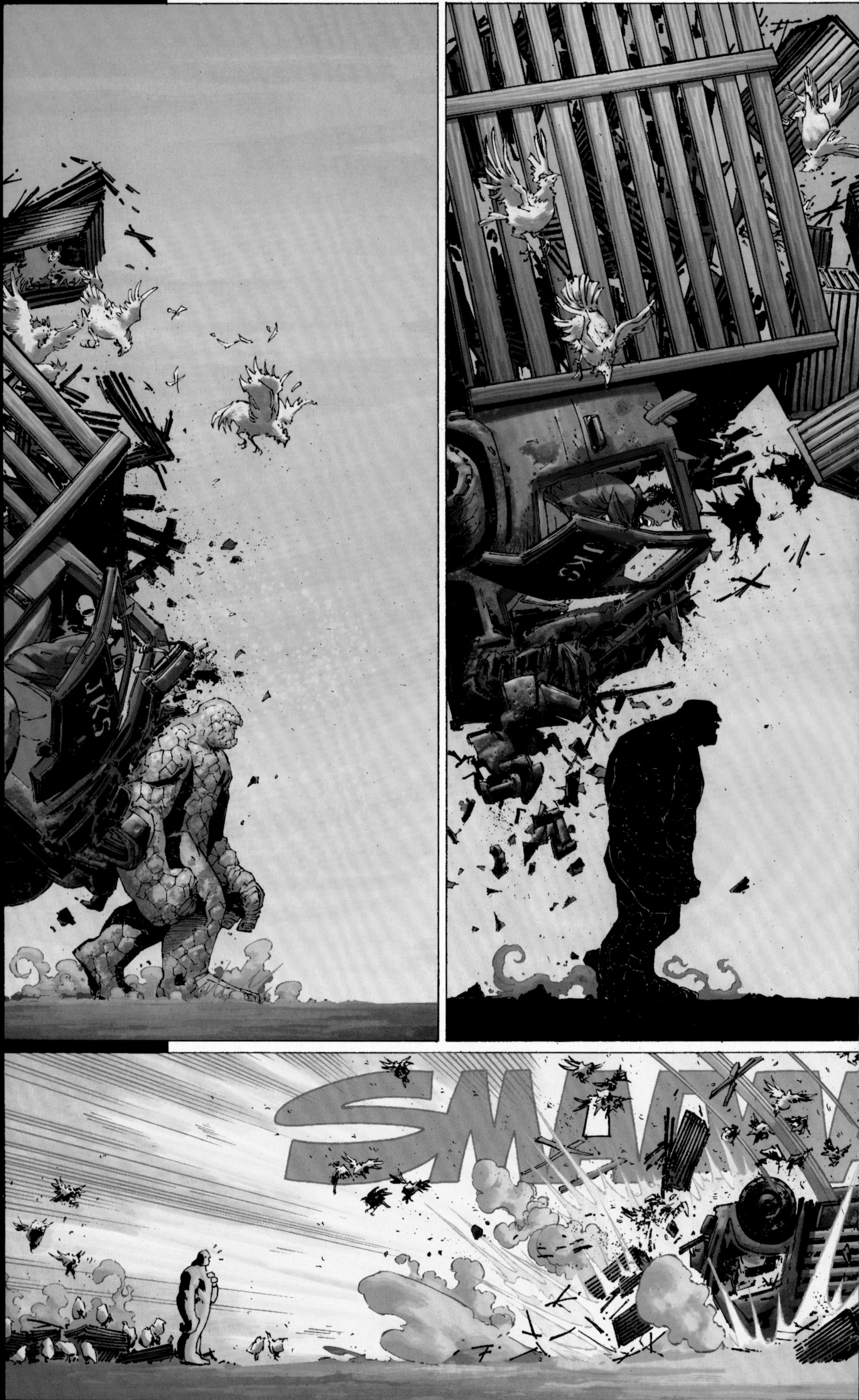
JKS

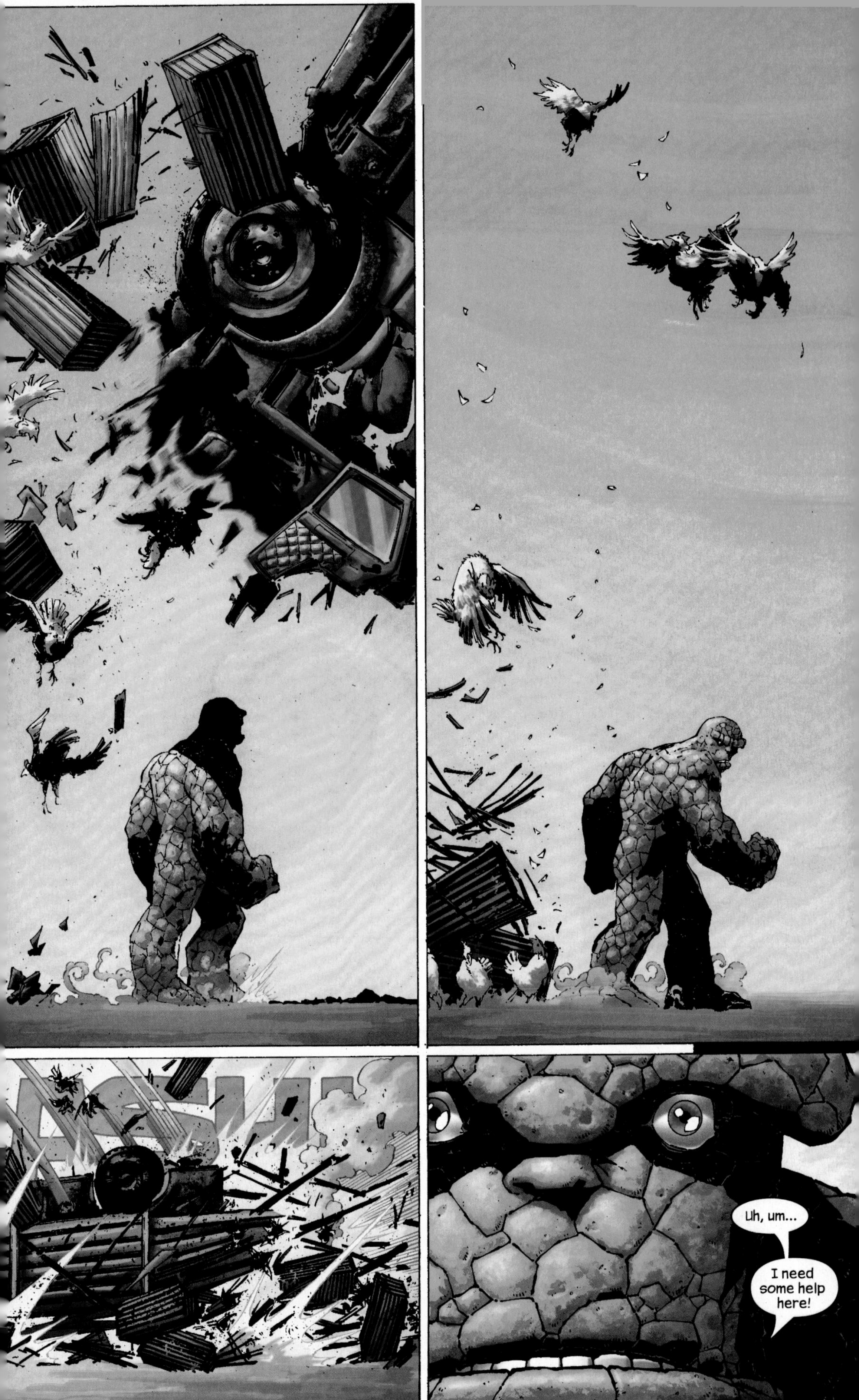
Uh, um...
I need some help here!

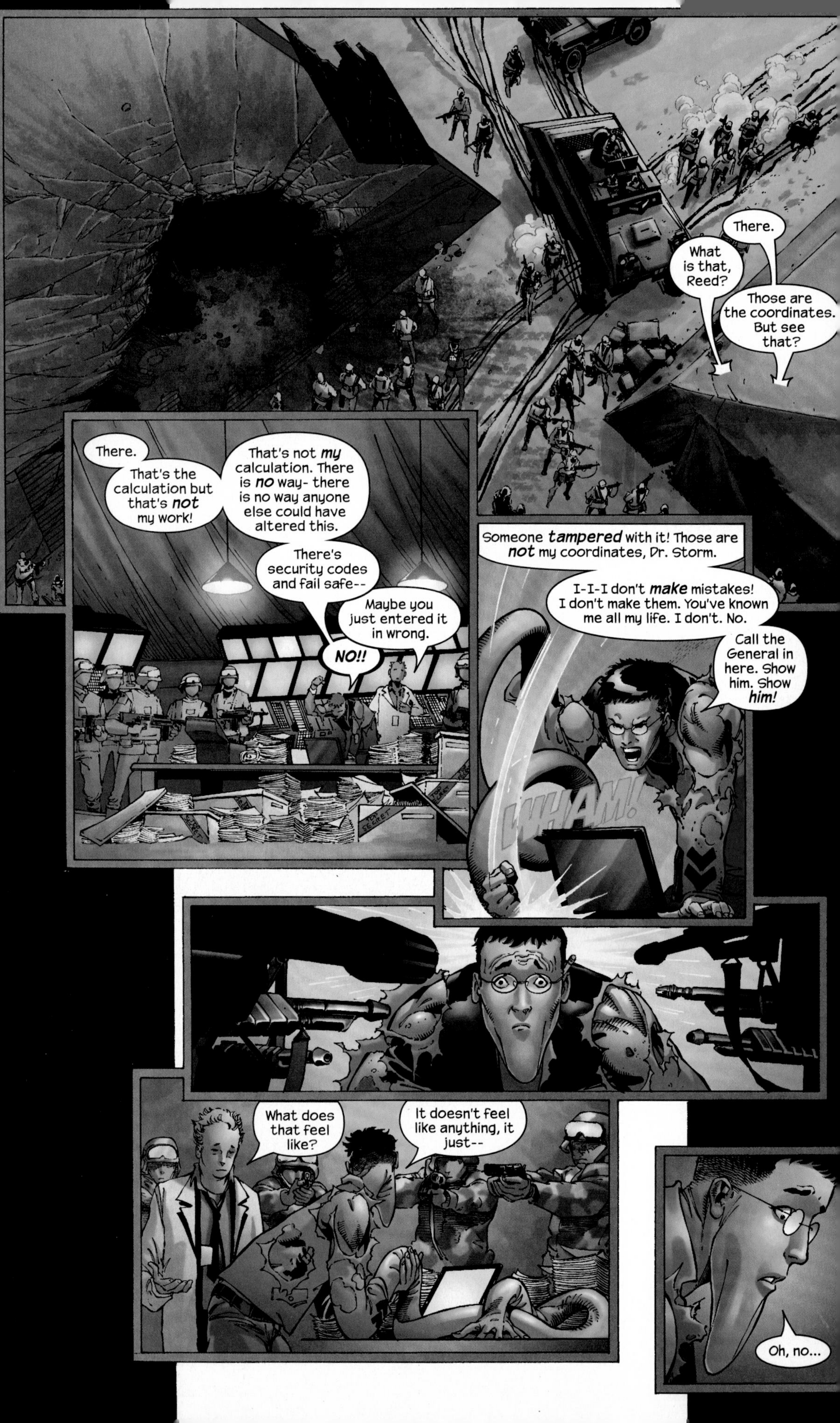
What is that, Reed?
There.
Those are the coordinates. But see that?
There.
That's the calculation but that's *not* my work!
That's not *my* calculation. There is *no* way- there is no way anyone else could have altered this.
There's security codes and fail safe--
Maybe you just entered it in wrong.
NO!!
Someone *tampered* with it! Those are *not* my coordinates, Dr. Storm.
I-I-I don't *make* mistakes! I don't make them. You've known me all my life. I don't. No.
Call the General in here. Show him. Show *him!*
WHAM!
What does that feel like?
It doesn't feel like anything, it just--
Oh, no...

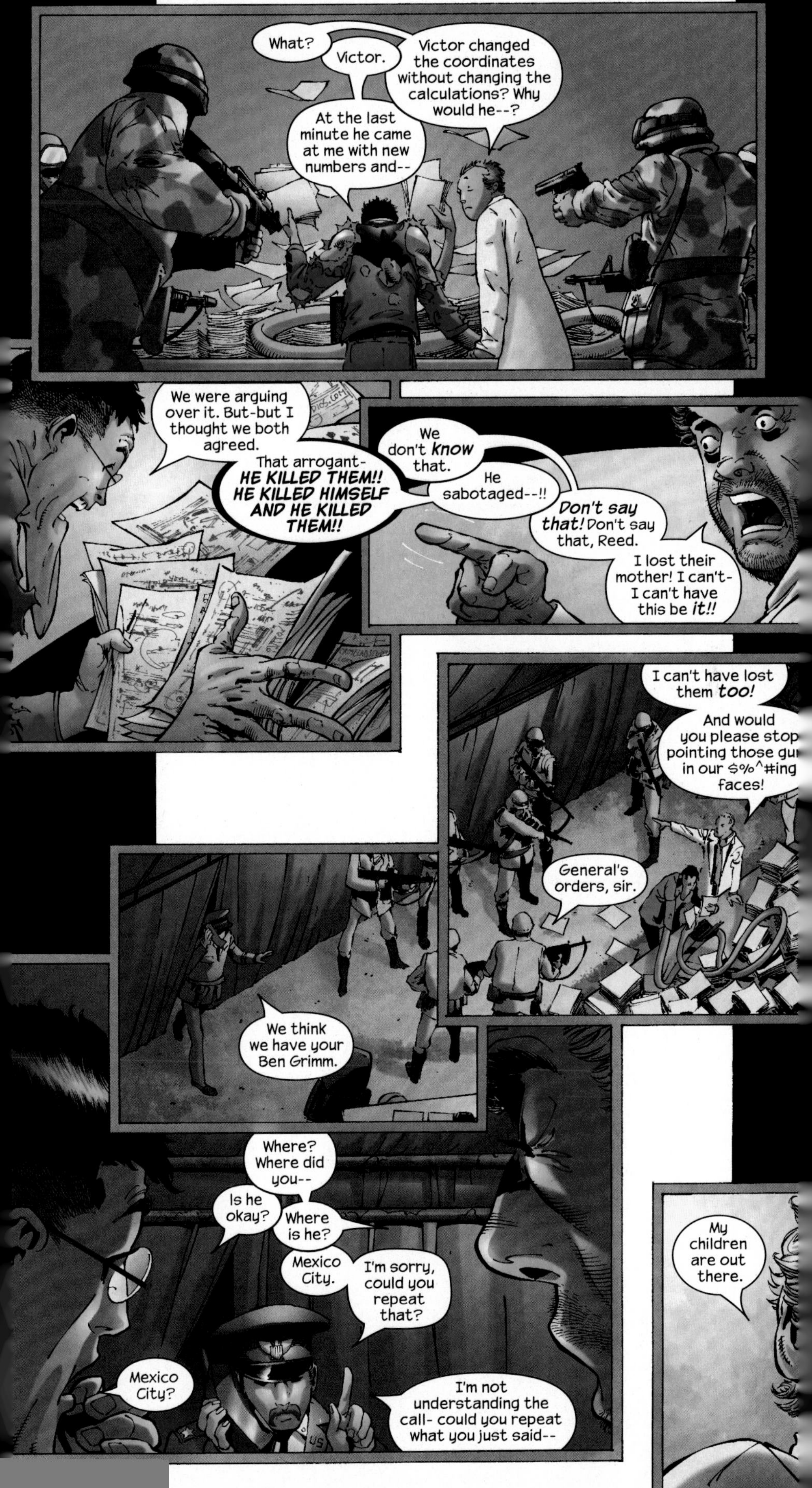
What?
Victor.
Victor changed the coordinates without changing the calculations? Why would he--?
At the last minute he came at me with new numbers and--
We were arguing over it. But-but I thought we both agreed.
That arrogant-
HE KILLED THEM!! HE KILLED HIMSELF AND HE KILLED THEM!!
We don't know that.
He sabotaged--!!
Don't say that! Don't say that, Reed.
I lost their mother! I can't- I can't have this be it!!
I can't have lost them too!
And would you please stop pointing those gu in our $%^#ing faces!
General's orders, sir.
We think we have your Ben Grimm.
Where? Where did you--
Is he okay?
Where is he?
Mexico City.
I'm sorry, could you repeat that?
Mexico City?
I'm not understanding the call- could you repeat what you just said--
My children are out there.

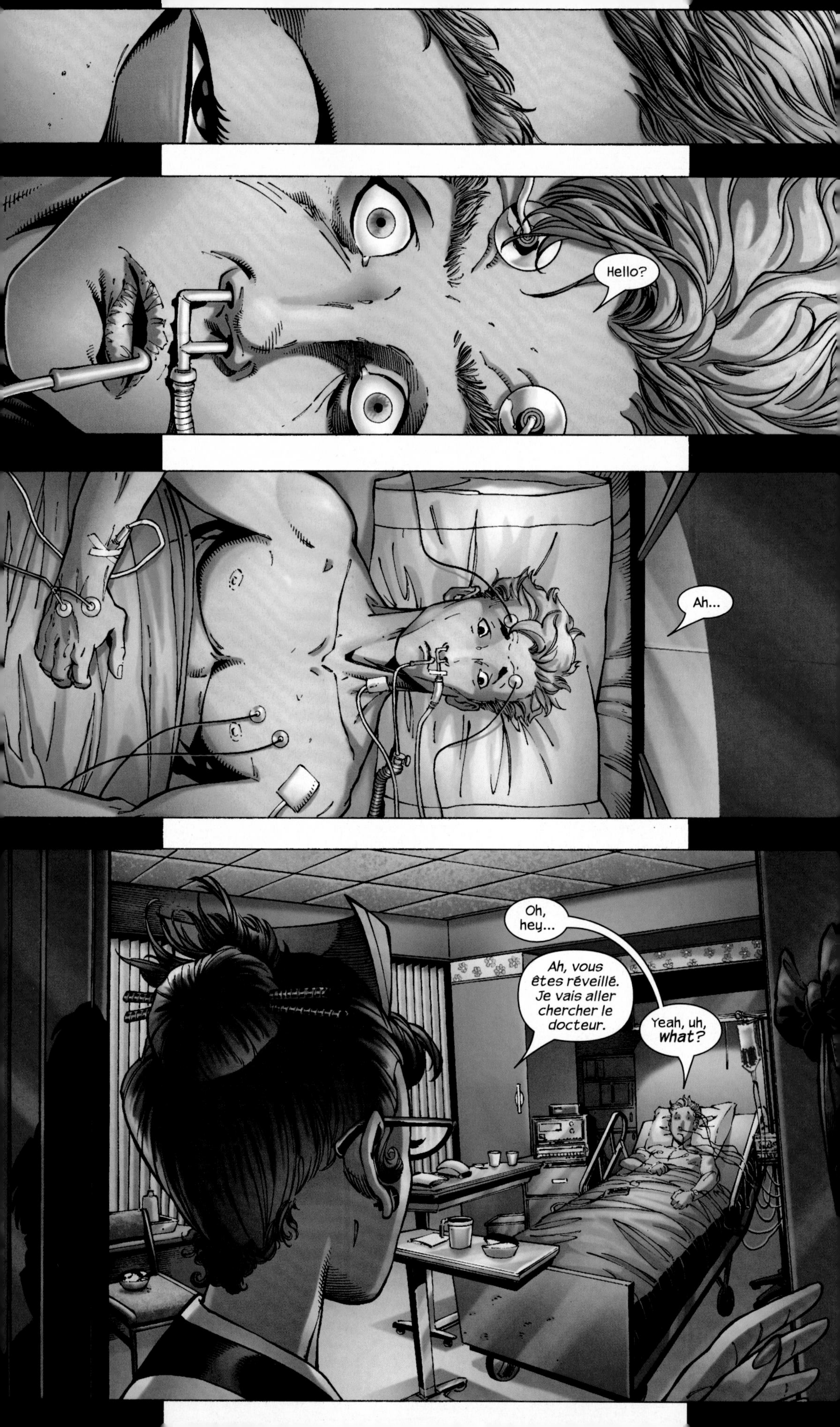
Hello?
Ah...
Oh, hey...
Ah, vous êtes réveillé. Je vais aller chercher le docteur.
Yeah, uh, what?

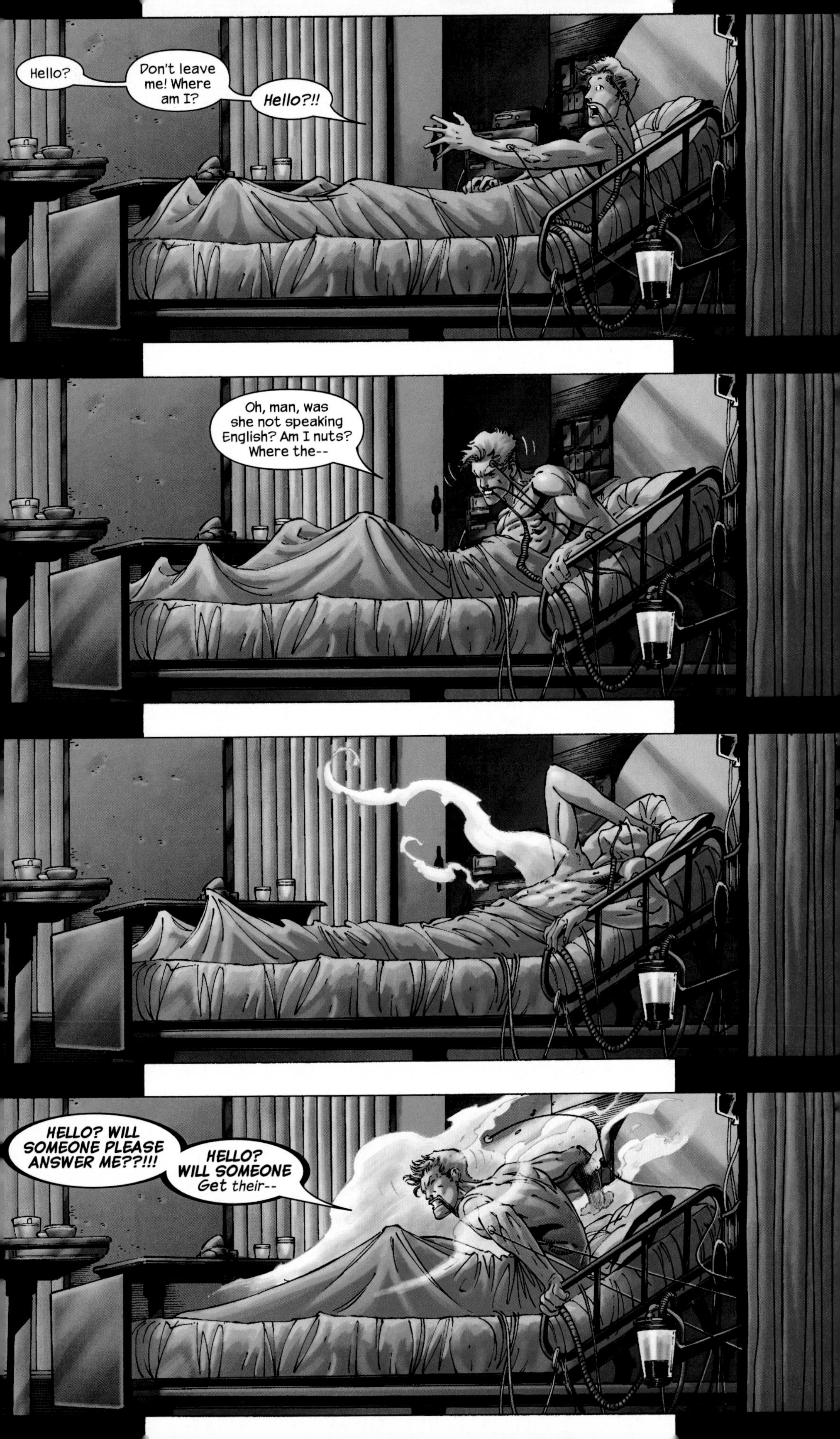
Hello?
Don't leave me! Where am I?
Hello?!!
Oh, man, was she not speaking English? Am I nuts? Where the--
HELLO? WILL SOMEONE PLEASE ANSWER ME??!!!
HELLO? WILL SOMEONE Get their--

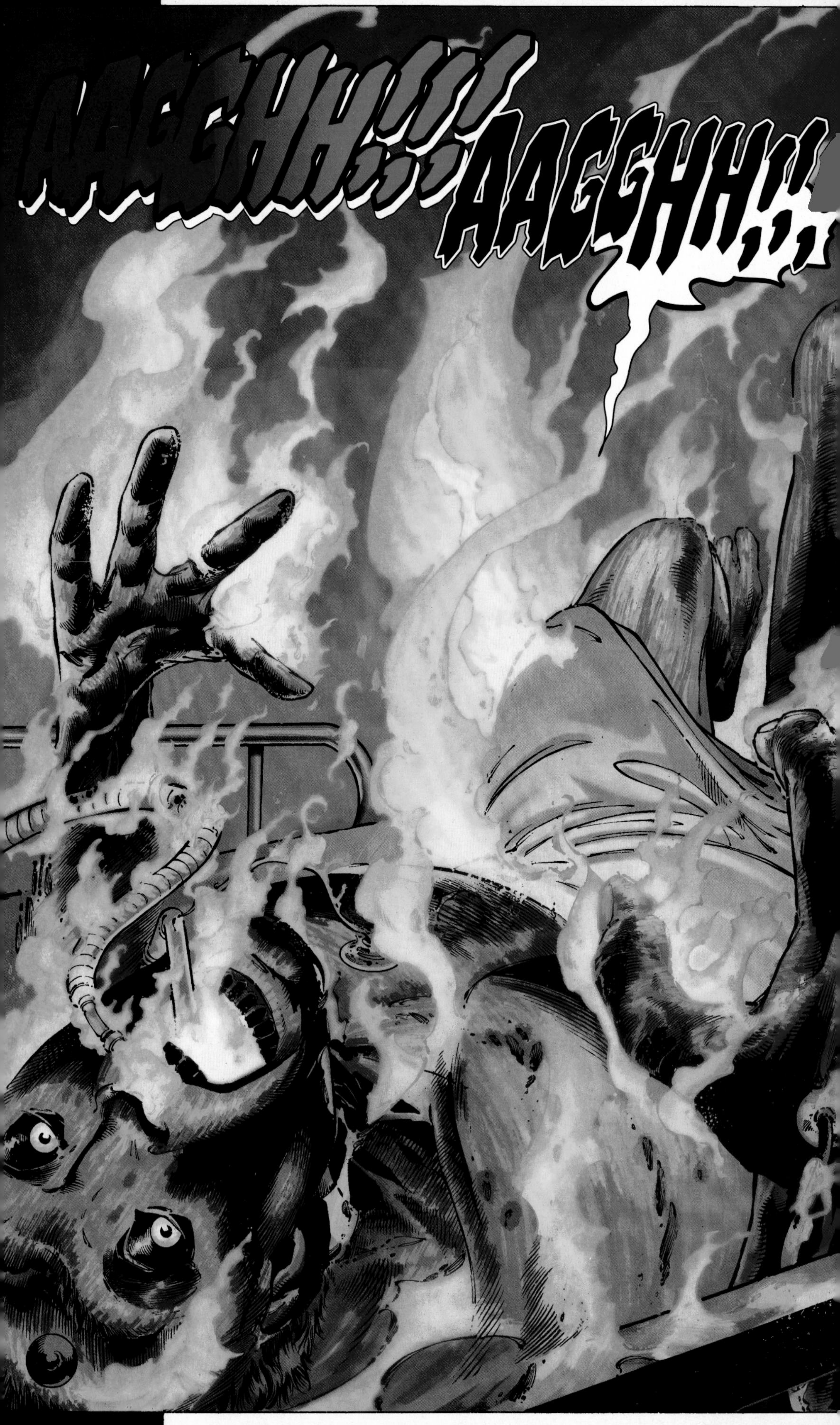
AAGGHH!!!
AAGGHH!!!

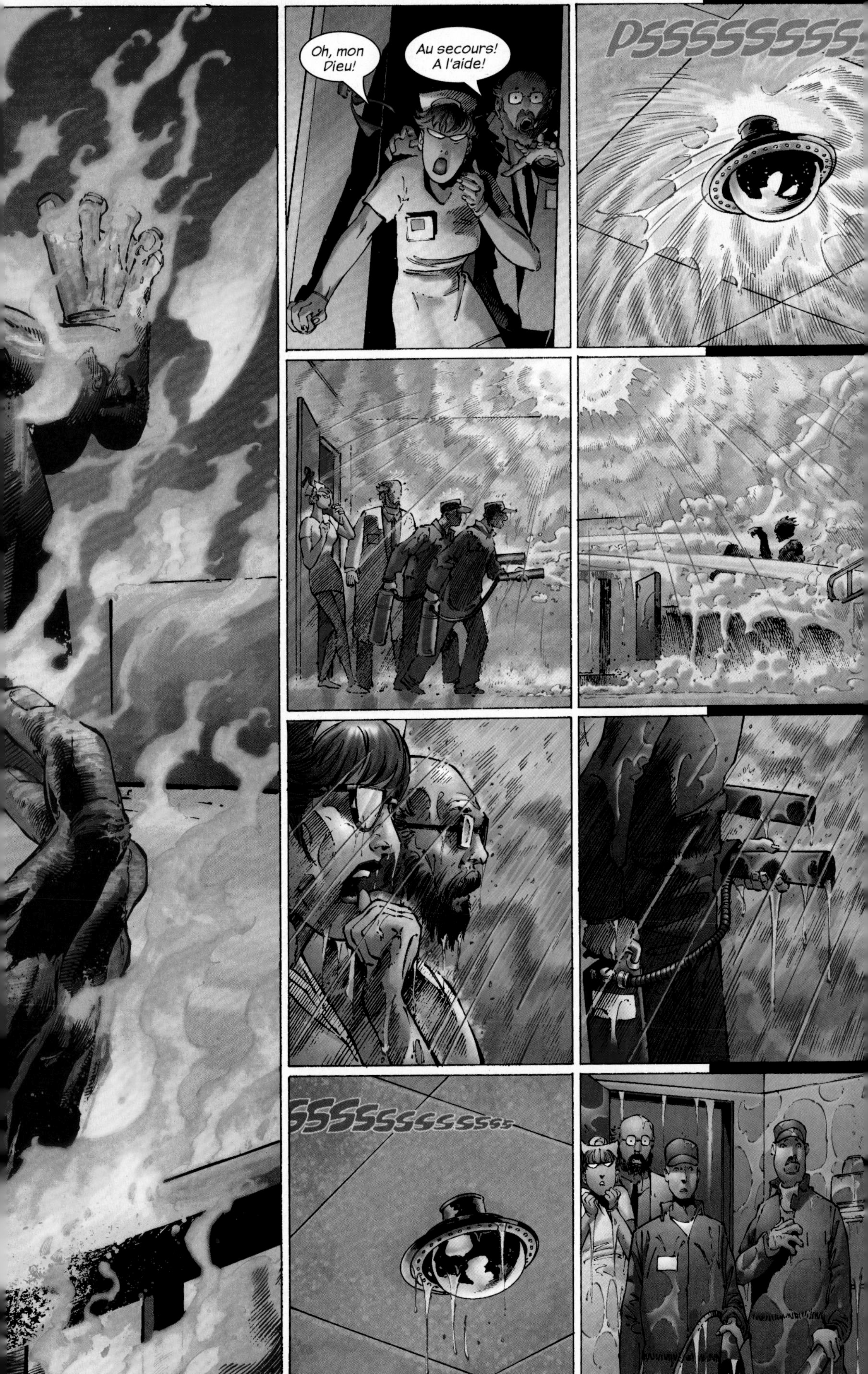
Oh, mon Dieu!
Au secours! A l'aide!
PSSSSSSSSS
SSSSSSSSSSSSSS

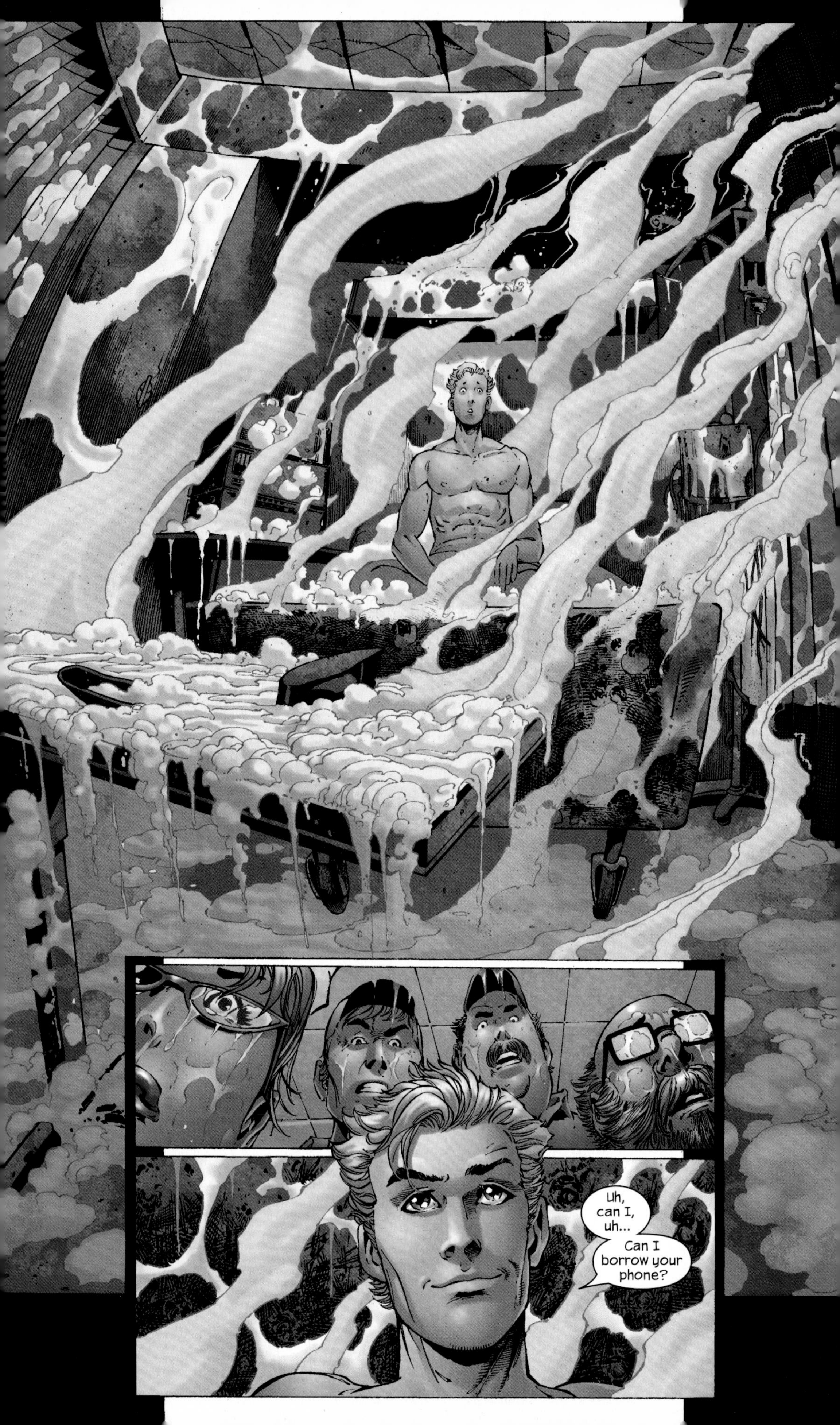
Uh, can I, uh...
Can I borrow your phone?

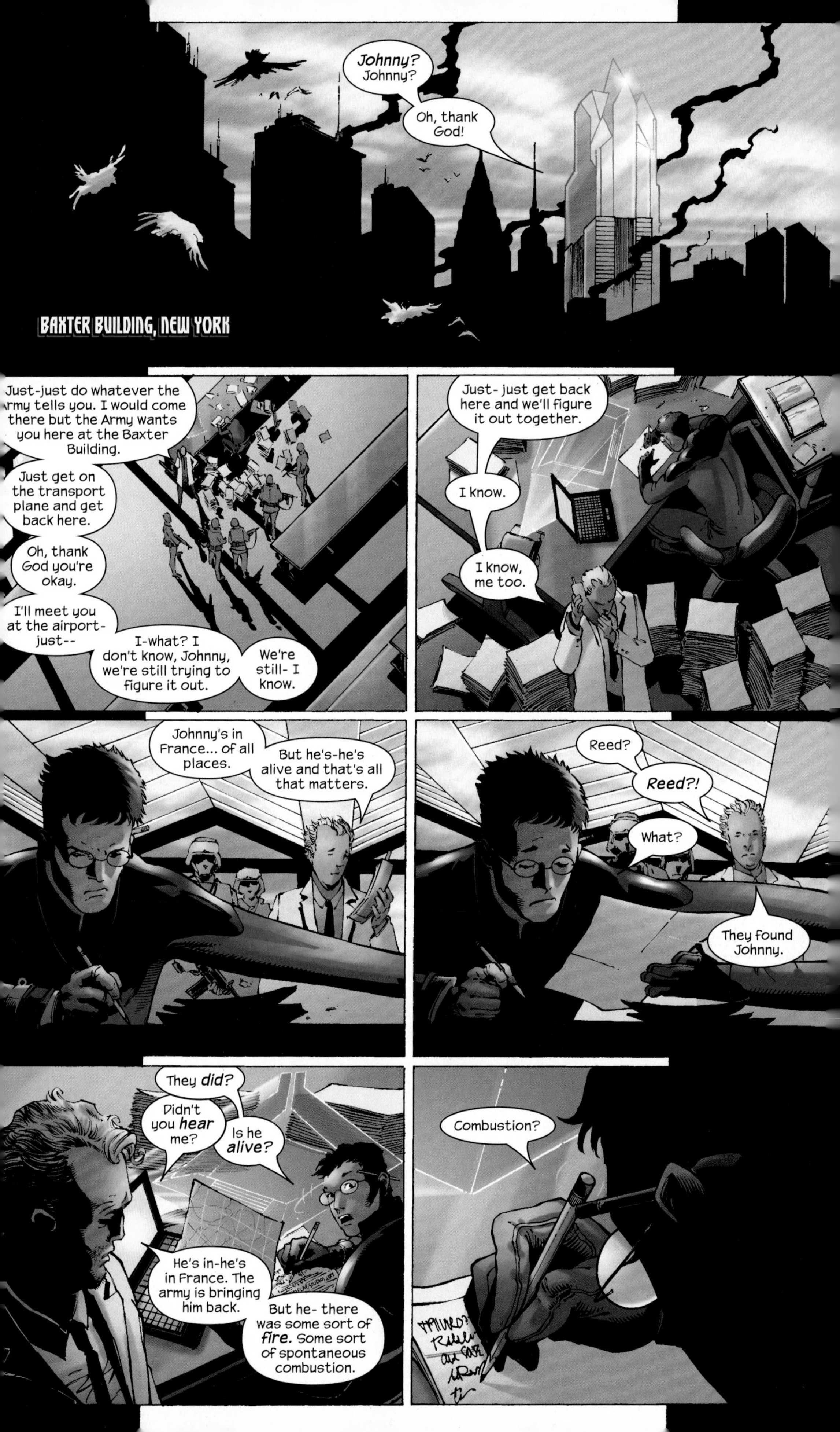
BAXTER BUILDING, NEW YORK
Johnny? Johnny?
Oh, thank God!
Just-just do whatever the army tells you. I would come there but the Army wants you here at the Baxter Building.
Just get on the transport plane and get back here.
Oh, thank God you're okay.
I'll meet you at the airport- just--
I-what? I don't know, Johnny, we're still trying to figure it out.
We're still- I know.
Just- just get back here and we'll figure it out together.
I know.
I know, me too.
Johnny's in France... of all places.
But he's-he's alive and that's all that matters.
Reed?
Reed?!
What?
They found Johnny.
They did?
Didn't you hear me?
Is he alive?
He's in-he's in France. The army is bringing him back.
But he- there was some sort of fire. Some sort of spontaneous combustion.
Combustion?

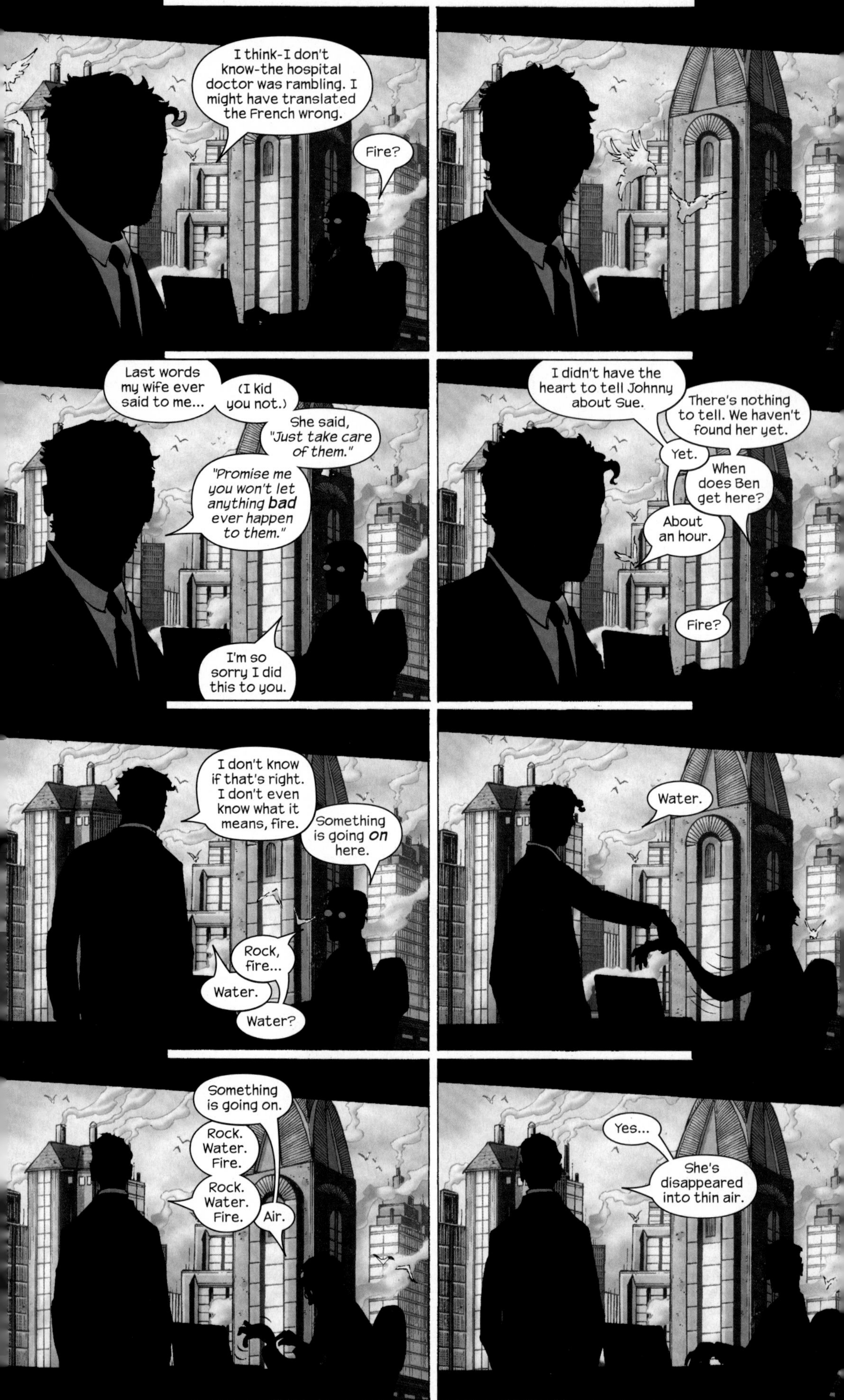
I think-I don't know-the hospital doctor was rambling. I might have translated the French wrong.
Fire?
Last words my wife ever said to me...
(I kid you not.)
She said, "Just take care of them."
"Promise me you won't let anything **bad** ever happen to them."
I'm so sorry I did this to you.
I didn't have the heart to tell Johnny about Sue.
There's nothing to tell. We haven't found her yet.
Yet.
When does Ben get here?
About an hour.
Fire?
I don't know if that's right. I don't even know what it means, fire.
Something is going ***on*** here.
Rock, fire...
Water.
Water?
Water.
Something is going on.
Rock. Water. Fire.
Rock. Water. Fire.
Air.
Yes...
She's disappeared into thin air.

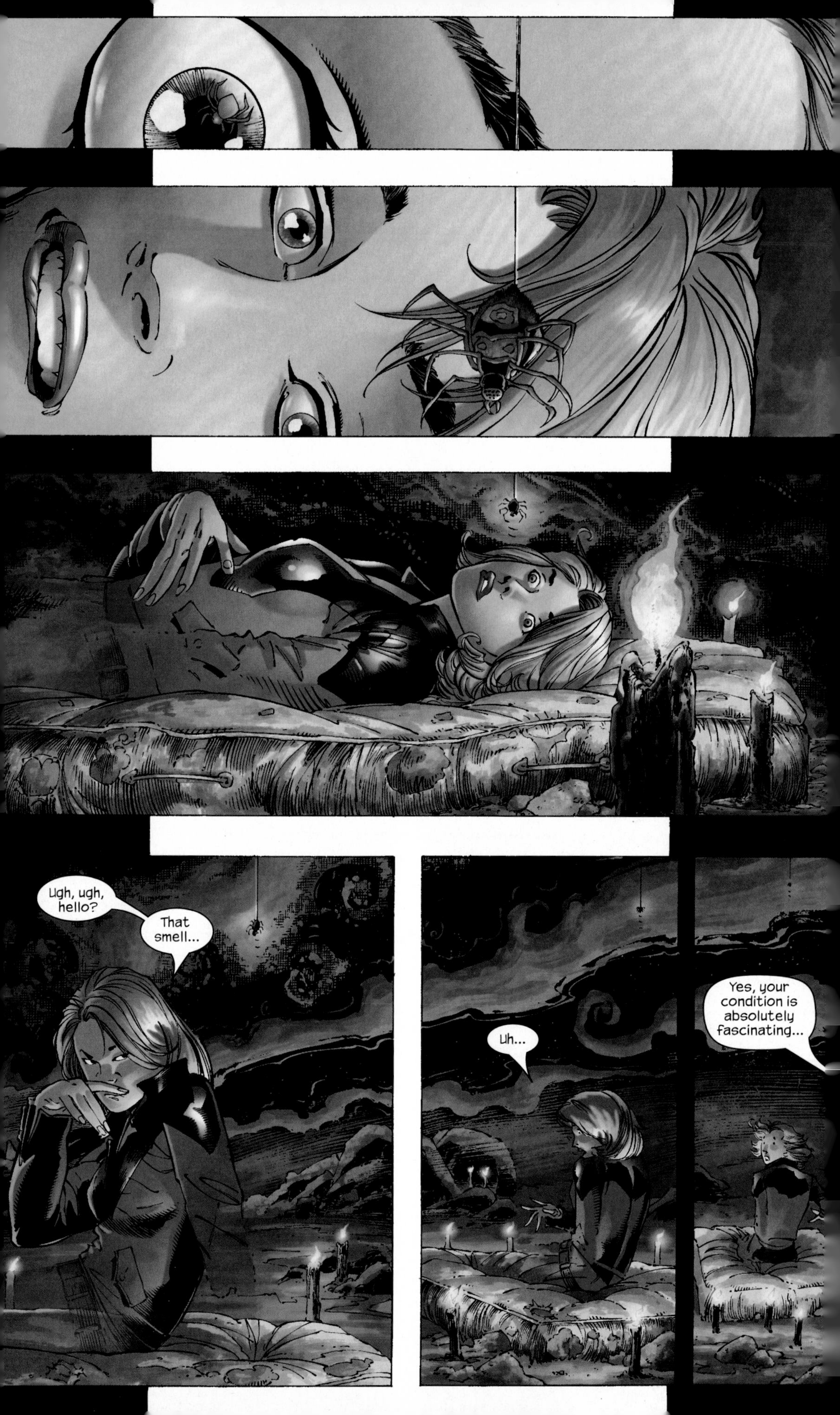
Ugh, ugh, hello?
That smell...
Uh...
Yes, your condition is absolutely fascinating...

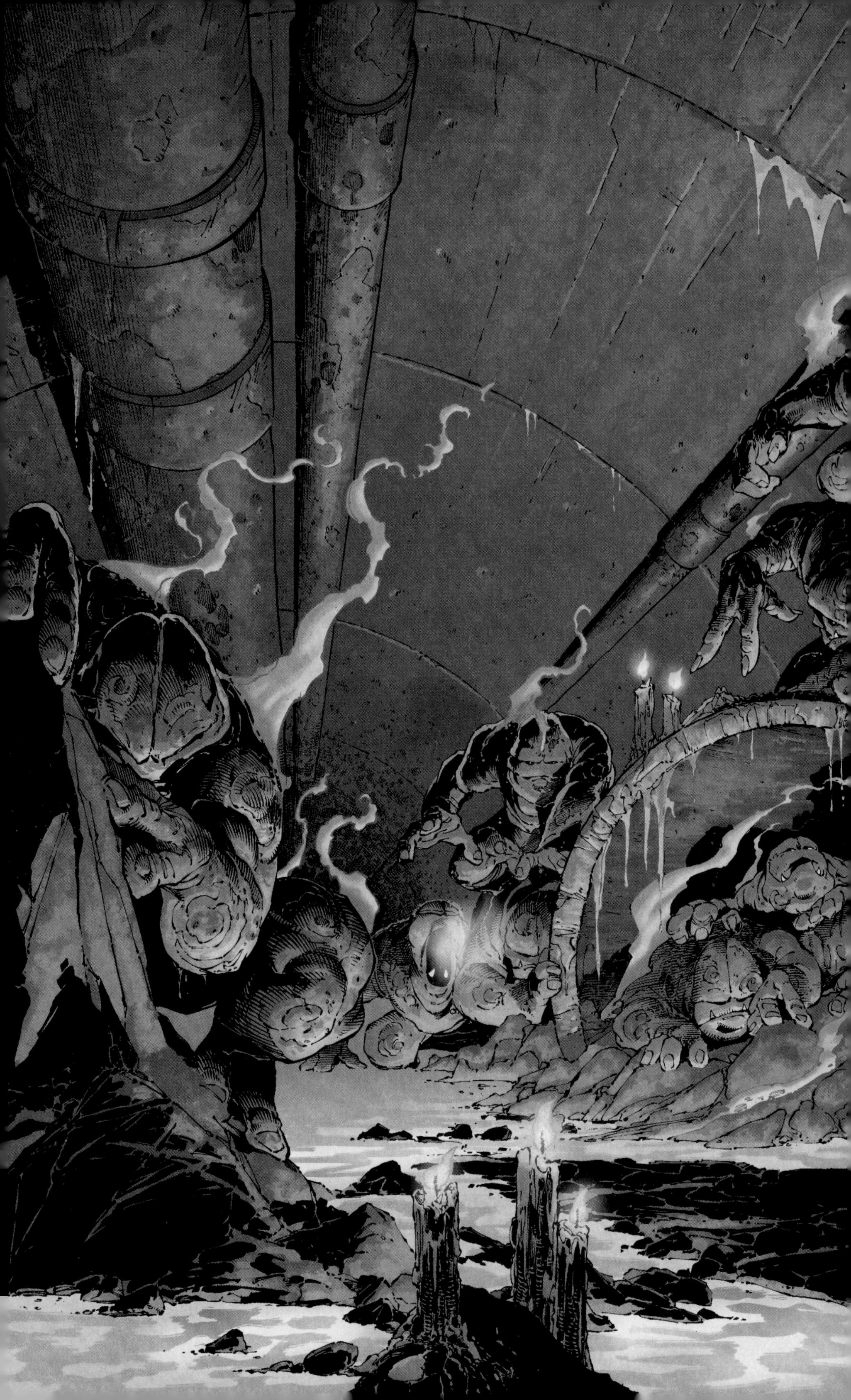

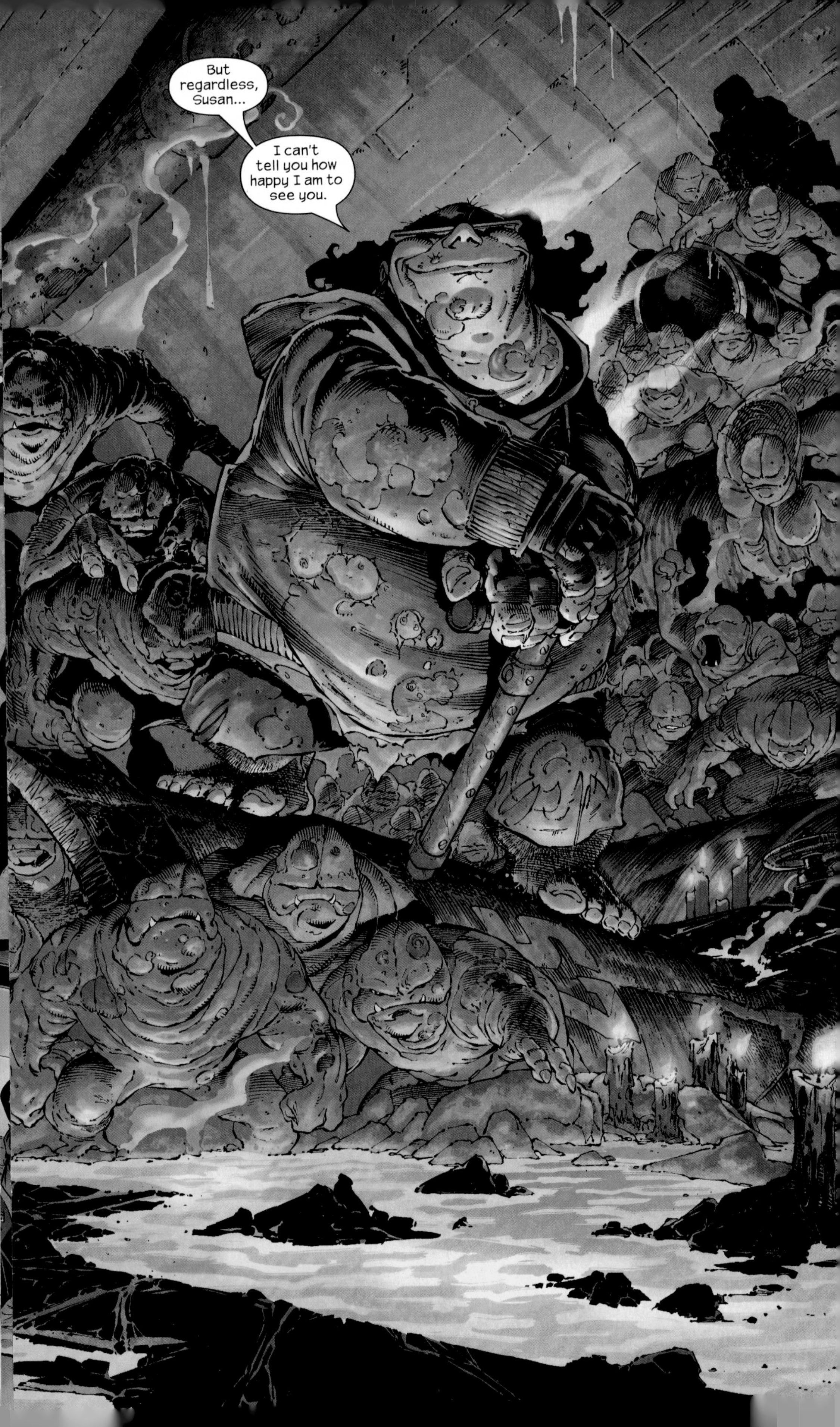
But regardless, Susan...
I can't tell you how happy I am to see you.

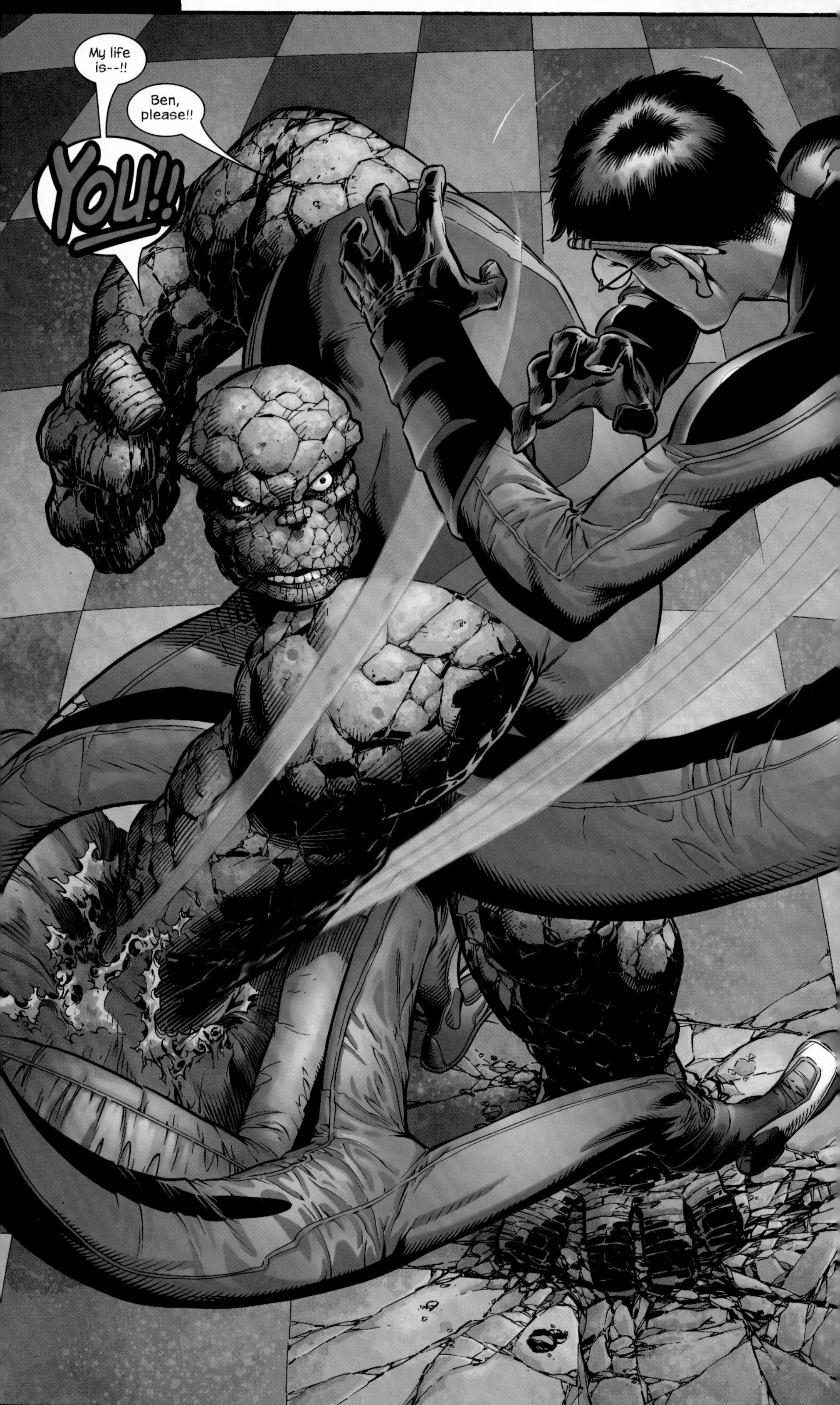

My life is--!!
YOU!!
Ben, please!!

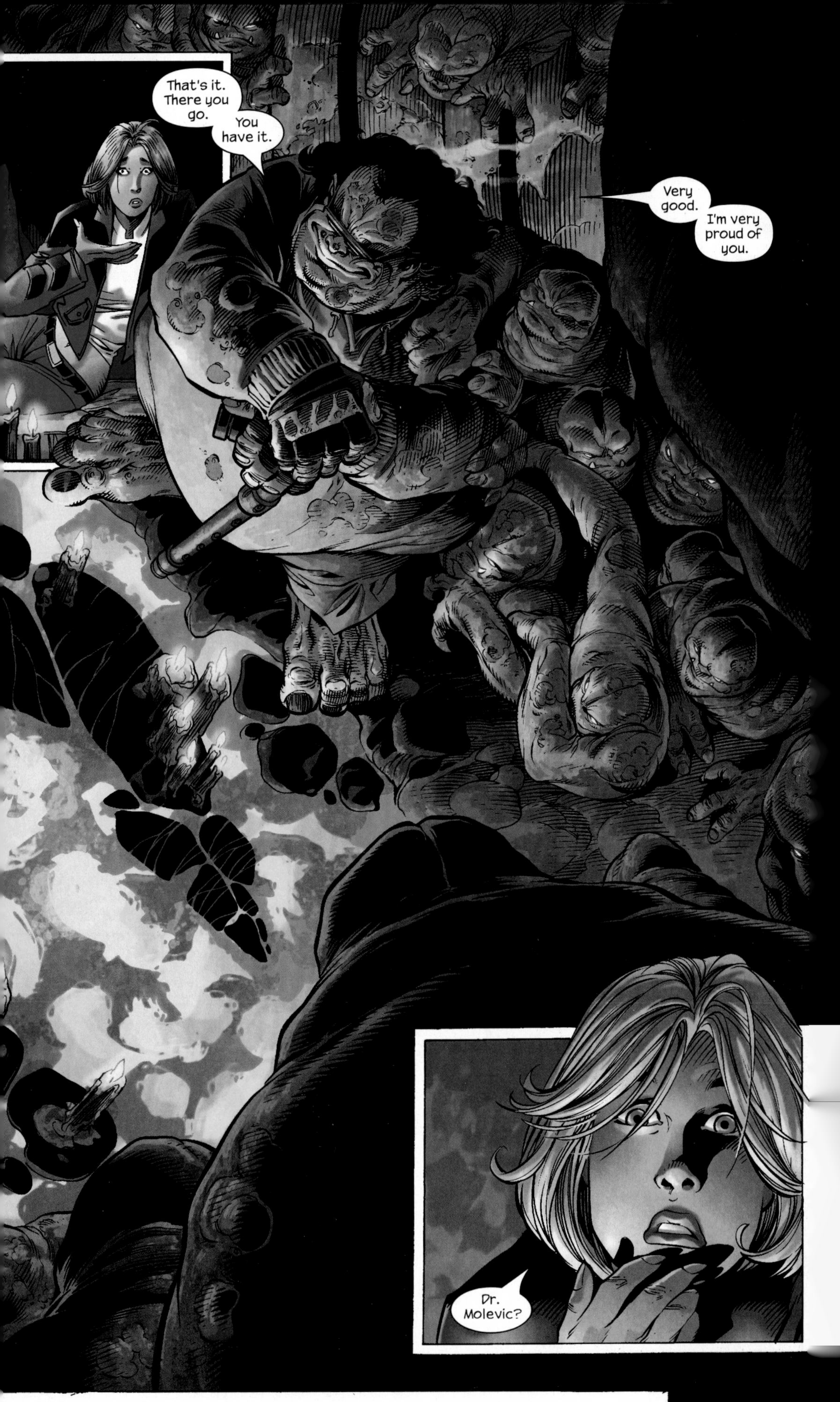
That's it. There you go.
You have it.
Very good.
I'm very proud of you.
Dr. Molevic?

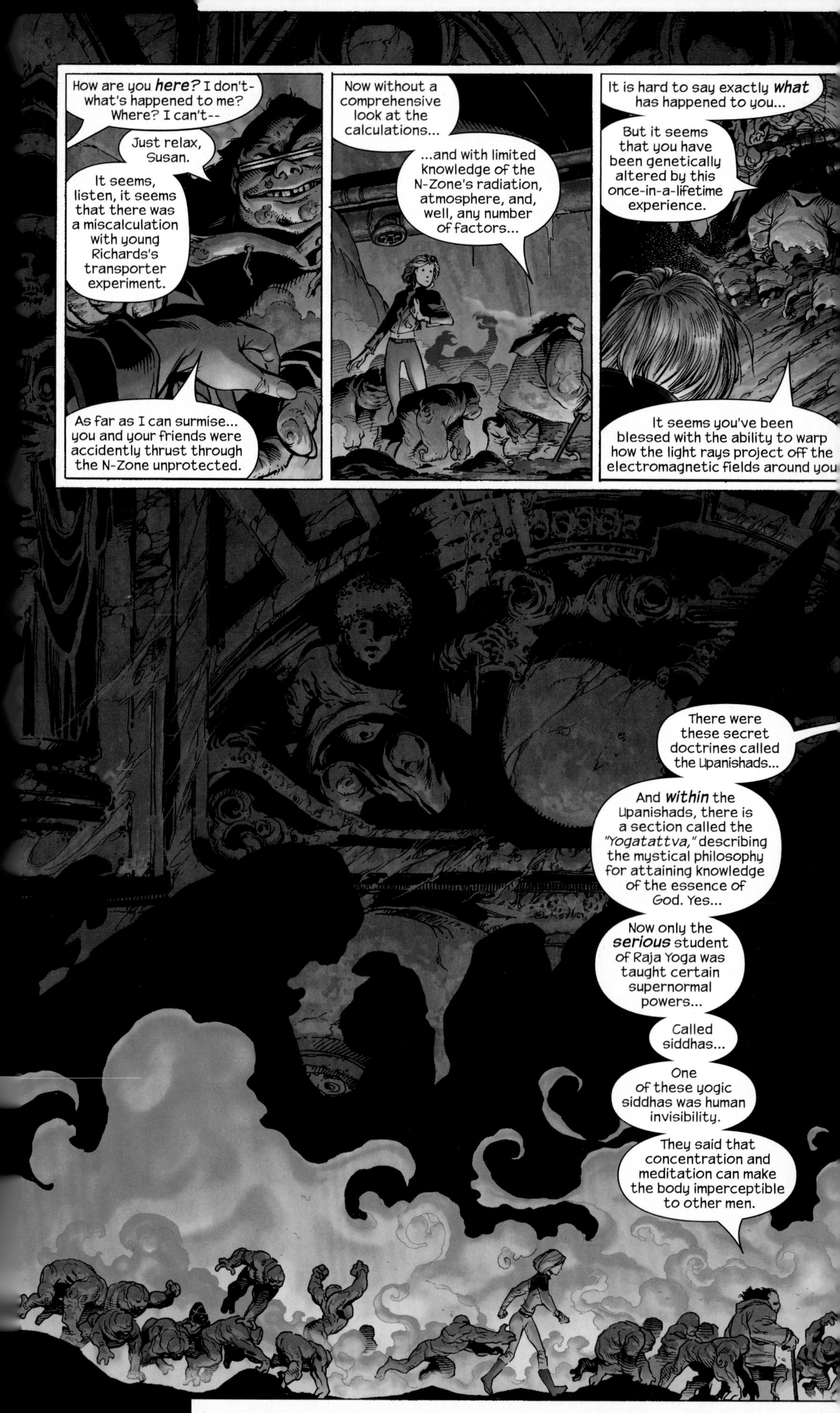
How are you here? I don't- what's happened to me? Where? I can't--
Just relax, Susan.
It seems, listen, it seems that there was a miscalculation with young Richards's transporter experiment.
As far as I can surmise... you and your friends were accidently thrust through the N-Zone unprotected.
Now without a comprehensive look at the calculations...
...and with limited knowledge of the N-Zone's radiation, atmosphere, and, well, any number of factors...
It is hard to say exactly what has happened to you...
But it seems that you have been genetically altered by this once-in-a-lifetime experience.
It seems you've been blessed with the ability to warp how the light rays project off the electromagnetic fields around you
There were these secret doctrines called the Upanishads...
And within the Upanishads, there is a section called the "Yogatattva," describing the mystical philosophy for attaining knowledge of the essence of God. Yes...
Now only the serious student of Raja Yoga was taught certain supernormal powers...
Called siddhas...
One of these yogic siddhas was human invisibility.
They said that concentration and meditation can make the body imperceptible to other men.

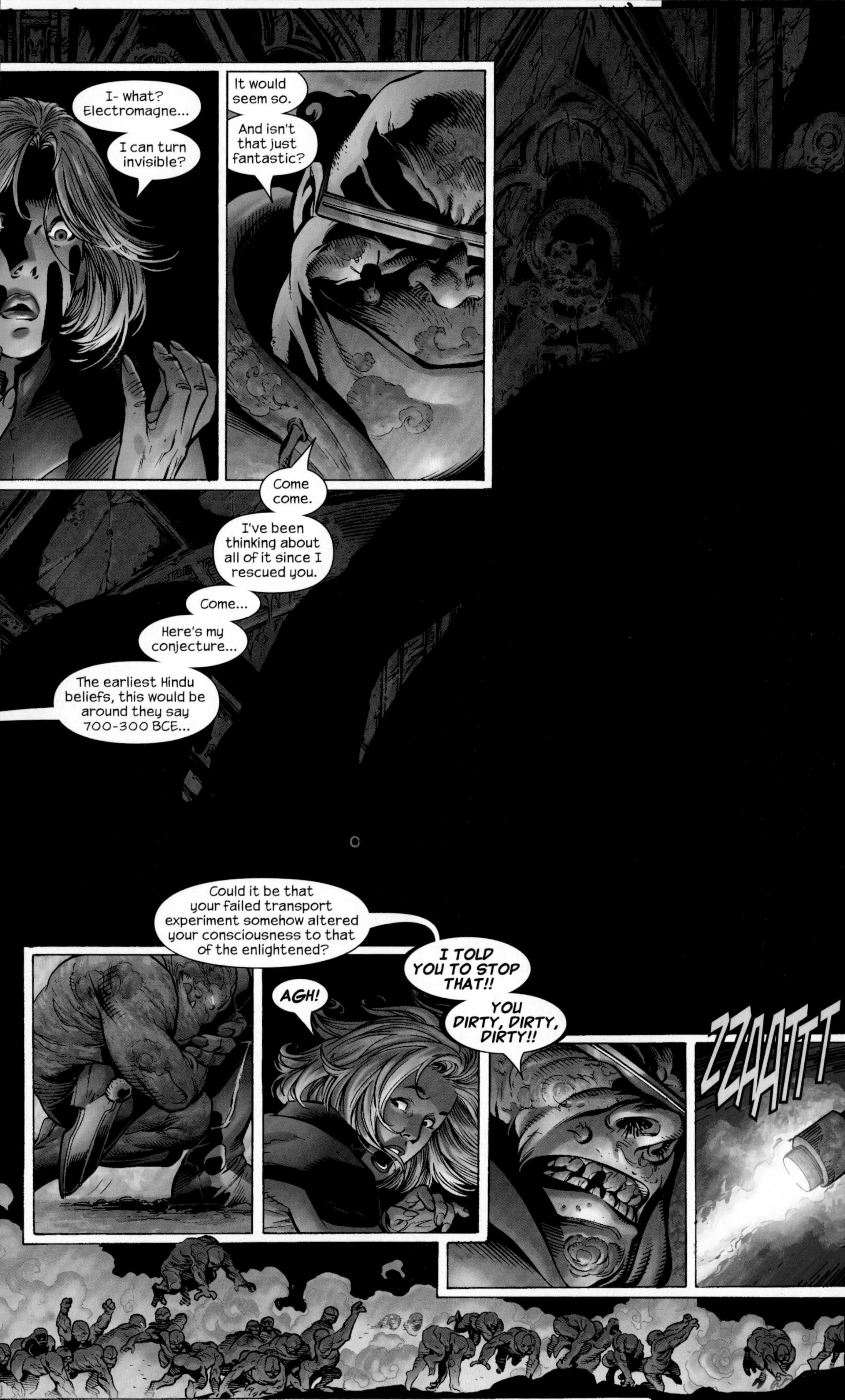
I- what? Electromagne...
I can turn invisible?
It would seem so.
And isn't that just fantastic?
Come come.
I've been thinking about all of it since I rescued you.
Come...
Here's my conjecture...
The earliest Hindu beliefs, this would be around they say 700-300 BCE...
Could it be that your failed transport experiment somehow altered your consciousness to that of the enlightened?
AGH!
I TOLD YOU TO STOP THAT!!
YOU DIRTY, DIRTY, DIRTY!!
ZZAATTT

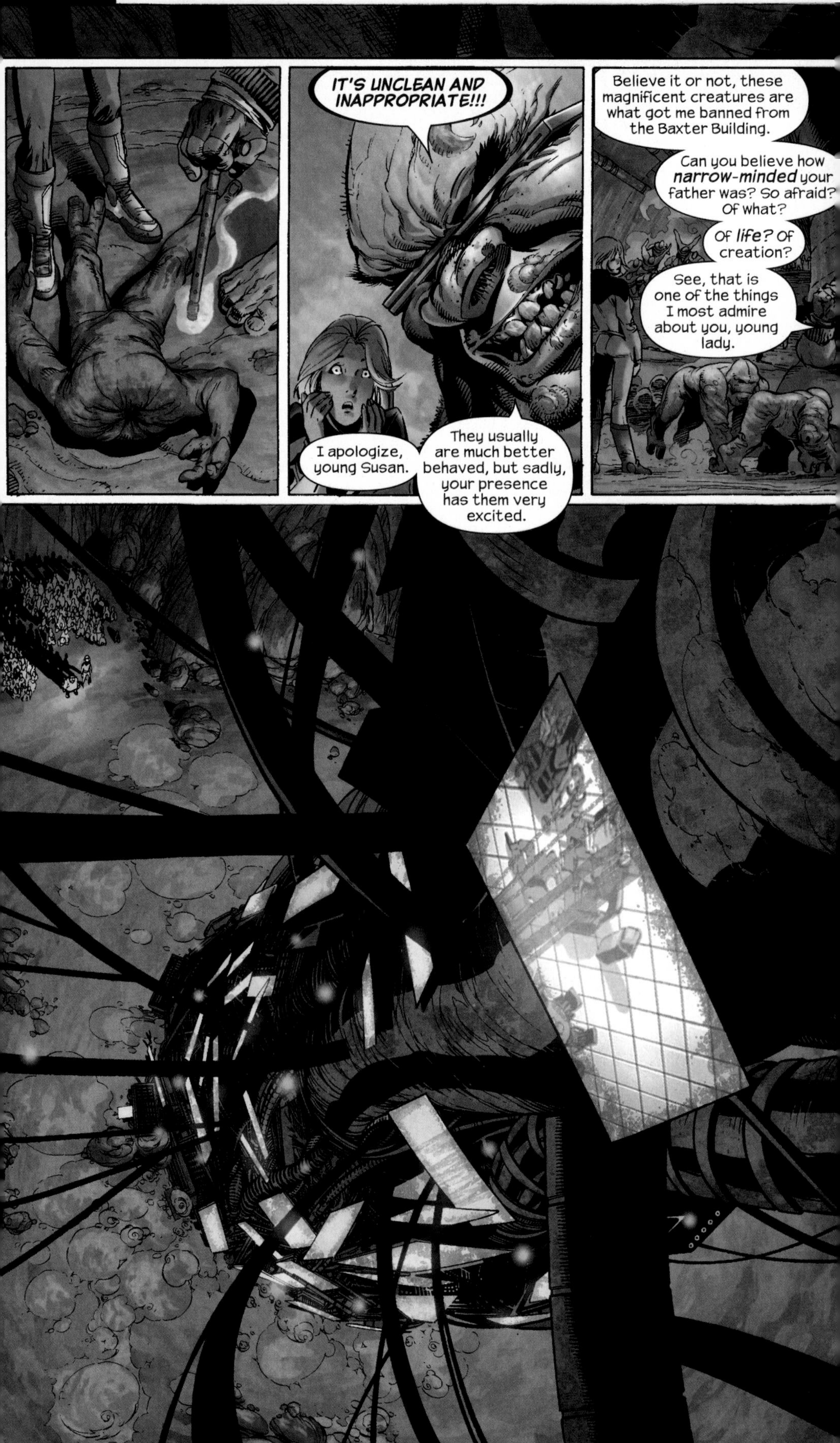
IT'S UNCLEAN AND INAPPROPRIATE!!!
I apologize, young Susan.
They usually are much better behaved, but sadly, your presence has them very excited.
Believe it or not, these magnificent creatures are what got me banned from the Baxter Building.
Can you believe how narrow-minded your father was? So afraid? Of what?
Of life? Of creation?
See, that is one of the things I most admire about you, young lady.

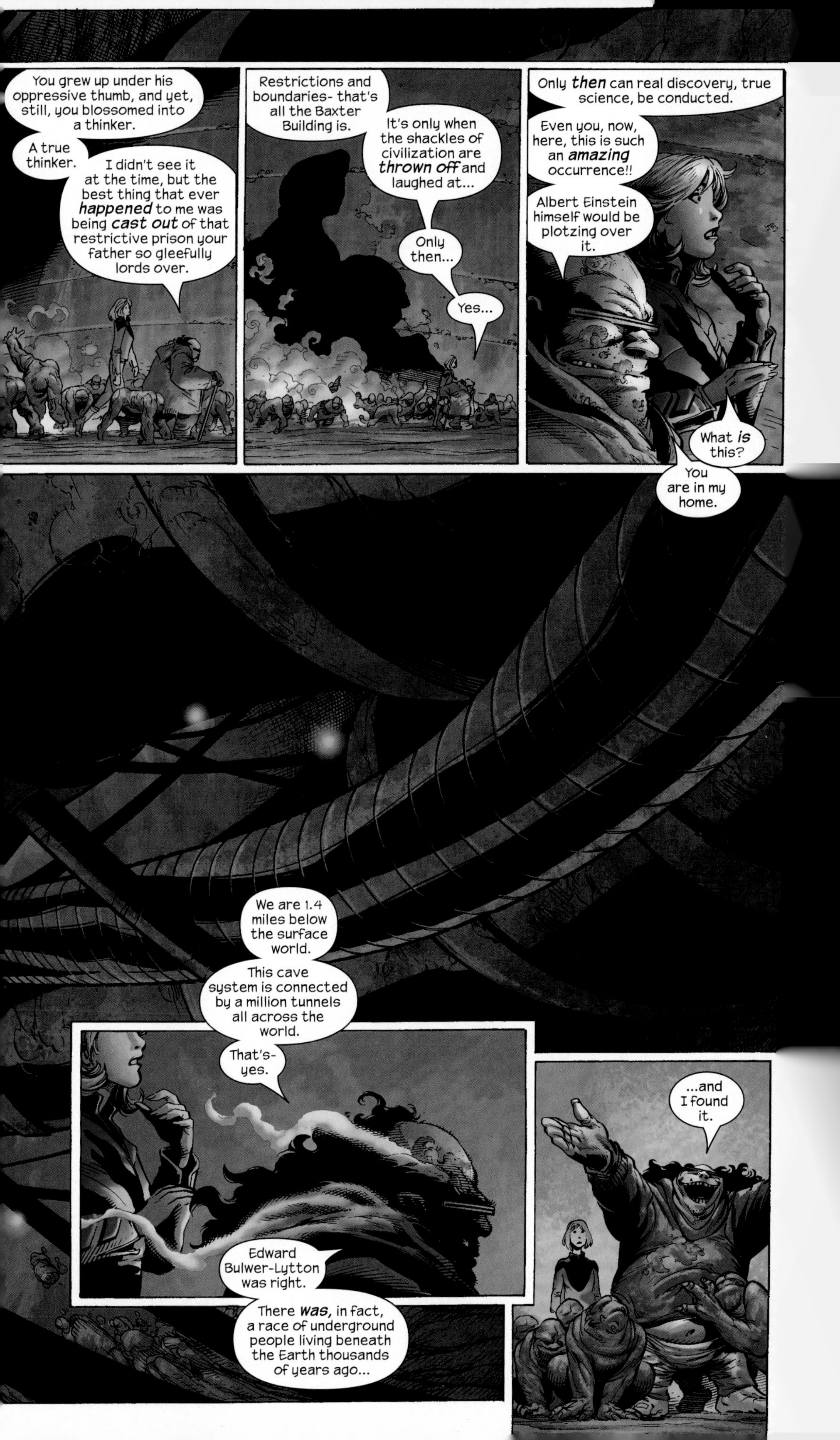
You grew up under his oppressive thumb, and yet, still, you blossomed into a thinker.
A true thinker.
I didn't see it at the time, but the best thing that ever happened to me was being cast out of that restrictive prison your father so gleefully lords over.
Restrictions and boundaries- that's all the Baxter Building is.
It's only when the shackles of civilization are thrown off and laughed at...
Only then...
Yes...
Only then can real discovery, true science, be conducted.
Even you, now, here, this is such an amazing occurrence!!
Albert Einstein himself would be plotzing over it.
What is this?
You are in my home.
We are 1.4 miles below the surface world.
This cave system is connected by a million tunnels all across the world.
That's- yes.
Edward Bulwer-Lytton was right.
There was, in fact, a race of underground people living beneath the Earth thousands of years ago...
...and I found it.

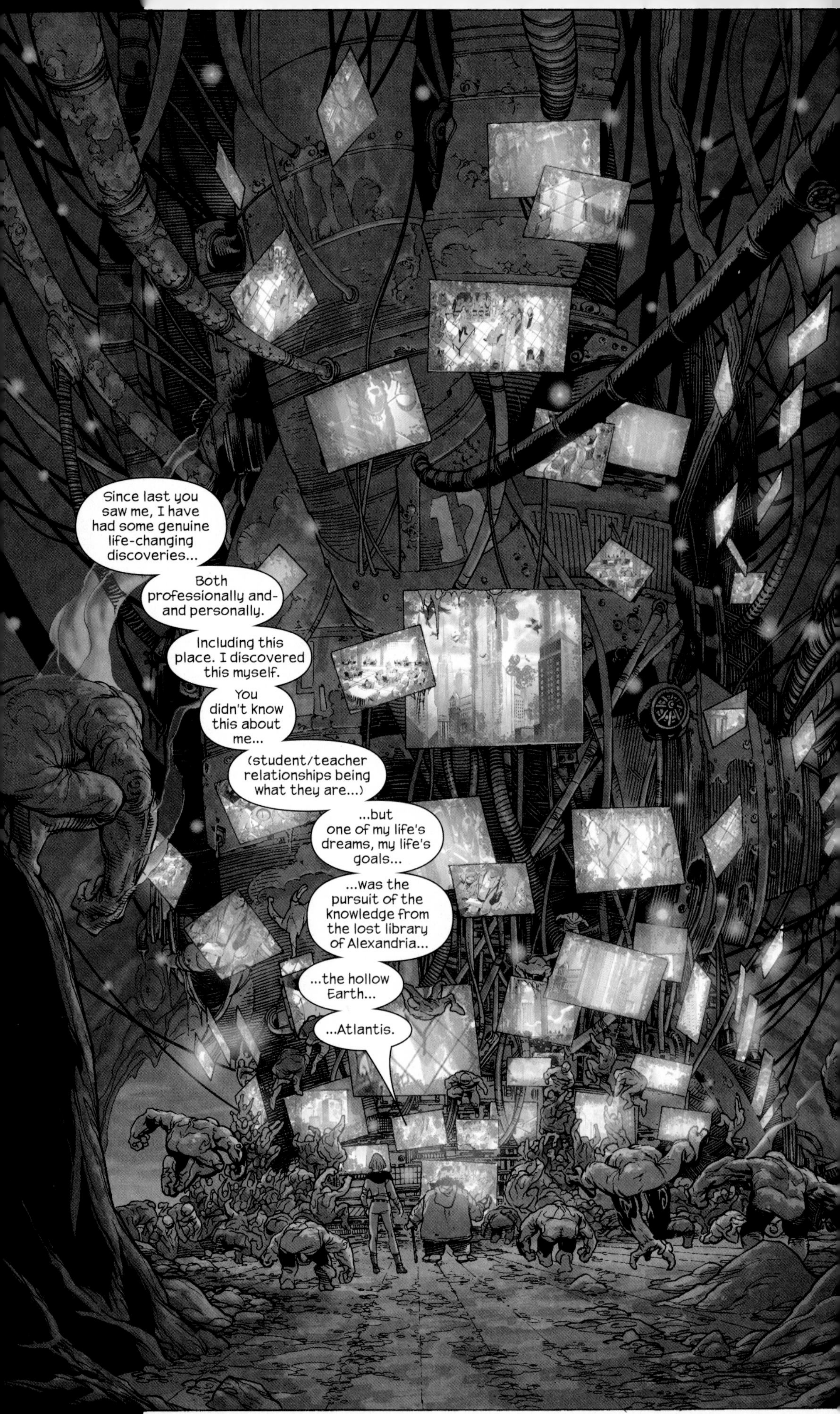
Since last you saw me, I have had some genuine life-changing discoveries...
Both professionally and- and personally.
Including this place. I discovered this myself.
You didn't know this about me...
(student/teacher relationships being what they are...)
...but one of my life's dreams, my life's goals...
...was the pursuit of the knowledge from the lost library of Alexandria...
...the hollow Earth...
...Atlantis.

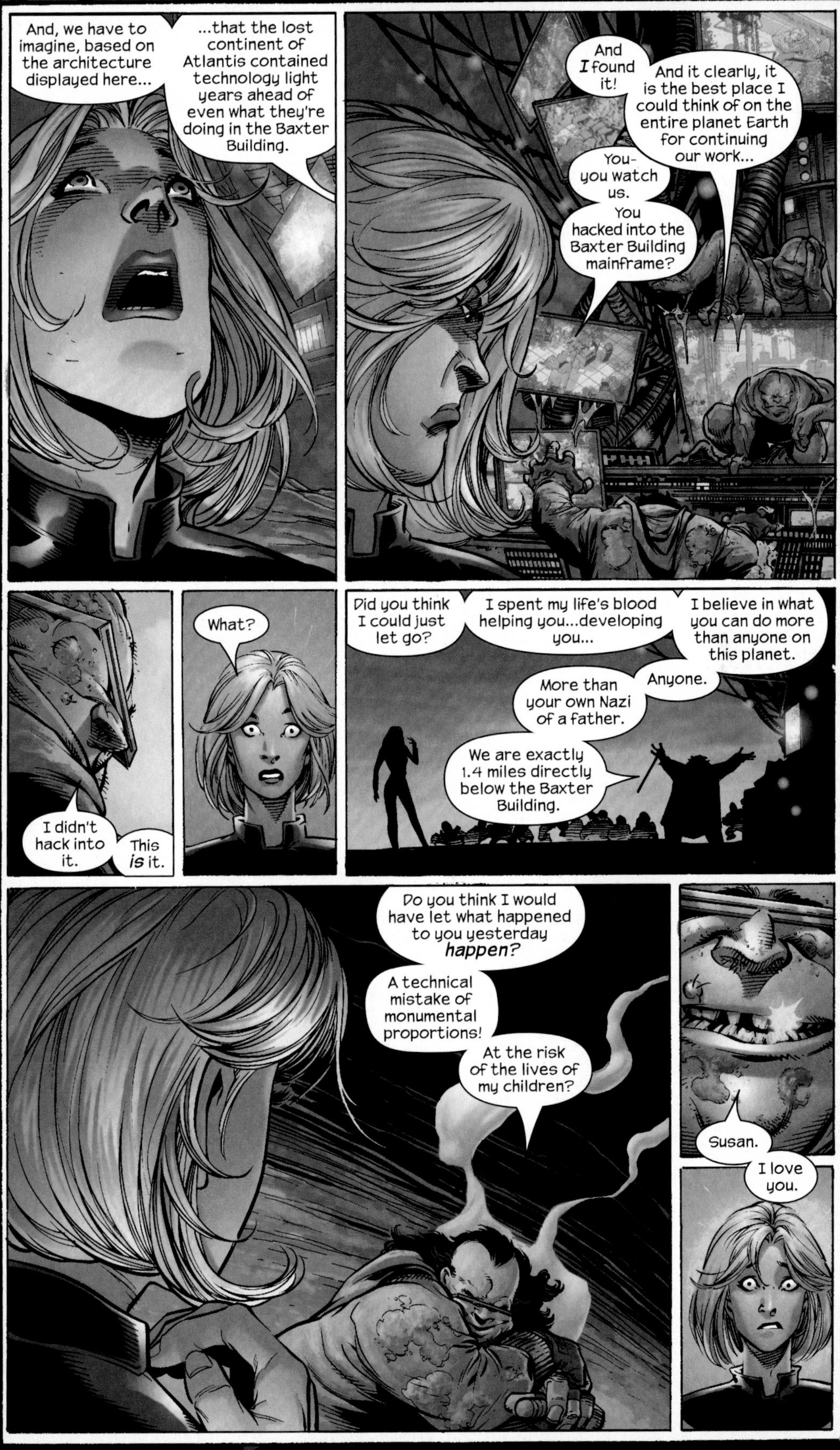
And, we have to imagine, based on the architecture displayed here...
...that the lost continent of Atlantis contained technology light years ahead of even what they're doing in the Baxter Building.
And *I* found it!
And it clearly, it is the best place I could think of on the entire planet Earth for continuing our work...
You- you watch us.
You hacked into the Baxter Building mainframe?
I didn't hack into it.
This *is* it.
What?
Did you think I could just let go?
I spent my life's blood helping you...developing you...
I believe in what you can do more than anyone on this planet.
Anyone.
More than your own Nazi of a father.
We are exactly 1.4 miles directly below the Baxter Building.
Do you think I would have let what happened to you yesterday *happen?*
A technical mistake of monumental proportions!
At the risk of the lives of my children?
Susan.
I love you.

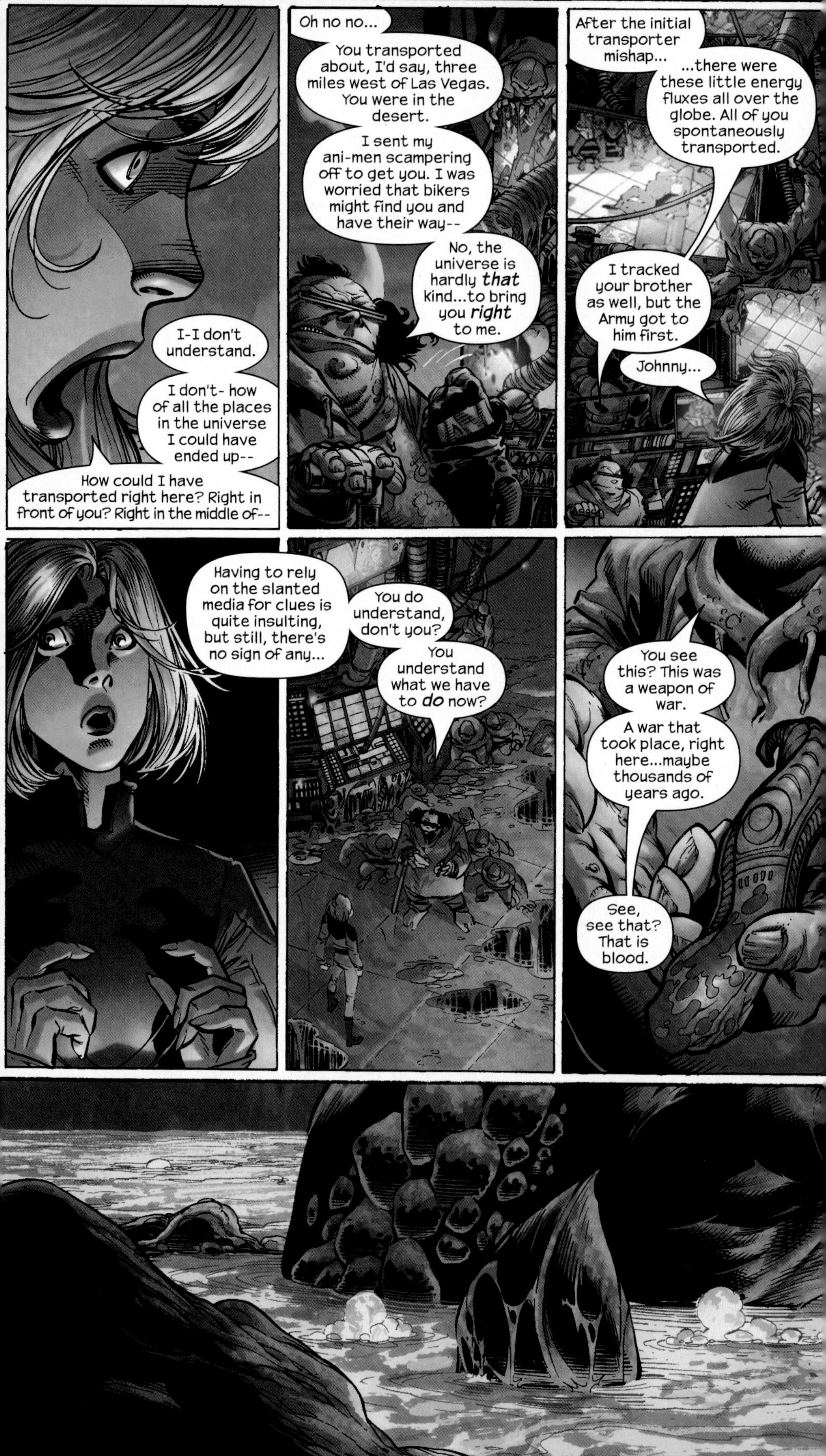

I-I don't understand.
I don't- how of all the places in the universe I could have ended up--
How could I have transported right here? Right in front of you? Right in the middle of--
Oh no no...
You transported about, I'd say, three miles west of Las Vegas. You were in the desert.
I sent my ani-men scampering off to get you. I was worried that bikers might find you and have their way--
No, the universe is hardly *that* kind...to bring you *right* to me.
After the initial transporter mishap...
...there were these little energy fluxes all over the globe. All of you spontaneously transported.
I tracked your brother as well, but the Army got to him first.
Johnny...
Having to rely on the slanted media for clues is quite insulting, but still, there's no sign of any...
You do understand, don't you?
You understand what we have to *do* now?
You see this? This was a weapon of war.
A war that took place, right here...maybe thousands of years ago.
See, see that? That is blood.

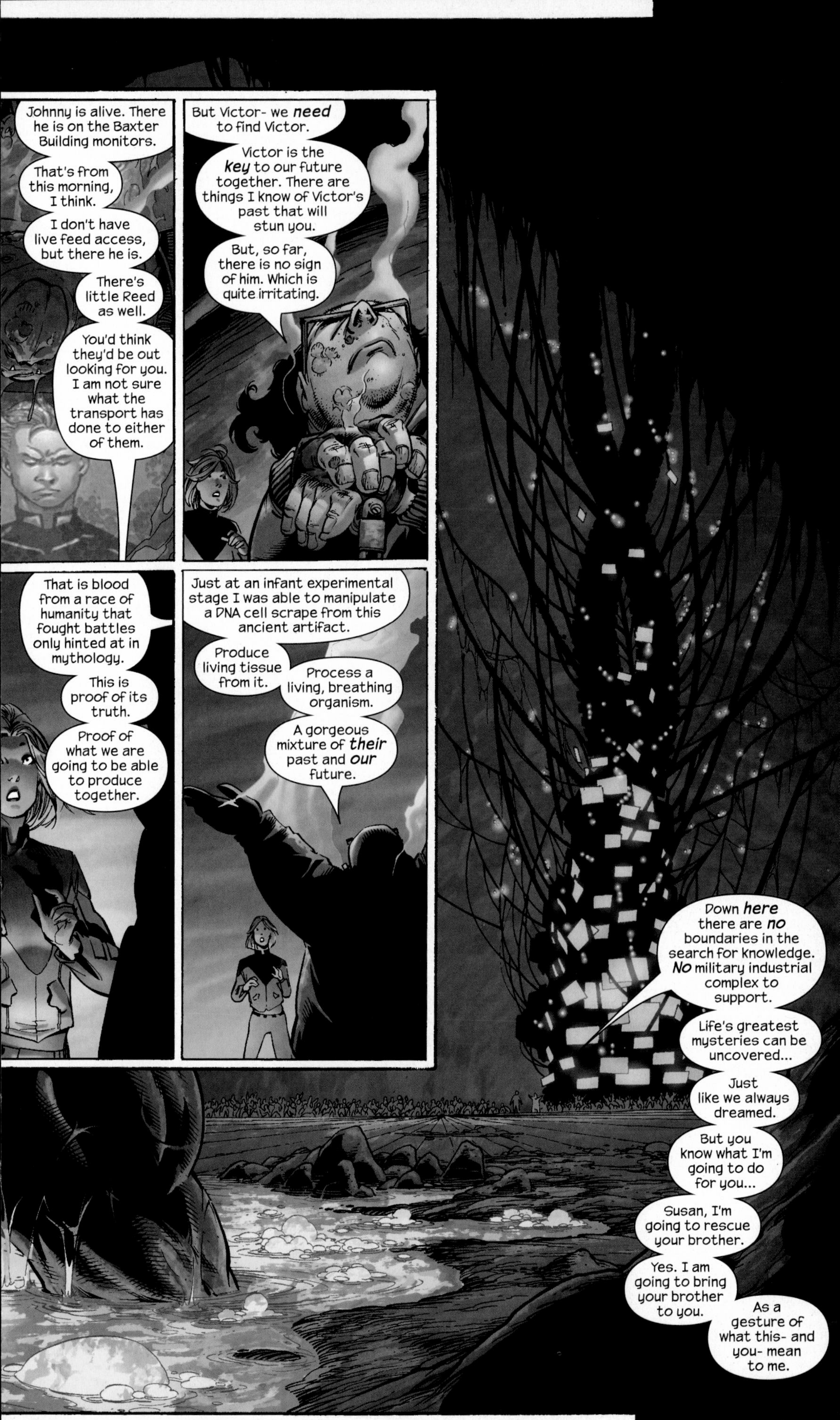

Johnny is alive. There he is on the Baxter Building monitors.
That's from this morning, I think.
I don't have live feed access, but there he is.
There's little Reed as well.
You'd think they'd be out looking for you. I am not sure what the transport has done to either of them.
But Victor- we *need* to find Victor.
Victor is the *key* to our future together. There are things I know of Victor's past that will stun you.
But, so far, there is no sign of him. Which is quite irritating.
That is blood from a race of humanity that fought battles only hinted at in mythology.
This is proof of its truth.
Proof of what we are going to be able to produce together.
Just at an infant experimental stage I was able to manipulate a DNA cell scrape from this ancient artifact.
Produce living tissue from it.
Process a living, breathing organism.
A gorgeous mixture of *their* past and *our* future.
Down *here* there are *no* boundaries in the search for knowledge. *No* military industrial complex to support.
Life's greatest mysteries can be uncovered...
Just like we always dreamed.
But you know what I'm going to do for you...
Susan, I'm going to rescue your brother.
Yes. I am going to bring your brother to you.
As a gesture of what this- and you- mean to me.

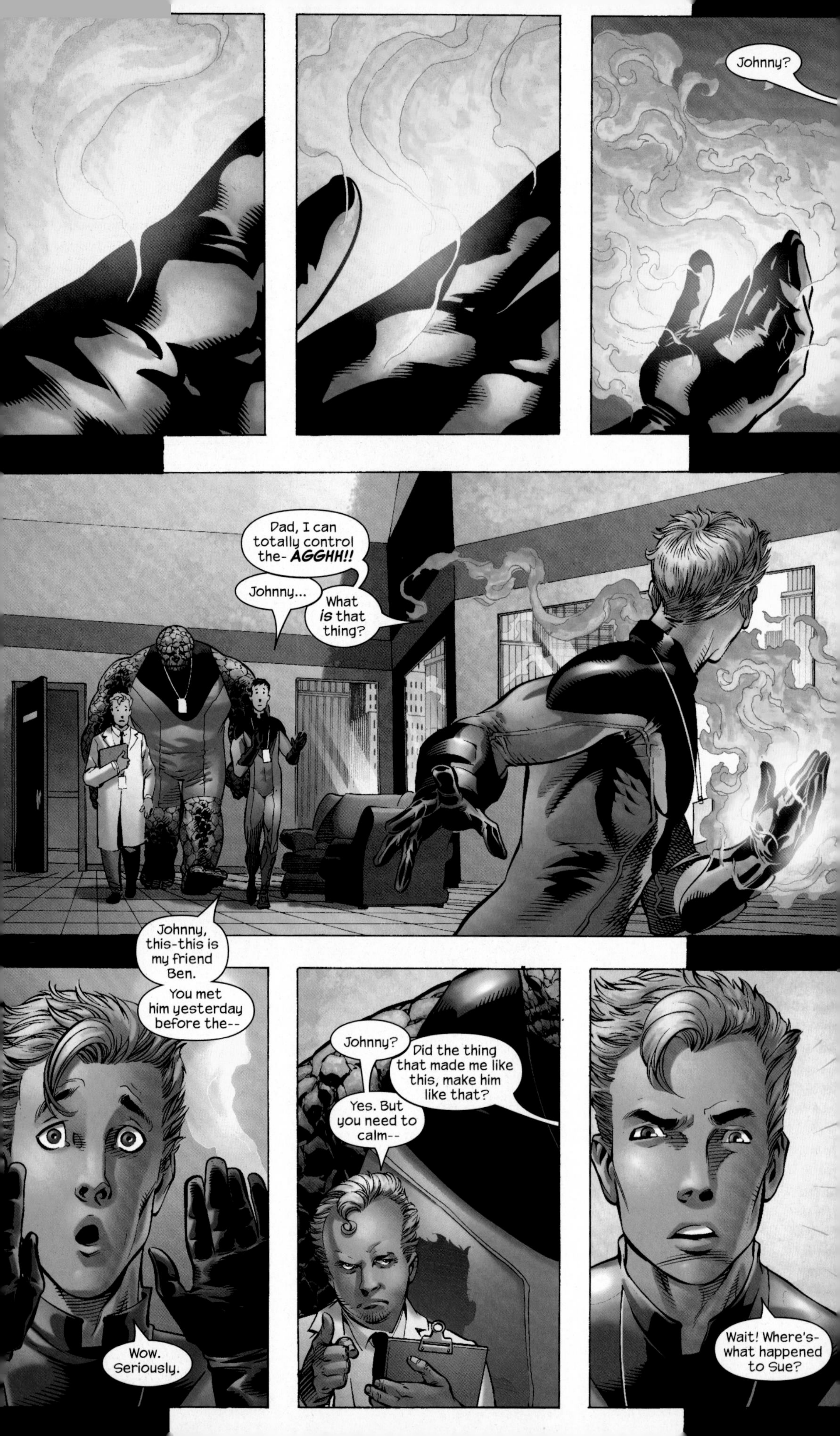
Johnny?
Dad, I can totally control the- AGGHH!!
Johnny...
What is that thing?
Johnny, this-this is my friend Ben.
You met him yesterday before the--
Wow. Seriously.
Johnny?
Did the thing that made me like this, make him like that?
Yes. But you need to calm--
Wait! Where's- what happened to Sue?

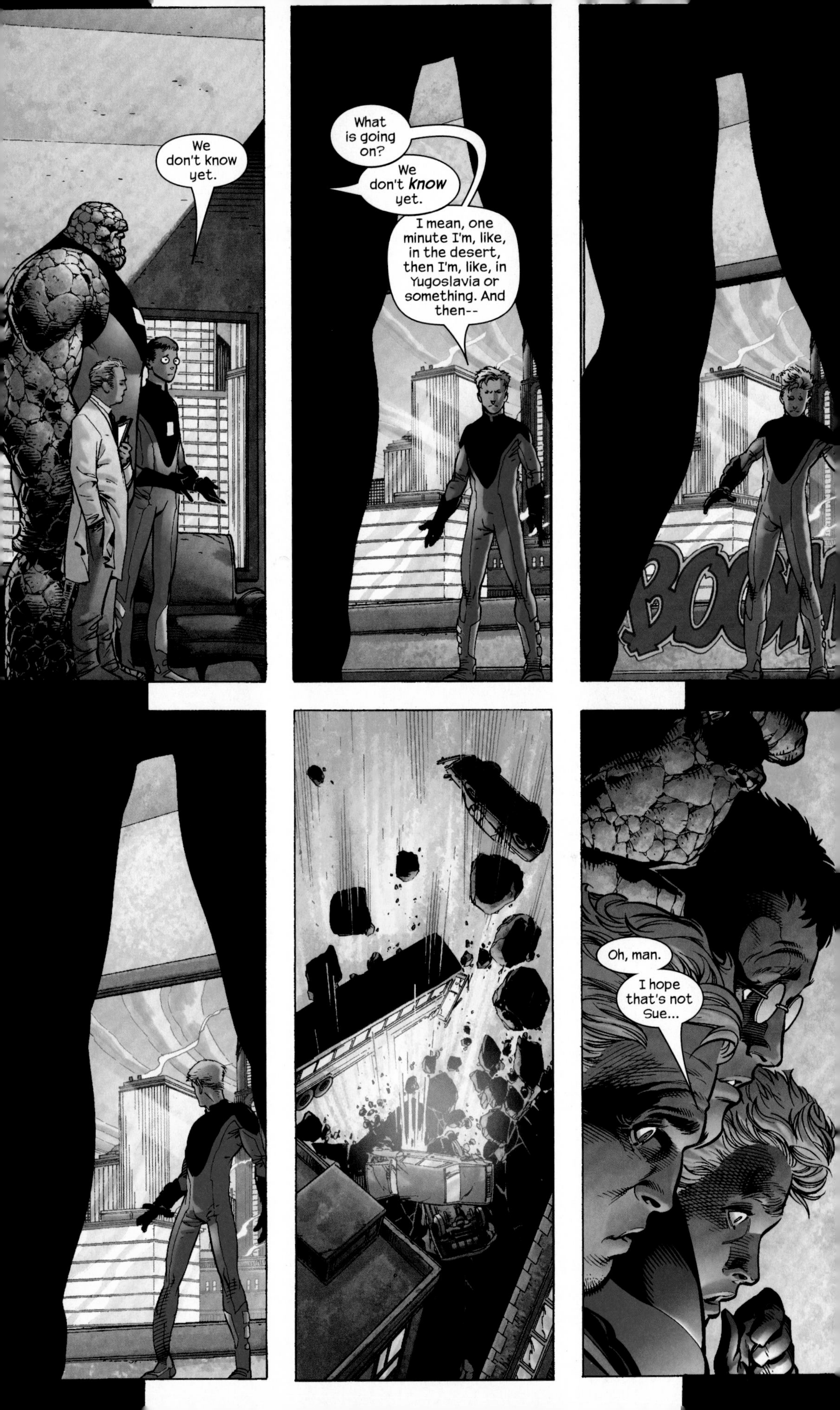

We don't know yet.
What is going on?
We don't *know* yet.
I mean, one minute I'm, like, in the desert, then I'm, like, in Yugoslavia or something. And then--
BOOM
Oh, man.
I hope that's not Sue...

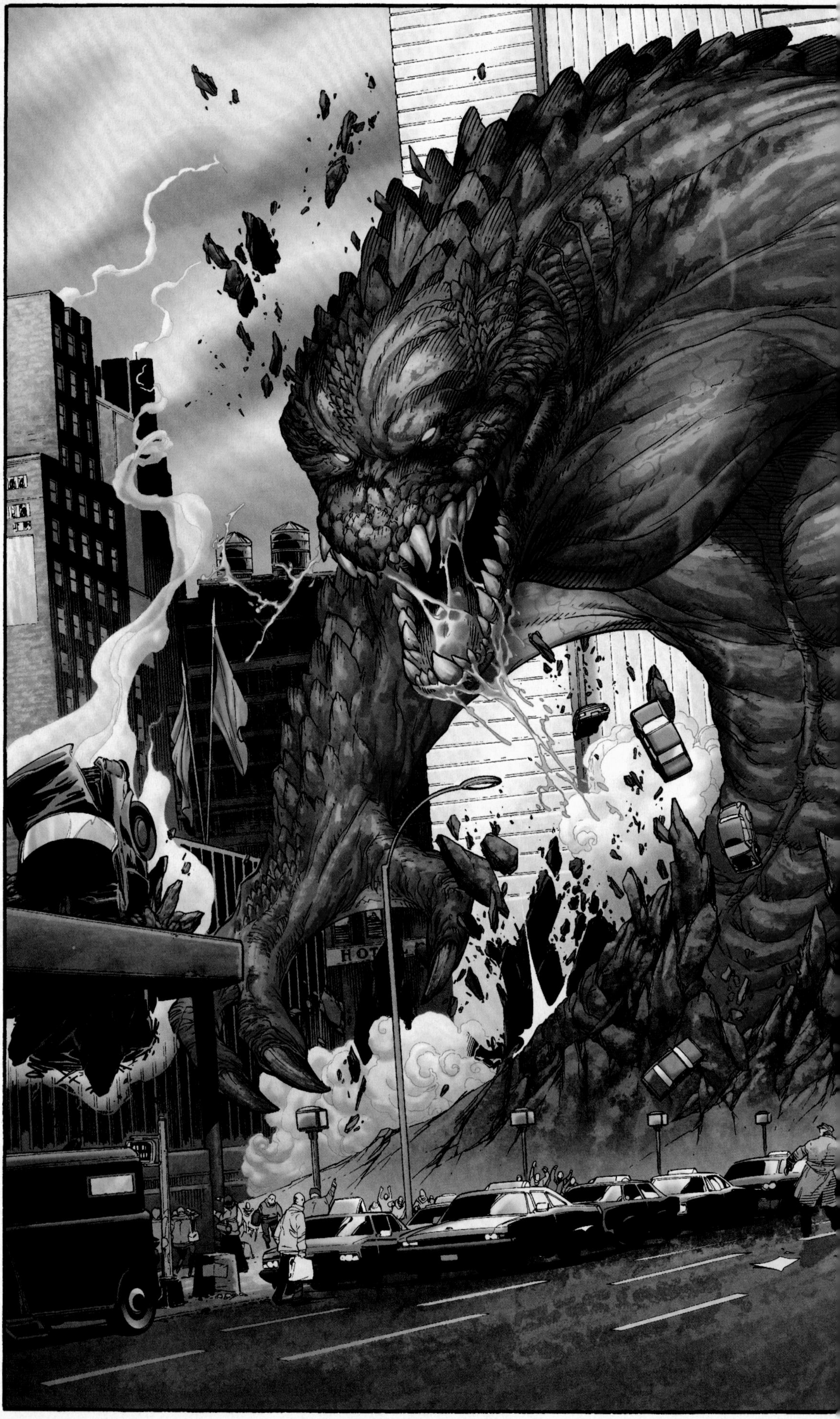

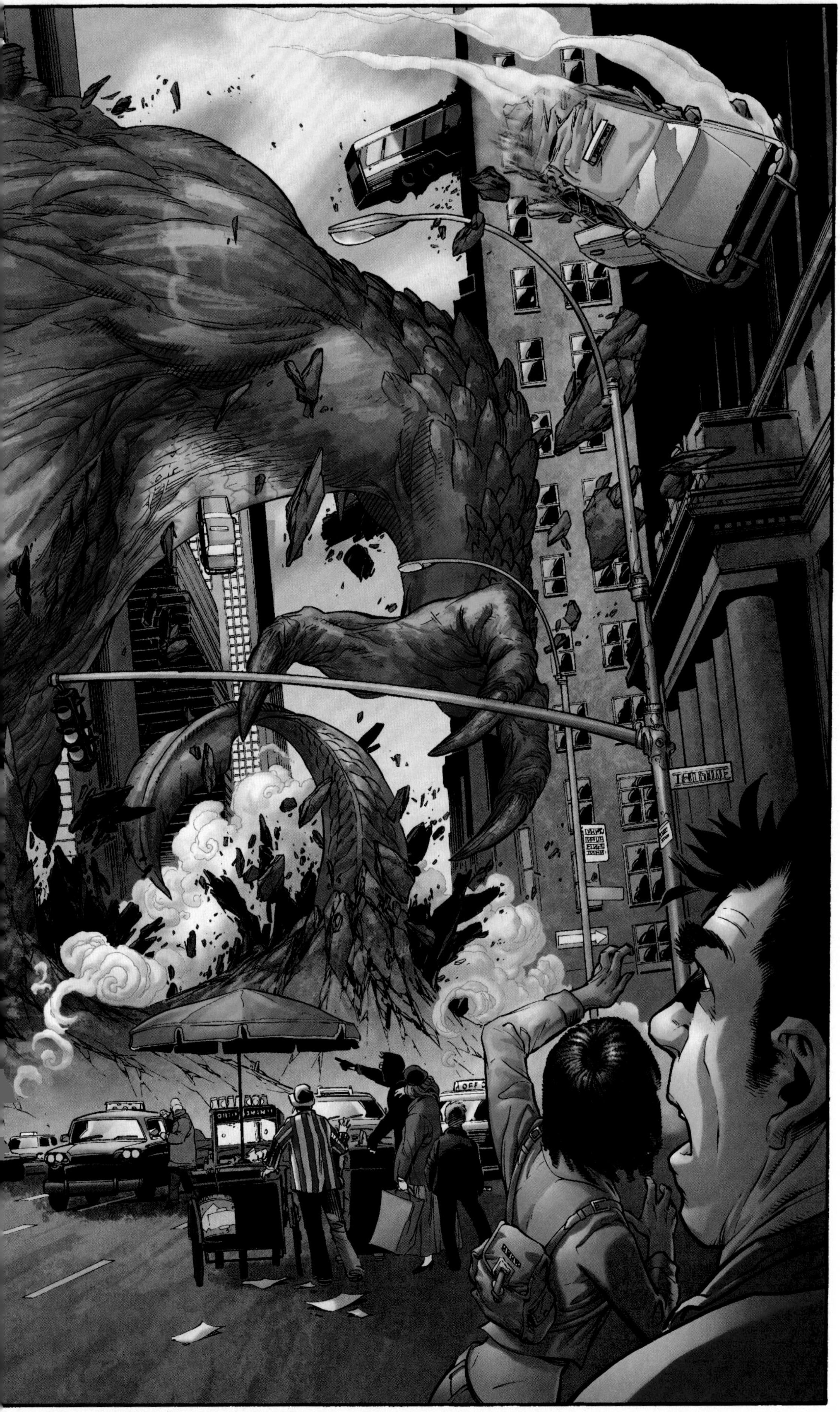

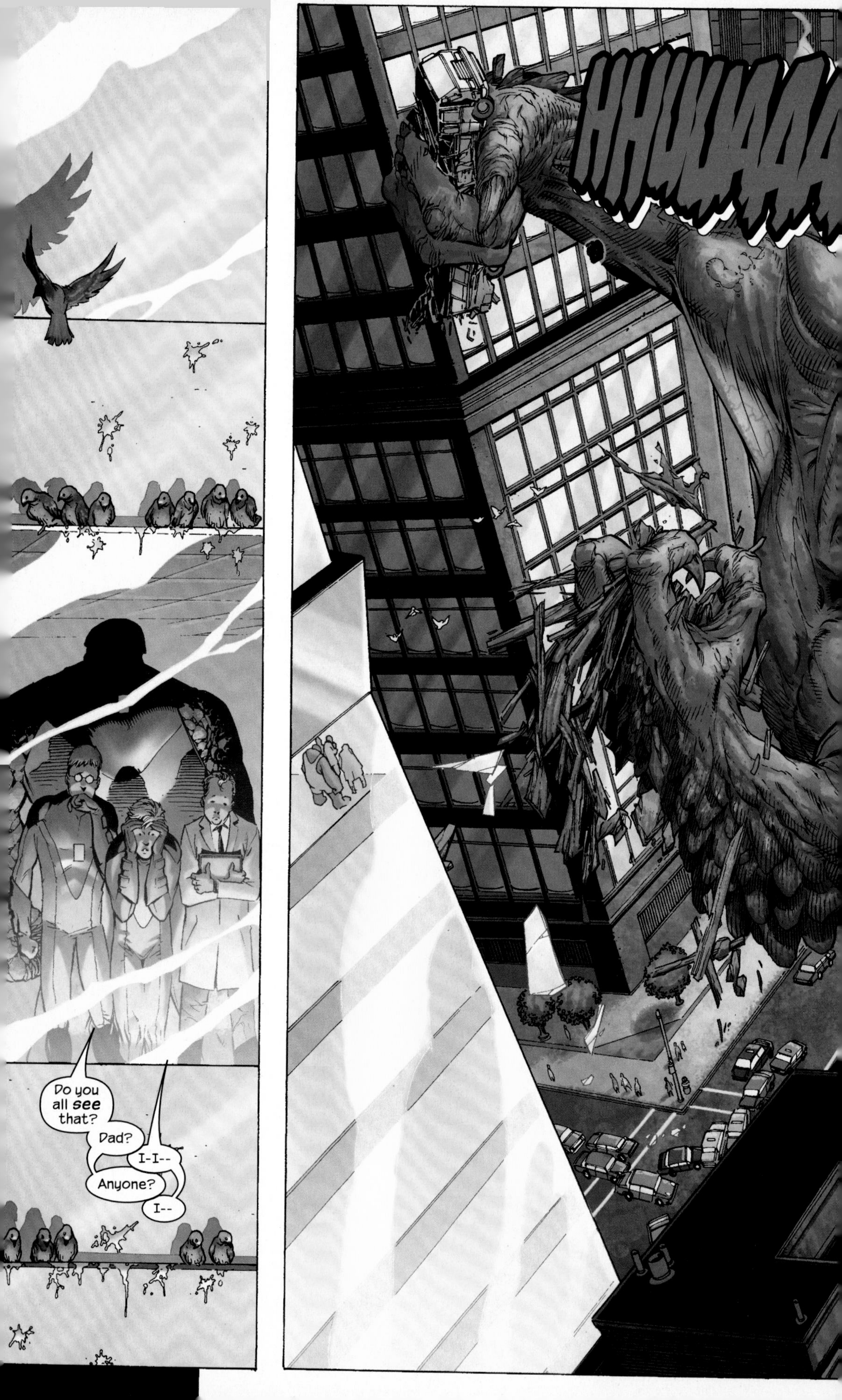
Do you all see that?
Dad?
I-I--
Anyone?
I--
HHUAAA

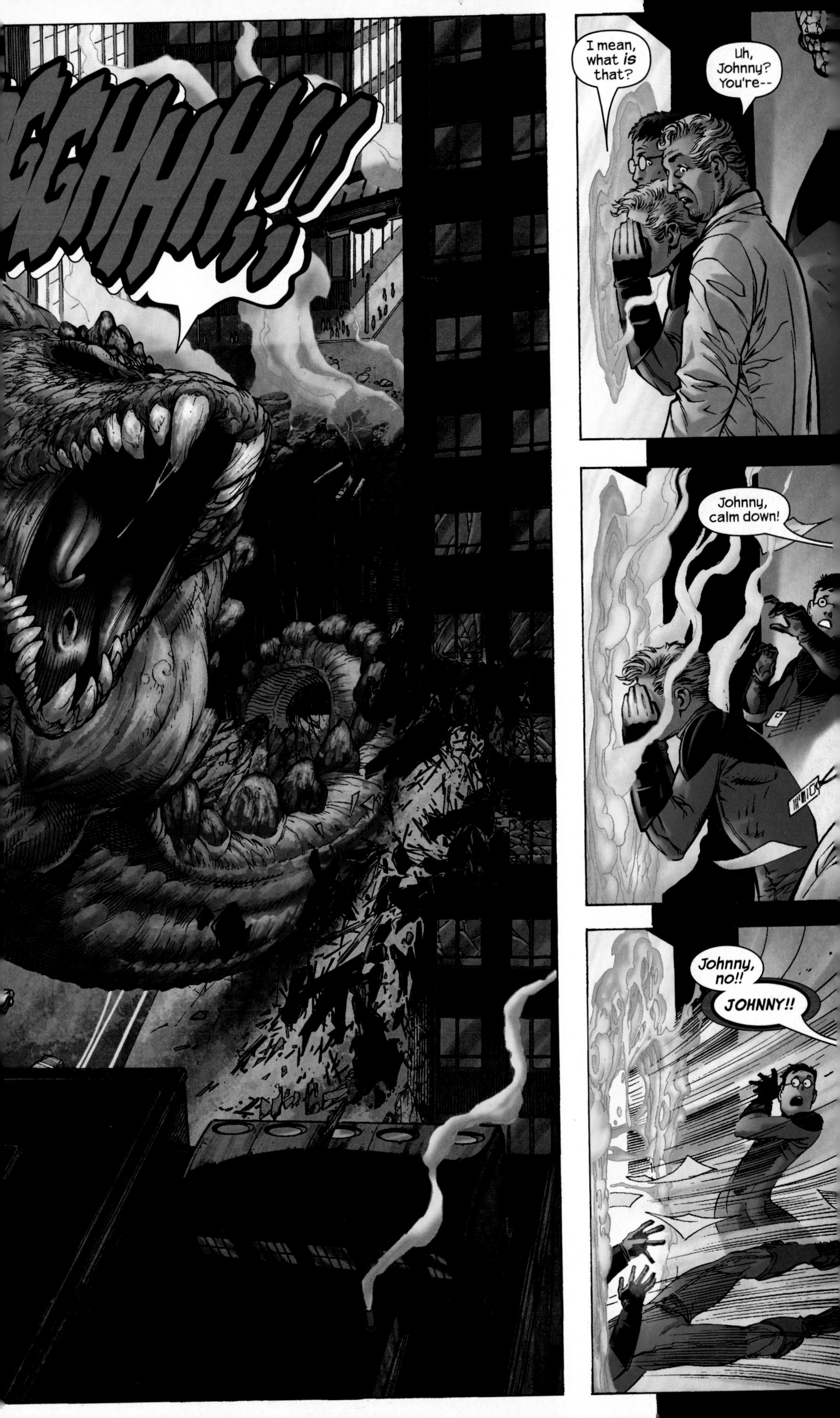
I mean, what *is* that?
Uh, Johnny? You're--
Johnny, calm down!
Johnny, no!!
JOHNNY!!

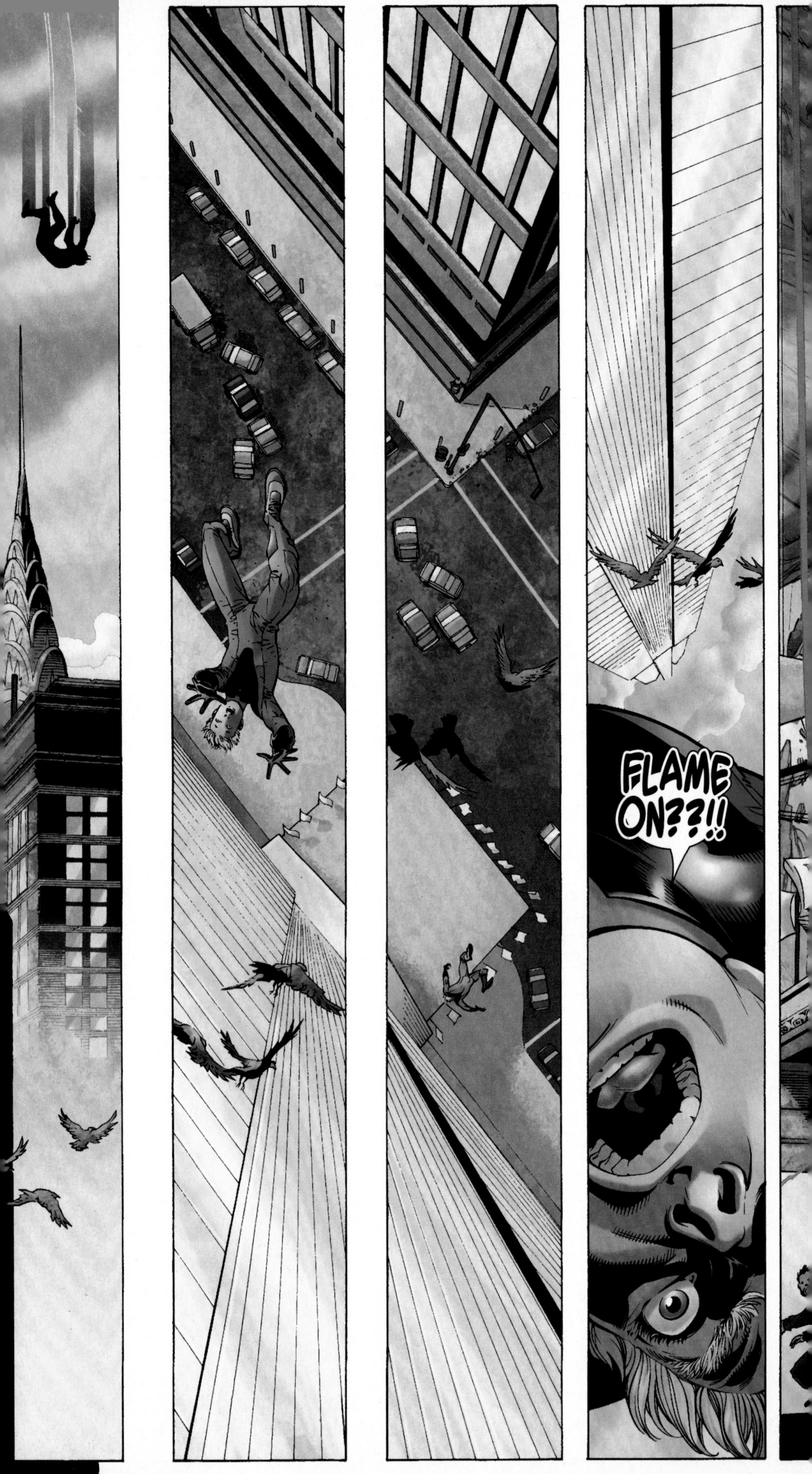
FLAME ON??!!

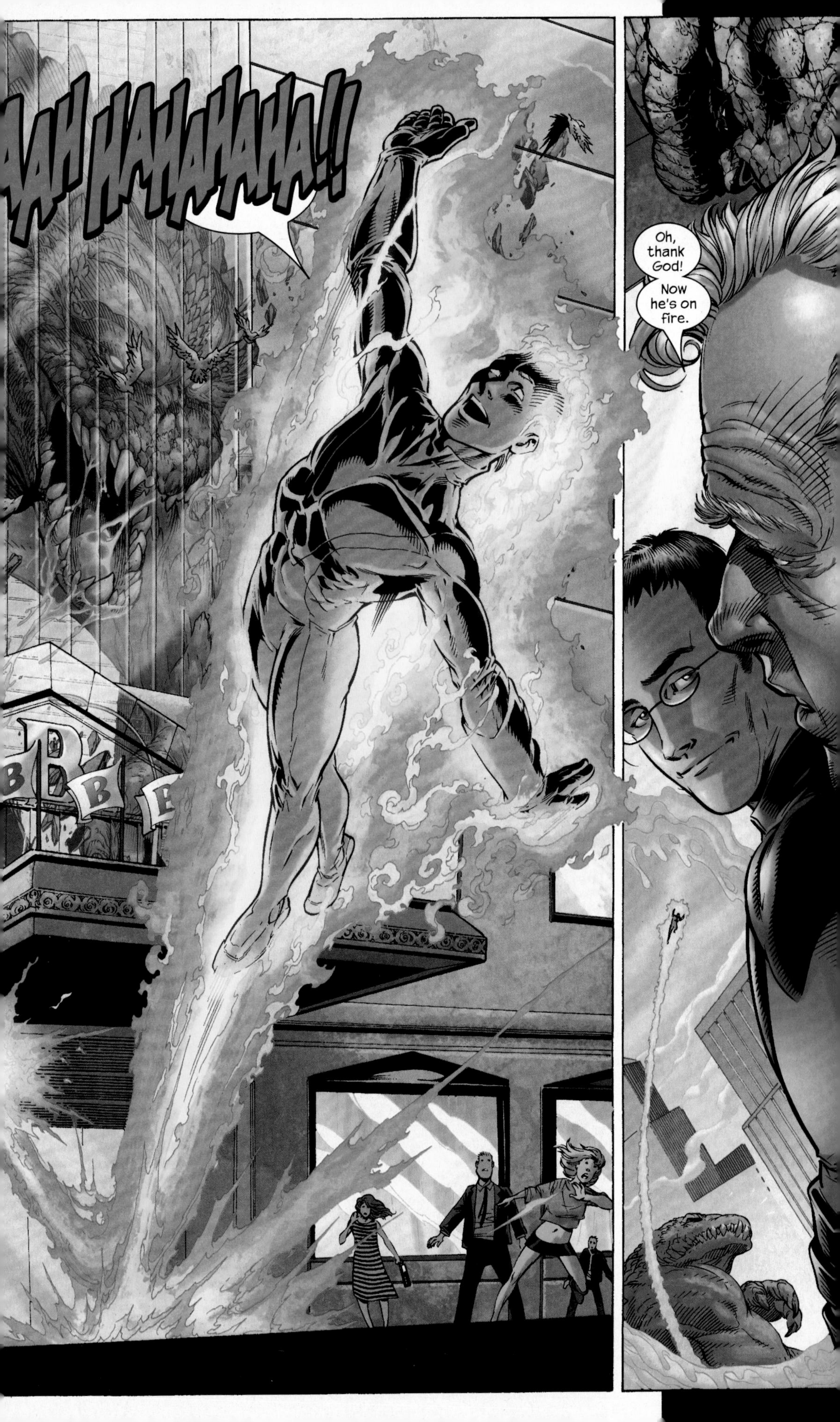
AAH HAHAHAHA!!
Oh, thank God!
Now he's on fire.

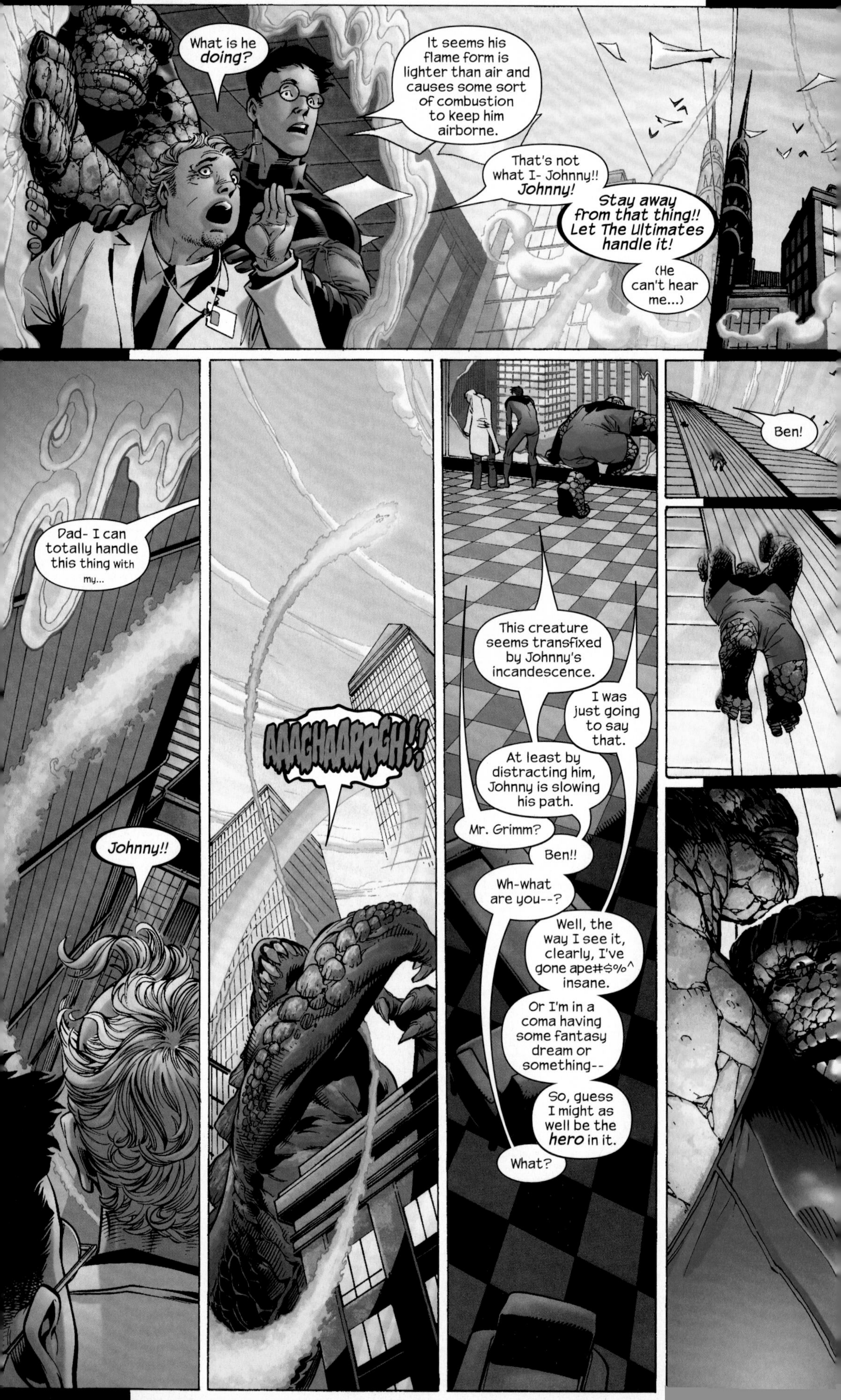

What is he doing?
It seems his flame form is lighter than air and causes some sort of combustion to keep him airborne.
That's not what I- Johnny!! Johnny!
Stay away from that thing!! Let The Ultimates handle it!
(He can't hear me...)
Dad- I can totally handle this thing with my...
Johnny!!
AAAGHAARRGH!!
This creature seems transfixed by Johnny's incandescence.
I was just going to say that.
At least by distracting him, Johnny is slowing his path.
Mr. Grimm?
Ben!!
Wh-what are you--?
Well, the way I see it, clearly, I've gone ape#$%^ insane.
Or I'm in a coma having some fantasy dream or something--
So, guess I might as well be the hero in it.
What?
Ben!

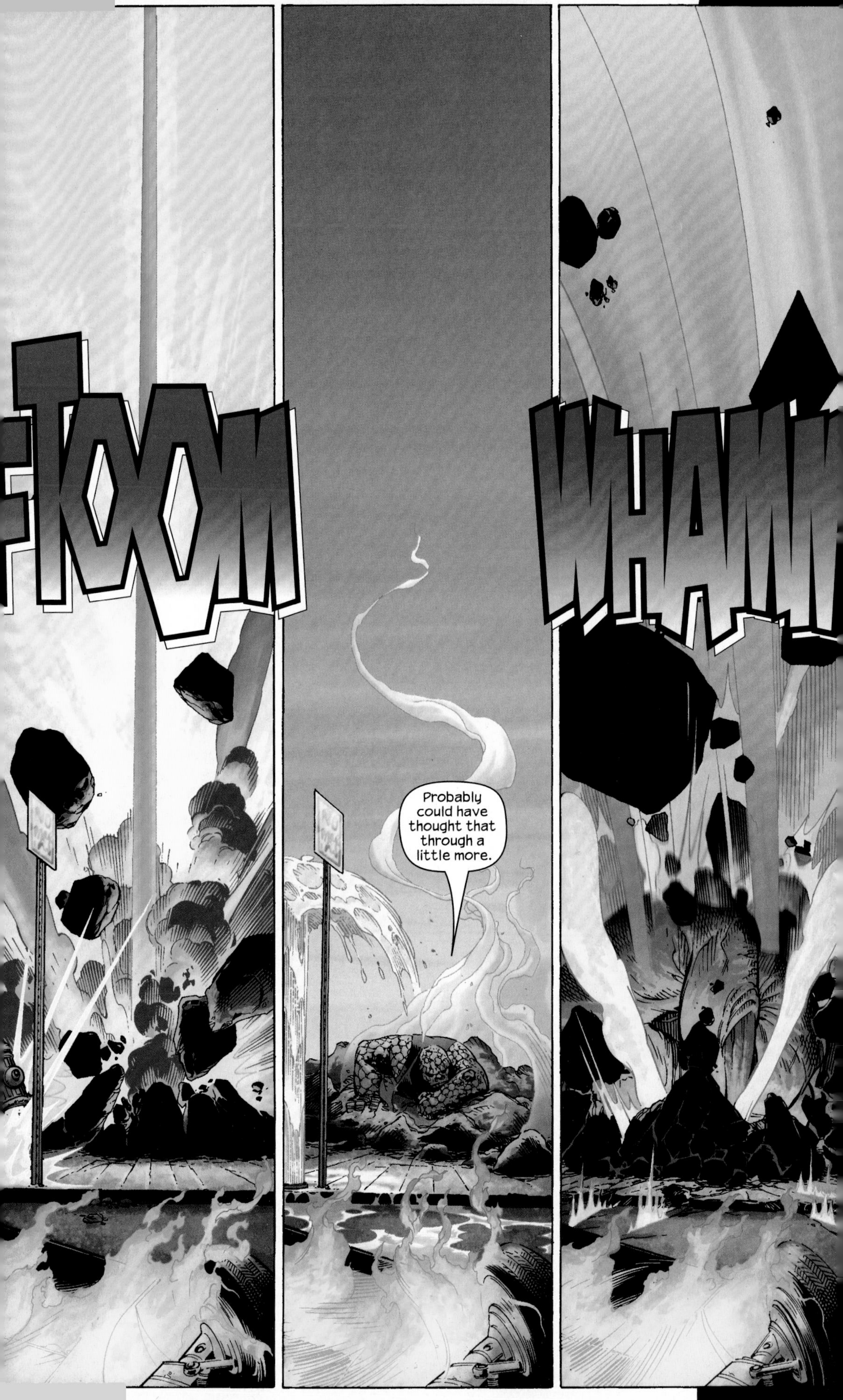
TOOM
Probably could have thought that through a little more.
WHAM

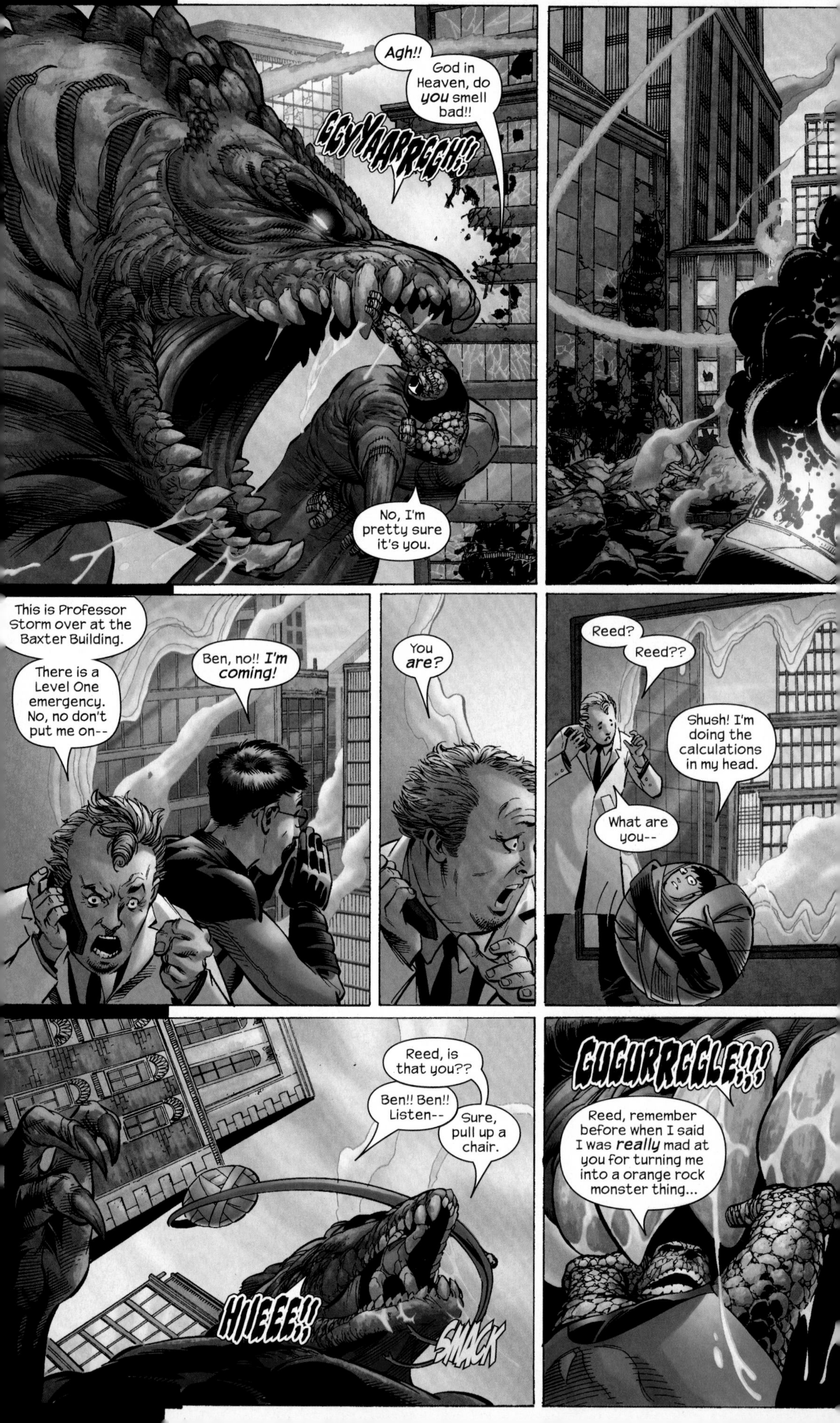
Agh!!
God in Heaven, do you smell bad!!
EEYYAARRECH!!
No, I'm pretty sure it's you.
This is Professor Storm over at the Baxter Building.
There is a Level One emergency. No, no don't put me on--
Ben, no!! I'm coming!
You are?
Reed?
Reed??
Shush! I'm doing the calculations in my head.
What are you--
Reed, is that you??
Ben!! Ben!! Listen--
Sure, pull up a chair.
HIIEEE!!
SMACK
GUGURRGGLE!!!
Reed, remember before when I said I was really mad at you for turning me into a orange rock monster thing...

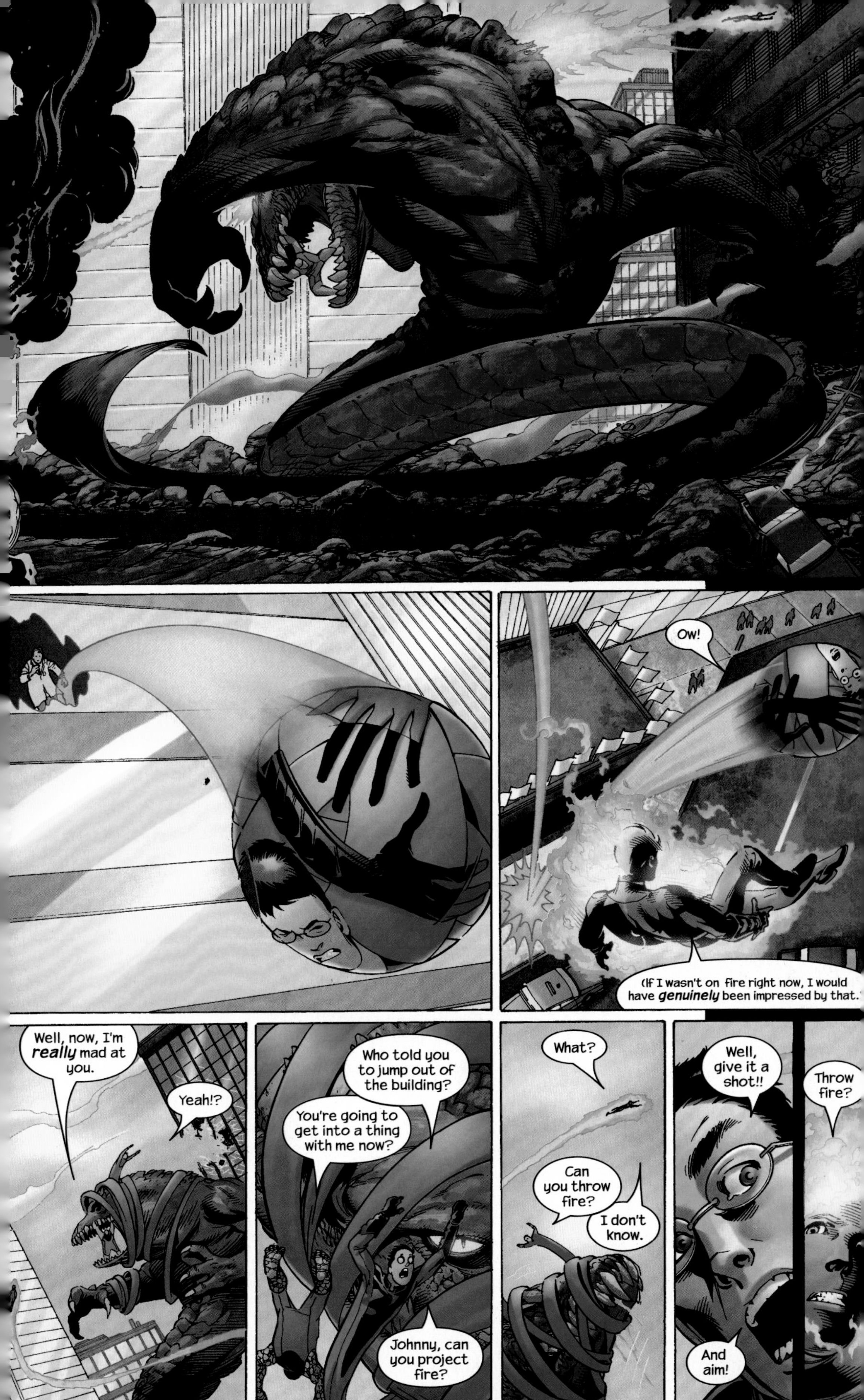

Ow!
(If I wasn't on fire right now, I would have *genuinely* been impressed by that.
Well, now, I'm *really* mad at you.
Yeah!?
Who told you to jump out of the building?
You're going to get into a thing with me now?
Johnny, can you project fire?
What?
Can you throw fire?
I don't know.
Well, give it a shot!!
Throw fire?
And aim!

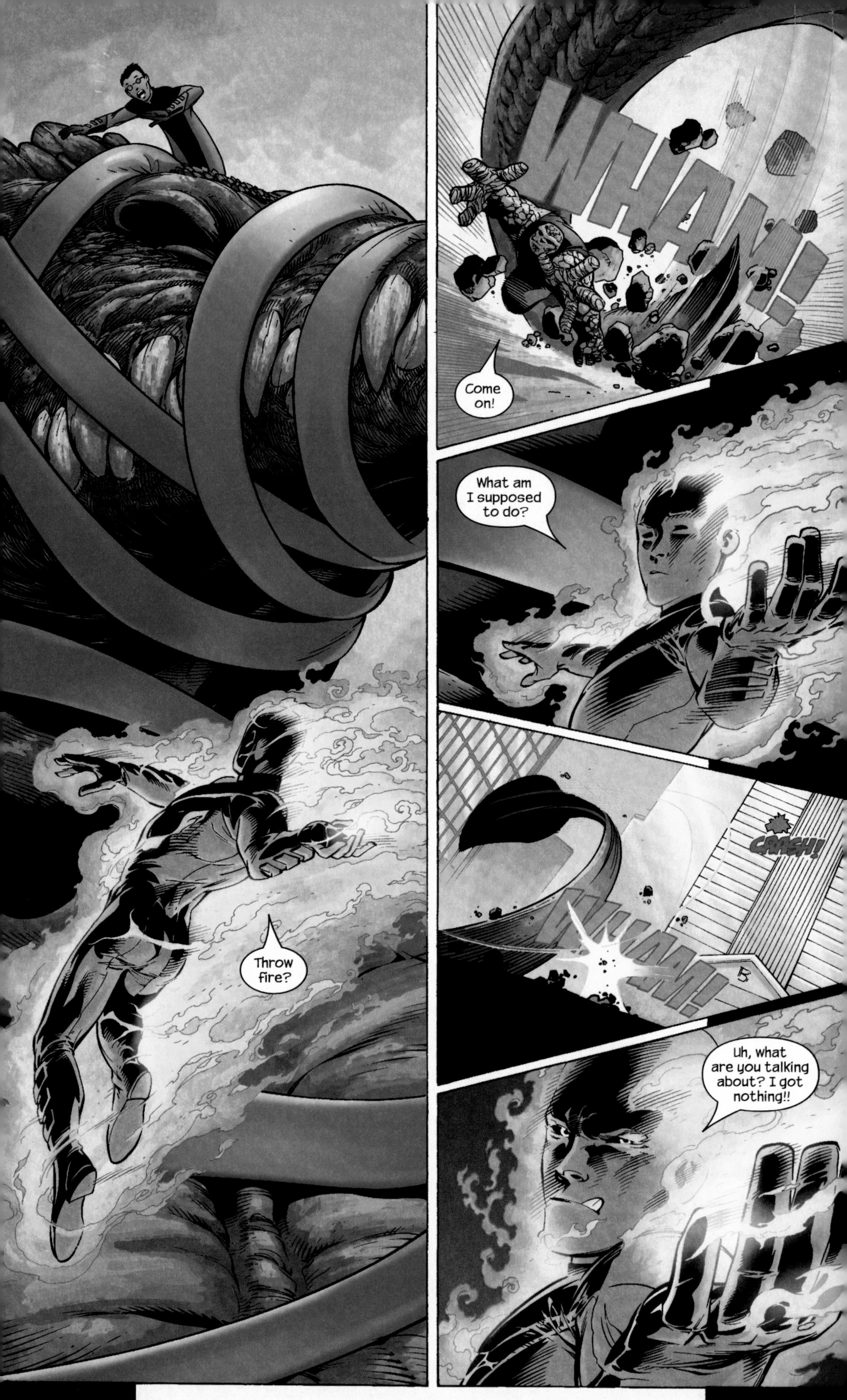
Throw fire?
WHAM!!
Come on!
What am I supposed to do?
CRASH!
WHAM!
Uh, what are you talking about? I got nothing!!

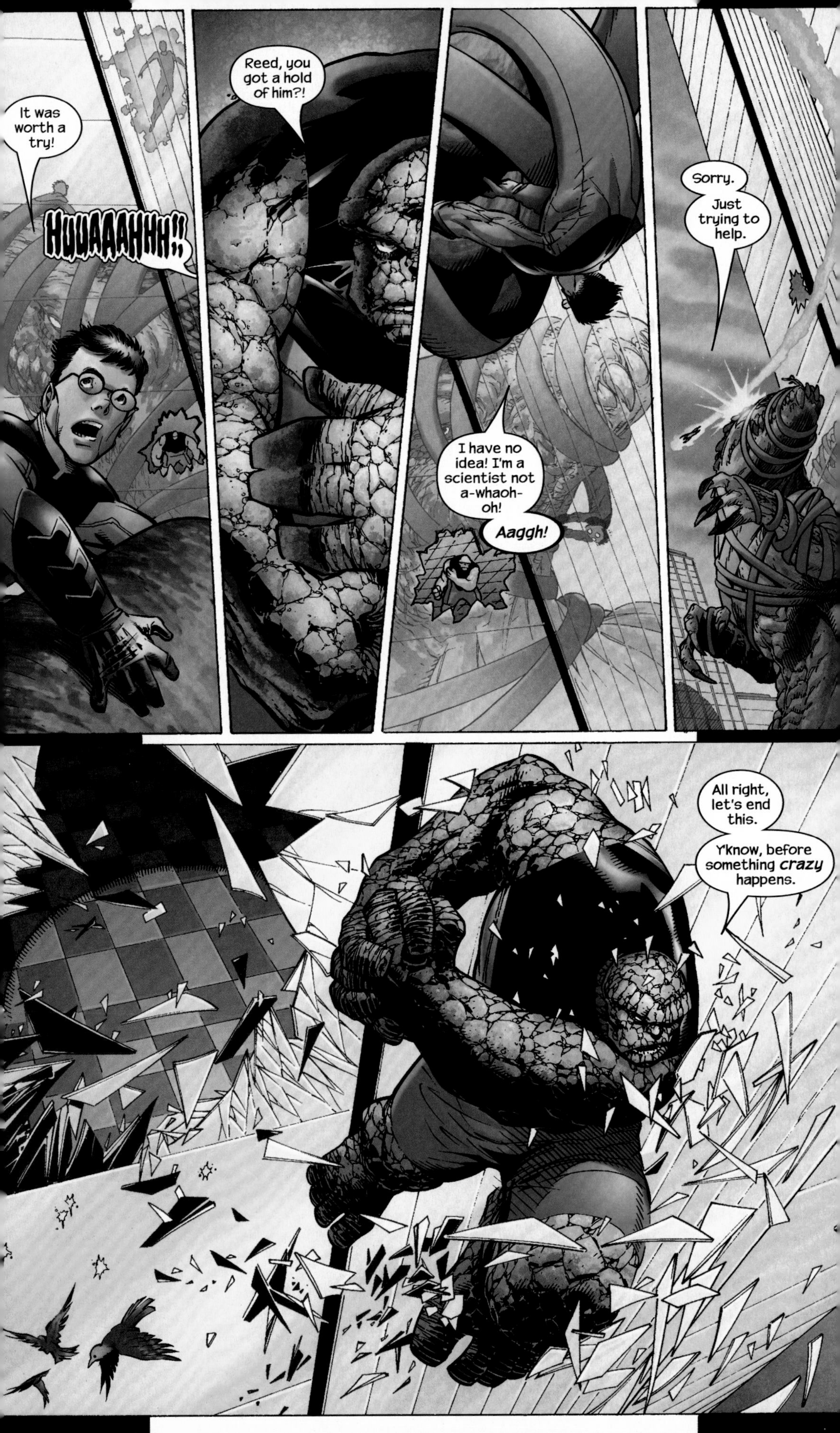

It was worth a try!
HUUAAAHHH!!
Reed, you got a hold of him?!
I have no idea! I'm a scientist not a-whaoh-oh!
Aagh!
Sorry.
Just trying to help.
All right, let's end this.
Y'know, before something *crazy* happens.

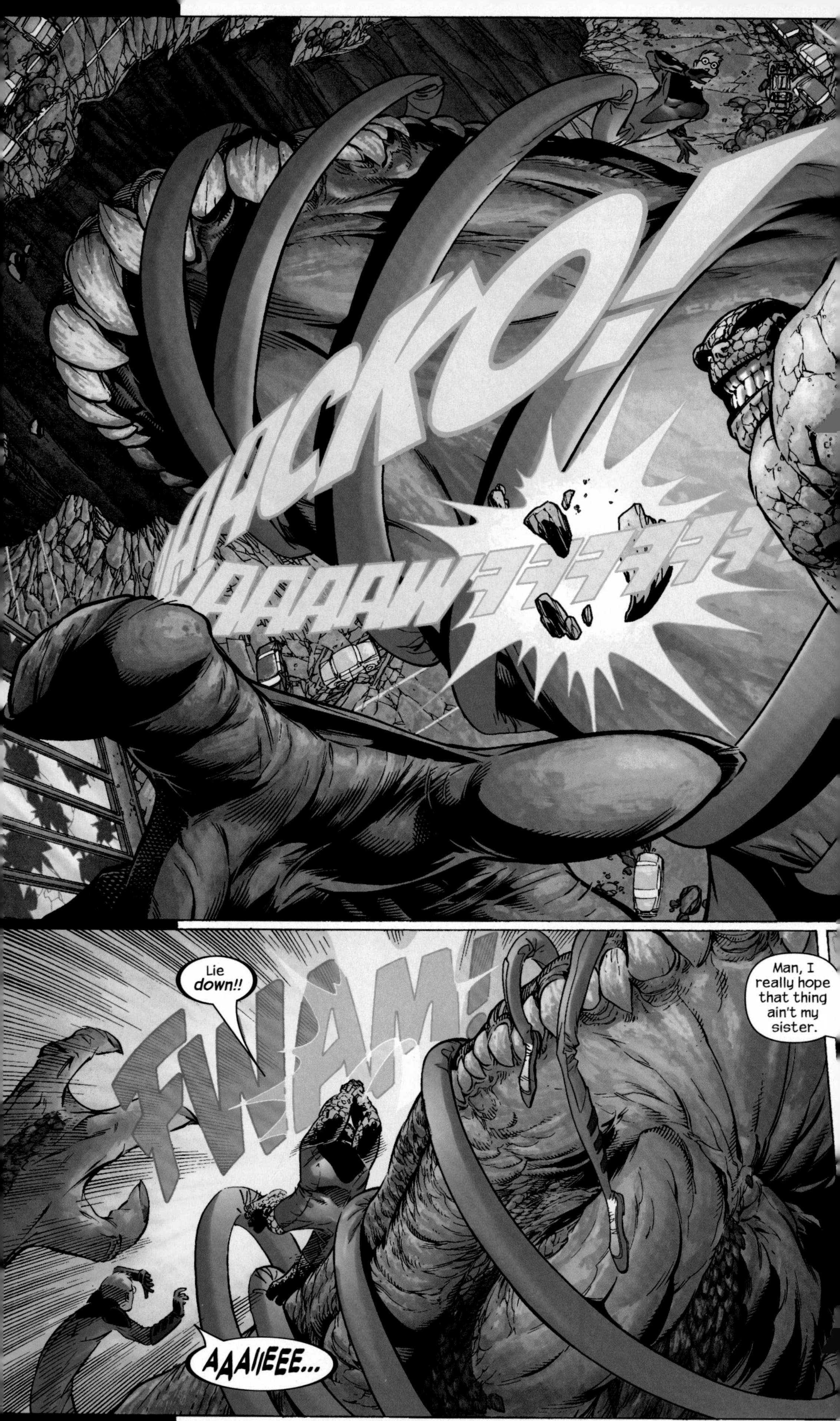
Lie down!!
FWAM!
Man, I really hope that thing ain't my sister.
AAAIIEEE...

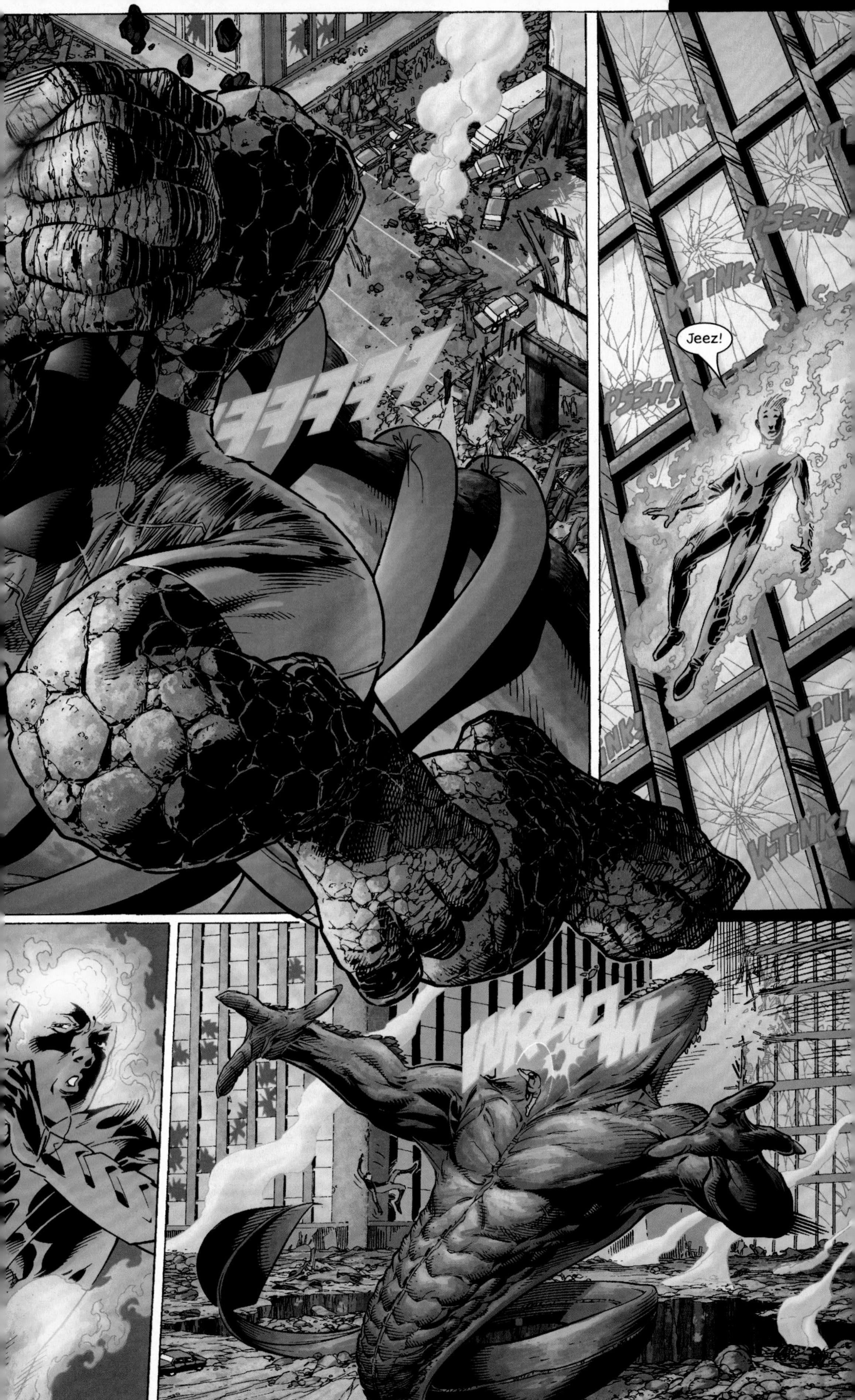
K-TINK!
PSSSH!
K-TINK!
Jeez!
PSSSH!
TINK!
K-TINK!

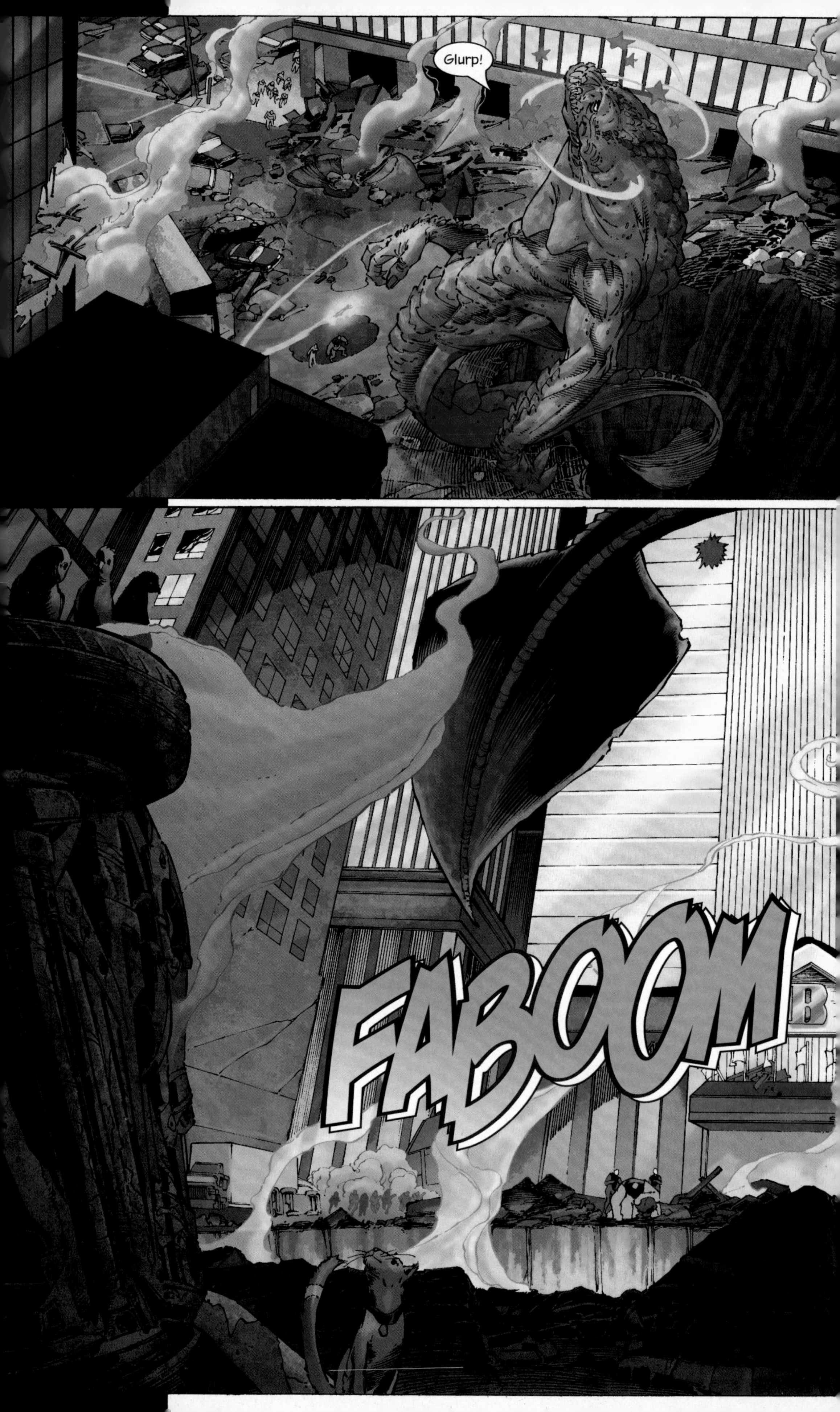
Glurp!
FABOOM

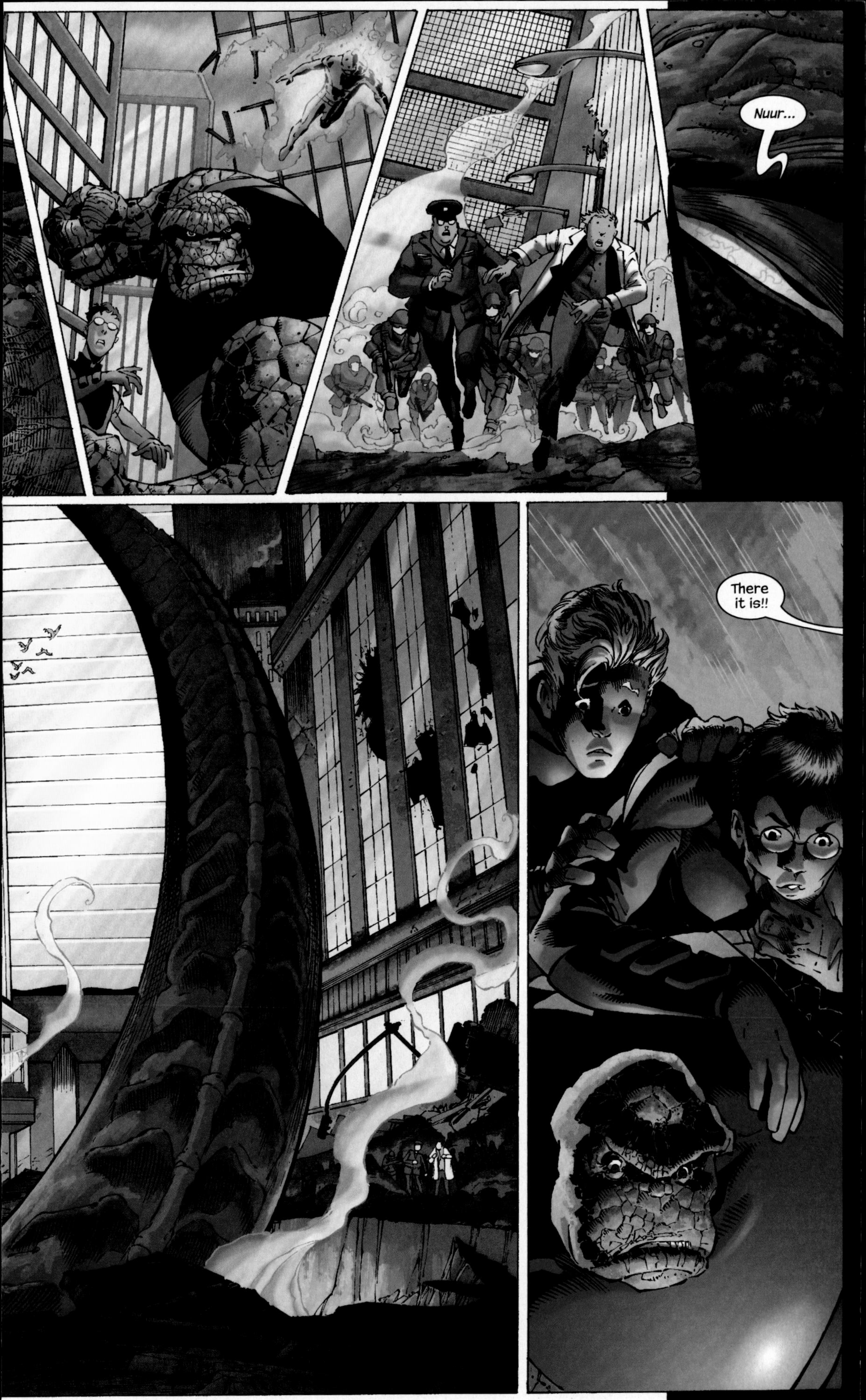
Nuur...
There it is!!

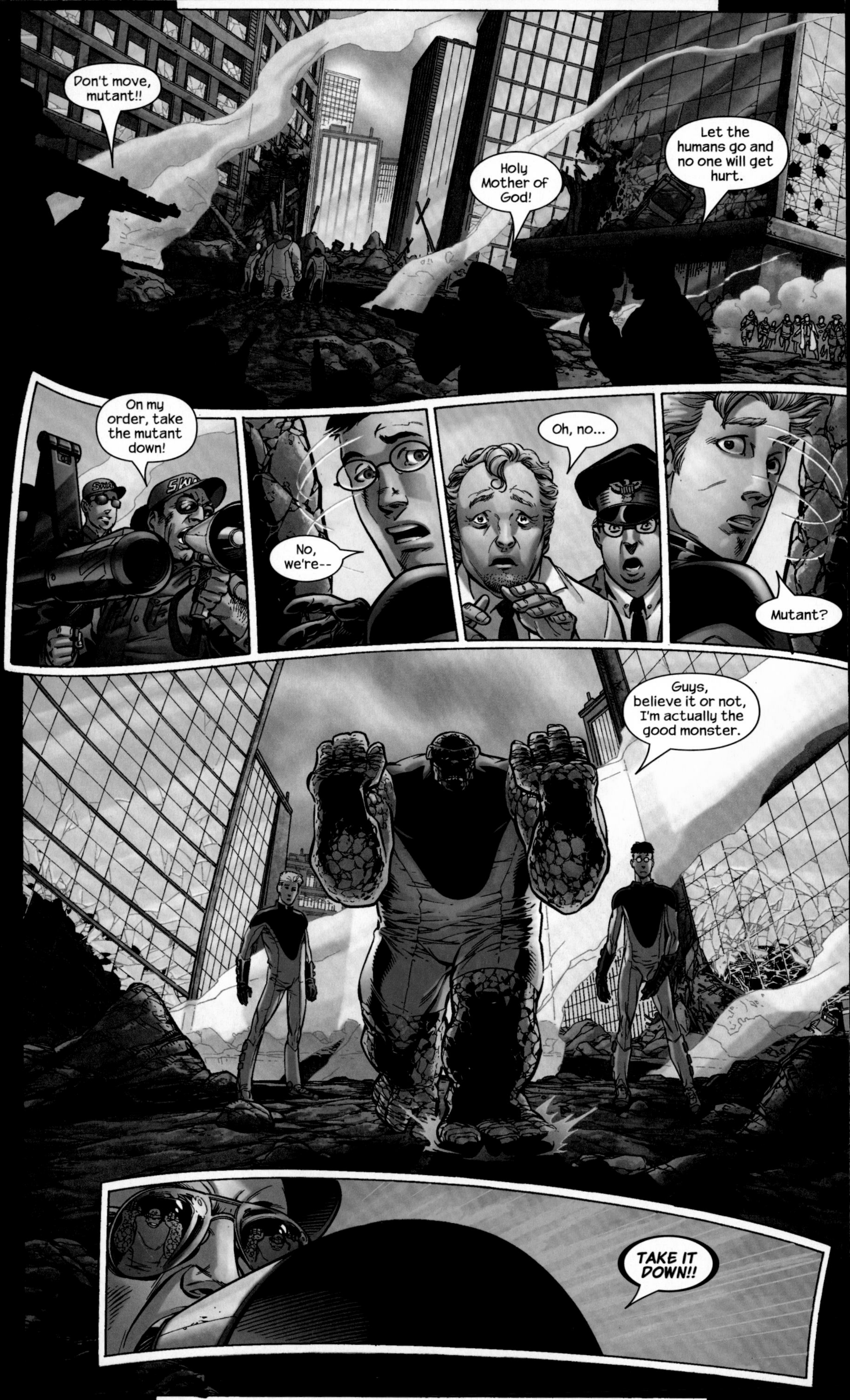
Don't move, mutant!!
Holy Mother of God!
Let the humans go and no one will get hurt.
On my order, take the mutant down!
No, we're--
Oh, no...
Mutant?
Guys, believe it or not, I'm actually the good monster.
TAKE IT DOWN!!

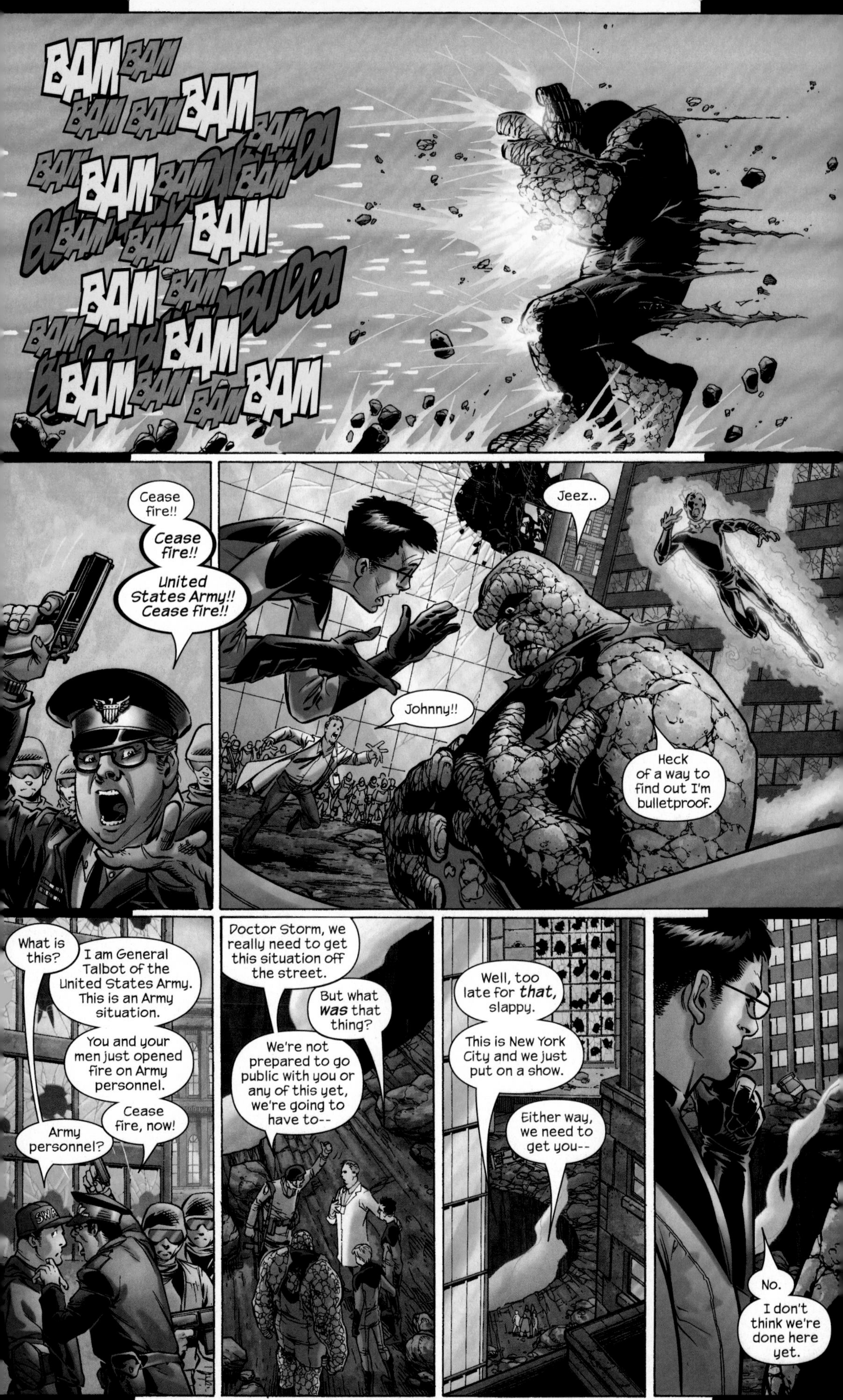
BAM BAM BAM BAM BAM BAM BAM BAM BAM BAM BAM BAM BAM BAM BAM BAM BAM
Cease fire!!
Cease fire!!
United States Army!! Cease fire!!
Jeez..
Johnny!!
Heck of a way to find out I'm bulletproof.
What is this?
I am General Talbot of the United States Army. This is an Army situation.
You and your men just opened fire on Army personnel.
Cease fire, now!
Army personnel?
Doctor Storm, we really need to get this situation off the street.
But what was that thing?
We're not prepared to go public with you or any of this yet, we're going to have to--
Well, too late for that, slappy.
This is New York City and we just put on a show.
Either way, we need to get you--
No.
I don't think we're done here yet.

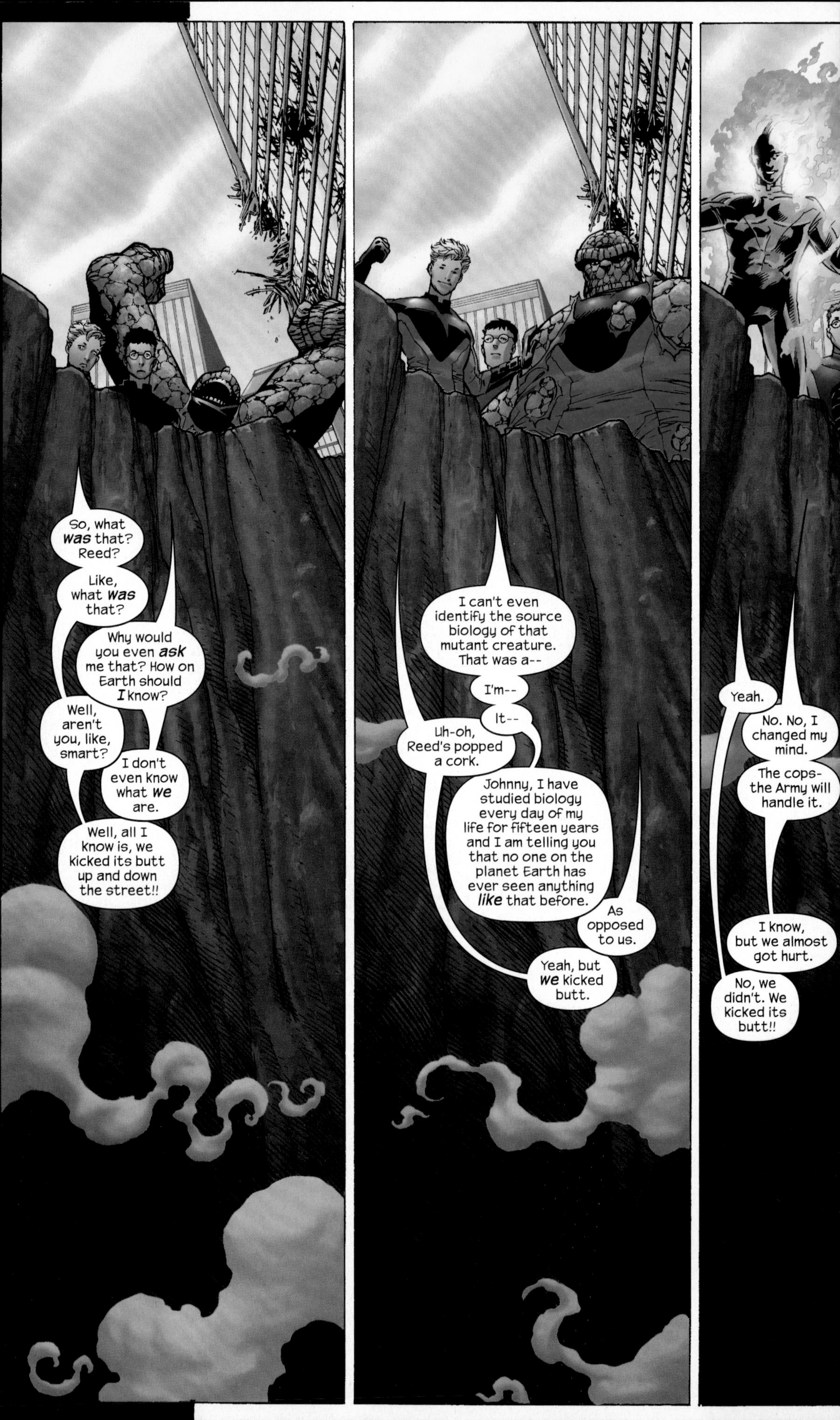
So, what *was* that? Reed?
Like, what *was* that?
Why would you even *ask* me that? How on Earth should *I* know?
Well, aren't you, like, smart?
I don't even know what *we* are.
Well, all I know is, we kicked its butt up and down the street!!
I can't even identify the source biology of that mutant creature. That was a--
I'm--
It--
Uh-oh, Reed's popped a cork.
Johnny, I have studied biology every day of my life for fifteen years and I am telling you that no one on the planet Earth has ever seen anything *like* that before.
As opposed to us.
Yeah, but *we* kicked butt.
Yeah.
No. No, I changed my mind.
The cops-the Army will handle it.
I know, but we almost got hurt.
No, we didn't. We kicked its butt!!

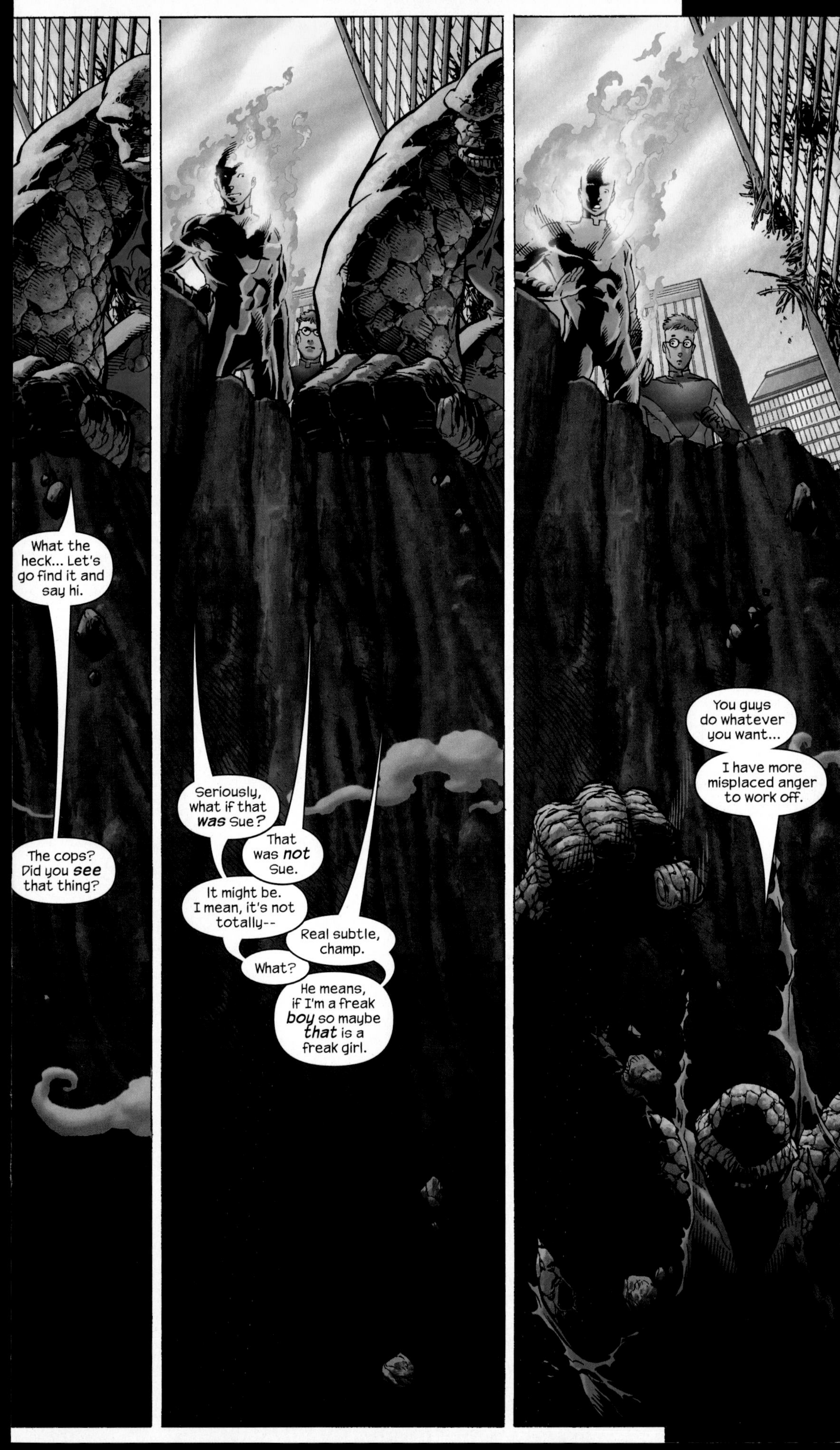
What the heck... Let's go find it and say hi.
The cops? Did you *see* that thing?
Seriously, what if that *was* Sue?
That was *not* Sue.
It might be. I mean, it's not totally--
Real subtle, champ.
What?
He means, if I'm a freak *boy* so maybe *that* is a freak girl.
You guys do whatever you want...
I have more misplaced anger to work off.

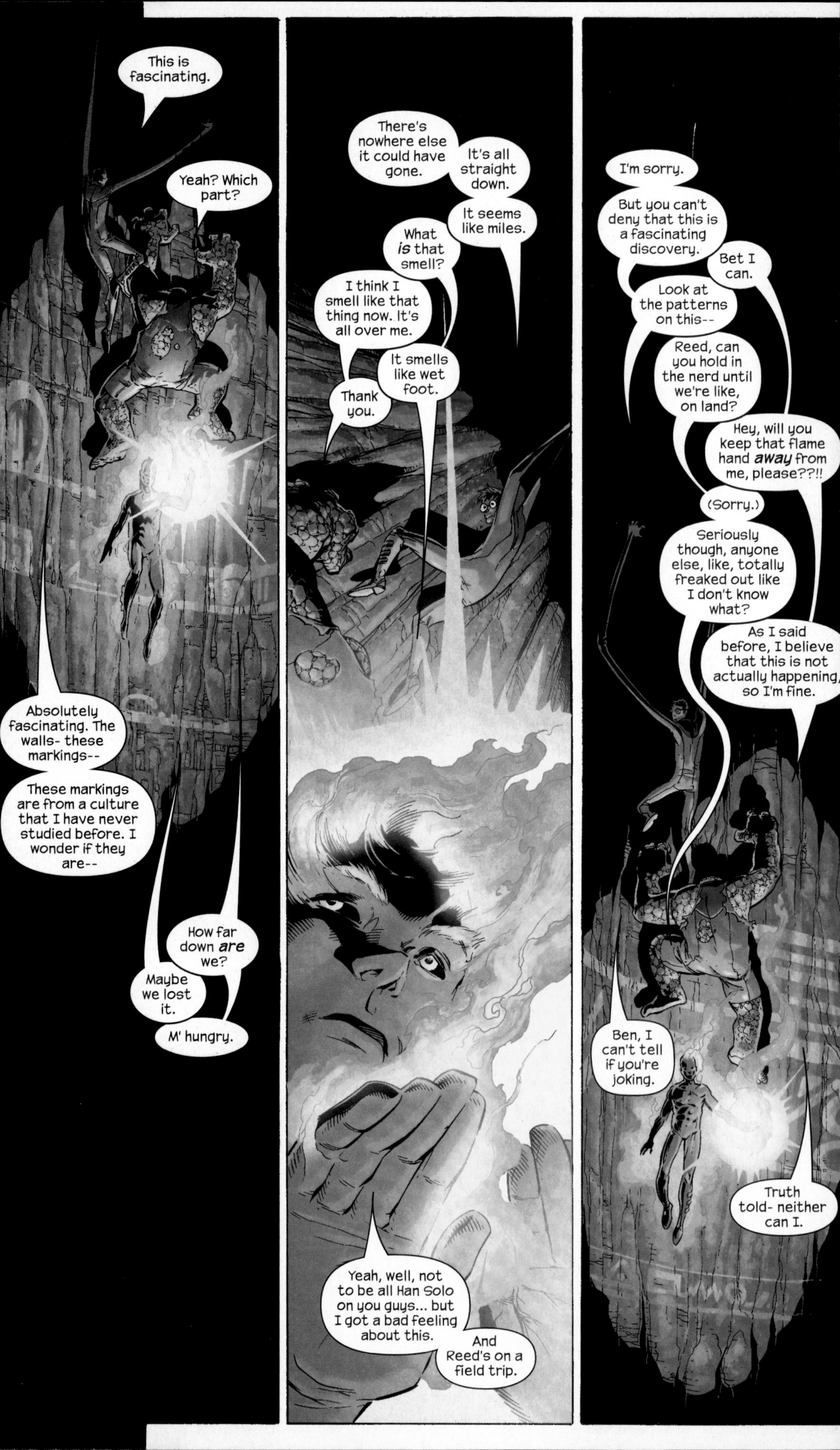
This is fascinating.
Yeah? Which part?
Absolutely fascinating. The walls- these markings--
These markings are from a culture that I have never studied before. I wonder if they are--
How far down are we?
Maybe we lost it.
M' hungry.
There's nowhere else it could have gone.
It's all straight down.
It seems like miles.
What is that smell?
I think I smell like that thing now. It's all over me.
It smells like wet foot.
Thank you.
Yeah, well, not to be all Han Solo on you guys... but I got a bad feeling about this.
And Reed's on a field trip.
I'm sorry.
But you can't deny that this is a fascinating discovery.
Bet I can.
Look at the patterns on this--
Reed, can you hold in the nerd until we're like, on land?
Hey, will you keep that flame hand away from me, please??!!
(Sorry.)
Seriously though, anyone else, like, totally freaked out like I don't know what?
As I said before, I believe that this is not actually happening, so I'm fine.
Ben, I can't tell if you're joking.
Truth told- neither can I.

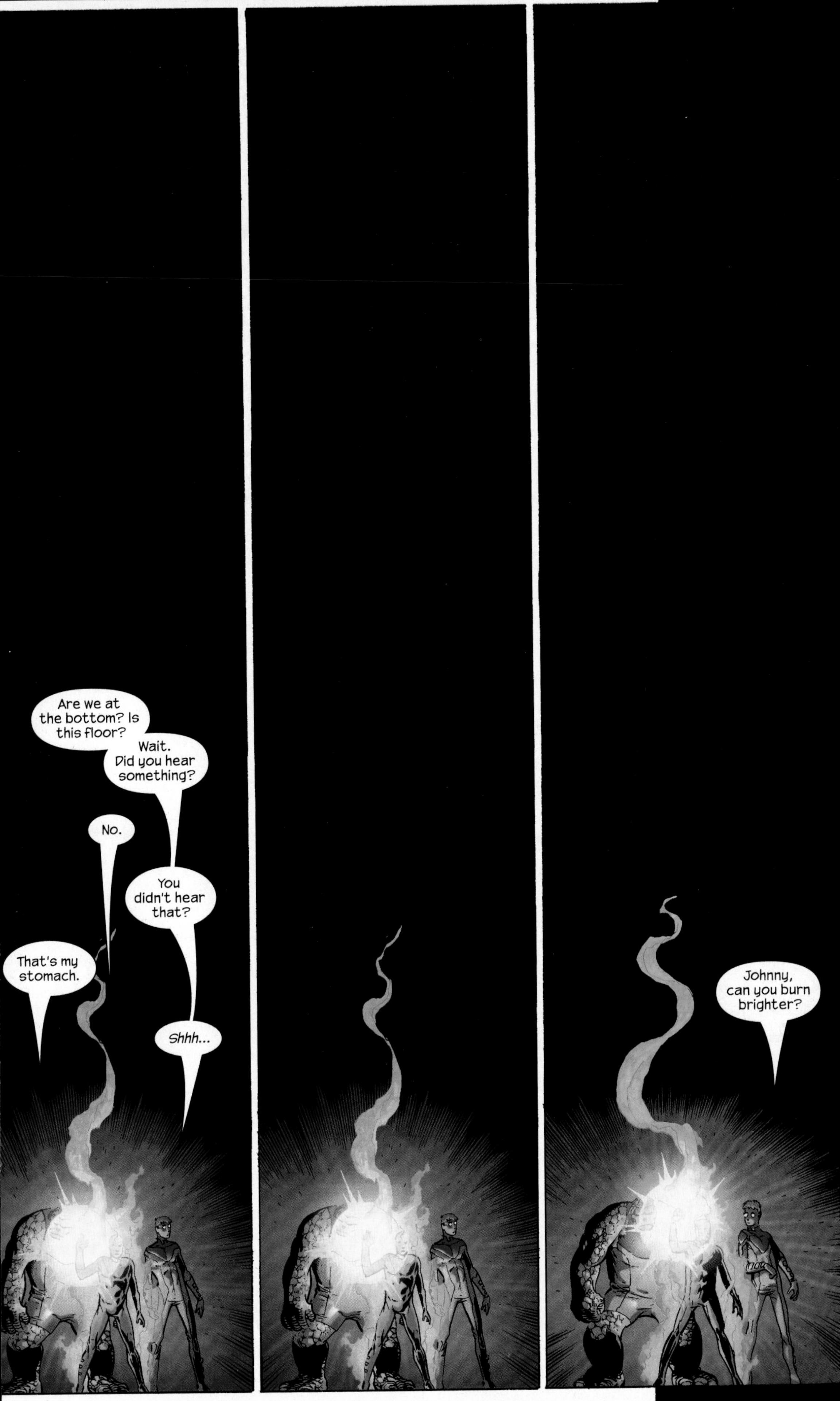
Are we at the bottom? Is this floor?
Wait. Did you hear something?
No.
You didn't hear that?
That's my stomach.
Shhh...
Johnny, can you burn brighter?

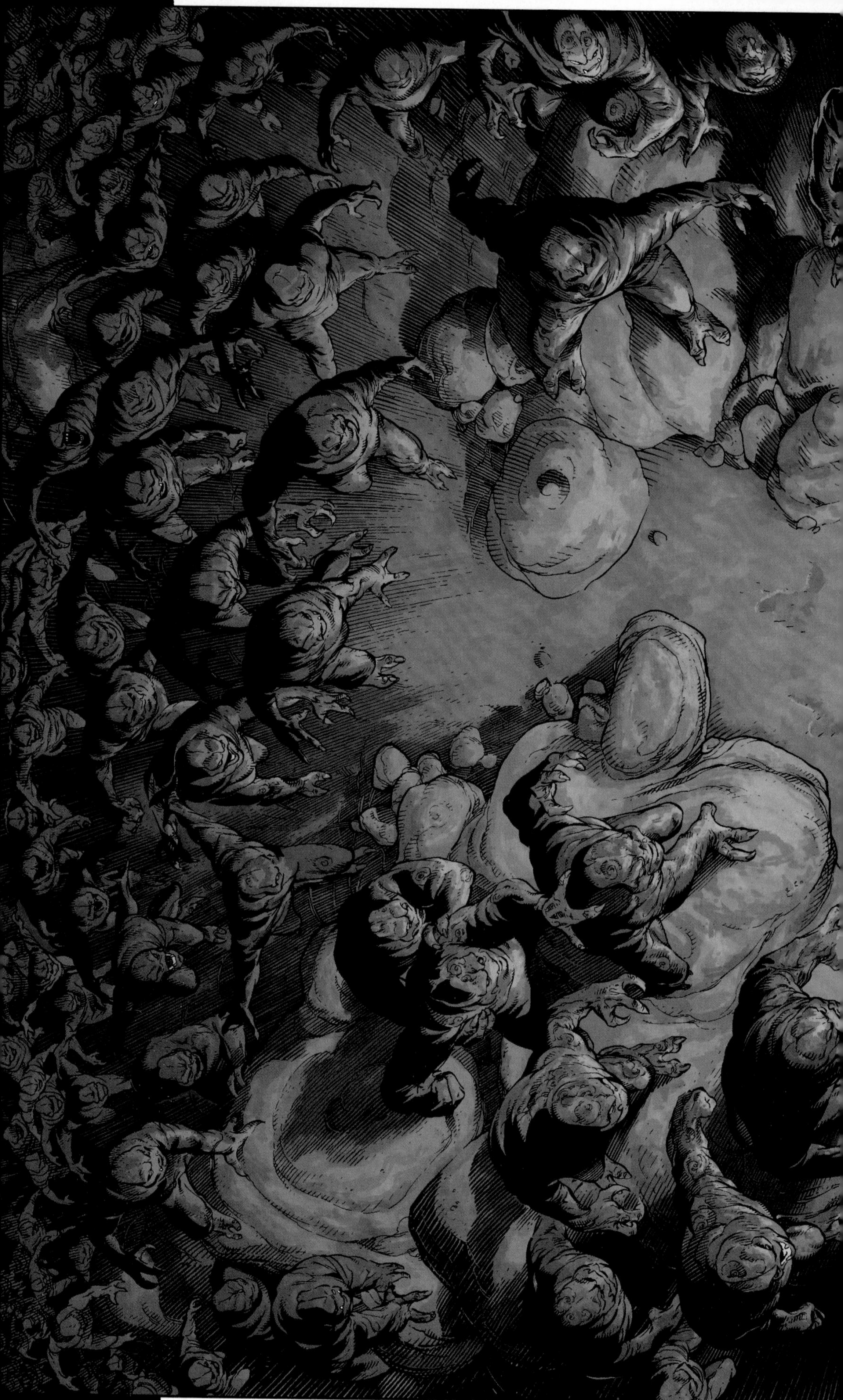

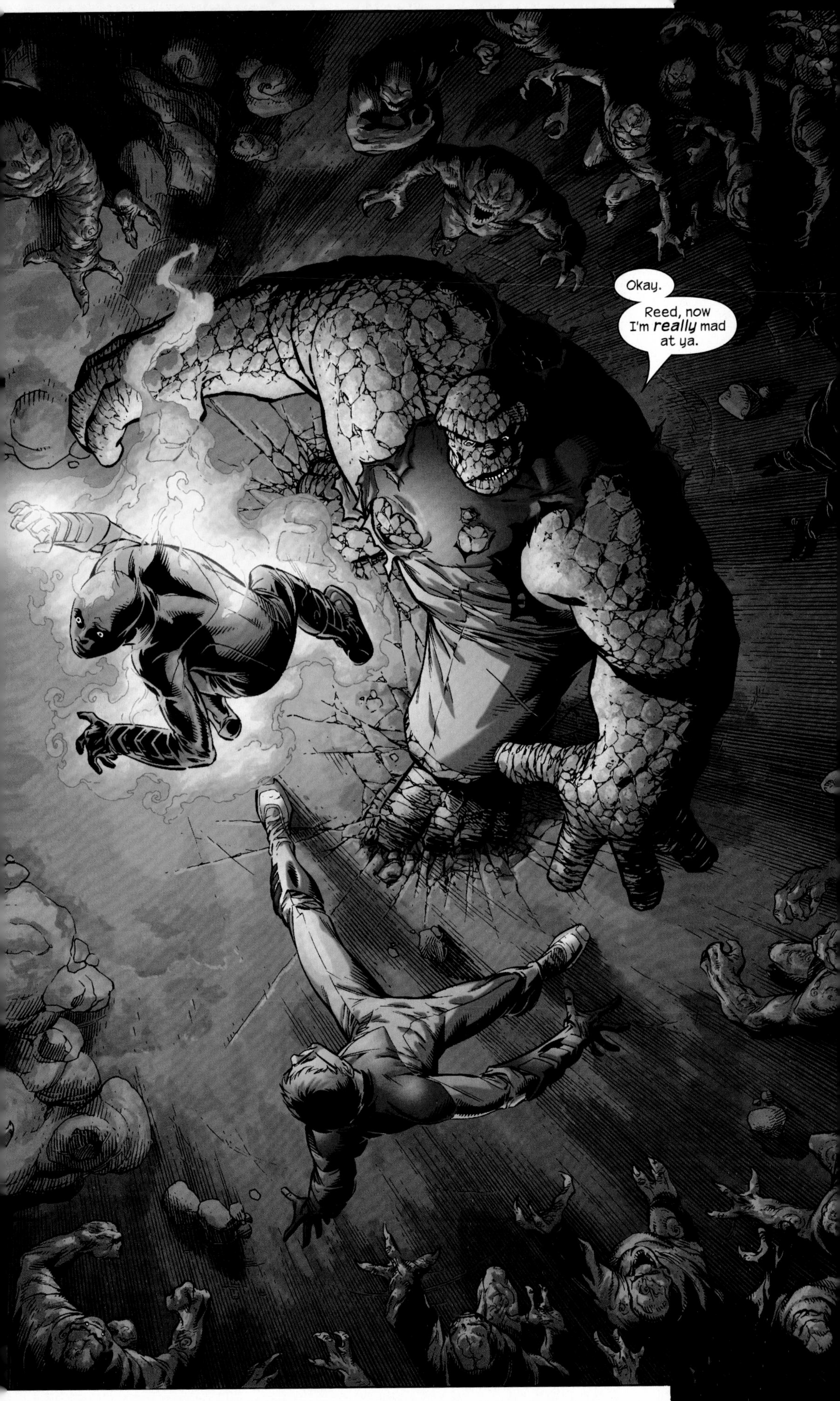
Okay.
Reed, now I'm *really* mad at ya.

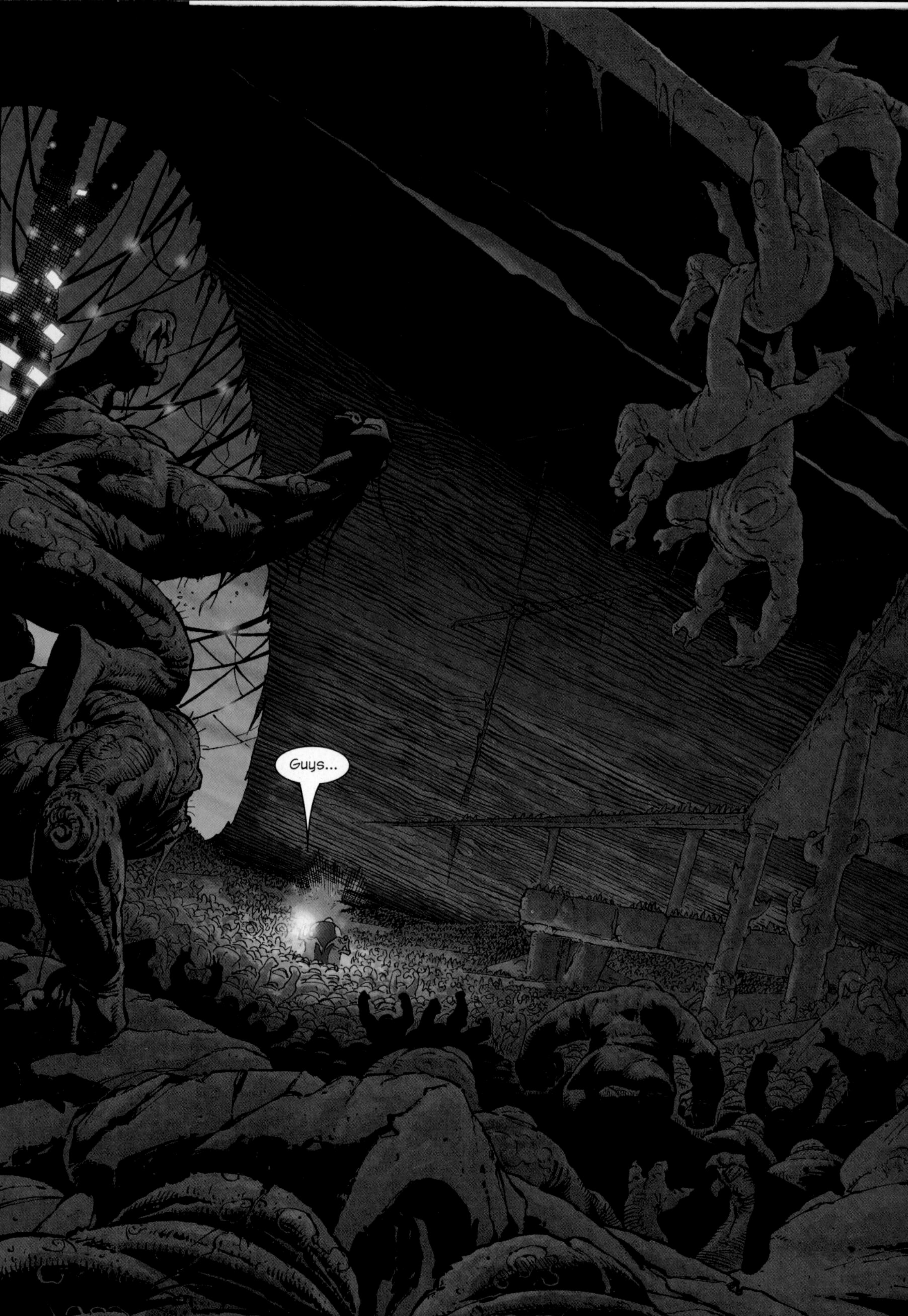
Guys...

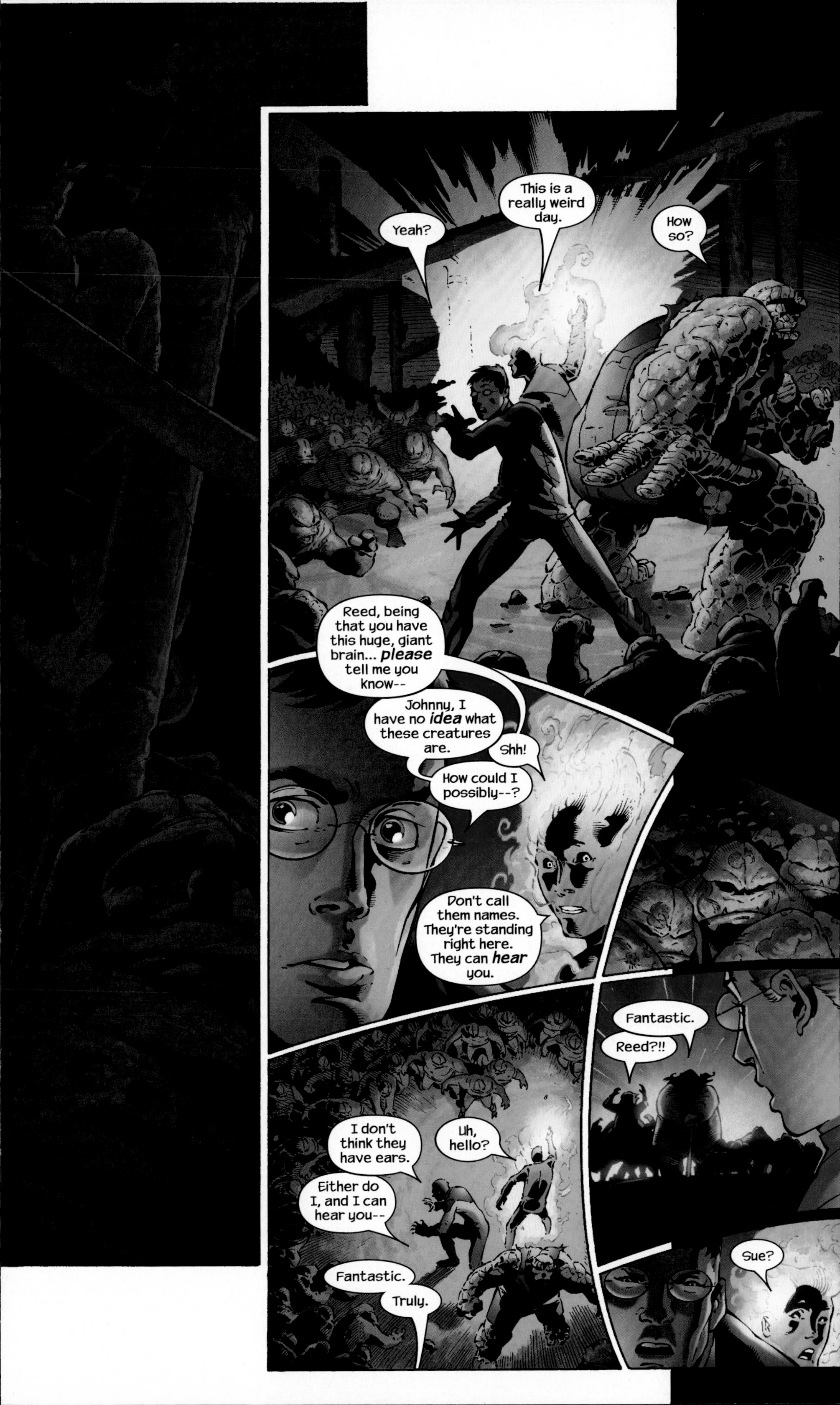
Yeah?
This is a really weird day.
How so?
Reed, being that you have this huge, giant brain... *please* tell me you know--
Johnny, I have no *idea* what these creatures are.
Shh!
How could I possibly--?
Don't call them names. They're standing right here. They can *hear* you.
I don't think they have ears.
Uh, hello?
Either do I, and I can hear you--
Fantastic.
Truly.
Fantastic.
Reed?!!
Sue?

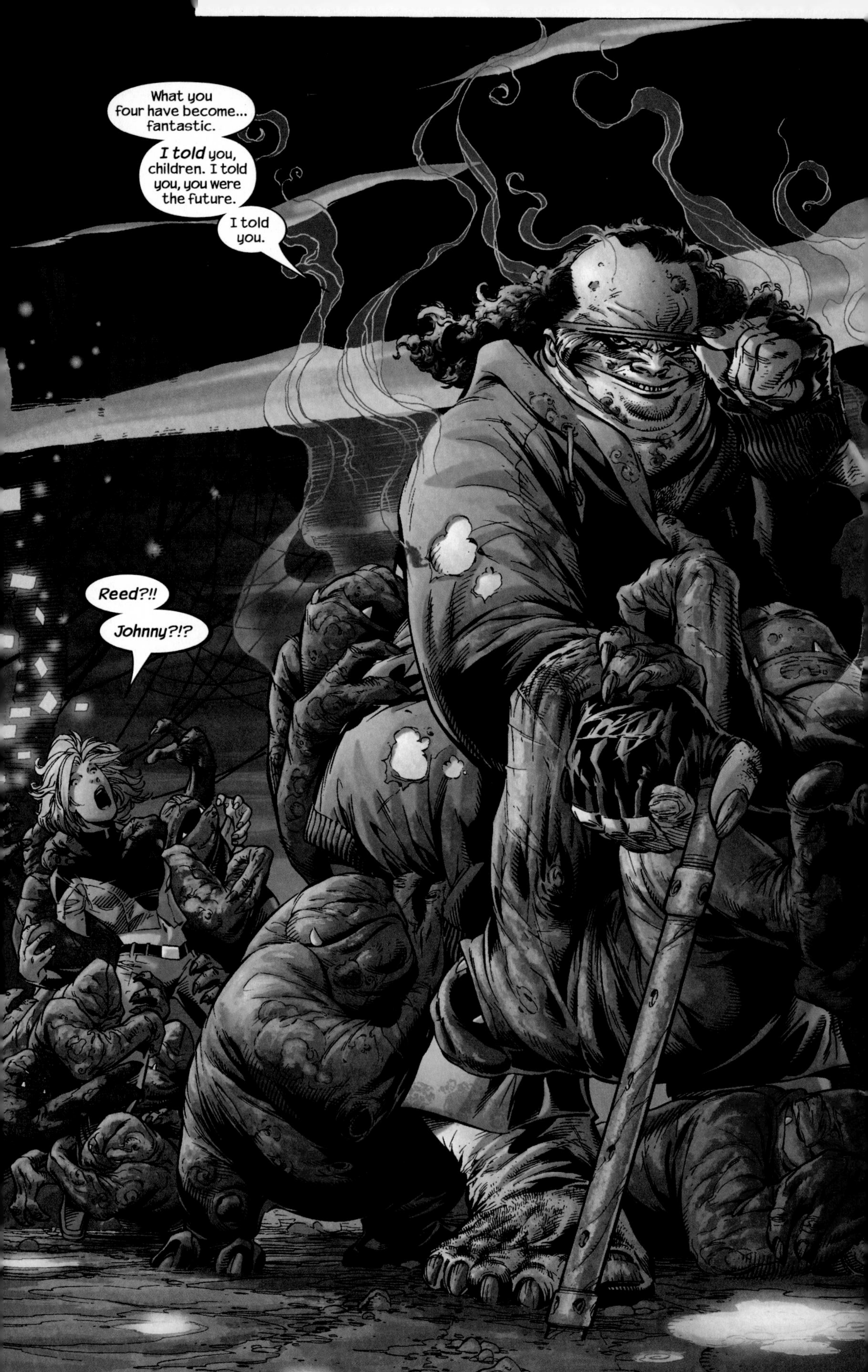
What you four have become... fantastic.
I told you, children. I told you, you were the future.
I told you.
Reed?!!
Johnny?!?

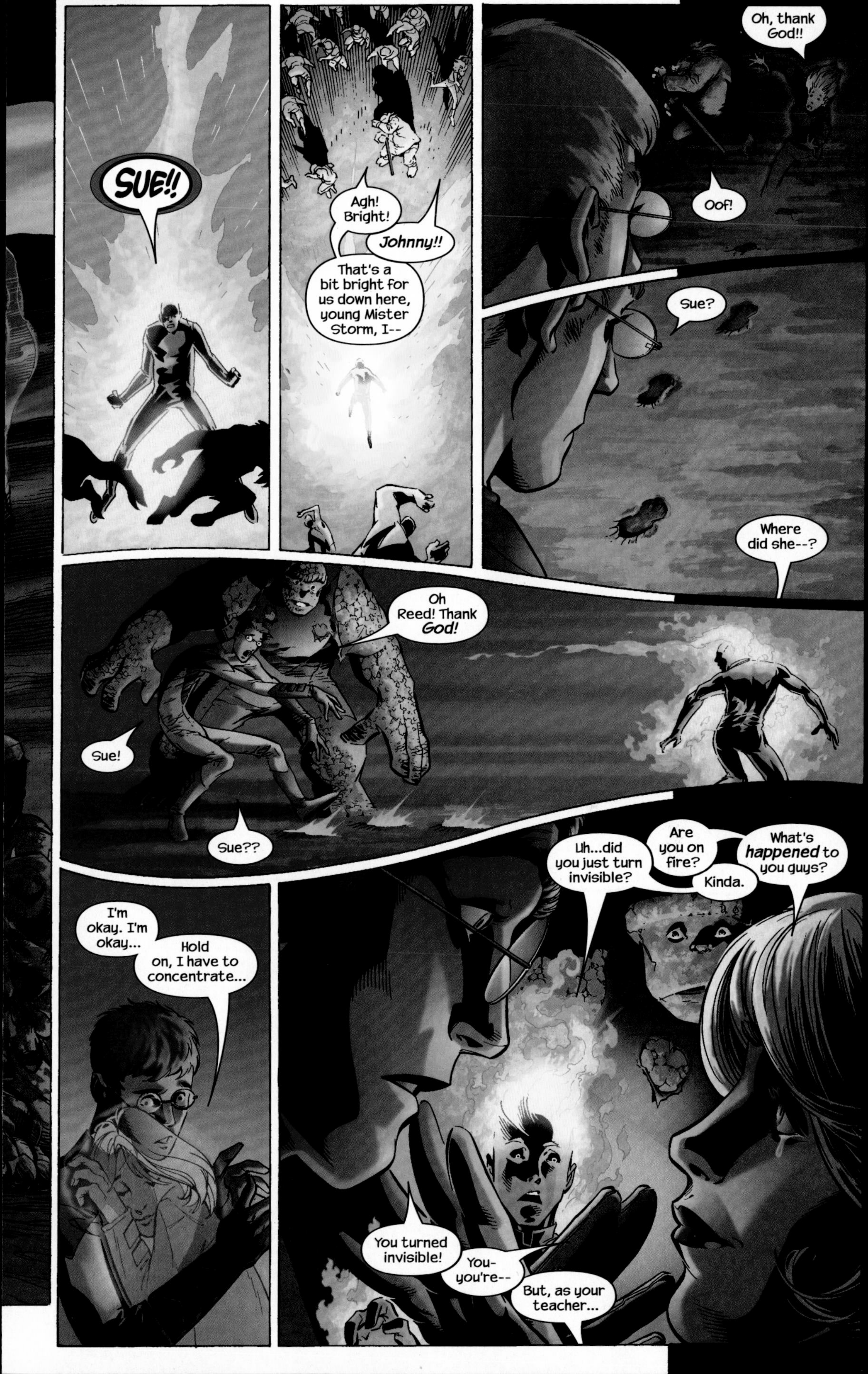
SUE!!
Agh! Bright!
Johnny!!
That's a bit bright for us down here, young Mister Storm, I--
Oh, thank God!!
Oof!
Sue?
Where did she--?
Oh Reed! Thank God!
Sue!
Sue??
I'm okay. I'm okay...
Hold on, I have to concentrate...
Uh...did you just turn invisible?
Are you on fire?
Kinda.
What's happened to you guys?
You turned invisible!
You-you're--
But, as your teacher...

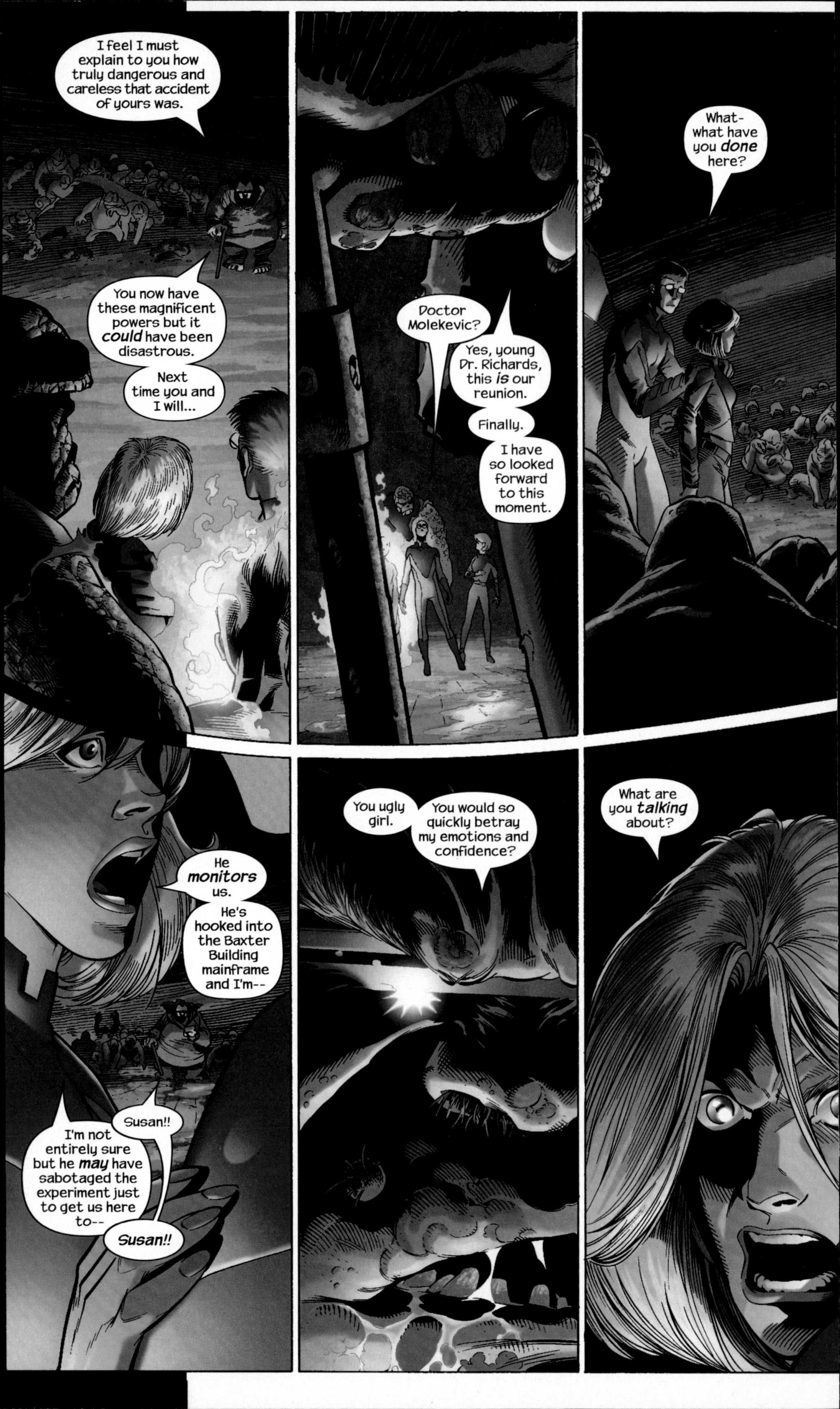
I feel I must explain to you how truly dangerous and careless that accident of yours was.
You now have these magnificent powers but it *could* have been disastrous.
Next time you and I will...
Doctor Molekevic?
Yes, young Dr. Richards, this *is* our reunion.
Finally.
I have so looked forward to this moment.
What-what have you *done* here?
He *monitors* us.
He's hooked into the Baxter Building mainframe and I'm--
Susan!!
I'm not entirely sure but he *may* have sabotaged the experiment just to get us here to--
Susan!!
You ugly girl.
You would so quickly betray my emotions and confidence?
What are you *talking* about?

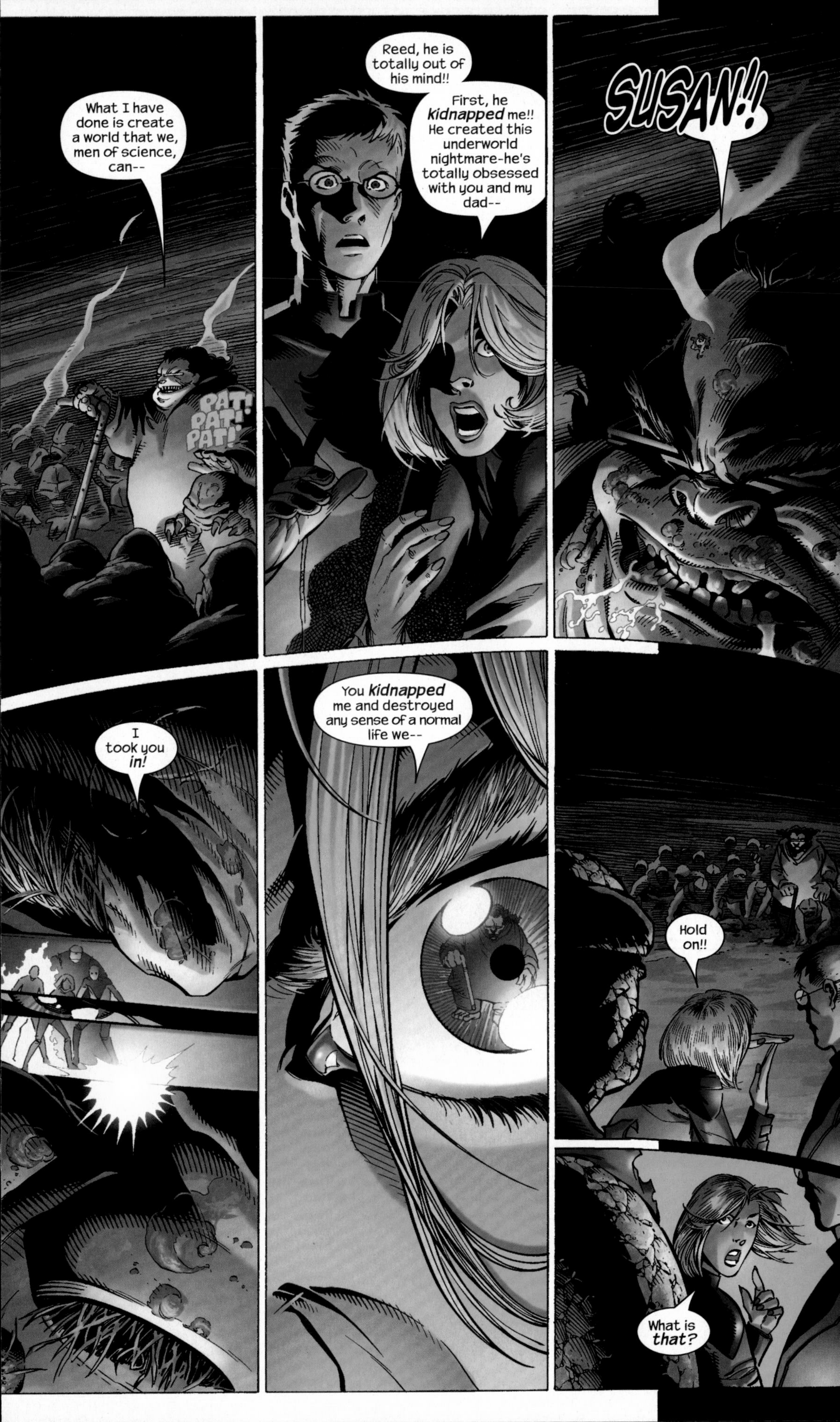
What I have done is create a world that we, men of science, can--
PAT! PAT! PAT!
Reed, he is totally out of his mind!!
First, he *kidnapped* me!! He created this underworld nightmare-he's totally obsessed with you and my dad--
SUSAN!!
I took you *in!*
You *kidnapped* me and destroyed any sense of a normal life we--
Hold on!!
What is *that?*

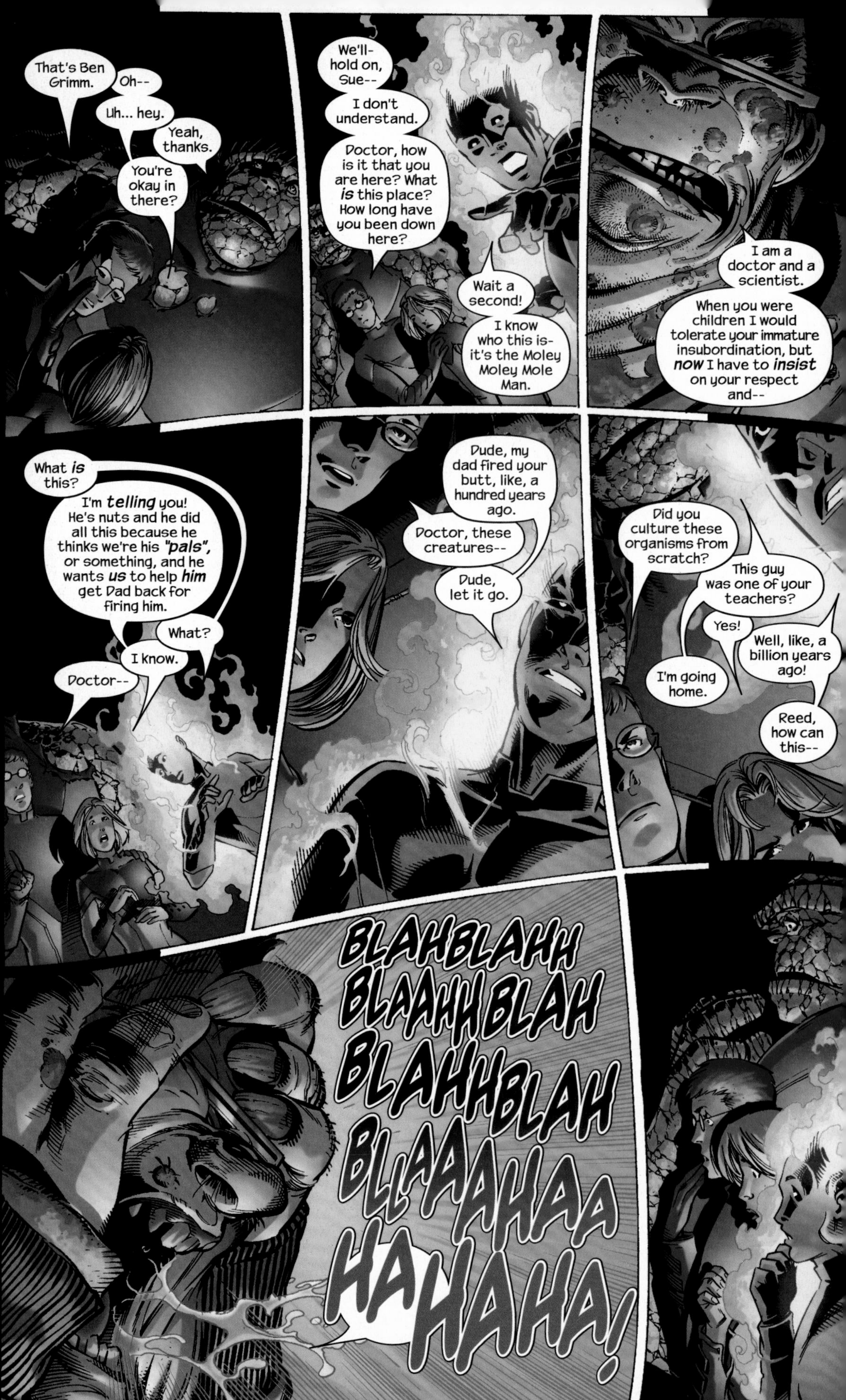
That's Ben Grimm.
Oh--
Uh... hey.
Yeah, thanks.
You're okay in there?
We'll- hold on, Sue--
I don't understand.
Doctor, how is it that you are here? What *is* this place? How long have you been down here?
Wait a second!
I know who this is- it's the Moley Moley Mole Man.
I am a doctor and a scientist.
When you were children I would tolerate your immature insubordination, but *now* I have to *insist* on your respect and--
What *is* this?
I'm *telling* you! He's nuts and he did all this because he thinks we're his *"pals"*, or something, and he wants *us* to help *him* get Dad back for firing him.
What?
I know.
Doctor--
Dude, my dad fired your butt, like, a hundred years ago.
Doctor, these creatures--
Dude, let it go.
Did you culture these organisms from scratch?
This guy was one of your teachers?
Yes!
Well, like, a billion years ago!
I'm going home.
Reed, how can this--
BLAHBLAHH BLAAHHBLAH BLAHHBLAH BLLAAAHAAA HAHAHA!

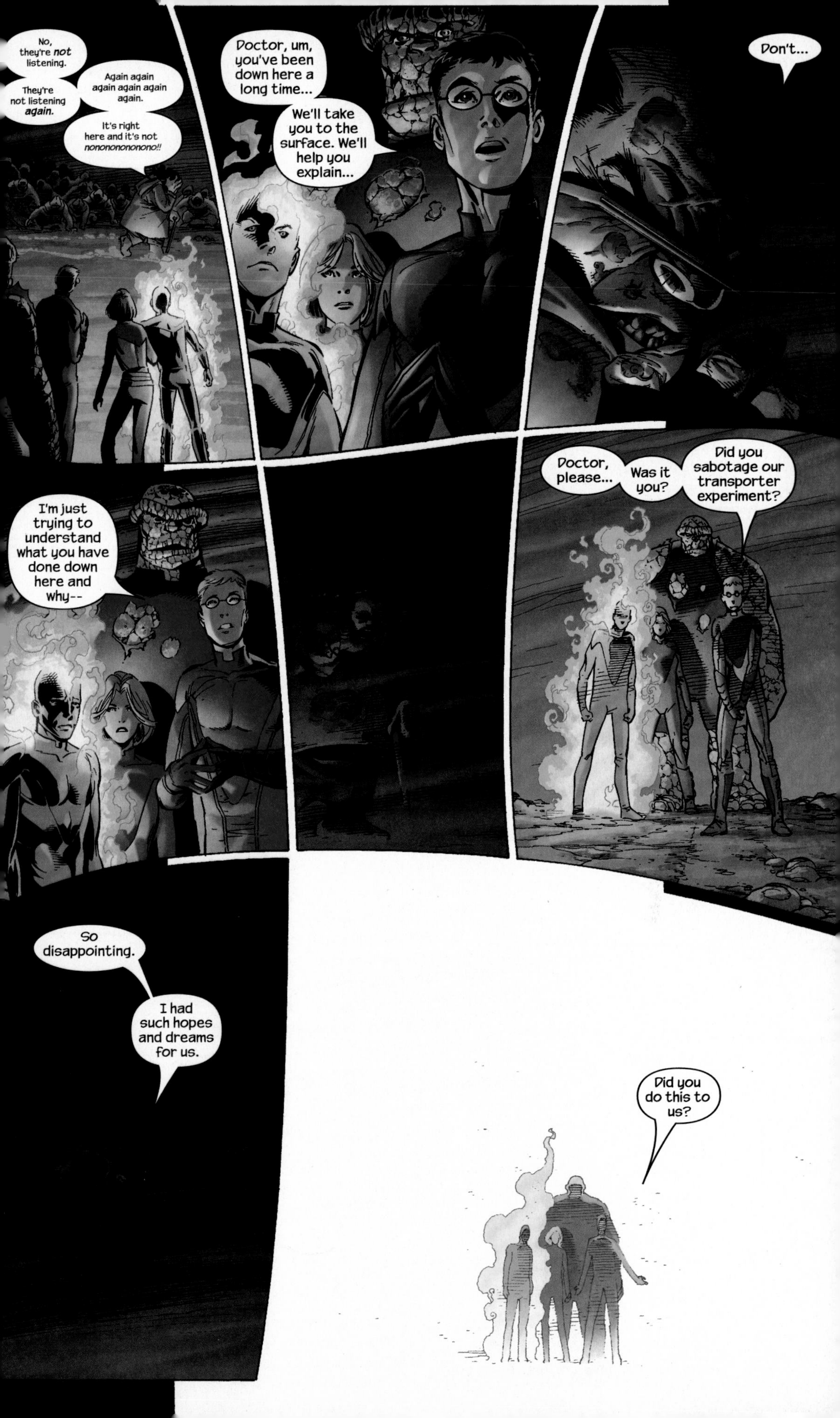
No, they're *not* listening.
They're not listening *again*.
Again again again again again again.
It's right here and it's not *nononononononono!!*
Doctor, um, you've been down here a long time...
We'll take you to the surface. We'll help you explain...
Don't...
I'm just trying to understand what you have done down here and why--
Doctor, please...
Was it you?
Did you sabotage our transporter experiment?
So disappointing.
I had such hopes and dreams for us.
Did you do this to us?

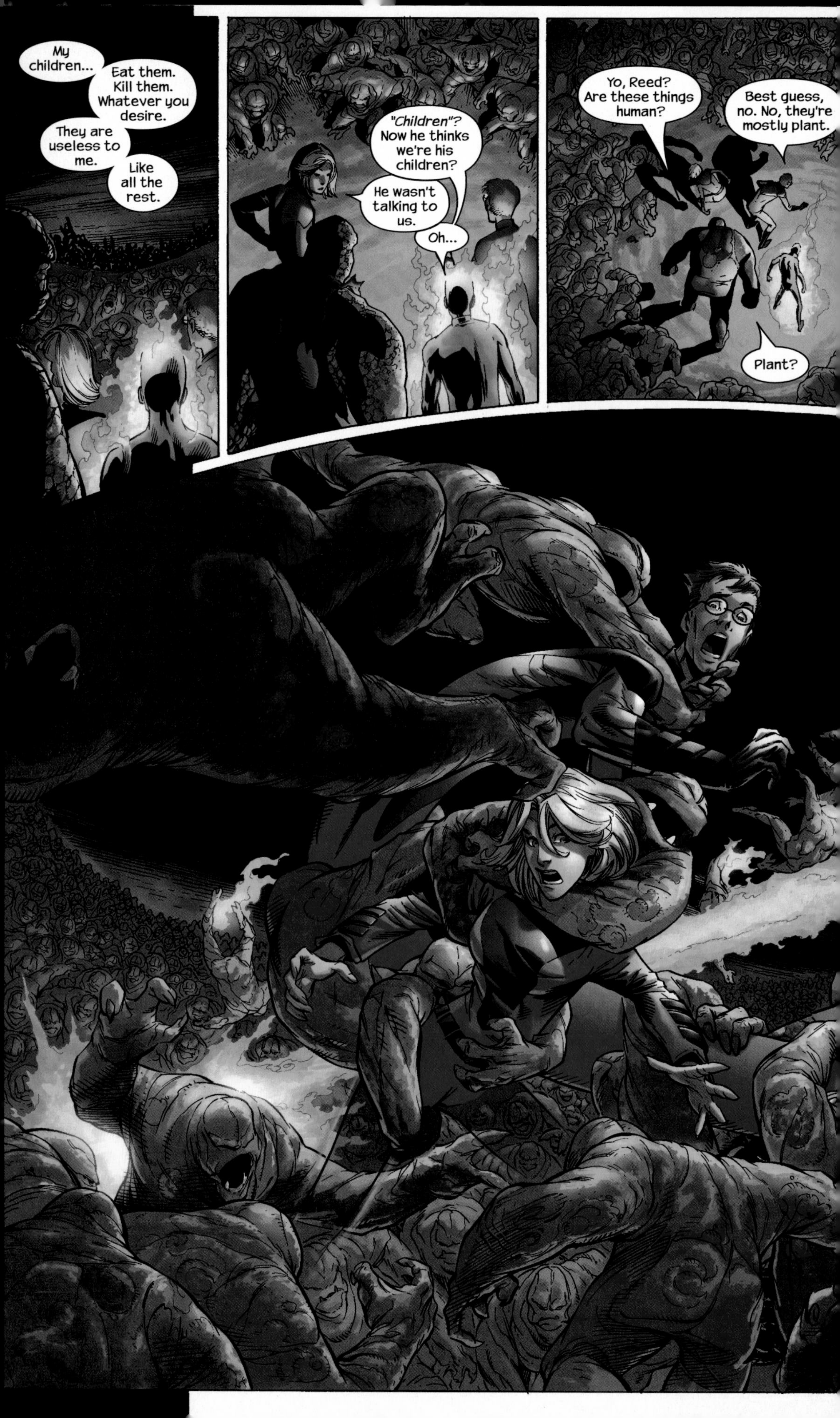
My children...
Eat them. Kill them. Whatever you desire.
They are useless to me.
Like all the rest.
"Children"? Now he thinks we're his children?
He wasn't talking to us.
Oh...
Yo, Reed? Are these things human?
Best guess, no. No, they're mostly plant.
Plant?

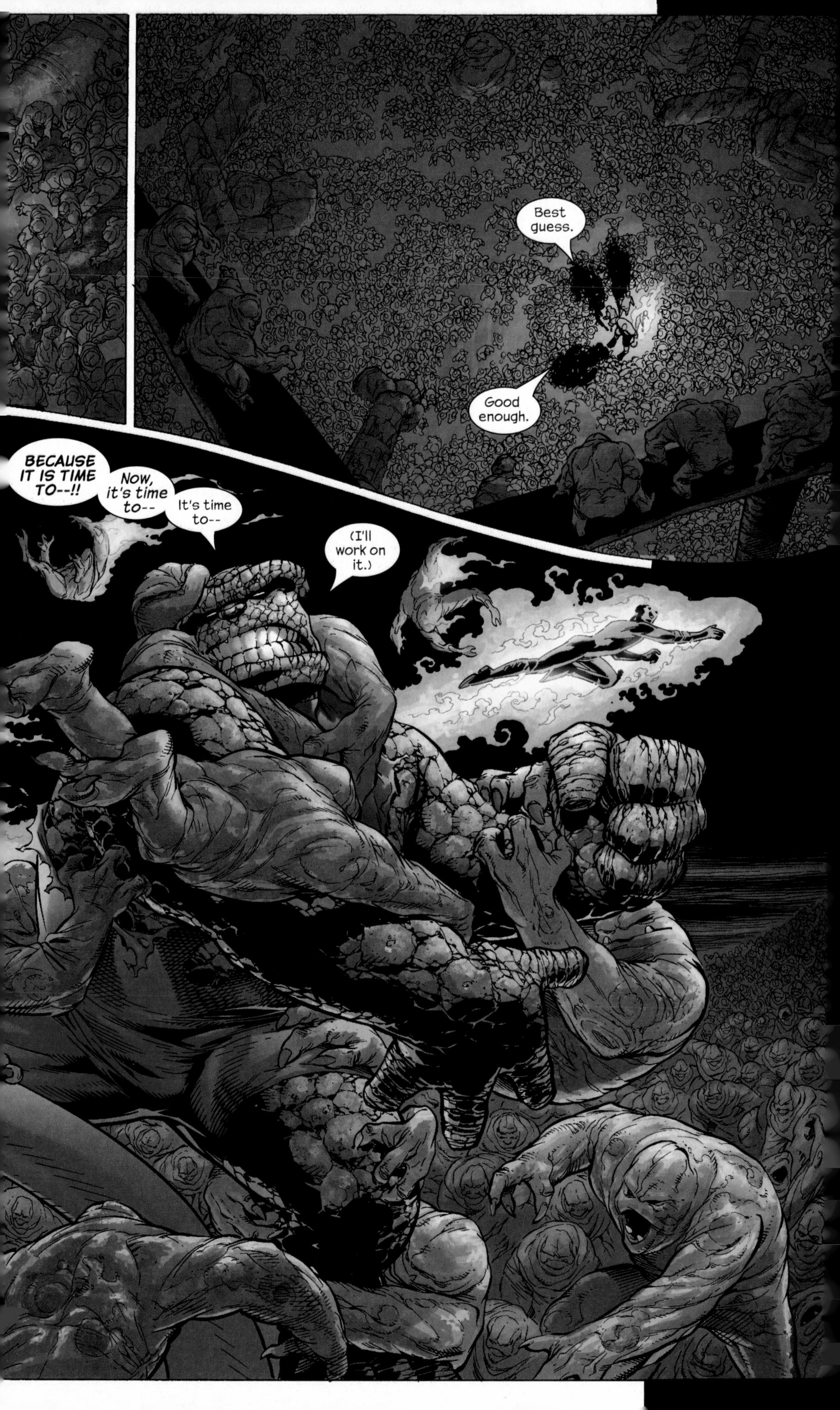
Best guess.
Good enough.
BECAUSE IT IS TIME TO--!!
Now, it's time to--
It's time to--
(I'll work on it.)

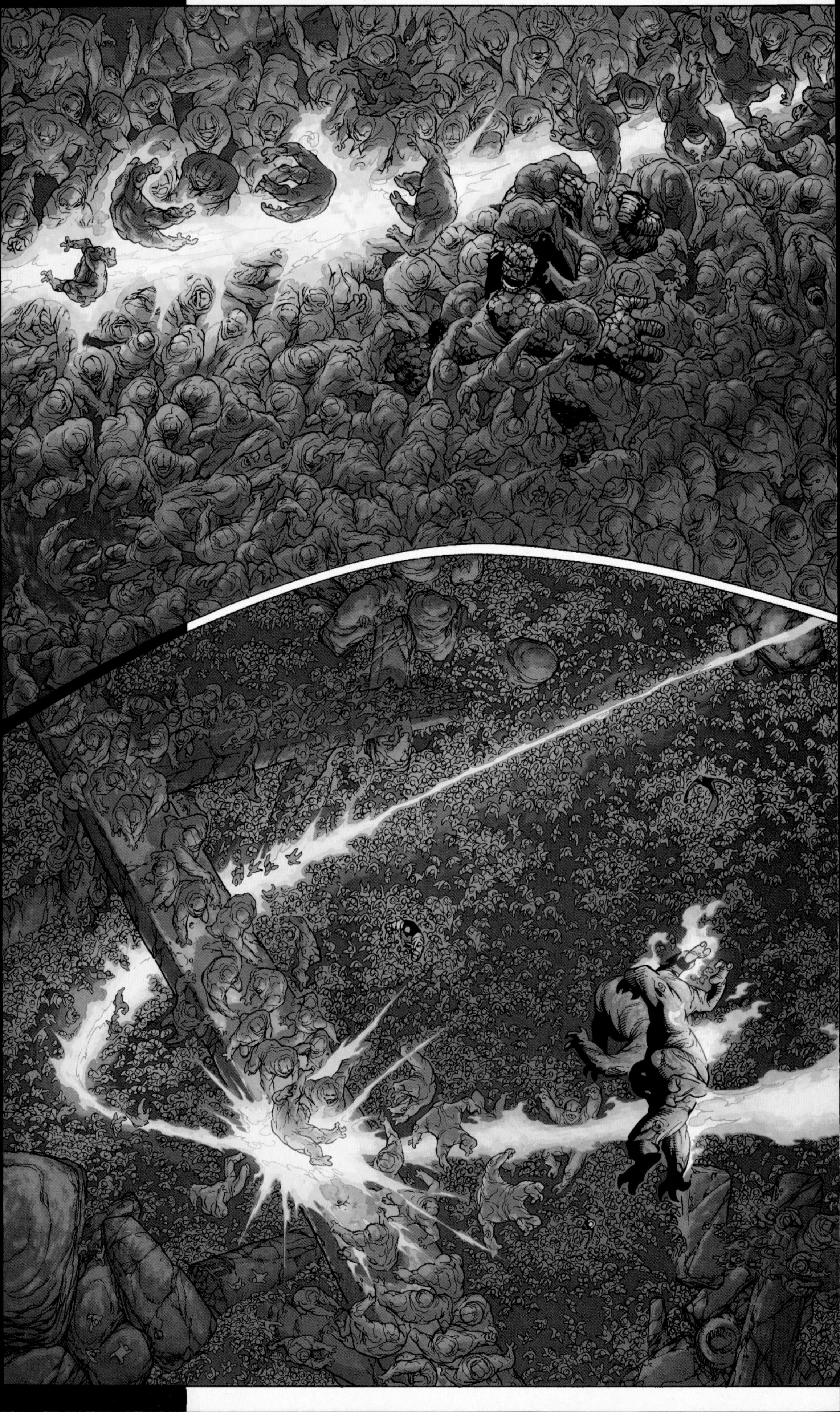

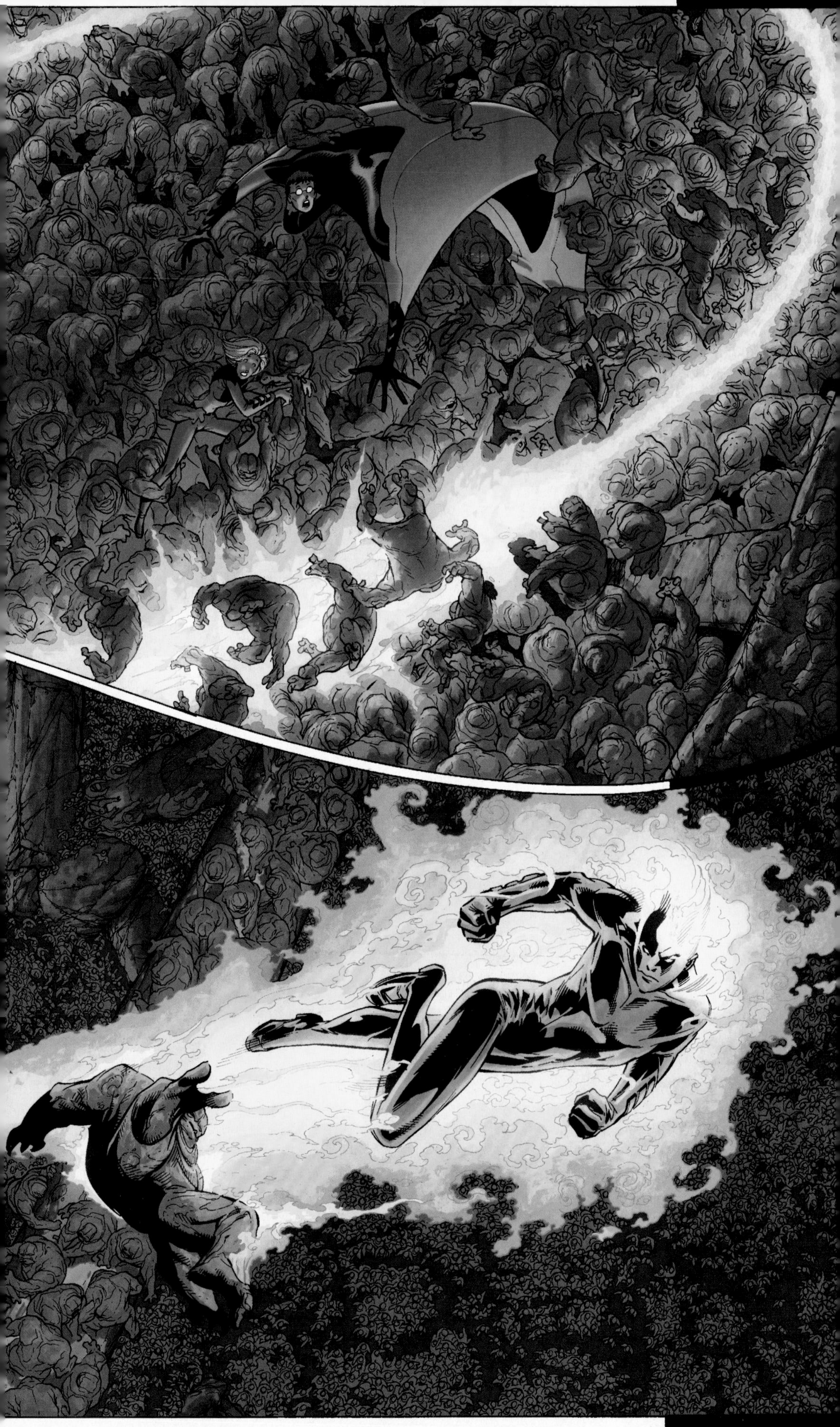

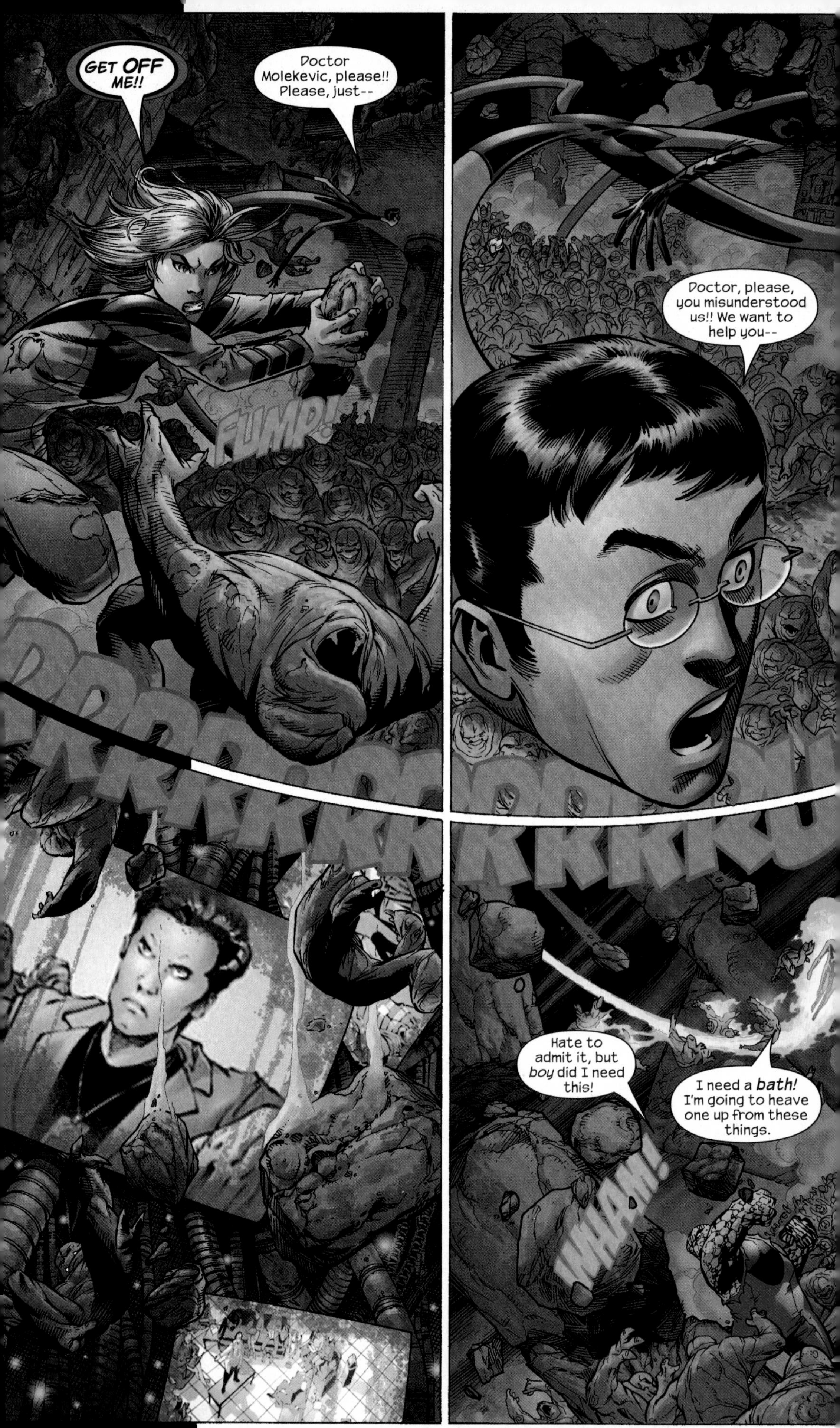
GET OFF ME!!
Doctor Molekevic, please!! Please, just--
FUMP!
Doctor, please, you misunderstood us!! We want to help you--
Hate to admit it, but boy did I need this!
I need a bath! I'm going to heave one up from these things.
WHAM!

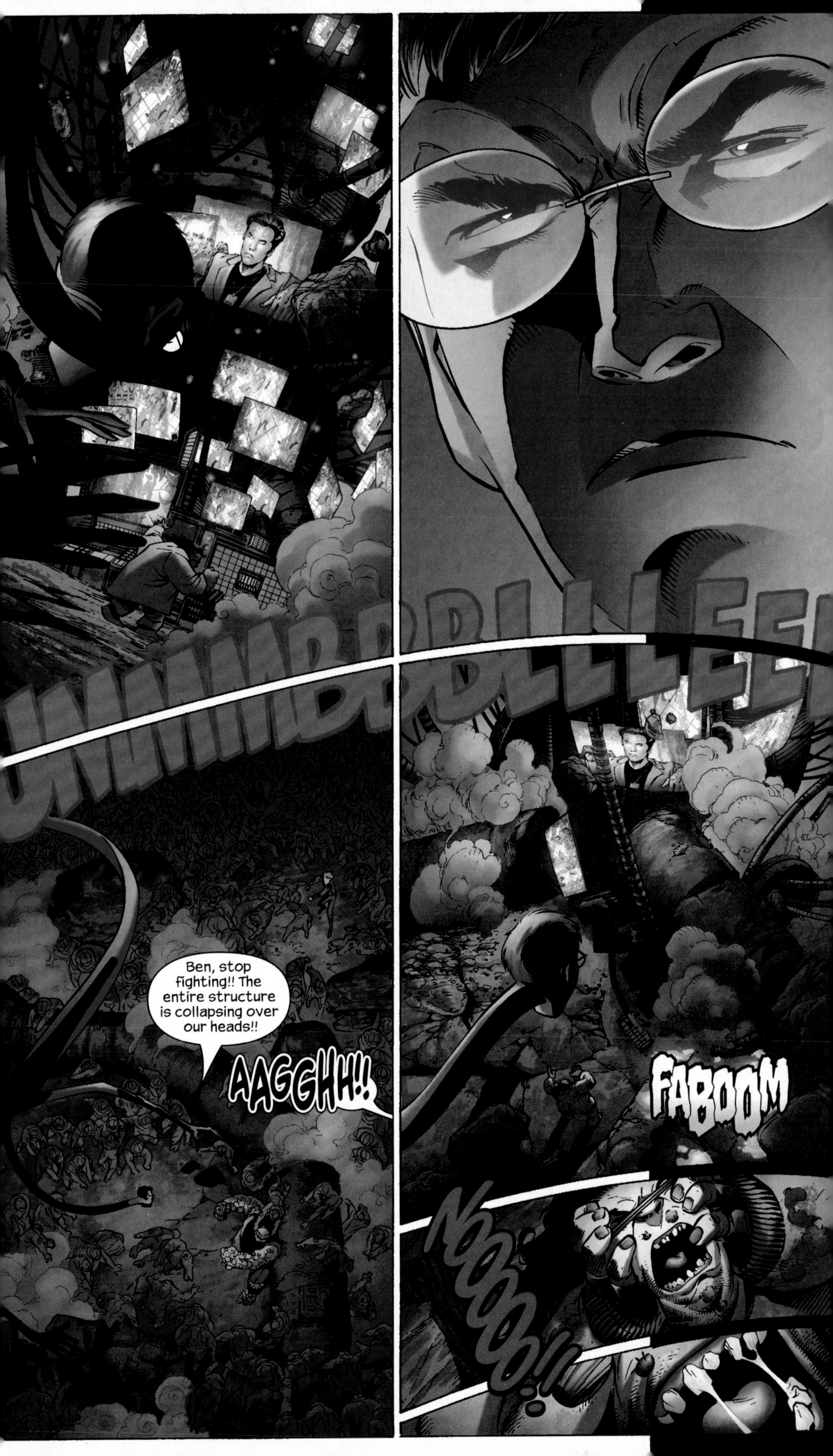
Ben, stop fighting!! The entire structure is collapsing over our heads!!
AAGGHH!!
FABOOM
NOOOOO!!

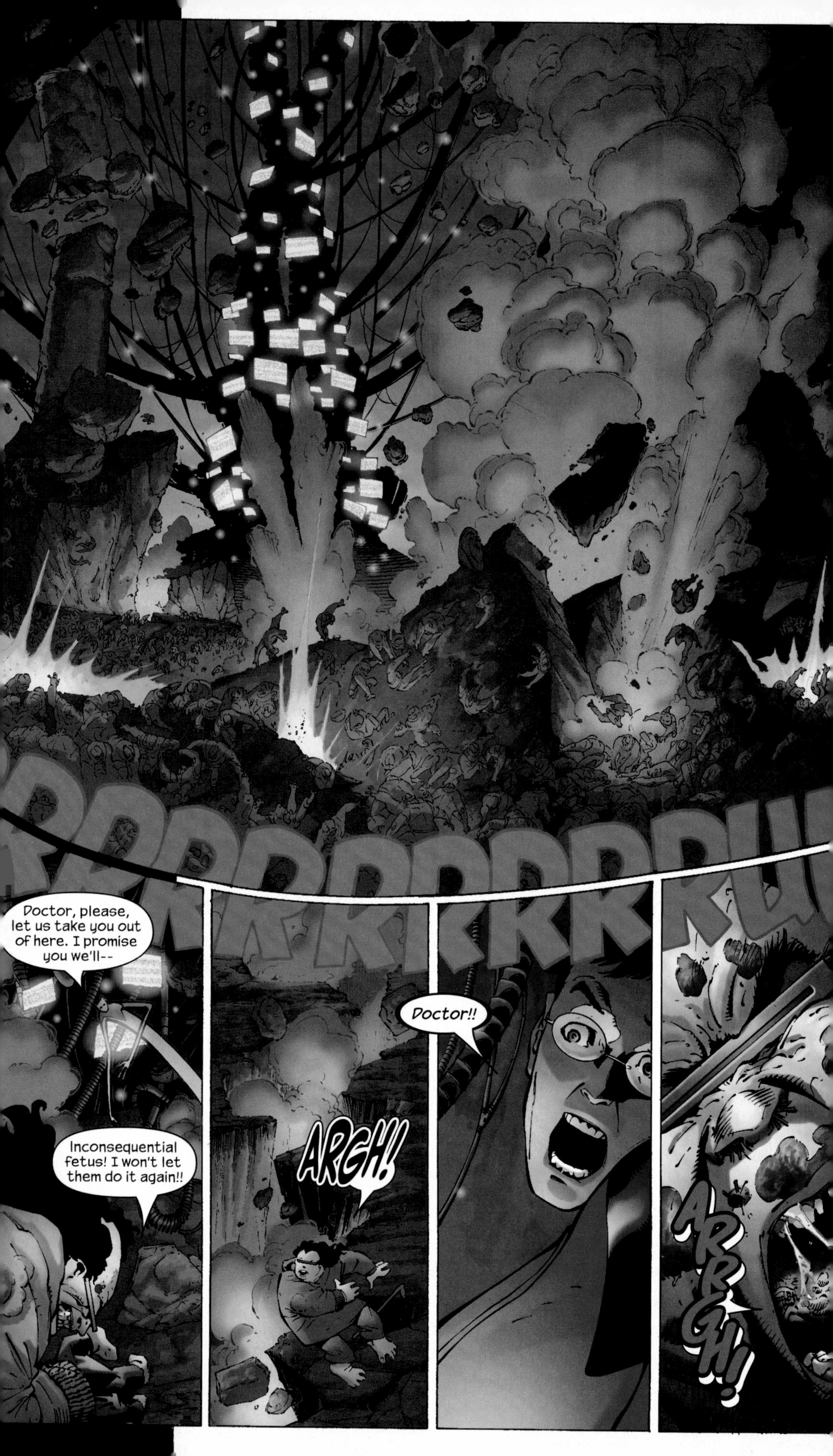
RRRRRRRRRRRU
Doctor, please, let us take you out of here. I promise you we'll--
Inconsequential fetus! I won't let them do it again!!
ARGH!
Doctor!!
ARRGH!

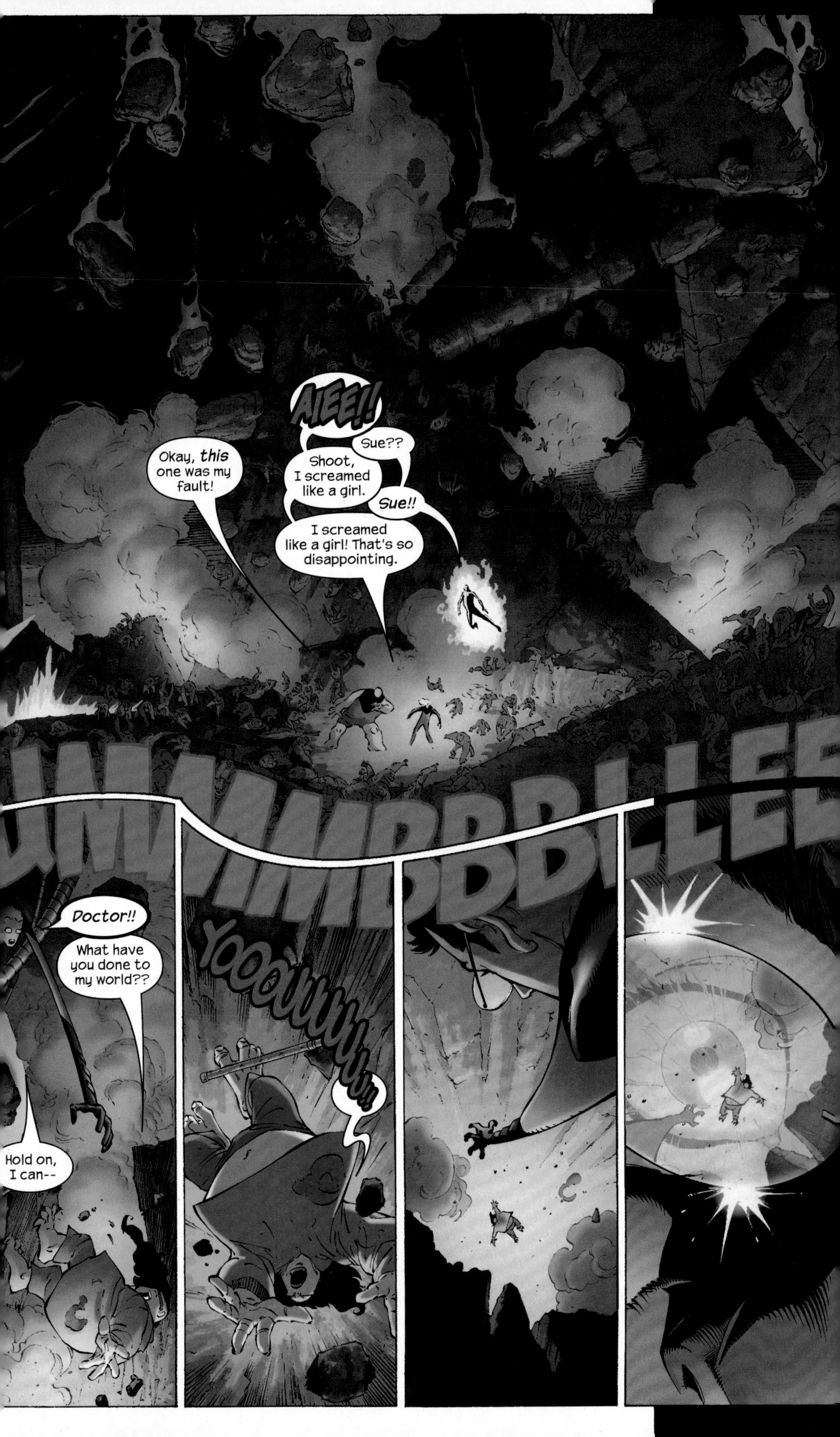
AIEE!!
Okay, this one was my fault!
Sue??
Shoot, I screamed like a girl.
Sue!!
I screamed like a girl! That's so disappointing.
RUMMBBLLEE
Doctor!!
What have you done to my world??
Hold on, I can--
YOOOUUUUUU!!

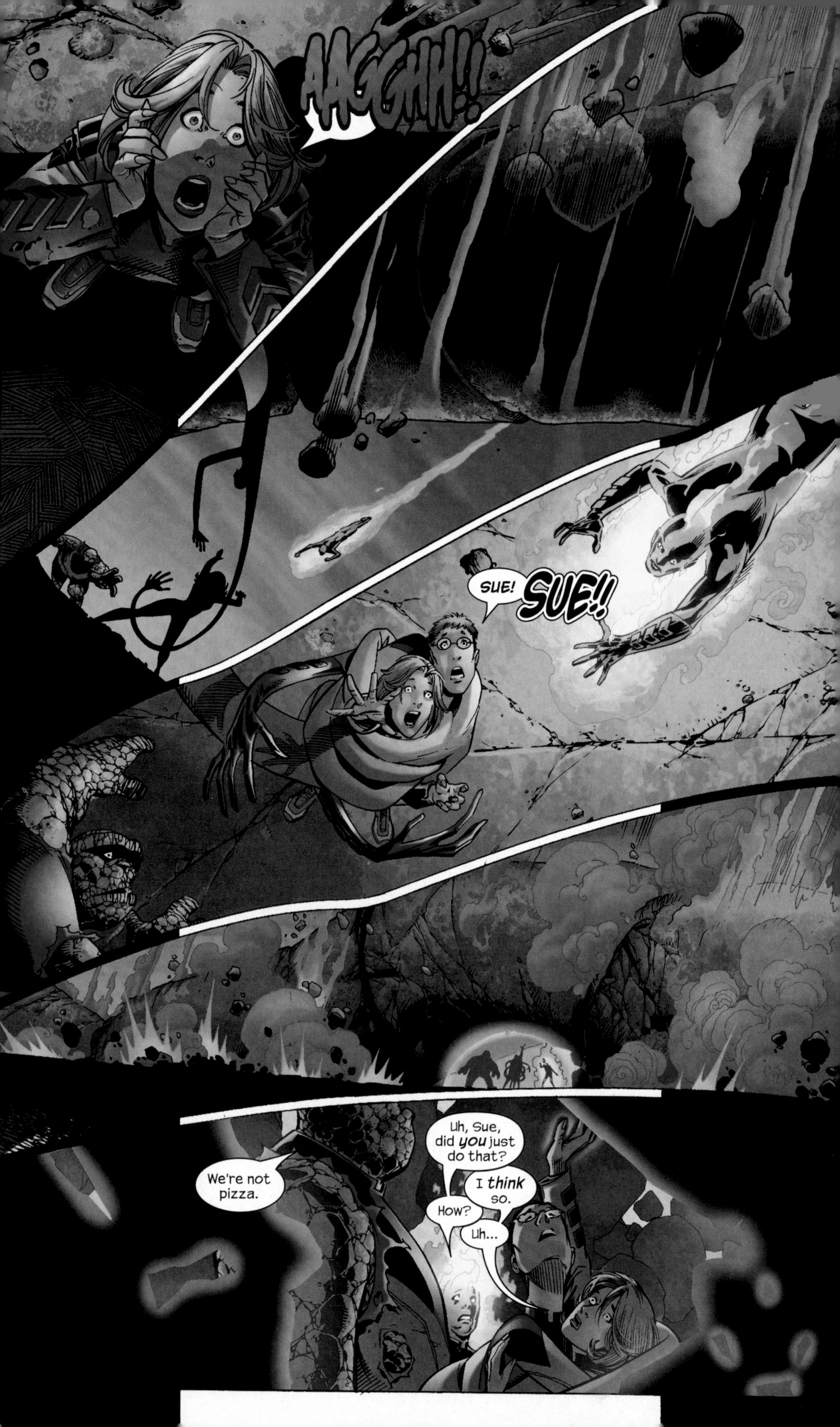
AAGGHH!!
SUE! SUE!!
We're not pizza.
Uh, Sue, did *you* just do that?
I *think* so.
How?
Uh...

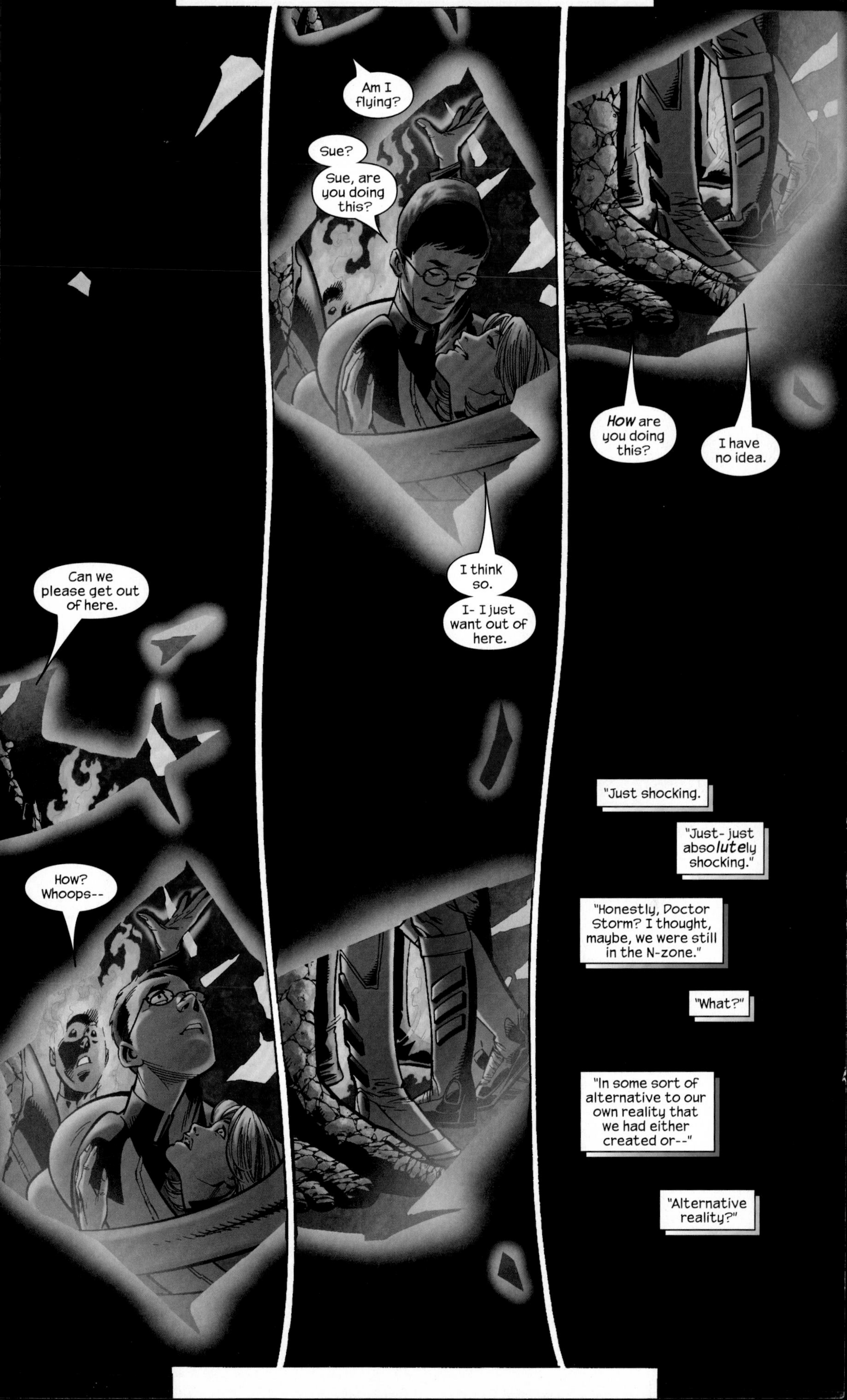

Am I flying?
Sue?
Sue, are you doing this?
HOW are you doing this?
I have no idea.
I think so.
I- I just want out of here.
Can we please get out of here.
How? Whoops--
"Just shocking.
"Just- just abso*lute*ly shocking."
"Honestly, Doctor Storm? I thought, maybe, we were still in the N-zone."
"What?"
"In some sort of alternative to our own reality that we had either created or--"
"Alternative reality?"

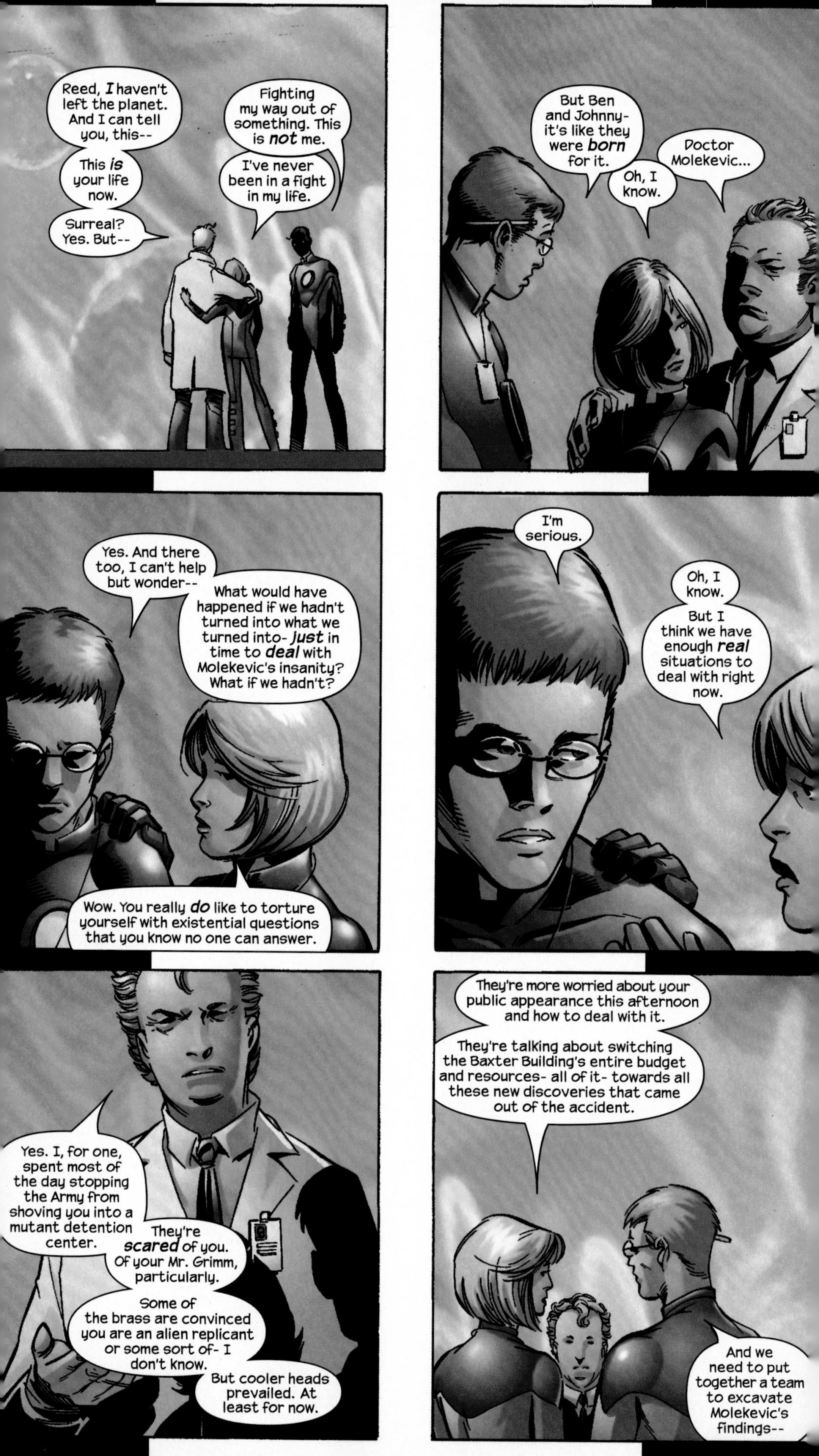
Reed, I haven't left the planet. And I can tell you, this--
This is your life now.
Surreal? Yes. But--
Fighting my way out of something. This is not me.
I've never been in a fight in my life.
But Ben and Johnny- it's like they were born for it.
Oh, I know.
Doctor Molekevic...
Yes. And there too, I can't help but wonder--
What would have happened if we hadn't turned into what we turned into- just in time to deal with Molekevic's insanity? What if we hadn't?
Wow. You really do like to torture yourself with existential questions that you know no one can answer.
I'm serious.
Oh, I know.
But I think we have enough real situations to deal with right now.
Yes. I, for one, spent most of the day stopping the Army from shoving you into a mutant detention center.
They're scared of you. Of your Mr. Grimm, particularly.
Some of the brass are convinced you are an alien replicant or some sort of- I don't know.
But cooler heads prevailed. At least for now.
They're more worried about your public appearance this afternoon and how to deal with it.
They're talking about switching the Baxter Building's entire budget and resources- all of it- towards all these new discoveries that came out of the accident.
And we need to put together a team to excavate Molekevic's findings--

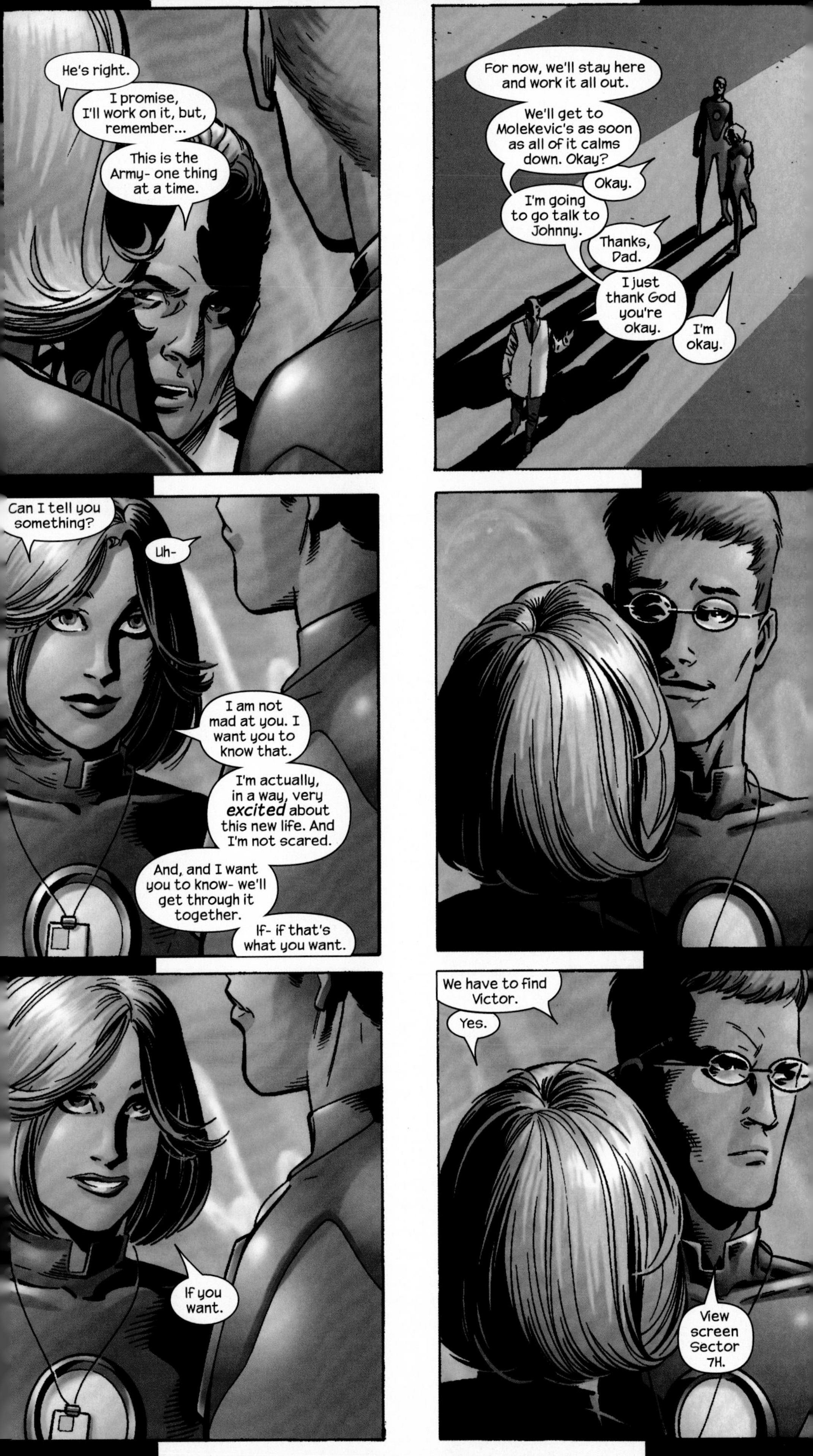
He's right.
I promise, I'll work on it, but, remember...
This is the Army- one thing at a time.
For now, we'll stay here and work it all out.
We'll get to Molekevic's as soon as all of it calms down. Okay?
Okay.
I'm going to go talk to Johnny.
Thanks, Dad.
I just thank God you're okay.
I'm okay.
Can I tell you something?
Uh-
I am not mad at you. I want you to know that.
I'm actually, in a way, very *excited* about this new life. And I'm not scared.
And, and I want you to know- we'll get through it together.
If- if that's what you want.
If you want.
We have to find Victor.
Yes.
View screen Sector 7H.

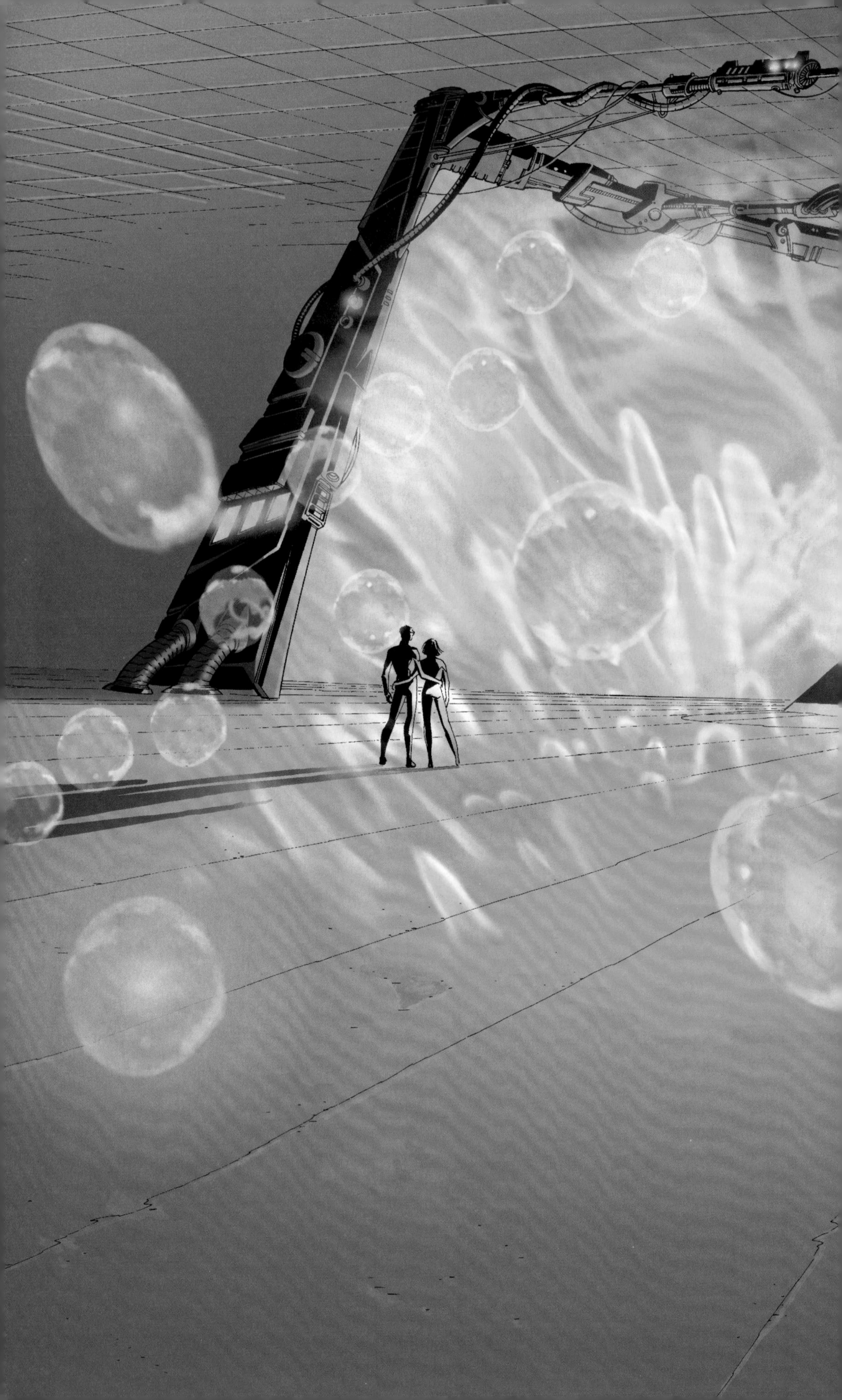

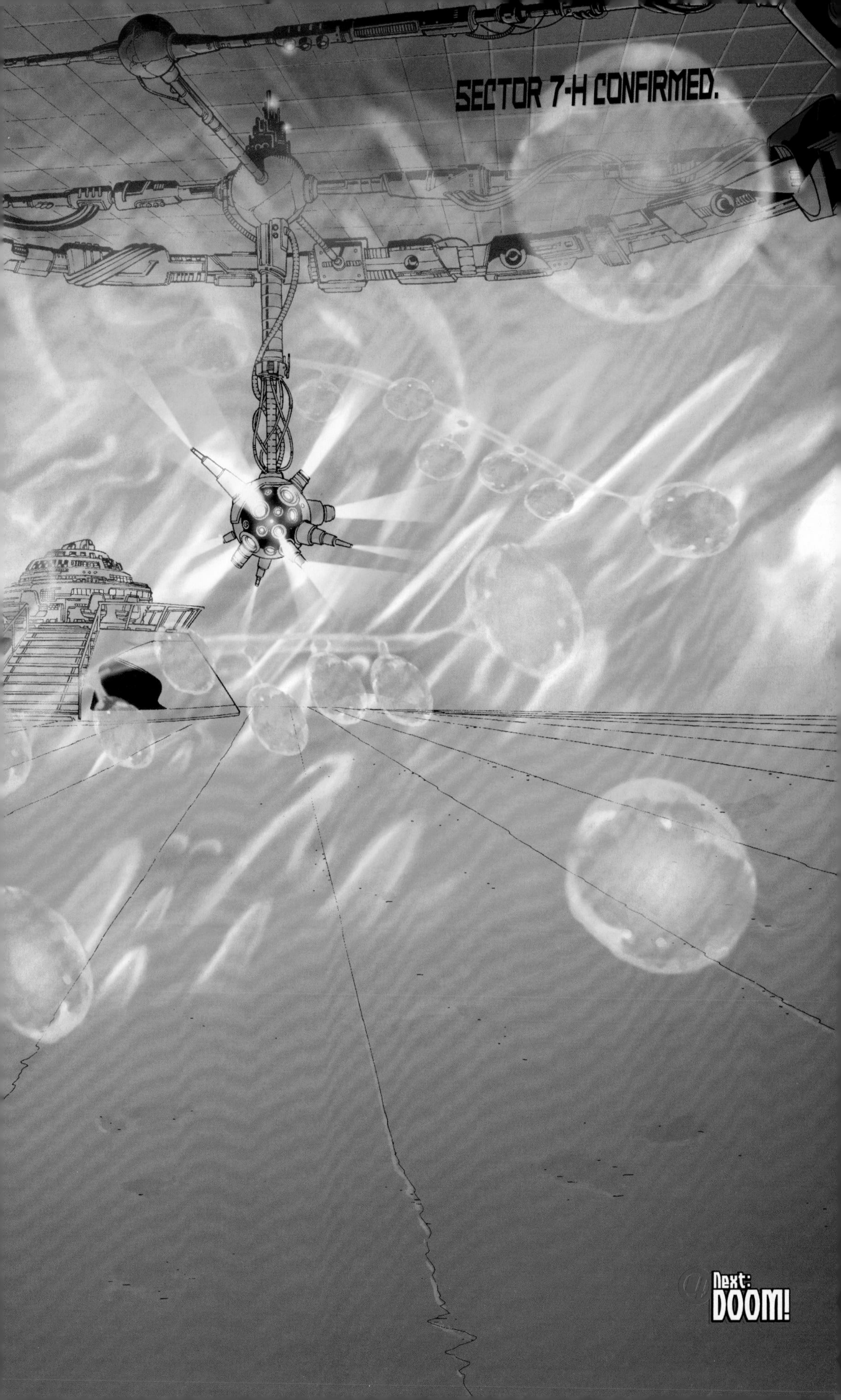
SECTOR 7-H CONFIRMED.
Next: DOOM!

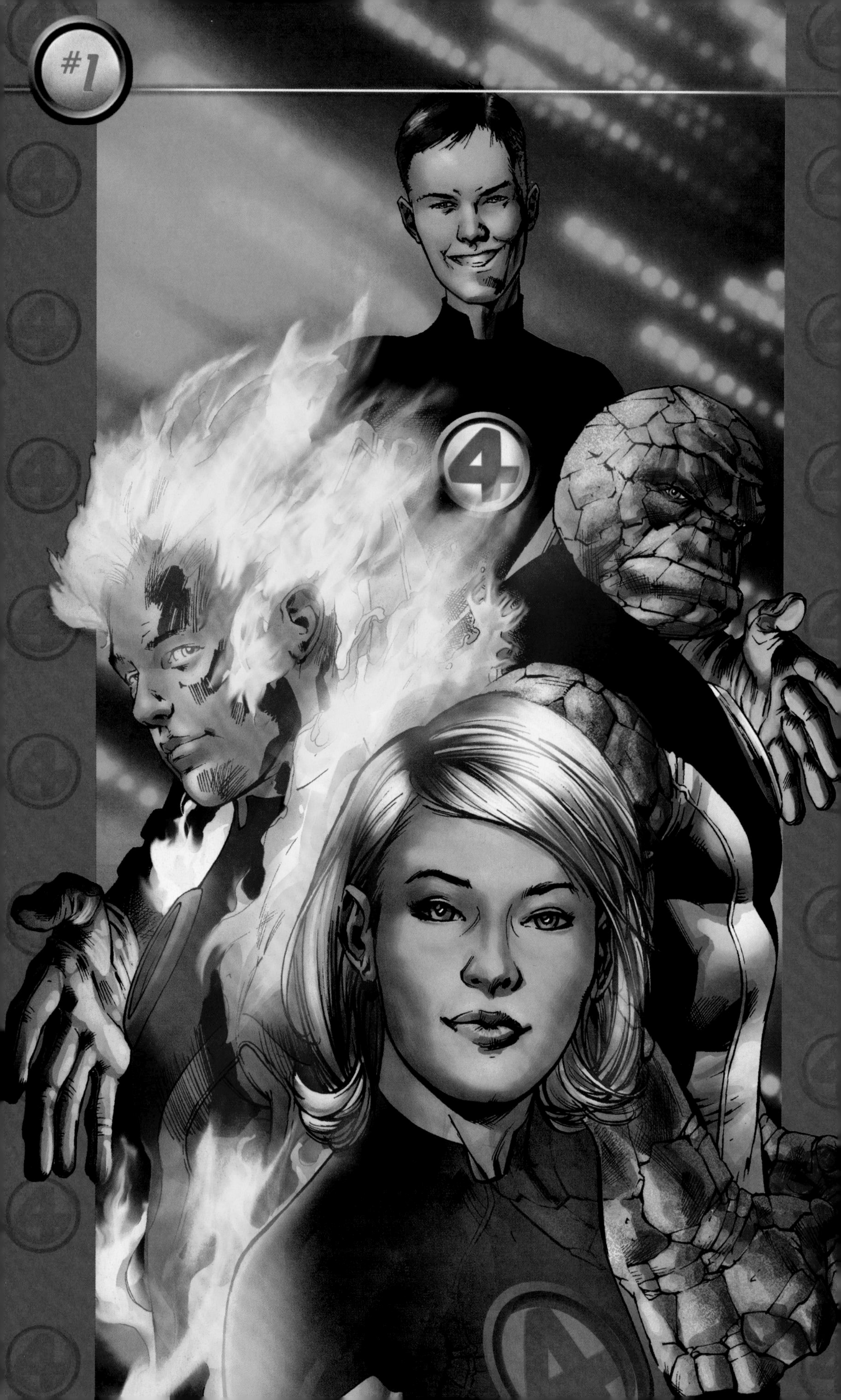
#1

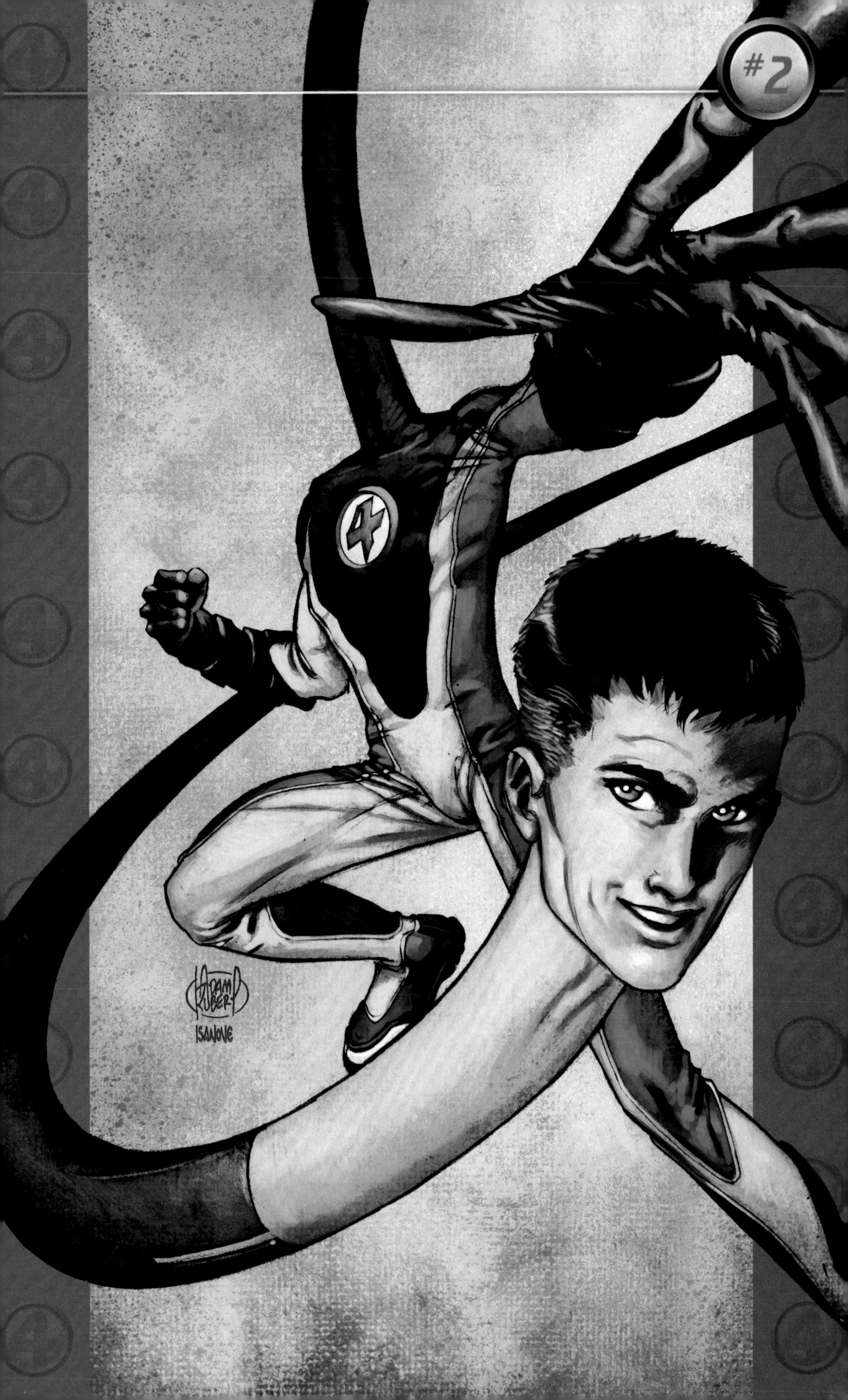
#2
ADAM KUBERT
ISANOVE

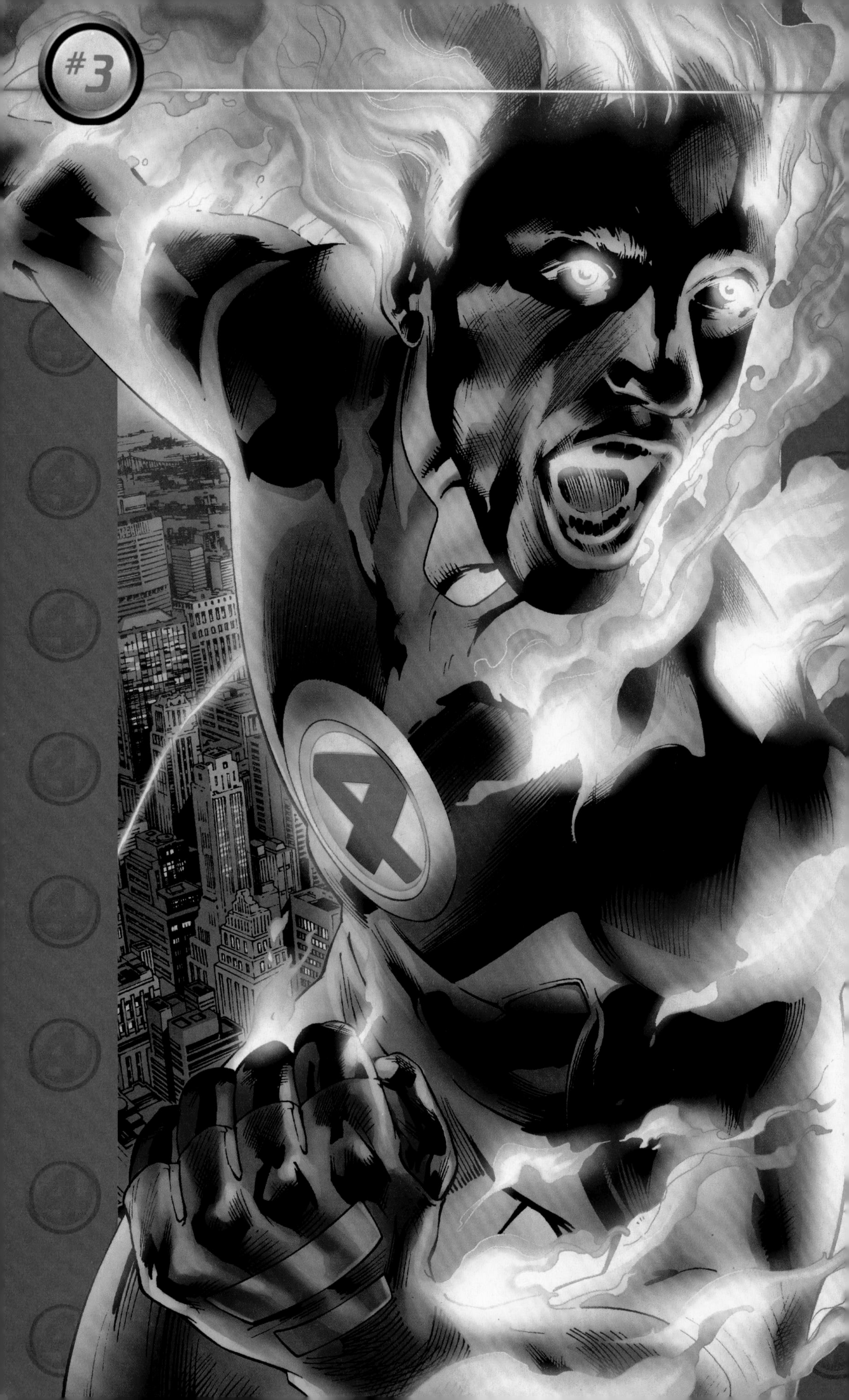
#3

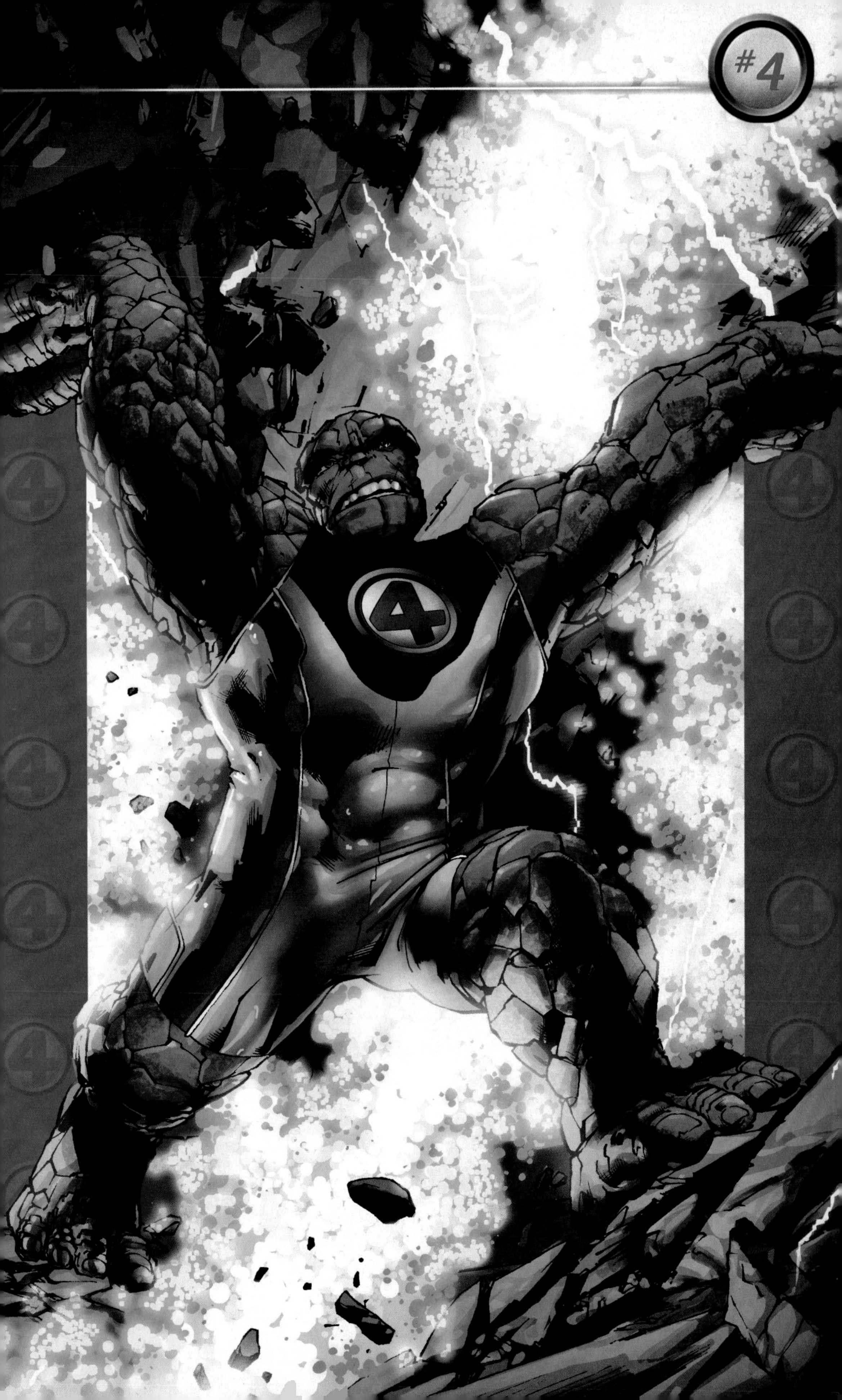
#4

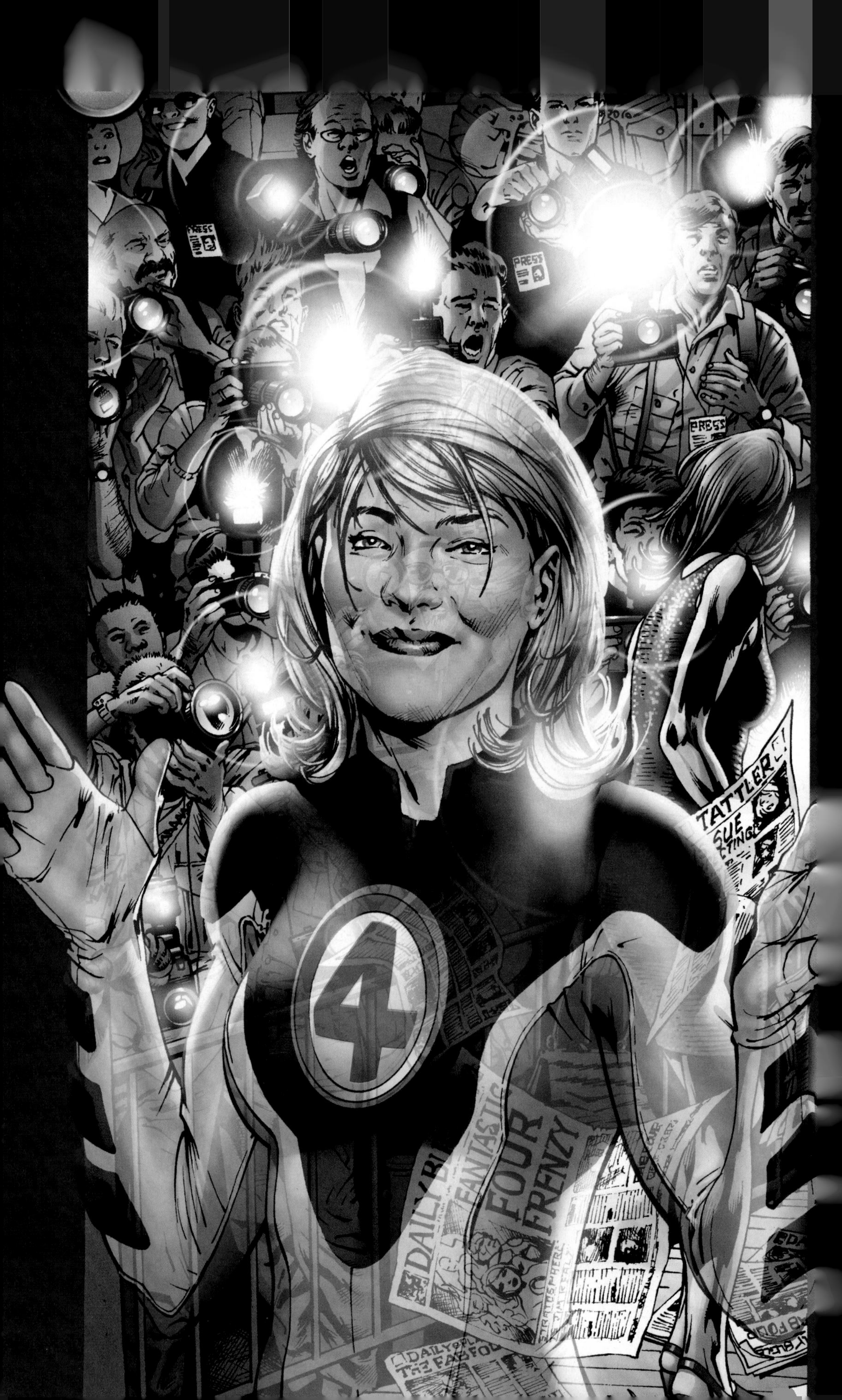
PRESS
PRESS
PRESS
TATTLER
SUE
FANTASTIC
FOUR
FRENZY

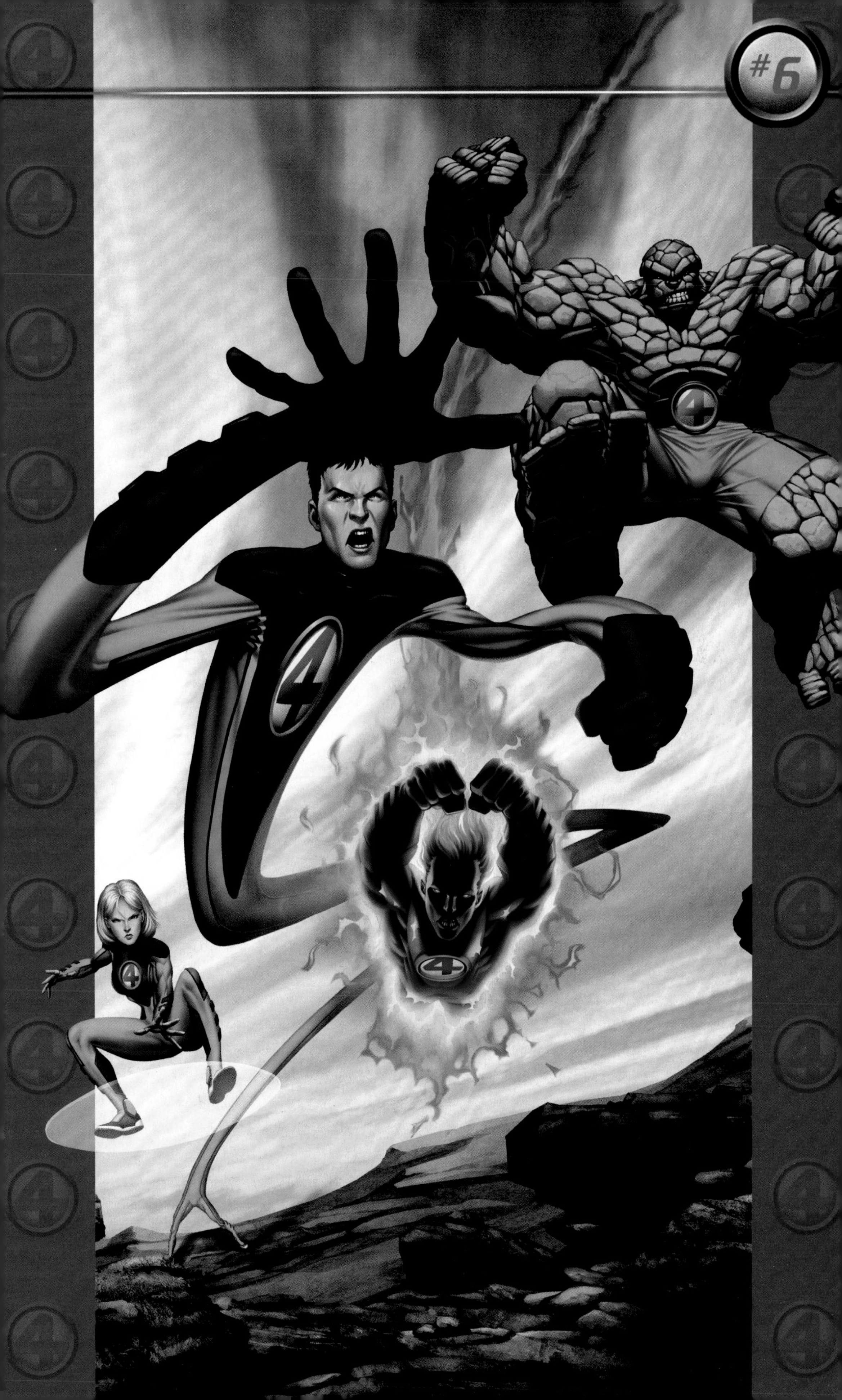
#6

Ultimate Johnny Storm designs by Bryan Hitch

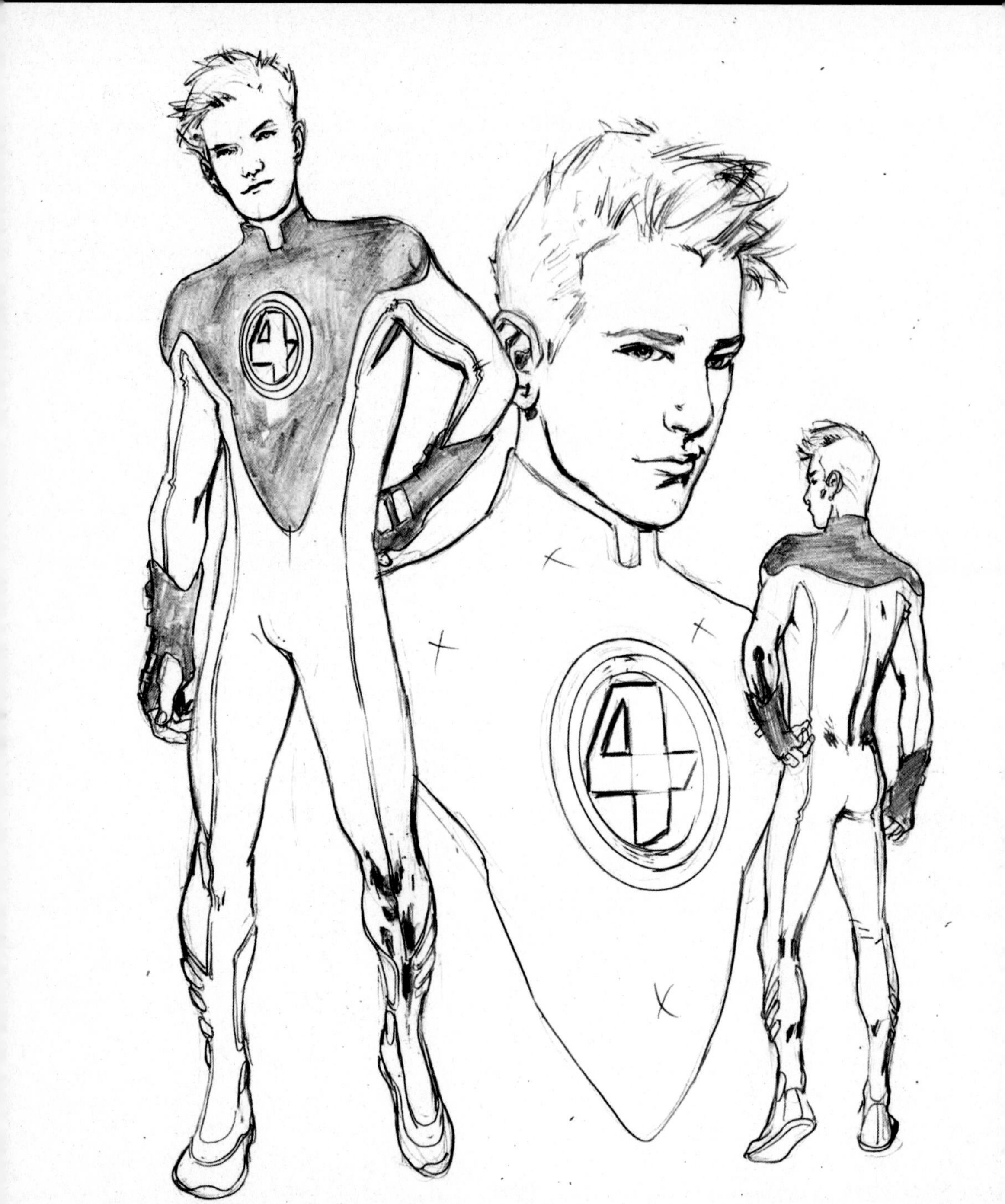